# TIME RUNNING OUT

Darvin kept her van within his line of sight for the first three miles, losing it on some of the twisty sections of road. He wasn't worried. Following someone on a highway was easy. Unless they turned off on one of the tiny secondary roads, or into a campground, they weren't going anywhere but straight. Four miles from the parking lot he touched the accelerator and closed the distance between his vehicle and the van.

"Almost there," he said. "What's it like to have a minute left to live? But then, you wouldn't know that, would you?"

He slipped a remote control from his windbreaker pocket. He entered a four digit code and waited. The road climbed slightly, then crested and began a long downward slope. His index finger touched one of the buttons, triggering a deadly sequence of events. A tiny receiver under the driver's seat in the van picked up a radio signal, electronically closing a circuit and sending a current from the battery to the solenoid coil. A small electric magnet opened the canister, releasing the pressurized cyanide gas into the passenger compartment of the van.

"Good-bye…"

Other *Leisure* books by Jeff Buick:

**SHELL GAME**
**AFRICAN ICE**
**LETHAL DOSE**
**BLOODLINE**

# JEFF BUICK

# DELICATE CHAOS

LEISURE BOOKS  NEW YORK CITY

A LEISURE BOOK®

February 2008

Published by

Dorchester Publishing Co., Inc.
200 Madison Avenue
New York, NY 10016

ISBN 10: 0-8439-6038-8
ISBN 13: 978-0-8439-6038-9

Printed in the United States of America.

10 9 8 7 6 5 4 3 2 1

Visit us on the web at www.dorchesterpub.com.

*To my first grandchild, Mikayla,*
*in my humble, and unbiased opinion,*
*the cutest little girl on the planet.*
*How fascinating it is to rediscover*
*our world through a child's eyes.*

# DELICATE CHAOS

# 1

A vast plateau of scrubland stretched out before the group of armed men. Heat waves rose off the parched earth, distorting their view of the elephants gathered on the edge of the tree line that marked the start of the forest. Overhead, the cloudless sky was deep blue, scarred only by the intense, noonday sun. The mercury was pushing one-ten and still rising. Africa at its finest.

"The large male closest to the acacia tree is the leader," one of the men said, pointing a long, thin finger in the general direction of the animals. "We call him Albert."

"Albert?" the woman asked. "Why Albert?" Her name was Leona Hewitt, and as the only woman, and white person, in the group, she stood out. Her off-blond hair fell to her shoulders in ringlets, and her face was tinged red from the relentless, scorching sun. Her greenish brown eyes were quick and lively, and when she smiled or laughed, her lips curled back, revealing slightly crooked, but very white teeth. A youthful thirty-seven, she welcomed the tiny lines around her eyes and mouth. They were the only sign she was pushing forty, and they gave her character.

The man smiled, his white teeth in stark contrast to his black skin. "He's very smart, so we named him after Albert Einstein."

Kubala Kantu's arm dropped back to his side. A native of the Samburu region of central Kenya, he was Leona's key man; the one who managed the African end of Save Them, Leona's wildlife foundation. A sketchy high school education was the strong point on his short résumé, even that probably embellished, but Kubala had an elusive mixture of street smarts and natural intelligence. It was a blend of talents that kept him alive while he protected the elephants from poachers. Kubala was tall, six-four, but rail thin with bushy hair and intense brown eyes that belied his easygoing nature. The loaded AK-47 slung loosely over his shoulder was another clue that he was not a man to mess with.

"They are unsettled today," he said quietly, his voice carrying easily through the hot, dry air.

"Why is that?" Leona locked her gaze on the animals, some two hundred yards in the distance.

"Poachers, perhaps?" Kubala shrugged. The gun moved with the motion. "They can smell danger. It is in the air."

"Have the poachers tried to kill Albert?"

Kubala laughed, but there was no humor in the sound. "Many times, but he is too smart. The poachers try to frighten the elephants, to trap them in a remote area where they can massacre them before we arrive. Albert will not be fooled by such tricks. He keeps his herd where we can watch them."

Leona turned slightly so Kubala came into her peripheral vision. "Animals act by instinct, not reason."

Kubala stared straight into her eyes. "Whatever you say, Ms. Hewitt. Whatever you say."

A slight gust of wind pulled at his robes and he cinched them tight. For six years he had watched over Albert's herd, and six others. Courtesy of the money Leona Hewitt raised in the United States, his group of twenty-seven park rangers was well organized and even better equipped. The poachers knew it, and they mostly stayed away from the seven-hundred-square-mile tract of land the Kenyan government had ceded wildlife control of to Save Them. It was a huge step to preserving the elephants, and one that had not come easily. Leona's concession to the government was that for every dollar she spent on conservation, she had to spend two on improving the quality of life for the local people. It was her idea, and had met fierce resistance at first. But new water wells, schools, and even a medical clinic appeared as she pumped money into the village of Marsabit, and the central government in Nairobi had backed off. Now, in the village that housed one thousand African men, women and children, she was a hero.

The elephants turned and disappeared into the trees, a few wisps of dust the only sign that they had visited the savannah. Within eyesight, a pride of lions lounged in the afternoon sun, and across the endless stretch of arid land was a massive herd of wildebeests and zebras. The elephants and the villagers weren't the only ones that benefited from the foundation.

"We should head back for the village," Kubala said. "Your plane leaves Nairobi early tomorrow morning."

Leona nodded. "I'm glad we got to see this herd," she replied, taking a long draw on her water bottle. She grasped Kubala by his forearm. "Thank you for taking such good care of the animals."

Kubala grinned. "Thank you, Miss Leona, for taking such good care of us."

It was a powerful moment, but it didn't last. The unmistakable crack of gunfire rifled across the plateau. The lions were instantly on the move, as was the group of rangers. Kubala grabbed Leona and pulled her to the Land Rover.

They jumped in and he yelled instructions to the driver. Seconds later they were flying down the rutted dirt road toward the origin of the sound. The guns were off their shoulders and all eight men in both vehicles were checking their clips and snapping off the safeties. Thirty seconds and three bends in the road brought them to a horrific sight.

Two elephants were down and dying. A third was stumbling across the small clearing they had just entered. Albert and the rest of the herd were gone, having stampeded into the dense jungle bordering the west side of the clearing. On the east side, hovering over the two stricken elephants, was a handful of heavily armed men. One had a machete in his hand and was hacking at the skin and bone around one of the tusks. Rivulets of blood coursed down the dead animal's neck and the man's face was covered with spatters.

The moment their Land Rovers entered the clearing, Kubala's men were under fire. The poachers had automatic weapons and handguns. One of the bullets smashed out the glass on the side windows and embedded in the seat between Kubala and Leona. He pulled a pistol from his holster and thrust it into her hand, then grabbed her by the shoulder and pushed her to the floor. He leapt from the vehicle as it careened to a stop at the edge of the clearing. The driver was hit in the neck as he opened the door, and dropped heavily onto the dry grass, unmoving, blood gushing from the wound.

Kubala's team was out of the vehicles and behind cover in seconds. They returned the fire, bullets cutting through the dense jungle that had been peaceful only minutes before. One poacher took a round in the head, then another in the shoulder. Leona kicked open the door, giving her a view of where the poachers had dug in. Growing up as a farm girl meant she knew the basics of firing a rifle, and to her a handgun was the same, only shorter. She raised the gun and sighted. Before she could squeeze off a few shots, a swath of bullets tore through the vehicle, ripping into the seats and sending tufts of stuffing flying. She yanked the door shut and hugged the floor of the Land Rover as more rounds slammed into the side panels, the rifle bullets tearing through the vehicle just above her prone body. The slugs from the handguns were unable to penetrate into the cabin and dropped harmlessly into the rocker panels.

Gritty dirt on the floor mats cut into her hands and cheek, and the air was thick with the odor of scorched metal and plastic. The gun felt heavy and useless in her grip. Kubala and his men were under attack, but she was in no position to help. The poachers knew she was in the vehicle and opening the door was an invitation to a stray bullet. She lay on the floor, her head throbbing, her pulse racing.

Realizing they were up against men who were well armed and capable of using the guns, the poachers retreated into the wall of foliage, laying down a dangerous volley of covering fire as they disappeared. Eighty seconds from the moment the two Land Rovers entered the clearing, it was again quiet. But now two elephants were dead, another writhing in its death throes near the tree line. Kubala's driver was killed the instant the bullet cut through his neck and spine, and one other of his team was nursing a serious leg wound.

"Get a compress on this wound and drive him to the clinic in the village," Kubala said to the driver of the second Land Rover. "Call ahead and tell them you're coming so they can prepare."

The man nodded and slung his gun over his shoulder, then barked orders to the others who were assigned to his Land Rover. It took less than five minutes to stem the bleeding and load the injured man into the vehicle. A trail of dust marked the vehicle's exit, then it settled to the ground and the clearing was quiet, save for the labored breathing of the third elephant. Kubala pulled a high-caliber rifle from inside the truck and walked across to where the elephant lay dying.

"I am sorry you must die at my hand," he said to the animal as he chambered a round. "But this is only meant to ease your suffering." He raised the gun and fired a single shot into the broad forehead. The breathing stopped and a heavy silence fell over the clearing.

Leona stood beside the Land Rover, ten feet from the dead ranger, fifty from the elephant. Already, the stench of death was in the air. Soon the buzzards would feast. She looked down at the pistol in her hand. She hadn't fired a single shot. There was no opportunity. Kubala's men had driven the poachers back into the forest while she was trapped in the Land Rover. She handed the pistol back to Kubala when he returned to where she was standing. Their eyes met.

"You acted bravely," Kubala said, seeing the emotion in her eyes. "They would have killed you if you had opened the door."

Leona simply nodded. She pushed her hair back from her face and looked over the carnage. "Why does it have to be like this?" she asked. "Why is there always death?"

The expression on Kubala's face didn't change. He adjusted the shoulder harness on the AK-47 slightly and tucked the pistol in his holster. "TIA, Miss Leona. TIA."

"TIA? What does that mean?"

"This is Africa. This is the way things are."

Leona swallowed and the dryness in her throat hurt. Kubala's words were simple, but true. And sometimes, the truth hurt.

## 2

DC Trust was a small bank if you measured it against Chase Manhattan, but it had carved out its niche and was aggressive in finding and keeping clients. Corporate clients. No savings accounts for kids or tellers waiting for clients to walk through the front door. Only corporations with healthy balance statements and an insatiable need for more investment capital. The bank's bottom line was well into the black, the shareholders were happy and the staff was well paid.

Head office was in a twelve story brick building on F Street, about three blocks northwest of the White House. DC Trust occupied the top two floors, with the worker bees on eleven and management on twelve. The two floors were totally different worlds. Eleven was cubicle city, a maze of dividers and desks under the harsh glare of fluorescent lighting. Photocopiers buzzed and phones rang. Executive assistants drafted documents and moved papers from one desk to another, always with some degree of urgency. Quitting time was five, but anyone leaving on the stroke of the hour was given a sideways glance. DC Trust believed in maximizing everything they touched.

Leona Hewitt, Director of Corporate Acquisitions and Accounts, had earned a coveted corner office on eleven. Close to playing with the big boys but not quite there. The fluorescent lights in her office were turned off—she hated them. Natural sunlight filtered in through the two banks of windows during the day, and at night she flipped on a desk lamp and worked in relative darkness. Her work space was busy but tidy, most of the files out of sight in the cabinets. Her desk had a few piles of carefully stacked paper, a computer monitor and six framed five-by-seven photos. Two were of Kubala Kantu with the elephants and the other three were of her with some of the African kids in their village. She lived and worked in Washington, DC, but her heart was in the pictures. Leona glanced up from her desk as a man entered.

"Good morning, Leona," he said, a slight trace of southern drawl mixing with his deep baritone. His suit was muted Armani, his hair glowing silver and his face well tanned. At sixty-three years of age and one-eighty carried on a six-foot frame, he wasn't a physically imposing man. His name was Anthony Halladay, and what intimidated people was his position as president and CEO of DC Trust. "Do you have a minute?"

"Of course," she said, motioning to a chair opposite her desk. She waited until he was seated, then said, "What brings you down to the trenches?"

He smiled, teeth white against the dark skin. "Is that what the staff calls it? The trenches?"

She returned the smile. "Sometimes. On good days. You don't want to know what we call it on bad days."

Halladay sat in the offered chair and smoothed the creases in his suit pants. Leona knew he liked it when the staff treated him like one of the boys. Few of them were comfortable enough to do it, but she had no problem trading lighthearted banter with him.

"I'm here on business," he said, his voice taking on a serious tone. "I've got an offer for you."

Leona twisted and leaned forward in her chair, a habit she had picked up early in her working life. She tilted her head slightly to the right. "Go ahead," she said, more than a little intrigued.

"You've been with us for six years. Six very good years. I'm quite pleased with your performance."

"Thank you," she said when he paused for a moment.

"But in your current position as a director, any further movement up in your department is impossible."

"There's always your job."

Halladay grinned again. "Or a vice presidency," he said.

The room went silent for the better part of fifteen seconds. Finally, Leona said, "Are you offering me a position as a vice president?"

Halladay nodded. "I am. You're the kind of person we're looking for on our management team, Leona. Tell you something can't be done and you'll find a way to do it. I like that. The board of directors likes that. In fact, I've already decided which file for you to cut your teeth on if you accept our offer."

"What is it?" Leona said, her pulse quicker and her breath coming in short spurts. Despite trying to keep an even keel, she was shaking. She pushed her hands down on the desk and the trembling transferred to her shoulders. Less noticeable.

He shifted in the chair and ran his hand through his thick silver hair. "The firm is Coal-Balt Inc."

"I see documents on them all the time," Leona said. "They generate electric power from coal-burning plants. Coal-Balt is one of our largest clients."

Halladay nodded again. "And most profitable. Currently they're a publicly traded company on the New York Stock Exchange. They follow normal accounting procedures, nothing out of the ordinary. But they've proposed a change to that structure."

"What sort of change?"

"They want to convert to an income trust."

Leona leaned back in her chair, the slight trembles gone, replaced by a calm, but thoughtful expression. "An income trust," she said quietly. "What's their logic behind that?"

"Shareholder value. By converting to an income trust, they

can raise the value of their shareholders' stakes by almost forty percent overnight."

"I'm not sure I get their line of thinking. Income trusts aren't that desirable anymore. Not a lot of tax advantages."

Halladay smiled. "The guys at Coal-Balt found a way around the tax laws. Nothing illegal, simply good business."

"What are they proposing?" she asked, her interest piqued.

"There are three separate vehicles Coal-Balt can use—Enhanced Income Securities, Income Participating Securities and Income Deposit Securities—to tie together a share of stock and a high-yield debt. The junk debt and shares, stapled together, replace the trust in its truest sense."

"Interesting approach. Will it work?"

Halladay shrugged. "They've run the figures, Leona, and I've seen the breakdown. It does work. The restructuring is a stroke of brilliance."

"What about regulatory approval?"

"The regulatory guys at the stock exchange have given the transition a green light. They need some more paperwork, but approval is pending. That paperwork needs to come from us."

"Why do they need us onside?" Leona asked.

"We hold two hundred and eighty million in demand loans. Our agreement to the conversion is one of the caveats the exchange requires to okay the deal."

Leona asked, "Who do you have in mind for my team?"

"You pick the people you need. This is your deal."

"Okay."

"It goes without saying how important Coal-Balt is to us," Halladay said. "I don't foresee any problems with this conversion. I hope you don't either."

Leona glanced at her watch. It was ten minutes past twelve. "I have an appointment for lunch," she said. "It's too late to cancel."

"No, that's fine, you go ahead." Halladay rose from the chair. "When will you be moving upstairs?"

Leona couldn't stifle the smile. "Whenever you're ready for me."

"Then I'll see you Monday morning. Your personal effects and computer will be moved up after work tonight."

Leona nodded and Anthony Halladay turned and left her office. She liked and trusted the CEO and having the position of vice president dropped in her lap was more than a nice touch. But she didn't like offers that came with strings attached. Never had. And the Coal-Balt file felt like a major string. *I don't foresee any problems with this conversion. I hope you don't either.* That didn't sit right with her. Like Halladay was telling her the outcome of her team's findings before they began. It was out of character for the man.

Leona switched off her reading lamp and hurried to the elevator. Her lunch date was waiting. But she wasn't too worried. If the restaurant served beer, which they did, he would wait.

# 3

Mike Anderson sipped on his bottle of Budweiser and watched the lunch crowd. People-watching was one of his favorite pastimes, and there were few places better than downtown DC. Washington was all about power; if you had it you flaunted it. If you didn't, you either faked it or played the attentive pup listening to the master. The percentage per capita of sycophants in DC had to be the highest in the country. In the world, perhaps.

He glanced around Kinkeads, knowing he was the square peg in the round hole. The luncheon crowd in the upscale seafood eatery was mostly suit and tie or dark pantsuit, gender dependant. He was jeans and a white T-shirt. Ex–New York cop, now mixed in with politicians and lobbyists. Gasoline and a match if he drank enough. It wasn't a stretch to recognize Anderson as ex-cop—he looked the part. He was dead-on six feet, 210 pounds, most of it still muscle and bone. His waistline had finally settled in at thirty-eight, no belly hanging over his belt. No wrinkles creased his face, except for tiny crow's-feet that stretched back from the corners of his eyes. He had a full head of dark hair, a strong jawline and quick brown eyes. Anderson finished his beer and waved at the waiter for a refill. He'd be good today, he was meeting Leona and she didn't like it when he drank enough to get belligerent. He ran his hand over his chin, feeling the stubble. It was only one day but he already looked like he'd been on a six-day bender. It was common knowledge that that sort of thing happened when you hit fifty. For him, forty-five had happened a month ago. This meant he was five years ahead of his time—at looking old. Great.

The waiter dropped another beer on the table and gave the untouched glass a sideways look that said, *trailer trash*. Anderson shook his head, wondering how even waiters in DC could be such sanctimonious pricks. A few seconds later Leona entered the restaurant and he caught her attention by waving. He watched as she picked her way through the throng of tables. When she walked, her body was a dichotomy, different parts moving in different directions. The result was sultry. Her breasts swayed slightly, but not too much. Her hips moved with a wavelike motion and he could see the heads turning as she made her way through the tables. From the first moment he had met her, he'd thought she was sexy—her body and her smile. He liked working for her charity. It meant he got to see her and talk to her, one-on-one. She settled into the chair opposite him.

"Sorry I'm late," Leona said, flashing him one of her

natural, disarming smiles. Fact was, she was almost always late, despite setting her watch ten minutes early. It was a minor character flaw—one she felt could be overlooked. "Unexpected business at the office."

"I'm happy. I ask for a beer, waiter brings one."

Leona glanced at the bottle. "How are you, Mike? You okay with the booze?"

"Yeah, I'm fine. Sticking to beer these days. No hard stuff."

"How are things with Susan?" Leona asked.

Anderson shrugged. "She's an ex-wife I still love. And she's living with another guy. How do you think things are?"

"You have to let her go." Leona slid her hand across the table and rested it on his thick forearm. "Life goes on."

He didn't respond other than to take another sip of beer with his free hand. The waiter approached and asked Leona what she wanted to drink. His tone was nicer now, civil even. Leona was business class—she belonged. Christ, he hated the whole DC hierarchy thing. Maybe because he was on the outside looking in. The fat kid with pimples sitting by himself in the school cafeteria.

"How's Kubala?" Leona asked, concern creeping into her voice.

"Not good. The poachers are still pissed at him over what happened when you were there three months ago. Every day is dangerous right now."

Mike Anderson was Leona's point man for her nonprofit foundation. Save Them was dead in the water without him, and she knew it. Once the accountants finished totaling the donations from the fundraisers, Anderson took the money and made sure it got to the right people in Nairobi. Distributing cash from a nonprofit in the US was easy and safe, but in Africa it took on a whole new dimension. Arriving in Nairobi with a suitcase full of bearer bonds was an invitation to a permanent home in a small pine box. The first few times were scenes out of a bad movie. The corrupt immigration guards at the border, the dark cars that tailed them to the bank. Invitations, at gunpoint, to meet some of Nairobi's most important, and dangerous, people. Those who could ensure the foundation's money filtered down to those who needed it to protect the elephants. For a fee, of course.

By his fifth trip to the Kenya capital, he had established the pipeline. Thirty-eight percent of Leona's hard-earned donations went to three distinct groups who provided protection for the remaining sixty-two percent. The most difficult part of deciding who to pay was figuring out who was the most despicable. No sense paying someone in Nairobi who was subservient to somebody else, or you ended up paying two people. Find the most corrupt, most despicable, most loathsome guy on the block and deal with him. It was the approach Mike had taken, and it had worked well.

The poachers were another story. Since the incident back in April, they had been stalking Kubala and his team, taking potshots at them from the bush. Two of his men had been wounded, one in the arm, the other in the leg. Nothing fatal, but almost enough to scare them into submission. Almost, but not quite. Kubala Kantu was not a man who was cowed by adversity. Not even when the adversity came in the form of bullets and machetes.

"When are you heading back to Africa?" Leona asked.

Mike shrugged. "You've got a fundraiser tonight. I'll wait for the accountants to release whatever you raise at your function before I go. Probably a week or so."

"Should be a good one tonight," she said. "We've got a few new faces in the crowd. It's nice when donor fatigue isn't an issue."

"Donor fatigue?"

"You know, when the room is always full of the same

people. After a while they get tired of giving. New donors get their checkbooks out a little quicker."

Mike nodded as the waiter reappeared and took their food order. He surveyed the room as Leona pointed to the menu and made sure her fish wasn't going to be battered or deep-fried. He doubted there was a man in the room who would survive a week in Nairobi with five hundred thousand dollars in his briefcase. Most would be dead inside twenty-four hours. Yet here they sat in their thousand-dollar suits, ordering fifty dollar lunch entrées and drinking twelve-year-old scotch. Different skill sets. Theirs just paid better.

"Poachers seem to have forgotten about killing the elephants," he said as the waiter disappeared into the kitchen with their order. "No new carcasses since April."

"Too busy trying to kill people." Leona sipped on her soda water. She glanced around the restaurant for the first time, drinking in the clientele. "What's with us? As a species, I mean. Why are we constantly trying to kill each other?"

Mike peeled the label off the beer bottle. "It's easy to figure out why people want to kill lawyers. Determining motive for the rest of us is a little tougher."

"You had a good lawyer," Leona chastised him. "You still have your house."

"Lost my balls, though," Anderson snapped back. She didn't respond and he said, "Where's the fundraiser tonight?"

"At the restaurant. Eight o'clock. You should come. Tyler's cooking up something special."

"What?"

"It's a surprise. He wouldn't tell me."

"It's your restaurant. You own it. You'd think that if anyone could find out what's on the menu it would be you."

She grinned. "Doesn't work that way. You know what

chefs are like. Masters of their domain. I might own the place, but Tyler runs it." The grin slowly faded. "Try to make it this evening, Mike. You need to get out more. I'm worried about you."

He finished his beer and set the bottle on the polished table. "I'll try." They were quiet for a minute, the background noise in the restaurant suddenly louder. "What's new at the office? You said something unexpected came up."

"One of the big boys came down from twelve and dropped a file on my desk," she said, purposely omitting the promotion to VP. "It's a utility company. They generate electrical power."

"Coal or water?"

"Coal. Why?"

"Big issue these days, burning coal to produce electricity. Lots of it going on now that natural-gas prices are through the roof."

Leona leaned forward. Mike Anderson was well-read and intelligent. His opinion was usually worth listening to. "What's wrong with burning coal to produce power?"

"Depends on how it's done and what kind of coal they're using. You can burn coal cheap and dirty, or you can burn it clean and expensive."

"I don't know the difference." She leaned back as the waiter set their plates on the linen tablecloth. "But I can guess how you burn it affects the bottom line."

"Big-time," Anderson said. "Most of the older coal-burning power stations swallow tons of the stuff every minute to generate thousand-degree steam. The steam drives the turbines that produce the electricity." He tasted the salmon, then a couple of veggies. The place might be full of sycophants, but the food was good. "By-product of burning coal like that is carbon dioxide. Lots of it. One of these big plants can dump tens of thousands of tons of carbon dioxide into the atmosphere every day."

"Carbon dioxide is a greenhouse gas, isn't it?" Leona asked.

"The worst one. It traps the heat and won't let it escape. Carbon dioxide is the main reason we've got global warming."

"I'm assuming that's the cheap way to burn coal."

"Yeah, the expensive way produces almost no carbon dioxide because they don't actually burn it, they transform it to something called syngas. I don't understand the process, but it's definitely better for the environment."

Leona swallowed a mouthful of fish and said, "You mentioned what kind of coal they burn. I didn't know there was more than one type."

"Well, coal is coal, but it comes with a shitload of impurities. Bitumen, sulfur, that kind of stuff. There are even trace quantities of thorium and uranium in some coal beds. Clean coal is bad enough, but add in all this other crap and it's plain disgusting. Killing our planet, and not slowly."

"Why do you always know all this stuff?" She set her napkin on the empty plate.

He smiled. "Impresses the girls."

"Worked on me," she said.

"So where does this company fit in? Environmentalists or pillagers? There's not a lot of middle ground on this one."

"I don't know." Leona motioned for the check. "But I'm going to find out. And soon."

# 4

Reginald Morgan was a living icon. He was fourth-generation industrialist, and first-generation philanthropist. His great-grandfather, Ezra Morgan, had worked the Virginia coal mines for six years during the Civil War era as a *butty*, doling out the underground jobs and walking about the mine looking for sections that were susceptible to collapsing. It didn't take long to realize the coal dust was killing him. He asked for a transfer to the head office, and since he had a quick head for math, was assigned to the accounting and payroll department. The patriarch of the Morgan clan rose quickly through the ranks, and by the age of thirty-six he was in charge of mining operations.

Ezra changed the way things were done. Child labor, used to mine the coal from the seams and then pull it to collection points in a coal dram, was eliminated. He designed a complicated network of underground railways to move the coal, and an updated version of the mechanized pulley system to bring the coal back to the surface. His mines were patrolled by men who understood the causes and dangers of methane gas and who knew what to look for when a collapse was imminent. Ezra Morgan's mines were the safest in the country.

Over the generations, the family name became synonymous with not only coal but also electricity. They mined the coal, then transported it to their electrical generating plant a few miles away in the foothills bordering the Rich Mountains in West Virginia. Providing power to the eastern seaboard proved to be a very lucrative business and the Morgan family fortune grew exponentially. Control of the business was kept in the family, eventually settling on Reginald Morgan. But now it appeared the dynasty was about to end. He and his wife tried for many years to have children, something that had not happened. He remained at the helm, trying to stave off the day that his company would pass to an outsider.

But Reginald Morgan was getting old. His seventy-third birthday had come and gone and his physical strength was waning. His mottled scalp showed under remnants of what had once been thick silver hair and his face was almost without color. Veins were visible under the paper-thin skin. He spent time staring at the back of his hands, likening them to road maps of some county he'd never visited. It struck him as odd that he didn't know the back of his hand anymore.

A second man entered the room and Reginald Morgan looked up from the papers on his desk. It was Derek Swanson, president of the Morgan empire of companies. Swanson was midfifties but didn't look a day over forty-five. His daily regimen included a six-mile jog and weight training. And he ate properly. Vegetables, fruit, no fat and no sugar. His face was rugged and tanned, the result of the many hours he spent outdoors, and he carried a hundred and ninety pounds on a six-two frame. His deep brown eyes were focused and penetrating. If eyes were truly the window to the soul, Swanson's inner persona was all business.

"You wanted to see me, Reggie." He slipped into the soft leather chair facing the company's Chief Executive Officer.

"Yes, thanks for coming," Morgan said, his voice still surprisingly strong for the frail body. "And on short notice. I know you're busy."

"Making us money," Swanson said.

"Yes, of course. Money." Morgan steepled his fingers and cocked his head slightly. "I'm not sure about the conversion, Derek. I don't think I'm going to back it."

Derek Swanson's face didn't change. His breathing didn't alter from its even cadence and he didn't tap a finger or wiggle a toe. Nothing spoke of the internal turmoil those few words had set off. "What's your reasoning for that?" he asked, his voice normal.

Morgan waved a hand as he spoke. "This company was built on solid business practices. Slow, steady growth with an eye to the future. Income trusts are dangerous, Derek. They deplete companies of surplus cash, and right now we need that cash. Lombard II needs work. It was state of the art when we built it, but not anymore. On your recommendation, we've been holding off installing scrubbers and moving to new technology since we hired you. That's eight years, Derek. It's time to move ahead. It's time to clean up our act and stop polluting."

"Why the sudden surge of conscience?" Swanson asked.

Morgan shook his head. "Nothing sudden about it. I've been pushing for new technology for years now. You were against it. And your opinion was what the shareholders listened to. Higher share prices, larger dividends—all money driven. It's time for that to stop. My family never knowingly destroyed the environment. Not while we ran the company."

"Are you saying that since you hired me as president, your company's ethical position has changed?" Swanson asked, a slight edge to his voice.

Morgan measured his response for a minute, then said, "You put profits ahead of people, financial gain ahead of the environment. When we brought you on, we were ready for change. You're the reason that change has never happened. We're still burning our coal dirty and cheap. And it's having an effect on our community." He wet his thin, pale lips with a quivering tongue. "You can label it ethics if you wish, Derek. But this company has not moved in the right direction since you took over."

"We have plans to clean up our emissions," Swanson said. "But it's expensive. The conversion to an income trust will generate a lot of money. Money that can be used to upgrade our facility."

Morgan laughed, a full-bodied chortle that took a full thirty seconds to completely die out. "Now who's having an attack of conscience? You could have implemented those changes anytime over the past eight years. Phased in over time, the effect on our bottom line would have been almost negligible. But you didn't." He leaned forward on his desk. "And now, when you have fifty million dollars riding on this conversion, you tell me the real reason you want it to happen is to initiate changes that will benefit other people. That's bullshit and you know it."

"The conversion is a done deal," Swanson said. "We have regulatory approval from the stock exchange and DC Trust is behind it. There's no stopping it, Reggie."

"I still have some influence," Morgan said. "My great-grandfather built this company."

"And now the shareholders tell us what to do," Swanson snapped back. "And they like the idea of the value of their shares increasing by forty percent overnight. I couldn't stop this if I wanted to. And neither can you."

Morgan's face took on color. "Don't underestimate me, Derek. That would be a mistake."

Swanson sat back in his chair, his voice returning to normal, his demeanor composed. "The conversion is an excellent business decision. The wheels are in motion. It's out of our hands."

"Nothing about this company is ever out of my hands," Morgan said. "And you're forgetting one thing."

"What's that?"

"Senator Claire Buxton. Her new fresh-air initiative. If her bill goes through, our equipment will be obsolete. Overnight. That makes our company unattractive to investors. Unless we have the money for the necessary upgrades." He paused and stared hard at the younger man. "Which, at this precise moment, we have. But you convert to an income trust and pay out hundreds of millions of dollars, and that money is gone. Buxton's initiative could sink us."

"It'll never happen," Swanson said.

"Why? Because you've hired a handful of lobbyists to protect companies that pollute the environment?"

"Careful. You're grouping your own company in with the bad boys."

"I am," Morgan said emphatically. "We pollute the air. We create massive impoundment ponds filled with sludge. We strip the tops off mountains to mine the underlying coal seams."

"I don't think you want to repeat that outside this office," Swanson said.

The elder man's face contorted with rage. "I'll say whatever I want, Derek. I've been pushing for more environmentally friendly methods of mining the coal and burning it since we hired you. You, however, have managed to talk the shareholders into keeping the status quo." He slammed a weathered fist on his desk. "I swear to God, Derek, I'm not going to let you run roughshod over this company, my family name, or our legacy any longer. The conversion is out. It's not going to happen."

Swanson struggled to retain his composure. "Like I said, you can't stop it."

"Yes, I can." Morgan's eyes burned with a strange mixture of desire and hate. "And I will."

Derek Swanson stood up and adjusted the sleeves on his suit so a half inch of dress shirt cuff showed. "This is going nowhere right now. We'll talk about it when you get back from your vacation."

"Maybe," Morgan said. "By then Senator Buxton's bill could be tabled. That will kill your conversion on the spot. The regulatory body at the exchange and the bank will immediately pull their support."

Swanson turned and walked to the door without looking back. He closed the door quietly behind him, his mind a seething mass of hate and loathing. The old man was a dinosaur. The company may have originated with his ancestors, but the shareholders controlled its destiny now. And the shareholders wanted what he wanted: the hundreds of millions of dollars the conversion to an income trust would pump into the company's book value. That he would personally benefit by almost fifty million dollars was simply a convenient by-product of the restructuring. And without Senator Buxton's bill passing through the Senate and Congress, there was no reason to change the way they did business. Although he knew they should.

Coal-Balt was a poster child for environmental destruction. They tore mountaintops apart to reach the coal seams, then pumped millions of tons of carbon dioxide into the atmosphere when they burned the coal to produce electrical power. But people wanted air-conditioning in the summer and lights in the winter. They couldn't live without the thousands of megawatts of energy that the steam-powered turbines generated. And that was going to make him even richer than he already was.

Swanson slowed as he passed Reginald Morgan's executive assistant. She glanced up at him and smiled. "What are you going to do when your boss is gone?" he asked.

"Catch up," she said cheerfully. "The only time I get a chance to clear off my desk is when he leaves for a week or two."

"Where are Reginald and Amelia going?" Swanson asked her.

"Caribbean," she answered.

"Their place in the Caymans?"

"No, Mr. Morgan wanted to move around a bit. They're taking a cruise."

"Late in the season for a cruise." Swanson headed for the door. "Almost hurricane season."

"Mr. Morgan thought of that. He figures the best place

to be is on a cruise ship," she said. "They simply change course and miss the storm."

"Makes sense." Swanson gave the CEO's assistant a nod of his head. "Unless the storm comes looking for you," he said quietly under his breath.

# 5

Leona finally left the office at twenty minutes to seven. She had opted not to drive to work in the morning, and hailed a cab and gave the driver the address to her restaurant. Invited guests would be arriving by eight and she wanted to help Tyler with the setup. Her mind wandered as the taxi moved with the evening DC traffic, past Washington Circle on Pennsylvania Avenue. The tightly fitting buildings, like a precise jigsaw puzzle, melted away as they traversed Rock Creek Park. They came out on the west side and entered Georgetown.

Anthony Halladay had dropped quite the plum on her desk. She should be thrilled; they didn't hand out vice presidencies at the bank very often. Currently there were six. Now seven. Her take-home pay would go through the roof, and her profile in a city built on profile would increase exponentially. But his comments bothered her. The caveat attached to the position.

*It goes without saying how important Coal-Balt is to us. I don't foresee any problems with this conversion. I hope you don't either.*

His words were specific—don't screw this up. But his tone was normal, not malicious or threatening. She was probably reading too much into it. Monday was her first day on the twelfth floor, her first day on the income trust conversion. She'd worry about it then. Right now, she had a weekend ahead of her, starting with a fundraiser to host.

The cab slowed on M Street in Georgetown, then pulled

in behind a Foggy Bottom shuttle, finally arriving in front of Gin House. She paid the driver and checked her watch as she cut across the sidewalk to the front door. Seven-thirty. Plenty of time. The outside of the restaurant was in contrast to the name. Stylish taupe-colored acrylic pillars bordered each of the eight floor-to-ceiling picture windows. A portico of the same color and texture jutted out over a stylish patio packed with diners listening to light rock on the Boettger sound system as they ate or drank.

She glanced at the menu posted inside the front door. It was the food, and how they prepared it, that set Gin House apart from every other DC restaurant. Everything was organic, and locally grown. The chickens were free range, the beef grassfed and the vegetables had somehow reached maturity without being sprayed with chemicals. The concept had caught on, not just with tree huggers, but with average people who liked fresh, well-cooked food and didn't mind paying a premium. Leona Hewitt loved to cook, and owning a restaurant was a dream that had happened more by happenchance than good planning.

Mildred, her favorite aunt, had bought the building that housed the restaurant twenty-five years ago when DC real estate was still reasonable. For the next quarter century, a deli occupied the main floor and a tailor ran his business from the upper level. Her aunt had never bothered getting involved with running either business. Instead she collected the rent every month, paying off the mortgage in fifteen years. Until her death, about a year ago, the building provided her with a steady form of income. When her will was read to the family, one line was a shock to almost everyone. It was the line where she left the building to Leona, with the provision that it could not be sold for at least five years, and that Leona would use the hundred thousand dollars also allocated to her in the will to convert the building to a restaurant. It had cost almost five hundred thousand for the build-out, but with the building as collateral, the bank had been only too willing to lend the other four hundred. Leona had the restaurant she had always dreamed of owning. But with her job at the bank, which she needed for the income, she didn't have time to run it. So she relied on the chef, Tyler Matthews.

Leona waved to her serving staff as she wound her way through the crowd and got smiles and waves in return. Another thing that made Gin House stand out was how she and Tyler treated their staff. The restaurant had a separate lounge with a plasma television and comfortable chairs for the servers and cooks. Each staff member had a private locker and there was always tea, coffee and fresh sandwiches on the counter. Her staff turnover was almost zero. She reached the kitchen, took a deep breath, and pushed open the door.

Tyler's domain was organized mayhem. With a hundred and twelve seats plus the rooftop patio, a lot of dishes got plated every night. Leona caught Tyler's eye as he tested a sauce, nodded to the cook and headed straight over. Only twenty-eight, Tyler was already an excellent chef. He was self-taught, from years on the job working with a slew of different chefs, each with their own strengths and quirks. There was little he hadn't cooked, and nothing he couldn't cook. The menu reflected his, and her, eclectic nature. She hated boring, and the restaurant was anything but that. The name, Gin House, reflected the fusion of French and Thai cuisine. Translated to English, Gin, in Thai, meant *let's eat*.

"Hi," he said, and they hugged. Tyler was a bit over six feet and wiry, with blond hair that tended to red. His eyes were shocking blue and honest. He had a quick grin, and a couple of scars from some of his rougher drinking nights. He'd learned a lot of lessons over the years, but backing down from a fight wasn't one of them.

"Busy tonight," she said.

"Always. Good food, lots of business. People come back."

A cook waved him over and he crossed the kitchen in short jerky moves. He tested the sauce, nodded, and returned to Leona. "We're ready for the fundraiser. The gals have it set up on the patio. Nice weather for it."

"What are you serving?"

"Roasted lamb short loin with sugar snap peas and chanterelle risotto." The excitement in Tyler's voice grew as he talked about the food. "And if they like seafood, a little grilled lobster tail with heirloom tomato and arugula salad to start. Plus sweet corn and okra fritters with preserved lemon sabayon. Should be delicious."

"Well, the kitchen's your domain. Whatever you think."

"This will get them in a giving mood. Great food always does."

Leona left her head chef and climbed the back stairs the kitchen staff used to ferry food and drink to the rooftop patio. The steep stairway was old, but well lit with bright lights her contractors had mounted in the ceiling. Still, the walls felt constricting. Her breathing was quick and shallow when she reached the upper landing. The early evening air was warm and the potted ferns swayed about in the soft breeze. The terra-cotta motif was perfect for the weather, and each table was garnished with a hand-carved elephant, no two the same. The tablecloths were white linen, the wineglasses cut crystal. The clientele for this one were some of Washington's most generous philanthropists. She expected to raise a quarter million dollars. Minimum. More was always better.

Three staff members were putting finishing touches on the tables, but there was a fourth person on the patio. He was dressed in business casual and standing next to the roof edge, looking down on the street scene. She threaded her way through the tables and approached him. He was tall, well over six feet with a friendly face and wire-rim glasses. She figured him a couple of years older than her, maybe forty.

"Hi. I'm Leona Hewitt."

He extended his hand. "Ross Carpenter."

"Are you here for the fundraiser?"

He nodded. "I'm early. I flew in from London a couple of hours ago and set my watch wrong. An hour late. Which got me here an hour early."

"Not a problem." Leona waved over one of the servers and they ordered drinks. "So where are you from and what brings you to Washington?"

"Pittsburgh. And I'm here for a video-game conference."

Leona tilted her head slightly and narrowed her eyes. "You're here to play video games?"

"I wish," Ross laughed. He accepted the Perrier water from the server and thanked him. "I'm in town on business. My partner and I come up with new concepts for video games and then develop them and get the new games on the market."

"Video games," she said, interest creeping into her voice. "Can't say I understand the appeal. I never played them and grew up in a house with no brothers and sisters, so I had very little exposure to them."

He nodded and looked away for a few seconds, scanning the street scene below. Two cars jockeyed for one parking spot. "Well, lucky for us, most people have at least tried playing them." He took a sip of water and switched the conversation. "I'm very interested in your fundraiser. A friend of mine called and passed along the invite to come as his guest. He knows I'm passionate about Africa. And from what he said, your foundation not only provides protection for the elephants, but it pumps money into helping the villagers as well."

Leona grinned. This was her turf. Her strength. "I've worked a deal with the Kenyan government where they've given me a tract of land around Samburu, with about eighty to a hundred elephants."

"Kenya?" Ross asked. "I though they had a functional park system. More than functional, actually. It's touted as being the best in Africa."

She nodded, her ringlets bobbing with the motion. "They do have a great parks system, but even the best conservation efforts in Africa need help. The poachers are always better funded and armed. If they really want to kill the elephants, they do."

"Except in Samburu."

"Exactly. The money we raise pays a team of ex-police and military to patrol the roads and plains. They're well armed and know how to use the guns. And the poachers know this. That's the biggest deterrent to them coming around. So they mostly leave us alone."

"What do you do for the villagers?" Ross asked.

Leona spent the next ten minutes giving him the details she had hammered out with the government. How they had agreed to bring in engineers and drill wells for drinking water and irrigation. The number of schools they had built and the increase in the local hospital's capacity. When she was finished, he stroked his chin thoughtfully and nodded.

"Wise use of the money. I like it."

"Thanks." Leona glanced about the rooftop. Twenty-plus people had arrived and were standing about with drinks. She looked back to Ross. "I've got to mingle. You don't mind?"

"Of course not." He extended his hand. "This is your party. That's your job tonight."

She shook his hand. "It was really nice meeting you."

"You, too."

For the next two hours she worked the crowd one-on-one, then gave them ten minutes of prepared words. The applause was long and loud, and people were nodding and reaching for their checkbooks. She had them. She'd make her goal of a quarter million dollars, perhaps more. It was a lot of work to set up a fundraiser like this, but worth the cost in hours and dollars. The difference she was making in Africa was substantial—life altering to many of the poor villagers. Lifesaving for the elephants.

Leona worked the room until the last guests had left for the night. She made a special note of thanking Ross Carpenter for stopping by, then headed down to the main floor. One of her helpers was totaling the donations and glanced up when she entered the small room off the kitchen. He ripped the paper tail off the adding machine and handed it to her.

"Five hundred and twenty-three thousand dollars," he said. "Pretty good night for the elephants."

"Wow." Leona looked down the tape. Her eyes stopped on one of the entries. "Who gave fifty thousand?"

"That fellow from Pittsburgh you were talking to when we were setting up. You must have impressed him."

"Not me." She let the tape drop to her side. For a moment she was back on the arid African plains, the dry wind coursing through her hair. Vast open spaces under cloudless skies—eerily quiet and deceptively peaceful. Kubala by her side, the elephants splashing in the water hole. Life as it could be. Life as it should be. "The kids. The elephants. They were the reason he gave the money."

# 6

Derek Swanson sat on the deck of his home in Morgantown's most exclusive subdivision. Behind him was sixty-four hundred square feet of eight-bedroom, seven-bath, West Virginia luxury. In front of him was an acre of landscaped gardens, complete with a duck pond and waterfall. The muted sound of splashing water drifted across the grass and the morning sun poked through the thick branches of the mature sugar maple trees. Two ovenbirds flitted about and a squirrel chattered at the distractions. Swanson's mind registered none of it.

He sipped his coffee, thinking of nothing but Reginald Morgan. The old man was a fool. A fool who was developing a conscience. And that attack of conscience was going to cost Swanson a lot of money. Somewhere in the range of fifty million dollars. His face took on color as he envisioned the money. Fifty million dollars. He was already rich, but that bump would put him in with the superrich. The ones who owned two-hundred-foot yachts and Caribbean mansions and never looked at price tags.

His housekeeper appeared and quietly refilled his coffee, then disappeared back into the house. His train of thought retreated to the income trust conversion. His experts all but guaranteed a 40 percent rise in stock value, which would pump about thirty-five million dollars into his portfolio. It would also kick in a fifteen-million-dollar bonus that was tied in to company performance. But without the conversion, it was all up in smoke. He needed the conversion, and to get it, he needed three things.

Reginald Morgan onside was number one. Without the old man the deal was dead. The CEO had the power to crater the deal—they both knew it. Morgan had connections inside the bank and at the stock exchange that could kill the deal in almost zero time. Getting him onside was imperative. The second was the bank. DC Trust held close to three hundred million dollars in demand notes, and if they decided the conversion was flawed, then it wouldn't happen. The bank should be okay. He had a person on the inside, and the file had been dropped on some woman with the promise of a vice presidency if all went well. The bank wasn't a problem.

That left the Senator Claire Buxton, the pain-in-the-ass politician from Utah. She was on some sort of personal crusade to reduce the levels of carbon dioxide spewing from the Pacificorp's Hunter 4 plant, close to Castle Dale. And if she were successful, it would affect emission levels from coal-burning plants across the country. If her bill passed through the Senate and Congress, the cost to upgrade their facilities would be astronomical. The additional cost of renewing their infrastructure would send the bank running and stop the approval by the regulatory body at the NYSE. It would drive a sword into the heart of the income trust conversion and cost him fifty million dollars.

But that was one sword that should never get out of the sheath. He had hired one of Washington's top lobbyists to sway the vote once it hit the committee that determined whether the bill would ever see the inside of the Senate or Congress. The jury was out on the results, but so far things were looking okay.

The problem was Reginald Morgan.

Swanson looked down at his hands. They were soft and manicured and seldom saw manual labor. He wielded great power with those hands by simply holding a pen or typing on a keyboard. Words, contracts, numbers—they were his weapons. He controlled the unions, the mine and plant workers and the financial advisors, with business acumen. Only once had he deviated and used force to resolve a dispute. A violent and militant union rep, a man who had incited the plant workers into a feeding frenzy, had fallen victim to his own tactics. It took his body six weeks to work free of the twine attached to the concrete and float to the surface of a nearby lake. By then the corpse was so bloated it was unidentifiable except through DNA records. Even then, Derek Swanson's hands had not been the instruments that dealt the blows. That, as almost everything else in Swanson's life, had been delegated.

Swanson slowly turned his gaze from the peaceful garden to the cordless telephone sitting on the table. One call, that's all it would take. One call and Reginald Morgan would no longer be a problem. He stared at the phone. The number was still etched in his memory. Four years had passed, yet he still remembered pushing the numbers that had started a series of events that culminated in the death of another man. Could he make the call again? He wasn't sure.

He sipped on the coffee but it tasted bitter. The sounds from the waterfall seemed louder, and filled his head with white noise. His head pounded from the stress. Could he do it? Could he sentence Reginald Morgan to death? The blood pumped through his veins, pushing against his skin, throbbing. His breath was coming quicker now. Shallower. He knew what the answer had to be. There was no other way. His hand reached out and he felt the cool touch of the plastic.

He dialed the number and waited.

Decision made.

# 7

When Utah's voters elected Claire Buxton to the Senate, they sent a pit bull to Washington. She was attractive, dressed well and wore lipstick, but Claire Buxton was still a pit bull. She was young for the Senate, only forty-three, with two out of three kids still living at home. Her oldest daughter was at the University of Utah, living in residence and studying the sciences, as her mother had done twenty-four years earlier. Claire's husband, Eric, was the lawyer in the family, but she was the one who had sought public office.

Claire Buxton was never a tree hugger. She ate fast food when she was in a hurry, drove an American-made SUV and begrudgingly recycled her glass and metal containers. But when some of her constituents who lived near the Hunter electrical power plant came to her with health concerns, she took their situation seriously.

The Hunter 4 plant burned coal to produce electrical power. And they burned a lot of it. Fourteen thousand tons a day. And that produced pollution. Pollution that was slowly killing people, including children. And the Hunter plant was merely the tip of the proverbial iceberg. There were hundreds of coal-burning electrical plants peppered across the US, many of them ignoring the Clean Air Act while pumping thousands of tons of carbon dioxide and sulfur dioxide into the atmosphere every day. And what went up the six-hundred-foot-high stacks eventually came down—as acid rain or snow.

And the mines that fed the plants' insatiable appetites for coal produced slurry, a toxic sludge of coal residue, water and oil that was held in huge retention ponds near the mine site.

Claire was on the last section of the Saturday morning paper when her husband padded into the kitchen, still wearing his dressing gown and slippers. A day's growth of stubble covered his chin. He poured some coffee and joined her at the table.

"You're up early," he said. "And dressed. On a Saturday."

"I fly to Lexington today. On Sunday I'm in Pikeville, Kentucky, to talk with Amanda Chisholm. She's the young girl who is dying because of the leaks in the retention ponds around Silo Six mine." She gave him a crooked smile. "Did you forget?"

He slapped himself on the forehead. "Right. Trying to get some leverage on the committee members for your environmental bill."

"Anything to see this bill pass through committee. It's going okay so far, but we've got some well-connected lobbyists working against it." She pushed her dark shoulder-length hair behind her ear. She had never been an overly attractive woman, rather nondescript with no outstanding features. Her face was well proportioned, with wide-set eyes and broad cheeks. She fit a size ten after a small struggle with the zipper and wore sensible shoes. "Jack Dunn is leading the charge. And he and his wolves are being well paid."

"I'm sure they are. I think you've pissed off a lot of utility companies." Eric sipped the coffee and winced slightly as the hot liquid burned his lips.

Claire smoothed the newspaper and folded it back into its original shape. "Some of these plants are complying with the Clean Air Act and the Clear Skies Act and burning their coal clean. Others aren't. They're the ones I'm after. The two acts have been around long enough now for these companies to have begun complying. The problem is, when they don't, the regulators at the Environmental Protection Agency aren't doing anything. And if the EPA isn't breathing down your neck, why spend hundreds of millions of dollars to upgrade your facilities?"

"But if your bill passes through the house, they start to pay," Eric said. "Big-time."

She nodded. "Every ton of emission they pump into the air or dump into a retention pond is going to cost them money. A lot of money. Enough that every plant burning its coal cheap and dirty will be scrambling to install new technology to cut down the crap they're dumping in our air."

"Crap?" Eric said, grinning. "You going to use that word when you table the bill?"

"Maybe," she said. "It got your attention."

"What about the lobbyists? Can they kill it?"

She shrugged. "Jack Dunn is the guy I'm worried about. He's tied in at every level from the years he spent in Congress. A lot of people owe him favors and he might call in a few on this one."

"Who hired him?"

"A company in West Virginia is the main player. Coal-Balt. They've got a few smaller producers in bed with them, but they're spearheading the push to kill it."

"I don't get it. Why don't they just comply? Under the Clear Skies Act, their emissions have to be down substantially by 2020. Why not do it now?"

"The rumor I've heard is that Coal-Balt is restructuring. They're in the process of converting to an income trust."

"What does that matter?"

"I don't understand the economics, but one of my aides gave me a quick briefing last week. If they shift from standard accounting practices to an income trust, the value of the common stocks will rise significantly. And the company will start paying out excess profits to the shareholders. That works well with a utility company, because they have a steady cash flow. But the downside is that allocating large sums of money to fix outdated equipment makes the conversion risky. Payback to the shareholders could dry up and if that happens, the big boys who control the pension funds will dump the stock. That'll start a freefall. And then they're in serious trouble."

"Why don't they fix their equipment, come into line with the current regulations, then convert in a few years?"

She gave him a sideways look. "You've got to be kidding. You can't figure that one out?"

"Money," he said. "Someone inside the company stands to profit."

"Huge. Hundreds of millions of dollars are on the table. The largest benefactors will be Reginald Morgan, the CEO, and Derek Swanson, the president. Morgan could care less—he's in his seventies and would probably like to see the company move ahead. It's Swanson. He's the one who brought in Jack Dunn and his team of sharks."

"So what do you do?"

"Get the bill through committee, then table it in the Senate. If it passes, it's off to Congress, then into the Oval Office. That's what I do, Eric. I get the damn thing through the proper channels."

"It's that important to you?" he asked quietly.

"People are dying. Children are dying. Amanda Chisholm is only one of many. It's got to stop."

He nodded. "Not to mention what these plants contribute to global warming."

"Pound for pound, these coal-burning plants are the absolute worst. A lot of the coal they use is either Midwestern or Appalachian, both of which are extremely high in sulfur. Acid rain, global warming, sludge seeping into the groundwater—nothing about these plants using outdated technology is nice. Nothing."

"And you're going to stop them." Eric tested the coffee against his lips, then took a sip.

"Damn right I am," she said. "2020 is still a long way off. I want them upgraded or shut down now."

"That's my gal. That's why you were elected. You care."

"Rare trait in DC. Don't go running about telling anyone. They'll think I'm the soft egg in the basket."

"Don't see that happening."

Claire Buxton sat quietly for a minute, thinking about the last four years in the Senate. The backroom battles, her doggedly sticking to her convictions while others fought to influence her decisions. Men sitting across the table, powerful men, knowing when they dealt with her they had to make concessions. A reputation built on integrity and honesty. No graft, no all-expense-paid junkets to the Caribbean, no wavering on her principles. No compromises.

She smiled and said, "No soft eggs here, Eric. No soft eggs here."

# 8

Traffic was light, almost nonexistent, and the town's churches were filled. The elderly citizens of Morgantown were dressed in their Sunday finest and the slow toll of the belfry bells echoed across the manicured parks and freshly painted clapboard houses near the city center. The scent of magnolia blossoms tinged the hot July air, and there was a stillness to the leaves that spoke of quiet country living. That little piece of America that existed mostly on postcards. A perfect Sunday morning.

It was also a perfect morning to plan a murder.

Derek Swanson sat in the park, alone on the wooden bench, watching a gaggle of young girls play with the geese next to the pond. The sound of their laughter drifted across the grass, a bitter reminder of the evil nature of his business. He didn't want this. It wasn't part of his plan, never had been. Reginald Morgan was a decent man, perhaps a bit too honest for his own good. There would be no pleasure in knowing the old man's blood was on his hands. None at all.

A nondescript rental car pulled up to the curb and an equally nondescript man exited and walked across the grass to the bench. His stride was more a movement of his legs that propelled his upper body simply because it was attached at the waist. Like Clint Eastwood. He'd always thought Darvin's gait totally aped Eastwood's. But his face was much less memorable. He had light brown hair, cut to the top of his ears and always perfectly groomed, and was clean shaven.

His skin was pasty white despite the hot July weather. There were no redeeming features, just average eyes, puffy cheeks and slightly thinning brown hair topping off a five-ten body. The kind of person no one ever remembered. Perfect if you were a hired killer.

Darvin reached the bench and sat down next to Swanson. Neither of them offered to shake hands. Darvin spoke first. His voice was tinged with an East Coast accent. Nearby, Virginia, West Virginia perhaps.

"So you have need of my services again, Mr. Swanson," he said. There was a coolness, almost a detachment, of the voice from the body.

"I do."

"Did you bring what I asked?"

Swanson handed over the legal-size envelope. Darvin tilted it and the contents slid into his free hand. Inside was an eight-by-ten photo of Reginald Morgan—the one they gave to the media for press releases. The itinerary for one of the Royal Caribbean ships, the *Brilliance of the Seas*, was detailed on a separate sheet of paper. Two bundles of money, one hundred thousand dollars in one-hundred-dollar bills, appeared briefly, then disappeared into the inside pocket of the man's light summer jacket.

Darvin studied the face on the photo. "He's an old man. Why not wait for him to die of natural causes?"

"I don't have the luxury of time."

Darvin's lips curled imperceptibly. "Yes, that's usually the problem." He glanced at the schedule for the cruise ship. "Do you want this to be an accident, or would you like to send someone a message?"

"No message. No reason to make sure everyone knows he was murdered. Over the side of the ship is fine."

Darvin nodded. "Then over the edge it will be."

"*Brilliance of the Seas* has already had one passenger go

over the side. George Smith. He was a Canadian on his honeymoon. You think this will raise any flags?"

The killer chuckled, a cold clucking sound. "Anytime someone disappears flags are raised. But when it's on a cruise ship, there's really nothing they can do unless someone catches the person throwing the victim over the railing. The ship, which is invariably registered to some country like Panama, is in international waters. Maritime law rules, and until they dock, the ship's captain is the only person who can apply that law. Cruise ships are wonderfully easy places to kill people."

"Then why is it costing me a hundred large?" Swanson asked.

Darvin leaned back against the bench. "Do it yourself. Save the money." He pushed the envelope that was sitting on his lap an inch closer to Swanson. The other man made no move to take it. "Didn't think so. You have your reasons for wanting Reginald Morgan dead and I'm not about to ask what they are. All you have to do is pay me. *Dirty deeds done dirt cheap*, as AC/DC would say."

"Who? What?"

"They're a rock band. It's a song. Never mind." He stood and walked back toward his car. Then he stopped and looked back. "Hope you said good-bye to Mr. Morgan. You won't be seeing him again."

Derek Swanson almost threw up. He choked back the bile and sucked in a few sharp breaths. A solitary cloud touched the edge of the sun and cast a blanket of shade over the park. What had he done? Killing the union rep was reprehensible, and sleep had been difficult for months after. But this, this was completely different. He knew Reginald Morgan. In some ways, he knew the man like a father. And now he was the instrument of the man's death. For money.

Fifty million dollars. He envisioned the scope of what

fifty million could buy. The yacht, the house in Europe and the Caribbean, a position in society only a handful of people ever achieve. And fifty million was seed money for more. Stocks, real estate, new businesses that needed capital, franchises, new technology—the list was astounding. He could parlay fifty million into a quarter billion inside five years. If he played his cards right, he could hit the elusive billionaire status sometime in his late sixties.

But at what price? Reginald Morgan's death was going to be a stone around his neck for the rest of his life. The old man was simply sticking to his convictions—that Coal-Balt needed to clean up its act, and that it was a poor time for the income trust conversion. Both points had merit. Hell, everything about Morgan had merit. Killing him was nothing but a selfish, unilateral action with no upside but money.

But it was a lot of money.

Swanson pulled himself up off the bench onto shaky legs. The deal was done. Darvin had Morgan's picture and a hundred thousand dollars. There was nothing he could do now to stop it even if he wanted. Reginald Morgan was a dead man.

# 9

Pikeville is a tiny jewel set in one of the undulating sways of the Appalachian Mountains. Its tallest building, an imposing brick structure, is six stories. Less than seven thousand people call it home, but ask them, and every person is adamant it's the best small town in America.

It was almost four o'clock when the car finally reached the outskirts of town. Claire Buxton expected the mayor, who had met her at her Lexington hotel earlier in the day, to drone on with a travelogue, but he sat quietly, letting her take in the town. The trip had taken almost two hours and most of their dialogue was already in the bag. Now it was time to take care of business.

The driver turned off US 23 onto Daniels Creek and crept up the quiet, secluded road. On either side were towering hills covered with leafy green trees and shrubs. The air was quiet and warm, with a stillness that seemed almost surreal. The sky was deep blue and barren of clouds. They turned into the second driveway and pulled up to an imposing brick house. Total silence descended on them as the driver turned the key in the ignition switch and the motor died. Claire exited the car and stared at the house.

It was beautiful. But beyond the façade was a story. A sad one. Amanda Chisholm lived here. She was eleven years old, and she was dying. Inoperable brain tumor was the official prognosis. Killed by a slow leak from the Silo Six retention pond was the unofficial version. That was the one everyone in town went with. But the problem was, many of the good people who lived in Pikeville relied on the coal mine for their biweekly paychecks. Coffee shop conversations were muted, words carefully chosen, opinions kept to a minimum. The facts were the facts and those could be recited. And they were. Often.

The retention pond for Silo Six held approximately two hundred million gallons of slurry. When it let go, it did so in a very sneaky way. In contrast to the leak at the Big Branch retention pond near Inez, Kentucky on October 11, 2000, where three hundred million gallons of slurry dropped into an abandoned mine shaft and flowed down the hills like molten lava, no one knew the Silo Six pond was leaking. The slurry migrated through the soft rock formations, down the incline to where the Chisholm house sat nestled into the trees. It surrounded the foundation of the inground swimming pool, and slowly leached through tiny cracks into the water.

Amanda was nine, almost ten, and swimming every day. She was working hard on her freestyle stroke for the upcoming swim meet against Williamson, and it wasn't uncommon for her to spend three hours a day in the pool. In water with a high parts-per-million count of arsenic, mercury and selenium. She ingested the water as she swam, tiny bits every time she took a breath or licked her lips. Eight months after her long hours in the pool, she was hit with a series of debilitating headaches. They wouldn't stop. And the pain was excruciating. Trips to the local doctor were unsuccessful in pinpointing the cause, until he ordered a CAT scan at the Pikeville Medical Center. The tumor showed up on the scan and Amanda was immediately sent to a specialist in Lexington. The news wasn't good. In fact, the news was awful.

Amanda was dying.

It took another three months to pinpoint the source. At first the management team at Barringer, the parent company for the Silo Six mine, denied everything. But it didn't take long to amass conclusive proof that the chemicals from the slurry were responsible. They changed their tune and offered to cover all expenses and the best medical care possible. And a generous cash settlement for Amanda's family. What the people at the mine didn't get was that nothing could replace Amanda.

Nothing.

Senator Claire Buxton rang the doorbell and waited. A man in his early forties answered, tall, with intelligent blue eyes. Intelligent, but sad.

"Senator Buxton, I'm Gary Chisholm." He offered his hand. "Thanks for coming."

"Of course. Thank you for having me."

They walked into the house, the mayor following behind

them. They reached a room in the back of the house that overlooked the empty swimming pool. A woman and a child sat close together on one of the couches. Both rose as Claire entered the room. The woman was thin, with long off-blond hair and sharply defined cheeks and chin. Her eyes were rimmed with red. The child was thin. Too thin. She wore a ball cap to hide her bald head. Her eyes were penetrating blue and honest. They held a knowledge and understanding that no child should have to bear.

"Senator Buxton, this is my wife, Sarah, and my daughter, Amanda," Gary Chisholm said.

"Call me Claire." She grasped Sarah's hand with both of hers. Then she looked down and locked eyes with the young girl. "Hello, Amanda. I am so honored to meet you. I've heard so many wonderful things about you."

"Really? Like what?" Her voice was little more than a whisper.

Claire sat on the couch with Amanda between the two women. "How brave you are. How you haven't let this stop you from getting straight A's in school. And how you beat every swimmer from Williamson in freestyle and backstroke at the last meet."

Amanda smiled, and a tiny fire danced in her eyes, sunk deep in their sockets. "First in both. Second in the medley."

"Very well done," Claire said.

"Coffee or tea?" Gary Chisholm asked.

"Water is fine, thank you." She turned back to Amanda and talked about school, boys, swimming and football. Amanda had yet to hit her teen years, but she knew NFL football. Especially the Denver Broncos. Her dad's team— now her team. Finally, the conversation drifted around to her health. "You look very thin, Amanda," Claire said. There was no sense patronizing the young girl by telling her she looked good. They both knew she didn't. "Were you always thin?"

"Not this skinny. It's ridiculous. My clothes fall off me now. Mom and Dad are going broke trying to keep me in clothes that fit."

Claire smiled and glanced at Amanda's parents. They sat stone-faced, watching. She'd seen it before on her trips through the children's hospital in Salt Lake City and it never ceased to amaze her. The child was the one with the disease, yet she was the one who reassured the parents that everything would be all right. They joked and cajoled their way through the day, while the parents struggled to come to terms with the fact that their child was dying.

"How are the treatments?"

Amanda scrunched up her nose. "Terrible. Worse than eating liver." She pointed to her head. "I used to have long, blond hair."

"Saves on shampoo," Claire said.

Amanda laughed, the sound echoing through the room. "That's funny. I didn't think senators were allowed to be funny."

"We are at times." Claire wondered how this could be one of them. "Amanda," she asked, leaning forward, "what would you like to be when you grow up?"

"That's easy. A doctor."

Claire's lips turned up ever so slightly. "To find new cures?"

"No, to be the only doctor who warms up her stethoscope before she sticks it on her patients."

Claire stared into the girl's eyes, alive and mischievous. She saw the determination. She saw the strength. She saw the life yet to be lived. And she knew at that moment that she couldn't fail. Her bill, once through the full house and signed by the president, would make the guilty companies responsible and would demand they clean up their acts immediately. It would close loopholes and demand action. It would make a difference.

It would save lives.

She leaned forward and grasped Amanda's hands, and although she tried, she couldn't stop the tears.

# 10

Leona's team consisted of four members plus herself. Each of her assistants had specific strengths they brought to the table. Their first meeting was after lunch on Tuesday, July 10, in the boardroom on the twelfth floor. She brought them up to speed with their assignment.

"Coal-Balt is one of our oldest and most loyal clients," she said, standing at the whiteboard that stretched across the front of the room. The other four, two men and two women, were seated in the leather chairs that ringed the long, polished walnut table. "And if you've read the printed material that was on your desk this morning, you already know why we're here. Coal-Balt is looking to restructure into an income trust. They have loans from our bank totaling two hundred and eighty million dollars, and according to the agreement we have attached to those loans, we have the right to veto any change in their operating procedure if we think it's going to adversely affect our position. So what we need to do is figure out whether their proposed conversion to an income trust is a good idea.

"This one is a little different than some of the other conversions we've seen. Coal-Balt is multifaceted in that they mine the coal and then produce electrical power by burning it in their power plant. Most companies do one or the other. Our guys do both. That has an upside and a downside. They never have a problem procuring the coal to burn, because they're mining it. But it also means they're subject to fluctuations in more than one commodity market. And labor concerns are increased at least twofold. Along with government regulations and requirements.

"Jarrod," she continued, looking at the youngest member of the team, a new hire fresh out of graduate school with a master's in economics, "you're going to look at the regulatory side of things. What legislation is out there that will require Coal-Balt to purchase new equipment in the next few years. Income trusts pay out excess profits to their shareholders and big financial hits cut into those payouts and erode investor confidence. Find out what's existing and what's new. I don't want any surprises down the road."

"You got it." Jarrod Geneau brushed a wisp of blond hair back from his forehead.

"Angela, you're accounting and taxes. Make sure our client's books are in good shape and that the IRS won't be knocking on the door soon. Most of the information you'll need is in-house. They have a substantial loan with us, which required them to submit their audited financial statements. But I want you to poke around the edges—find out if they've got any financial skeletons in the closet."

Angela Samarach, midforties and ultraconservative, simply nodded and made a few notes in her appointment book.

"Sean, you're labor. Coal-Balt is hugely labor intensive. It takes a lot of men, and some women, to mine the coal, transport it, and burn it. They do everything from blasting the tops off mountains to get at the coal to maintaining the equipment at the mine site and the plant. There are twelve unions representing workers and each union is pushing for high wages and good pensions. All of that costs money. Find out where Coal-Balt is in each of their contracts with the different unions, which ones are up for negotiations in the next year or two, and how militant they are. I'm especially interested in seeing the projected figures for their pensions. I don't want to get submarined by escalating pension payouts. Okay?"

"Okay." The task wasn't new to Sean Grant. His background before joining the bank was on the financial end of things with one of the major construction unions on the east coast. He knew labor and could read and understand the small print on the contracts between management and labor. Grant was heavyset, pushing forty and when he slipped into a pair of jeans, he fit in well with the union guys. Dress him in a suit and he was equally as comfortable with management.

"Tracey," Leona said, looking to the final member of the team. Tracey Mendez was thirty-two, married with two kids in every community sport ever devised, and drove a minivan with enough bumper stickers to wallpaper an average-size bedroom. "I want you to look at everything Sean, Angela and Jarrod aren't looking at. Is there any possible litigation on the horizon? Who dislikes Coal-Balt, and why. Anything that could potentially sneak up and bite us in the ass."

Leona leaned on the table and locked eyes with each one of them for a couple of seconds. "We've worked together before. There's no reason why my new title should get in the way. I'm still me. Everybody okay with that?"

There were nods, and Sean Grant said, "Vice presidents don't scare me. They're little fish struggling to get up the river to the spawning grounds and become big fish."

"Could care less about that VP thing," Tracey said.

Jarrod swallowed, his Adam's apple bobbing up and down, and Angela's eyes stayed focused on the paper in front of her. Even though she treated it with a certain degree of deference, the fact was, Leona Hewitt was now one of the most powerful figures at DC Trust. She worked on twelve, and that alone put her next to God. He was on thirteen.

"Thanks, and keep me posted. You've got thirteen working days, which means I need full reports on my desk by Friday the twenty-seventh. Interim reports are welcome if you think there are details I need to see as you dig them up."

They filed out and headed for the elevator. She turned the other direction and walked down the hall to her office. The walls on the top floor were paneled below the wainscoting and painted a tasteful shade of light brown above the wood. Portraits of the bank's founders and former presidents lined the long hall, and the muted lighting highlighted each painting and portrait. The carpets underfoot were thick and her heels didn't make a sound as she entered her office and slipped off her suit jacket. She draped it over the back of her chair and sat down. The office was twenty-five feet square, with a sitting area against the wall farthest from the window. Two heavy leather loveseats lined with rivets faced each other, a dark walnut table between them. The abstract art on the wall was mostly deep taupe with black and gray slashes and an occasional red splash. It reeked of testosterone.

Leona hated it.

She started slightly as the phone rang, then checked the caller ID. It was long distance, 380 area code. Ohio. She answered on the third ring, one before it went to voice mail. "Hi, Dad," she said, swiveling to look out the window. "How are things at home?"

"How'd you know it was me?" Joseph Hewitt asked.

"Ohio area code," she said.

"Could have been your mother. She's still in Ohio."

"She'd never call me at work."

"Well, work is where you're at during the day. God only knows where you are at night."

"At home."

"Not when I call. Anyway, do you like your new office?"

"You'd love it." She focused her gaze on the phone.

"Great. Don't let them push you around, Leona. They're men. They'll run roughshod over you if you let them."

"Yeah, like all the boys at home."

"Lucky you're a tough woman or they would've ground you into the dirt."

"Lucky me. Listen, Dad, I'm busy. I can't talk right now. Call me later at home. I'll be there."

"Right. You'll probably be out to dinner with some politician or lawyer."

"Talk to you later," she said, and replaced the phone in its cradle.

Her father meant well, he always had. But instead of raising a daughter, he'd created a textbook version of a tomboy. The girl who beat the boys at their own games or faced that look of disappointment on her father's face. Always the look. It took any joy out of coming in second. Perhaps her father's drive for her to succeed was the reason she had started traveling. Between her second and third year of university, she took a break and ventured to Australia and New Zealand. Just her. No friends, no family, no strings. To earn money she taught economics and finance in Perth. Teaching others was the greatest learning curve of her life, and it was when she was called on to explain the concepts to others that she truly understood them.

The beaten path didn't interest her. She shied away from the usual touristy places. Instead, she forged friendships with the outback doctors who flew small planes to places like Lightning Ridge, famous for black opal deposits. She had an affinity for flying and often piloted the plane as they floated over the vast tracts of sparsely inhabited land of the Australian outback. It seemed so long ago now.

She stared out the window at the snippet of Washington that comprised her view. It was a city of power, both financial and political. Some parts of her psyche worked here, others were more at ease in the Australian wilds. She could wear her strengths on her sleeve, but never the weaknesses. This city would eat you alive if you showed a chink in the armor. And she certainly hadn't achieved VP status by allowing Anthony Halladay to see the scared kid trapped inside. She wondered if every person had one of those kids. She suspected they did. Some hid it better than others.

Leona glanced down at her hands. What sort of power did they wield now? She had discretionary powers over lending to one hundred million dollars. Her decisions could affect whether companies received financing, or if they left empty-handed. Lives would be affected. Businesses made or broken. She had reached the coveted position, but was it what she really wanted?

She felt like the great imposter.

The person who, to the world around them, appears to be in full control of their universe. But under the surface they have doubts and fears about their ability. About whether or not they deserve the position or fame or wealth they have achieved in life. The world was full of them. Singers, actors, composers, artists, developers—even bankers. The list was absolutely endless. Every discipline had them.

It was what drove her. The fire that burned inside and incited her to be the best at whatever she did. But the flames were never extinguished. The higher she climbed in life, the better her position with the bank, the more successful her charity, the larger the bonfire. It was a monster, created from inadequacy and fueled by a fear of failure. Of being unmasked and recognized for what she was.

Scared.

Scared of being the one left without a chair when the music stopped.

# 11

Mike Anderson stared at the dark liquid in the glass, thinking of how vile it was. Worse than vile, perhaps. Who had thought of distilling wheat or rye into bourbon? It was like Newton and the apple. If an apple had fallen on his own head, he'd have sworn and chucked it away. Newton formulated gravity. And someone had looked at a sack of grain and wondered what would happen if they distilled it. Jack Daniel's was the answer.

Mike wrapped his hand around the glass and pounded it back, the bourbon hot on his throat. The burn felt good, and some part of him thanked the heartless bastard who had come up with the concept of alcohol. Two drinks from now he'd hate them. He waved at the bartender for another round.

He pulled the bank draft out of his pocket and stared at the amount. Over five hundred thousand dollars. Leona's fundraiser at her restaurant had gone well. On the heels of the evening's success, he was now looking at another trip to Africa. Back through the nightmare that was customs and immigration, Kenya style. He was getting quite good at talking his way through the airport checkpoints, and every now and then recognized one of the guards. That made things easier. They tended to remember the travelers who tipped them well, and documents were never scrutinized quite as closely. But the trips were dangerous. Always.

The bartender dropped the drink on the wood, caught his eye and tilted his head slightly. "The woman at the end of the bar asked that this one be put on her tab. You okay with that?"

Anderson didn't have to look. He'd already made eye contact with her a couple of times. She was about his age, reasonably attractive and thin. He liked thin. "Yeah, that's fine."

He toyed with the glass without looking over at her. A vision of his wife's face—his ex-wife's face, he told himself—flashed though his mind. Women and booze. Two of life's most challenging obstacles. He pulled his cell phone from its hip holster and dialed Leona's home number. She answered after a few rings.

"I got your e-mail with the electronic ticket," he said. "Looks like I'm leaving on Friday."

"That work for you?" Leona asked.

"Yeah. It's okay. You know me, a couple of days to pack and stop the newspaper delivery and I'm fine."

"Return ticket is for August fourteenth. That should give you some time with Kubala." One reason Mike liked taking the money to Kenya was getting an opportunity to visit the villages in and around Samburu. She always booked his stays for at least two weeks longer than what he needed to deliver the money.

"Thanks," he said. There was a moment of silence over the line, then he added, "I've got a feeling about this one."

"What sort of feeling?" she asked.

"Not good. Like something is going to happen."

"Women have intuition. If men had it they'd all be at the racetrack. God does things for a reason."

"Yeah, you're right. It's nothing. Just a feeling."

"Well, be careful. Kenya can be dangerous."

"Really?"

"Anything else you need?" She ignored the sarcasm. "Money?"

"No, I'm fine. I've got cash. I'll expense whatever I spend. Which is almost zero once I reach Marsabit."

"Thanks, Mike. This wouldn't work without you."

"Then why don't you pay me better?"

She laughed. "It's a nonprofit. Nobody gets rich working for a charity."

"I'll talk to you when I get back."

"Take care."

"Of course." He killed the connection and raised the glass to his lips. He sipped the JD, enjoying the slow burn as it trickled down his throat. He turned to face the woman at the end of the bar and smiled. She smiled back. He slid off the seat and walked the twenty feet to where she sat. A month in Africa was a long time to be away from American women.

A very long time.

# 12

*Brilliance of the Seas* departed Miami on Thursday, July 12 at seven in the evening. Scheduled ports on the twelve-day cruise were St. Lucia, St. Martin, Grenada, Barbados, Martinique and St. Vincent. Reginald Morgan and his wife, Amelia, watched from their balcony as the Florida coast slowly diminished to the west. Reginald Morgan was frugal in some ways, but not when booking a cabin on a cruise ship. They were comfortably ensconced in an owner's suite on deck ten, complete with a queen bed, an overstuffed sofa, two upholstered chairs and a bar area.

"I'm going to get some fruit," Amelia said, kissing her husband on the forehead. "Do you want anything?"

"No, thank you," he said. He watched her walk through the cabin, amazed at her poise and grace. She was four years older than him, yet still in fine health with a sharp mind. They were fortunate, in a world where Alzheimer's was so common, to both be so healthy, physically and mentally. He looked back to the ocean, the coastline now a wavering glow of light in the thickening dusk.

The future of his company was foremost on his mind. Even the ambience of the cruise ship wasn't enough to shake the office from his thoughts. Derek Swanson was a problem, had been for some time now. His president's vision of where Coal-Balt should go was very different from his. He had been pushing for some time now for scrubbers and other environmentally friendly upgrades to the plant, but Swanson had concentrated on the bottom line, always focusing on profits over everything else.

It was time for it to end. Time for Swanson to leave.

The man wouldn't go willingly, and that was going to pose a problem. It was difficult to fire a top executive without giving them a huge severance bonus. And that was not going to happen. Swanson didn't deserve to collect millions as he got his ass booted out the door. It was going to get ugly.

Morgan picked up a book, a suspense thriller by a new Canadian author, and settled into the chair. Time to relax. The office would still be there when he returned.


Darvin sipped his rum and coke and watched the steady parade of passengers making their way to dinner. It was the first night on the ship and dress was business casual. He scanned the faces, seeing everything from trepidation to total relaxation. Rich people attempting to look average. Average people attempting to look rich. Studying people was his favorite pastime. It was the essence of his business. If you were going to kill someone, you needed to know them. Their habits, their weaknesses, their routine. Then the minute or two it took to kill them was so much easier.

There was a downside to watching strangers. He hated the happy ones, especially the spoiled kids who wanted for nothing and their doting parents who kept trying to give them more. A pregnant woman walked toward him and his stomach churned at the sight. Even from the moment of conception, the helpless child growing in the womb, women had the ultimate control. Simply by having a vagina they were empowered to destroy lives. His mind raced with hateful thoughts. *She's so small. Even the small ones can make life a living hell. Especially the small ones. His mother was small. But evil. Horribly evil. How can that much evil be packed into such a tiny package?* She noticed him staring at her belly and smiled as she passed. He simply returned her smile, his thoughts locked behind the façade and unknown to anyone but him.

He spotted Reginald and Amelia Morgan as they strolled through the lounge toward the restaurant. A quick gulp and the last of his drink disappeared. He stood and stretched slightly, then melded into the crowd, his pace slightly slower than the rest. As Morgan passed him on his right side, he turned and they touched. His hand slipped into the elderly man's jacket and pulled out a handkerchief. In the same motion he let it fall to the floor. He tapped Morgan on the shoulder and bent over. When he looked up, Morgan and his wife had stopped and were looking back.

"I think this fell out of your pocket." He stood and offered the monogrammed piece of cloth.

Reginald felt his pocket. "Yes, thank you."

"Not a problem." Darvin locked eyes with the man. "Enjoy your dinner."

"Thanks again."

Darvin let them go ahead, then fell in behind them. Cruise ships were wonderful places for people in his business. He knew exactly where his victim was for the next twelve days, and over the next week, he would occasionally run into the Morgans, striking up short, useless conversations. Building trust. They would remember him, but only vaguely. Not enough to generate suspicion.

And then one day, near the end of the cruise, Reginald

Morgan would disappear. No clues. Nothing to suggest anything but a tragic accident at sea.

Darvin entered the Minstrel Dining Room and gave the maitre d' his table number. He was hungry and cruise ships always had great food. So different from the world of his youth, when he wasn't sure which was worse: the hunger pangs or the slop his mother served for dinner. Some of the tables were already full and the first course was served. Well-dressed men and women tucking prawns and crisp salads into their puckered lips. They had never known the horrors, the hunger, that he had. They probably never would. He despised them for that, and if he had his way, the body count on this cruise would be far greater than one.

He pushed the thoughts from his mind and followed the maitre d' past the cascading waterfall to his table, wishing that all of his jobs could be this civilized.

# 13

Claire set her reading glasses on her desk and leaned back in her chair. Surrounding her were the trappings of power, DC style. The furniture was heavy oak, as were the window and door frames. The patterned carpet was firm underfoot and pictures of past presidents and other influential political figures graced the light brown walls. The only personal touches in the room were the pictures of Claire Buxton's family. She gave the doorway a perfunctory look as a young man entered.

"I think we'll get through committee." His name was Bradley Smythe and he was fresh out of Princeton, spending the summer as a senior intern for Senator Claire Buxton.

"You sound confident. What do you know that I don't?"

He held up a couple of sheets of paper. "These just arrived. Your brief on Section 406 of the Clear Skies Act has swayed Senators Watson and Grieve into siding with you. They came around once they saw the holes in the existing legislation. I think the part about Amanda Chisholm probably did the trick."

Arnold Watson was a sitting Republican representing Nebraska and the chairman of the committee responsible for hearing Claire Buxton's bill and deciding whether it held merit and should be sent ahead to the floor of the full house. Ralph Grieve, of Illinois, was the ranking member from the Democrats. Both men were pivotal to the success of her bill.

"And they responded well to terminating the twenty percent rule," Bradley added, handing her the letters.

"Finally," Claire said, her voice tinged with acid. "Allowing the older plants to keep producing unless they renovated their facilities, at which time they had to install new antiemission equipment, looked good on paper. But if their renovations were less than twenty percent of the value of the plant they didn't have to spend any money on scrubbers. And the scrubbers are crucial to substantially reducing the carbon dioxide and sulfur pouring out of their smoke stacks."

"There have been a lot of eighteen-and nineteen-percent renovations since that legislation passed," Bradley said.

Claire shook her head. "And those older, outdated plants are producing fifty percent of the country's power. It's ridiculous."

"Well, Watson and Grieve are both looking at your take on Section 406 and the twenty percent rule a lot closer now."

"They've been there from day one." Claire shook her head. She scanned the letters from the two senators and nodded. "My latest brief is nothing new, with the exception of mentioning Amanda. Section 406 replaced a one-time automatic penalty with a graduated one for plants with excess emissions. It's not rocket science. Under the old Acid Rain Program the bad guys were immediately accountable. Section 406 allowed them to burn dirty coal in plants with outdated technology for a longer period of time with smaller fines. So much for progress."

Bradley nodded. "It's the human touch that Amanda added. I'm sure you've got them."

"It would appear," she said, glancing again at the letters, short and to the point. They agreed with her bill, which modified the existing Clear Skies Act and shortened the time period for delinquent companies to clean up their acts. "Set up lunches with both of them. One at a time. Try for Tuesday and Wednesday next week. Pick somewhere quiet, close to here. Capital Grille is probably best. I want their attention over lunch, and a quick good-bye afterward."

"Done." Bradley spun on his heel and headed through the door into the anteroom.

Claire grinned at his youthful exuberance. She had been like that twenty years ago. Convinced that she could change the world. Now she was in a position to, and realized she couldn't. It was all too big, too convoluted, too screwed up for one person to fix. Hell, it probably wasn't even fixable. But one part of it was. The incredible damage the coal-burning plants were doing to the world's air supply. And the devastation heaped on the surrounding countryside by the mining companies. They had to be held accountable, and her new bill would do exactly that.

She thought of Amanda—of the young life lost—and tears pooled in the corners of her eyes. The girl had never asked to be sick. Her parents hadn't intentionally lived downstream from a leaking retention pond. No one wanted to see a young girl die, all her life's ambitions unfulfilled. But in this case, there was a culprit. An easily identifiable one. Even Schumberg, the parent company that ran the Silo

Six mine, was admitting they were culpable. Their solution was to throw money at the problem, but that wasn't going to save Amanda Chisholm from an early grave. It would help ease the Chisholm's financial burdens, but could never hope to compensate for the loss of their daughter. And the frustrating thing was, it never had to happen.

Under Clinton, the economy had grown and prospered. Environmental groups were encouraged to provide solutions to the nation's problems. The pendulum was swinging in the right direction. But when George W. Bush took power, everything changed. America went to war, a conflict that cost billions of dollars and widened the gap between Republicans and Democrats. The environment faded as the country's debt increased, to the point where no one wanted to talk about it. They had other things to worry about. Like keeping their jobs and their houses. Worrying about emissions from coal-burning plants was yesterday's problem. Even if those emissions were causing global warming and melting glaciers.

Bradley stuck his head in the door. "Watson is confirmed on Tuesday, July seventeenth and Grieve on the eighteenth. They're both anxious to meet with you."

She entered the dates in her BlackBerry and thanked her intern. Everything was coming together. With the senators from Illinois and Nebraska behind her, the bill should easily pass through committee. Then on to the floor of the full house, to the Oval Office for a signature, and it would be law.

Then maybe children like Amanda Chisholm would stop dying.

## 14

Leona stopped by the restaurant on her way home from work. Tyler had been working on a new recipe for halibut in preserved lemon beurre blanc sauce and insisted she stick around for dinner. He overran her objections with a vivid description of his newest creation, and she finally gave in and found a small table in the back corner, away from the street. She pulled a handful of loose pages from her briefcase and settled in, alternating between people-watching and perusing the initial notes her team had prepared.

They still had two weeks before their final reports were due, but one thing was already painfully clear. Coal-Balt was not the golden boy on the block when it came to their environmental track record. Their coal mine near Valley Furnace, West Virginia, was a major contributor to the state's pollution index. The retention pond, filled with over four hundred million gallons of slurry, was a disaster looking for a home. And their labor practices were abhorrent. Five of the labor unions that placed workers in the mine had outstanding grievances with the company. Serious ones, mostly centering on safety. Or the lack of it.

And Lombard II, their power-generating plant, forty miles to the south, made the mining operation look like a Boy Scout troop. The plant had been constructed prior to 1970, which meant it was exempt from emission controls unless it was renovated. But the government's idea of renovating was anything in excess of twenty percent of the current value of the plant. Coal-Balt had undergone seven renovations since 1970, all less than twenty percent of value. And no emission-reducing equipment had been installed.

Leona spied Tyler on his way with her dinner and cleared

a small space on the table. He set the plate down and brandished the pepper mill.

"This is how halibut should be served." He twisted the top of the mill and lightly dusted the food with pepper.

"Not too spicy, I hope," she said.

"I know what you like. It's perfect."

Leona watched her chef walk back to the kitchen. The man loved food. It excited him. He came alive in the kitchen. Her mind skipped back to the day he had dropped his application in the pile. It was a Saturday and she was sitting at one of the tables near the front of the restaurant going over the final touches with the interior designer. Gin House was slotted to open in a week and she had two major problems. The interior wasn't finished and the chef she had hired decided to take a job with a competitor. Something about Tyler caught her eye and she excused herself from the meeting and pulled his résumé off the pile and quickly flipped through it. He had experience running a kitchen and had worked in a handful of high-end restaurants. She ran out the front door and called him back.

"I need a chef," she said as they sat together at one of the tables. "And your qualifications look good. What else can you tell me that would make me want to hire you?"

Tyler thought for a few seconds, then said, "Is the kitchen working yet?"

"Yes. It's finished."

"Any food in the freezers?"

"Not yet."

"Give me ten minutes to find some food, and half an hour to prepare it. Then you can decide if you want to hire me."

Leona stared at him. He was confident, not arrogant. "Okay, you've got a deal. But it's not that easy. I'm a vegetarian."

"You eat fish?" he asked, and grinned when she nodded. "No problem."

An hour later she set her fork on the edge of her plate and waved him over. The sea bass he had found and cooked in less than an hour was excellent, but it was the vegetables and his presentation that absolutely floored her. It was one of the best meals she had ever eaten. "I need you today."

"Now *you've* got a deal," he said, grinning. The rest was history.

She tried a mouthful of the halibut and looked back to her paperwork. The condition of the mine and the plant and the labor problems were bad, but it was what Jarrod had uncovered that really worried her. New legislation could be coming into play inside the next twelve months, and it would require revamping the entire electrical generating plant. Claire Buxton, one of Utah's representatives to the Senate, was pushing for tighter controls on emissions, and her bill was drafted and heading for committee approval. Jarrod's feeling was that it may pass without being amended. If that happened, Lombard II would be facing a huge overhaul or be shutting down. One or the other. Either way, Senator Buxton's bill was going to cost the parent company a lot of money. If it passed.

Leona pushed the papers aside and worked on the halibut. It was beyond delicious. Tyler poked his head out of the kitchen and she gave him two thumbs-up. He retreated, a smile on his face. She popped another piece of fish in her mouth and chewed, thinking about the timing surrounding the income trust conversion. It was convenient to say the least. If the conversion went through, and Buxton's bill passed, the shareholders were in for a bit of a shock. The cost to rebuild Lombard II would be astronomical and the monthly beneficiary checks would shrivel or die entirely. If Coal-Balt had waited for the bill to pass before attempting the conversion, it would have fallen flat on its face.

Her first file as a vice president and she was already leaning toward nixing it. Which wasn't going to sit well with Anthony Halladay, the bank's CEO. Halladay had been quite blunt when handing her the assignment. *I don't foresee any problems with this conversion. I hope you don't either.* There was little room to read anything between the lines there. Halladay golfed with someone over at Coal-Balt; one of the big boys. She couldn't remember whom, but was sure they both had memberships at the same private course.

Leona finished her meal and leaned back in her chair. The back of the restaurant was much more dimly lit than the front and she felt a tinge of anxiety. She steeled herself against an attack, but it overwhelmed her. The walls tightened around her as the intenseness built. Her hands shook and her breathing was quick and shallow. She sucked in a couple of deep breaths and forced herself to focus on her situation. It was dark, but she wasn't in an enclosed space. She could get up and walk out the front door into the evening sunlight at any moment. There was no reason for an attack.

Logic won out. The attack diminished, then faded entirely. Her breathing returned to normal and she stopped shaking. Tyler breezed out of the kitchen and headed toward her table. Halfway there he quickened his stride, concern on his face.

"Are you okay?" He sat beside her at the table.

"That obvious?"

"Yeah, your face is totally white."

"I'm fine. A touch of a panic attack."

"Why? What's wrong?"

"I don't like enclosed or dark spaces. Guess it's a bit dark back here for me."

"Claustrophobia?"

She nodded. "Had it as a kid. Hated to be locked in small rooms."

"How are you in elevators?" he asked.

She laughed. "Horrible. I take the stairs up to the eleventh floor—twelfth now—every day."

"Keeps you trim," Tyler said.

"I'm a size eight," she replied snidely, "not a three. I'm hardly trim."

Tyler grinned. "You look better already. How was dinner?"

"Delicious. Are you going to put that on the menu?"

"As a special once a week for a month to see how people react. If it goes well, I'll add it on in early September. Spicy dishes do well in the fall and winter months, so the timing works."

"You're the chef. It's your call."

He leaned over and gave her a quick kiss on the forehead. "Glad you liked it. I've got to get back to work."

He headed back for the kitchen, his lanky legs moving jerkily. She watched until the door closed behind him, then packed up her papers. What to do? She had another few days, then a decision to make. But it was looking more and more like her recommendation was not going to jibe with Anthony Halladay's.

And that was not good.

# 15

Jack Dunn leaned forward, his elbows on the table, his tie dangling precariously close to the pork medallions he had ordered for lunch.

"It's partially conjecture, Derek." His deep baritone voice was a whisper that carried nowhere in Mendocino Grille and Wine Bar, the upscale Georgetown restaurant on M Street. "But we can assume it's accurate."

"Claire Buxton had lunch with Senator Watson on Tuesday and Grieve on Wednesday. And your sources say she's got their backing for her bill. That's what you're telling me," Derek Swanson said. His voice wasn't quite as hushed and his face was taking on a deep shade of crimson.

"Yes. You've got to realize that Senator Buxton's bill is attractive right now for a slew of reasons. The whole global warming thing is . . ."

"Don't fucking tell me about global warming, Jack," Swanson cut him off in midsentence. "Don't tell me her bill is good. Tell me that you've got enough support to kill it. That's what you do, Jack. You're a fucking lobbyist. You lobby. You tell people what they're supposed to think. You tell them how to vote on issues." Swanson leaned back in his chair, grinding his teeth. "That's what I'm paying you to do, Jack. Now go do it."

Dunn's jaw tightened and he let out a couple of long breaths. He had spent twelve years in Congress representing the interests of the voting public of Michigan, and was more comfortable telling people off than being told off. But life was different now. He was the paid lobbyist, working for the interests of big business. And Coal-Balt was not a company he wanted to alienate. They paid extremely well and Derek Swanson was tied in with a host of other high-level executives in the resource industry who could need a lobbyist at some point. Not a good bridge to burn. Jack Dunn relaxed and felt the tension melt from his shoulders.

"Okay, Derek, I'll work on it. I've got a couple of favors I can pull in, votes I can sway, but even with those in the bag it'll still be close."

"Do what you can, Jack. This one's important. I want

that bill killed in committee. If it gets to the floor, there are too many variables."

Dunn nodded. "Agreed. That's why Watson and Grieve are so important. They control the committee. If the bill has support from both the Democrats and the Republicans, it shows a united front. That makes it tougher to influence the swing vote."

"I understand all that. But the bottom line is to get the job done. I don't care how you do it."

"My fees may have to increase if I start calling in these aces. I've had these favors sitting around for a long time. I don't want to use them unless I have to."

"That's fine. Sometimes it costs money to make money." Swanson sipped his wine and set the empty glass on the table. "The financial upside to the bill dying in committee is worth the extra cost. See that it happens."

He slipped out from behind the table and left the restaurant without looking back. Outside the sun was warm and there was little or no breeze. He shrugged out of his suit jacket and folded it over his arm as he walked. Jack Dunn was one of the best in the business, and if he was having trouble, then stopping Claire Buxton was not going to be easy. He knew her by reputation, and the most common observation was that she didn't quit. Once Buxton got her mind set on something, she followed through and got results. That was an ugly character trait if you were on the other side of the table.

Swanson flagged down a cab and gave the driver an address. He had other business to take care of in Washington before heading back to West Virginia. The city flashed by, stone monuments to important men, important moments in American history. There would never be a monument to him; his legacy would be wealth in the bank. And that was fine. Public recognition was great for civil servants, which included everyone up to the president, but he wanted money. It was very simple. Money motivated him. It excited him.

And fifty million dollars was incredible motivation. Enough to disrupt the legislative process. Enough to order a man killed. Reginald Morgan flashed through his mind, then was gone. There had been no news from the police that the CEO was dead, and the only explanation was that Darvin had yet to kill him. Swanson wondered about that— about the timing. It was already July 19, only four days until the cruise ship was scheduled to dock in Miami. Why wait so long? Why not kill him a couple of days out of Miami? No answers to that, but it didn't matter. The task had been delegated and was being taken care of. Leave it alone and let the man do his job.

The cab stopped in front of the monstrosity that was the Old Executive Office Building and he paid the driver and strode quickly inside. Coal Bolt had numerous ongoing applications allowing them to expand their mining operations, and he had bureaucrats to see. Things got done quicker when he took care of them personally. All except for murdering people. That was best left to others.

# 16

At eleven o'clock, an hour before July 20 dropped into the history books, *Brilliance of the Seas* was twenty-nine hours out of Grenada, en route to Cozumel. The seas were calm with a quarter moon on the horizon. The night air held a chill and the few passengers who were on the upper decks wore light jackets.

Reginald Morgan leaned against the railing next to the

golf simulators on the twelfth deck, watching the waves generated by the bow as it cut through the dark, foamy water. It fascinated him, the power of massive cruise ships—how two propellers could push so much weight through such a dense medium with absolute ease. The engineer in him wanted to see the machinery that drove the ship, but with all the terrorist attacks in the past few years, any chance of being allowed into the engine room had vanished. He settled for enjoying the result of the diesel engines driving the props.

The wind was noticeable on the upper decks, where protection from the rushing air was negligible. Nonetheless, it was his favorite spot. Every night, long after the golf simulator and Seaview Café were closed for the evening, he had spent a few minutes alone, mesmerized by the immenseness of the sea. When in port, the ship looked huge. When at sea, it was merely a speck atop a living creature that could swallow it in a moment. The seabed was littered with wrecks, one of them deemed unsinkable. When dealing with Mother Nature, arrogance had a price.

He looked about as another person passed him, then stopped at the railing a few feet away. Reginald recognized him as the man who had noticed his handkerchief had fallen from his pocket. They had spoken numerous times since, but nothing more than a quick hello and a generic comment on how nice the weather was.

"It's wonderful up here," the other man said. "Very peaceful."

"Yes," the elderly man replied. "A nice place to think."

"I agree." There was a moment's silence, then the man asked, "What do you think about?"

Morgan turned slightly and leaned on the railing with one elbow. "Anything that comes to mind. That's what is so nice about being here. When I'm in the office, I think about work. At home, it's the family. Here, it can be anything."

"You still work?" Darvin asked. "You look old enough to be retired."

Morgan laughed. "Passed that milestone years ago. But I love going into the office. It's in my blood. And my wife understands, bless her soul."

"What sort of business?"

"Utilities. We generate electrical power."

"Now that's an interesting commodity," Darvin said. "Electricity. You can't see it, can't really touch it, but it powers all sorts of things, and it can certainly kill you."

"It's dangerous, but I can't imagine living without it. Everything we rely on needs power of some sort, and most of it is electrical."

"'Live Better Electrically,'" Darvin said, repeating the electrical industry's catchphrase from the 1950s.

"Have you enjoyed the cruise?" Morgan asked.

"Very much so. I liked the islands, but I think this is my favorite part. Standing on the deck late at night looking out over the water. It really does encourage abstract thinking."

"What do you think about?" Morgan asked.

Darvin moved closer, to within a couple of feet. Despite the wind, not a hair moved. "I think about my mom and dad a lot. About what my life was like when I was young."

"Where did you grow up?"

"In West Virginia, but that's unimportant. What *is* interesting is the family dynamics. You know, how Mom and Dad interacted."

"How was that?" Morgan asked, wondering where this was going.

"Not all that well. You see, Mom used to beat Dad. Now that's backward to most abusive relationships, but my mom was a mean-spirited bitch. And she was smaller than Dad. But meaner than you could ever imagine. I know I already said that, but repeating things is good for emphasis. And after she beat the shit out of my dad, then she went to work on me. It had quite the effect actually. I grew up hating women."

"That's an interesting story." A hesitation crept into Morgan's voice.

"Yes, it is. And surprisingly enough, it has relevance to our situation."

"What situation?" The distance between the two men suddenly seemed very narrow.

"This situation. Right here, right now. I don't think I would have been so violent if my mom had been nicer to me. I didn't like her hitting my dad, but I really hated her for beating me." Darvin leaned even closer to the CEO. "I finally hit her with a shovel. From behind, so she couldn't see me coming. Split her head wide open. You ever see a human brain, Reginald?"

Morgan licked his lips nervously. "How do you know my name? I never told you my name."

"Derek Swanson says hi," Darvin said quietly. His arm shot out and snaked around the old man's neck. He jerked his forearm toward his own body, snapping the brittle bones in Morgan's neck. The man went limp, and in one fluid motion Darvin heaved the lifeless body over the edge. There was no sound, no splash, nothing to indicate a person had dropped twenty stories into the water. Darvin glanced over the railing and stared at the water. The wake was covered with foam and it was impossible to see anything in the churning sea. The killer stood at the railing, watching the approximate spot where Morgan's body had landed, until it disappeared into the vast darkness behind the ship. He scanned the deck for any possible witnesses who may have happened onto the scene at the moment he killed the elderly man, but no one was watching.

He glanced at his watch. It was a few minutes before twelve. Perhaps the midnight buffet would be better tonight. He hoped so. Time to have a good meal with the rich and privileged.

# 17

Nairobi was a hole.

At least, that was Mike Anderson's take on the place. He hated the heat, the garbage and the poverty. But even more, he hated the shifty eyes, the untrusting nature of the people and the violence. Random violence with sickening results. He often operated in the wrong part of town, where mutilated bodies were dumped in the gutter and the police never came. Eventually the corpses disappeared. Weird how that happened.

The first stop after arriving was the bank. He deposited the bank draft, slipped the bank manager five thousand and took two hundred and sixty in cash in a worn leather briefcase. His bodyguards, Tuato and Momba, watched the street as he left the bank and slid in the backseat of the car. Since his third trip to Kenya he had been using the two men to escort him about Nairobi. Once he was on the outskirts of the city, Kubala took over. But inside the madness of the Kenyan capitol, he relied on them to keep him alive. White guys with money didn't last long on the streets by themselves. Anderson was resilient and street smart, but the odds were totally in the locals' favor.

"Nikala's place first," he said as the two large men piled in the front seat of the older-model Mercedes. He sat in the back, quietly splitting the money into two uneven piles. He stuffed the smaller pile, eighty thousand dollars in total, in a slit under the driver's seat. It fit tight against the bottom of the springs and padding. He glanced at the two men in the front, but both were concentrating on the street and neither had seen him hide the money. He replaced the remainder of the one hundred and eighty thousand in the briefcase and set it on the worn leather beside him.

The streetscape changed as they left the somewhat up-scale banking district and burrowed deeper into the sprawling legion of decrepit apartment buildings and shanties. The cracked streets were littered with garbage and stray dogs prowled about searching for scraps. In a city where people scavenged for food, there was little left over for the animals. They were skinny with unkempt coats. None were neutered or spayed. Anderson had this strange tape that replayed in his head, where Bob Barker showed up and gave the people a piece of his mind for not having their pets fixed. Then they shot him.

He blinked a few times to wipe out the bizarre images. Where the hell had that come from? He refocused on the briefcase and his thoughts turned to Leona. She placed such faith in him—absolute trust. The one thing he could never get from his wife. How did *that* happen? Maybe it all had to do with the commodity. Leona was about money. His wife was about emotion. No, not true. His wife hadn't trusted him with money either. Maybe Leona was a trusting person and his wife was a bitch. Ex-wife, he reminded himself.

The car slowed and stopped in front of a mellow pink four-story building. A line of bullet holes scarred the wall facing the street and a heavy iron gate barred the front door against the uninvited. Tuato stayed at the wheel while Momba knocked on the gate. A face appeared and a few words were spoken. The gate opened and Mike Anderson hustled from the car into the darkness of a long, low hallway. The stench of rotting garbage was heavy in the air. He followed the man up a rickety staircase to a small second-floor landing that led to another hall. The carpet was worn through to the wooden floor, and their steps echoed in the narrow space. Halfway down the hall, the man pointed to an open door and Anderson entered.

He'd been there twice in the past and knew the room and the man. Nikala Shambu was a giant of a man, well over six feet and almost as wide. His eyes were a jaundiced yellow against his jet-black skin. He smiled a lot, but it was all window dressing; there was no warmth in the gesture. Anderson walked across the bare floor and sat in a chair a few feet from the gang leader. Six other men, all visibly armed with handguns, stood about. They weren't smiling.

"My favorite American," Nikala said, the grin spreading across his face. His eyes dropped to the leather briefcase. "I see you've been busy raising money for your elephants."

"I don't raise the money, Nikala," Anderson said. "I just bring it to Africa. The messenger, so to speak."

"I like your message. It speaks to me of money." He laughed at his play on words. "What have you got today?"

"One-eighty," Anderson said. "We had a very good fundraiser."

"Yes, I would say you did." Nikala raised an eyebrow. He took the money as Anderson handed it across. The bills looked funny in his huge hands, too small to be real. He thumbed through a couple of bundles, then set them on the table in front of him. "Very well done, Mr. Anderson. I like it when you visit."

"Question," Anderson said.

"Yes?" Nikala steepled his fingers and leaned back in the chair.

"Why don't you fix this place up? It's a dump. I give you enough money to buy a palace, yet you live here."

Nikala leaned forward, his face darkening. "This is Kenya, Mr. Anderson, not the United States. This house is quite nice by our standards." He locked eyes with his visitor. "Are you trying to insult me?"

Anderson shook his head. "Nope. I was wondering, is all. I'd buy a big house and new furniture. Guess we're different."

Absolute quiet settled over the room as Nikala stared at him. Then the big man burst out laughing. "We're not so different. This is where I meet you—where you give me money. I have a house. A very nice house. I don't want you to know where it is."

Anderson nodded. "I thought so." He stood up, taking the briefcase with him. "I've got to go. See you in a few months."

"I'll look forward to it." Nikala didn't stand or offer his hand.

Anderson retraced his steps through the tenement and found Tuato and Momba waiting at the curbside. This was a part of the job he did for Leona and her foundation that he found repulsive. Paying off thugs to keep other thugs from killing him, Kubala, the villagers, the elephants and anyone else they thought should die. What a fucked-up country. Actually, the whole continent was fucked up. Some parts more than others. He slid into the car and gave Tuato the second address. One more stop, to deliver the other eighty thousand dollars, then off to the village. To Kubala and the elephants. The rewarding part of the job.

The car blended in with the congestion on the narrow street and moved with the flow. Ten minutes into the drive, Tuato said something to Momba and the second man turned and looked behind them. He blurted something out and a gun appeared in his hand. Anderson glanced behind the car and sucked in a deep breath. A car was right on their rear bumper, and four men were visible inside, each one with the barrel of an automatic weapon pointing up from their laps.

Pulling alongside them was a similar vehicle, also with four men, all armed. One of the men in the front passenger seat waved at them to pull over. He flashed a badge and a gun.

"What's going on?" Anderson asked. "Who are these guys?"

"Don't know." Momba handled the gun like it was a hot potato. It was obvious he didn't know whether to drop it or start shooting. "Maybe they are police. Maybe not."

"I think they are police," Tuato said. "All their guns are the same. Robbers would have different guns."

"Stop the car," Anderson said.

"If they are robbers, they will kill us," Momba said. He was perspiring now, beads of sweat forming on his forehead.

"If they're police and we shoot at them, we're all dead men for sure," Anderson said. "Stop the car."

Tuato pulled over to the curb and shifted into first gear. He left the car running and the clutch in. But at this point, the chances of them outrunning the other men or the bullets from their guns were zero. They sat quietly as all eight men from the other two cars surrounded their vehicle. The one who had been waving the badge approached the driver's door and spoke to Tuato in a foreign dialect. They talked for a minute, maybe two, then Tuato turned to Anderson.

"They are police. They want to speak with you."

The policeman stood back from the car a few feet. "Mr. Anderson, if you could please get out of the car." His English was accented, but fluent.

Anderson slowly left the relative safety of the backseat and stood on the uneven pavement. Faces peeked out of windows on the upper floors of the buildings that lined the street, but no one stood about at street level to watch. That was an invitation to catch a stray bullet when the shooting started.

"What can I do for you?" Anderson assessed the situation with a trained eye. None of the men wore uniforms, but

Tuato was right about the guns. The other thing that struck him were the men's shoes—all light combat boots, like the ones SWAT members wore. This was definitely not some ragtag outfit of robbers. They were police, elite police, but why did they want him?

"You are Michael Anderson?" the man asked.

"Yes."

"Can I see your passport please?"

Anderson handed over his passport and entry visa. The policeman gave it a quick glance and slipped both papers in his pocket.

"Mr. Anderson, I have some questions for you. I'll need you to accompany us to the police station."

"I'm not comfortable with that," Anderson said. "Nor am I comfortable with you having my passport."

The man moved closer, to within a couple of feet. "It doesn't matter what you are comfortable with. You are coming with us. If you resist, my men will kill your bodyguards. If you continue to resist, they will kill you. The choice is yours. You have five seconds to make a decision."

Anderson didn't hesitate. "I'm feeling much more comfortable now that you explained things. Let's go."

"So you have a sense of humor. That will benefit you."

"It's the one thing my ex-wife didn't get in the settlement."

"In the car. After you give me whatever gun you are carrying."

Anderson pulled the Smith & Wesson from under his loose-fitting shirt and handed it over. He waved off Tuato and Momba and slid into the backseat. Two men immediately flanked him. Both were armed and kept their guns aimed at him.

Carpe diem was dead. Any chance of escape was gone.

# 18

"Contact the FBI and the Mexican authorities," Captain Antonio Belgravio said. "Immediately. Advise them we have a missing person."

"Yes, sir," the junior officer in the crisp white uniform said. He spun on his heel and left the captain's cabin, heading back toward the bridge.

The captain, an elegant Italian man in his early sixties with olive skin and thick black hair, turned to Amelia Morgan. "The crew has searched the entire ship, Mrs. Morgan. Every deck, all the public areas including the spa, the swimming pools, the gift shops—everywhere. There is no sign of your husband."

Amelia Morgan nodded and looked down at her hands, her mouth set in a grim line. "This is totally out of character for Reginald," she said. "Is there any chance he may have fallen overboard?"

The captain gave his shoulders a long and uncommitted shrug. "The railings are high enough that it would be very difficult to fall, unless the sea was very rough or the person at the railing wished to go over."

"My husband did not commit suicide," Amelia said. "He's healthy and we have a wonderful life."

"Yes, of course."

Belgravio glanced at his watch. "It's after five. We will be docking in Cozumel in less than an hour. I must check on things."

"Can I return to my cabin?" Amelia asked.

He shook his head. "I'm afraid not. No one will be allowed in the cabin until the Mexican authorities have completed their investigation. And the FBI, if they are able to arrive in Cozumel quickly enough. Although, I don't think that will happen."

"What *is* the procedure, Captain?"

"At this point, since we are in international waters, maritime law prevails. That means jurisdiction rests with the man or woman in charge of the ship."

"That would be you."

"Yes. When we dock in Cozumel, things change. The Mexican police will come aboard. We will give them access to whatever parts of the ship they need, including your room, which was quarantined the moment we suspected your husband may be missing."

"In case I killed him," Amelia said.

Belgravio ignored the remark. "The Mexican police will determine whether they think foul play was involved. If that is the case, they have the jurisdiction to keep the ship docked until their investigation is complete. If they determine your husband's disappearance to be an accident, we will sail on time for Miami. The FBI will come aboard at that time."

"A man is missing, captain." Amelia's eyes flashed a strange mix of anger and sorrow. "And that man is my husband, whom I love dearly. I would think some kind of action might be a good thing right now. Like searching for him."

The captain raised an eyebrow. "We have done so, Mrs. Morgan. Quite extensively."

"Not on the ship. In the ocean."

He shook his head. "You didn't notice Mr. Morgan was missing until the middle of the night. If he did fall overboard, it may have happened two or three hours before that. It takes at least an hour to turn the ship around and begin to retrace our route. Then an additional two to three hours to return to the possible spot where your husband entered the water. If he fell overboard, and that is still in question, the search area would be massive. Impossible, in fact. It would make looking for the proverbial needle in the haystack very easy."

She nodded, slowly as his words sunk in. If Reginald had gone overboard, he was dead. "You said my cabin is off-limits."

"Yes." He rose from the chair and motioned to a younger man waiting by the door. "We have another cabin prepared for you. Julio will escort you."

"Thank you, Captain."

Belgravio watched her leave, then busied himself with the necessary paperwork documenting Reginald Morgan's disappearance. It took the better part of an hour before he finished. He walked to the bridge as the ship sidled up to the dock. Three Mexican police cars were at the end of the pier and seven officers were already through the security checkpoint and waiting for the gangplank. Belgravio left the bridge and went to meet them After the introductions, he and Enrico Valdez, the officer in charge, walked side by side to Morgan's stateroom. The rest of Valdez's team split up, each accompanied by a ship's officer to guide them in their investigation.

"Is there any chance Mr. Morgan may still be onboard?" Valdez asked. He was soft-spoken, midfifties with dark Mestizo skin and intelligent eyes.

"None. Unless he's sequestered in a cabin, which is highly unlikely. My crew is well versed in this type of exercise. We block the ship off into sections and position ourselves so there is no possible way for the missing person to move about without our knowledge. Roving crew members check everything from lifeboats to between each row of seats in the theater."

"Any sign of foul play?"

"No. We look for blood. Especially by the ship's railings, in case someone *did* go overboard and hit the railing on the way down."

"And . . ."

"We found nothing," Belgravio said as they arrived at Reginald and Amelia Morgan's cabin. The staff member watching the door allowed them access. "This is the room our missing person was staying in."

"Very nice." Valdez walked about, taking in the luxurious trappings that money could buy. A Steinway baby grand piano sat near the sliding doors to the oversize deck. He looked about the deck, then returned to the suite and went through every room carefully. "How old is Mr. Morgan?"

"He is in his seventies," the captain responded.

"Maybe he dipped into the Viagra. Found another cabin for the night."

Belgravio shook his head. "I've spoken with the staff members on this deck. The Morgans were very affectionate to each other and extremely polite to the staff. This is not the kind of man who does something like that. Especially at his age."

Valdez nodded toward the balcony. "The railings are high. Is it possible for a man to fall over?"

"It is possible," Belgravio answered, "but unlikely."

"If they were assisted?"

"It would be much easier."

"Did your staff find any indication of a struggle?"

"No," Belgravio said. "There is no evidence he was murdered."

"That's good for you. Makes it easier to release the ship."

"Yes, it does. But I would never conceal or cover up evidence of a murder in order to stay on schedule."

Valdez was silent, looking about the room. Finally, he said, "We have a few hours to look about while you're in port. If we don't find anything suspicious, you will be allowed to leave."

Belgravio nodded. "As you say, you have time to conduct a detailed search. My staff will be at your disposal."

"That would be appreciated."

Valdez joined up with one of his men outside the cabin and they headed off in search of their other team members. Belgravio returned to the bridge and watched the steady stream of passengers as they disembarked and walked the length of the pier to where Mexicans loaded with souvenirs stood waiting. Beyond that was the town of Cozumel, with a picturesque central square and streets lined with shops and boutiques.

But there was at least one passenger who wouldn't be shopping today.

# 19

The preliminary vote was in. Bradley, her Princeton intern, had totaled the votes for and against. If everyone who had promised to vote for her bill did so, it would pass by two votes. Tight, but who cared. The bottom line was what counted. And the bottom line was that Claire Buxton's pro-action bill on coal, both mining and electrical generation using it to power the turbines, was going to pass through committee. No more free rides for the environmental murderers.

Next step, the full house. Then the Oval Office. At which point, it would be law.

Claire closed the file, tucked it in her briefcase, then set it on the floor and pushed it under the seat ahead of her. The corner of a newspaper section poked out of the seat-back pouch and she pulled it out and perused the front page. An article on a passenger disappearing from a cruise ship caught her attention and she read the copy. She stopped dead at the victim; Reginald Morgan. She knew the name, but couldn't place it. She kept reading about the mysterious manner in which the man had disappeared. The seas were calm, no pitching action that might have thrown him overboard. No rain to moisten the deck and cause it to be slippery. No one on the ship had seen a thing. Royal Caribbean, owners of *Brilliance of the Seas*, was keeping their comments to a minimum. The article reminded the reader that *Brilliance* had lost another passenger a while back—George Smith, a Canadian on his honeymoon. The final paragraph was on Reginald Morgan, and that told Claire Buxton where she had heard the name.

Reginald Morgan was CEO of Coal-Balt.

Claire set the newspaper on her lap, lost in thought. What was going on? Three hundred and fifty million people in the US and the person who disappears from a cruise ship is the CEO of the company that hired Jack Dunn to fight her antipollution bill. What were the chances?

The *FASTEN SEATBELT* sign lit up and the flight attendant started down the aisle picking up newspapers and checking to see if seats were in an upright position and belts were fastened. The senator gave the woman a smile as she passed across the newspaper and an empty water glass. But her mind was elsewhere—aboard a cruise ship, late at night, on a deserted deck. What had happened? Had the man stepped up on the railing to get a better look, or was he thrown overboard? What would be the upside to someone removing Reginald Morgan? Would it affect his company's position of opposing her bill?

Questions. Too many questions. She needed to get back to Washington and find some answers.

Derek Swanson threw the copy of *USA Today* on his desk and ran his hands through his hair. Morgan's disappearance had made the front page. Partly because he had gone missing from the same ship as that Canadian on his honeymoon. The press was having a field day with it. His phone kept ringing and his voice mail was full, everyone wanting to know what had happened to the CEO of the company. Like he should know.

That he did was irrelevant. No one was asking if he was involved in Morgan's disappearance; only if he knew what was going on. Dumb question. How the hell would he know? Ask his wife, she was there. He gave every person his stock answer: *We're all in a state of shock right now. We have no idea what happened, but are in contact with the authorities.* What a crock of shit. He knew exactly what happened. But he sure as hell wasn't going to tell anyone.

In retrospect, taking the CEO out on the cruise ship had been a bad idea. Throwing people overboard from a deck on one of the floating hotels was being touted in the papers as a possible way to commit the perfect murder. But while the jurisdictional issue made it attractive, the profile it raised was exactly the opposite.

The phone rang and he checked the caller ID. This one was important. He picked up the receiver and said, "Give me good news, Jack. Tell me you shut her down."

"Not good news." The tone in Jack Dunn's voice was anything but optimistic. "It looks like her bill will pass through committee. I can't get the support I need to kill it."

Swanson's hand trembled slightly and his voice was shaky. "When will it go through? How long do I have?"

"About ten days at the committee level, then it gets tough to estimate. Another couple of weeks in the Senate, then Congress. Things are moving quickly these days once they hit the house floor. I'd say a month at the outside."

"Are you sure you can't sway them?"

"Ninety-nine percent. Claire Buxton has a handful of other senators riled up about some terminally ill young girl in Kentucky. The only way you're going to stop her is if she's out of office, but she still has two years left on her term so that's not going to happen."

"Okay," Swanson said. "If anything happens to change things, let me know."

"Immediately."

The line went dead and Derek Swanson leaned back in his chair and stared at the ceiling. Buxton's bill was at least a month from becoming law, which might be enough time to have the conversion in place. Unless there was an overzealous watchdog somewhere in the system who recognized the danger in the upcoming legislation, he should have time to dump a good portion of his stock after the price peaked, but before the impact of the new laws was felt. It would cut into the bottom line, but forty or forty-five million in his pocket was still possible. And that was worth the effort. Definitely worth the effort.

He glanced at the calendar. Wednesday, July 25. DC Trust was the last hurdle, and they should be onside very soon now, which would allow them to proceed with the conversion. The effect of Claire Buxton's bill would be disastrous, but only to the shareholders who held on to their stock. The ones in the know, like him, would be long gone.

With the money.

Derek Swanson closed his eyes and his office faded to black. He would be retired soon. A lot quicker than he had imagined, but what did he care. His motivation had always been money, and it wouldn't be long before he'd be in the big leagues. Well out of the multimillionaire slot, on his way to billionaire status. It would take time, but with a few smart investments, he could do it. A hazy vision of Reginald

Morgan floated through the darkness, but he pushed it away. The man was old, ready to go anytime. He hadn't sped things along all that much. Simply helped nature take its course. No more getting old with all the aches and pains that went with age. No more worries.

"You can thank me later, Reggie," he said quietly.

# 20

"What are the chances the unions will settle?" Leona asked.

She and her team were entrenched in the boardroom at the bank, piles of paper stacked on the polished wood. It was shortly after lunch on Friday, July 27, deadline day for their reports on Coal-Balt. All four of her team were ready. The mood in the room was anything but upbeat.

Sean Grant shook his head. "Two of them may, but the other three are going to walk unless management puts something better on the table. And it's not just wages. Coal-Balt has been screwing these guys on their pensions for a long time and it's coming back to haunt them. The plans are only forty to fifty percent funded. And unless the markets take some sort of huge surge and push their investments way up, they're in trouble. Coal-Balt won't be able to cover the pension checks."

He took a drink of water and pulled another file from his stack. "The Teamsters move the coal between the mine and the plant. And they're not happy. A couple of their members were fired and the company ran roughshod over the grievances. There's absolutely no way they'll settle when their contract is up."

"When is that?" Leona ran her fingers through her ringlets.

"Nine months."

"So it's about ready to hit the fan."

"Big-time. The Plumbers and Pipefitters are a couple of steps behind the Teamsters. And the electricians always want to earn more money than anyone else. So they're going to be pretty militant when their contract comes due for negotiation."

"All right, labor troubles are massing on the horizon," Leona said, then turned to Angela Samarach. "What about their accounting practices? Any Enrons in the mix?"

She shook her head. "Not that I can see. They've been aboveboard with all their income reporting and have been depreciating their equipment at a reasonable rate. Profits are good and appear to be legitimate. There aren't a lot of warning lights going off on the financial end."

"What about taxes?" Leona asked. "They owe the government anything?"

"A few million in current taxes, but nothing in arrears. They're right up to date. Like I said, financially, they look good."

"Well, they owe us some money. That's why we're doing this."

"I factored in all their loans. Their loan-to-asset ratio is fine."

Leona nodded. "Jarrod, what's up with the regulatory end of things?"

Jarrod cleared his throat and pushed back a strand of long hair from his face. "Right now, Coal-Balt is within the federal emission guidelines, but that could change soon."

"Why? What's up?"

"There's a new bill being drafted that is an extension of both the Clean Air Act and the Clear Skies Act. It closes loopholes in the Acts and gives them real teeth. And if it passes, Coal-Balt will be greatly affected."

"How?" Leona asked, chewing on the end of her pen.

"Right now companies that generate electrical power by burning fossil fuels can sidestep installing new technology to cut down pollution if they renovate less than twenty percent of their facilities at a time. It's a no-brainer that every renovation is pegged at eighteen to nineteen percent of the value of the plant. Claire Buxton's new bill would stop that in its tracks. Lombard II would have to comply with the current emission standards, which means a complete overhaul, including adding new scrubbers and other antiemission equipment."

"Do you have a dollar figure on what that would cost?"

"An estimate, but probably within ten percent." He checked his notes. "Eight hundred and thirty million dollars."

Leona let out a long breath. "That's a lot of money. And they would have to implement those changes in some sort of set time period?"

"One year."

"Now that's interesting," Leona said. "You said the bill hasn't passed yet. How did you find out about it?"

"I have some friends working as interns for a couple of senators. They let me know it's pending."

"I hope you did nothing wrong when you had your friends get this information for you," Leona said. "Like insider trading in Senate secrets?"

"No," Jarrod laughed. "No secrets compromised in the investigation."

"What are the chances of this bill becoming law?"

He shrugged. "Fifty-fifty. Might happen. Might not. It has some key support, but these things are always a bit of a crapshoot until they actually get through the house. There's a lot of influential people who don't want to see this become legislation."

"I can imagine." She turned to Tracey Mendez, the final

member of the team. "So what did you find that falls out-side what everyone else was looking at?"

"Quite a bit," Tracey said, referring to her notes. "Straight off the top, Coal-Balt is involved in six litigation suits, all as the defendant. None of them are huge, but alto-gether they total almost sixteen million dollars."

"Why are they being sued?" Leona asked.

"Two of the suits are from former workers who allege that the company provided them with unsafe working con-ditions. One was a miner, the other worked in the plant on the retention pond. The other four are all environmental. Property owners suing because the company's operations destroyed the land surrounding their houses or damage to their water supply. Coal-Balt is fighting all of them, but they'll probably settle out of court for about half the cost of the initial claim."

"So about eight million dollars, give or take. That's not bad."

"No, it's not. Litigation isn't a major concern. But they've got other problems."

"Like?"

"Well, one that recently ironed itself out. The company CEO, Reginald Morgan, was opposed to the conversion. But with his death, that's a bit of a moot point now."

"What are you talking about?" Leona asked, leaning for-ward. "There was dissension in the ranks?"

"Big-time. At least that's the rumor. Derek Swanson wanted the change, but Morgan was looking to oppose it."

Leona was quiet for a few seconds, then asked, "Who would have come out on top? Did the people you were talking with have any idea?"

"Morgan was the CEO, and his family founded the company. But it's now a publicly traded company, and the shareholders hold the trump card these days. Swanson's appeal would have been to sell the shareholders on the prospect of huge financial gains in their stock portfolios. But Morgan had a lot of clout with the longtime shareholders. I'd say the consensus was in Morgan's favor."

"Now that's interesting," she said. "Management on different pages. Doesn't make for smooth sailing." She mulled over the information for a few moments, then asked, "What else?"

"I'm not an expert, but from what I've been able to piece together, the whole operation is shaky. Straight off the top, the mine is running out of coal. They've got a very low Demonstrated Reserve Base, which is calculated on anthracite or bituminous coal beds a minimum of twenty-eight inches thick, or subbituminous coal beds greater than sixty inches that occur within a thousand feet of the surface."

"What's anthracite?" Leona asked.

"Coal is broken down into grades, and anthracite is the highest. It's very hard, has lots of fixed carbon and burns well with little residue. Bituminous coal is the most common grade of coal in North America and is used by power plants to generate electricity. It doesn't burn as clean as anthracite. Ninety percent of the coal the mine produces is bituminous."

"That's not a bad thing, is it?"

"No, it's common. But the industry sets an Average Quality of Coal based on trace elements, moisture, ash and fixed carbon among other things. Coal-Balt is producing low-quality bituminous coal from a quickly depleting supply."

"Which means they'll have to find another source of coal soon or they won't have any fuel for their power plant."

"Exactly. And the ten percent of the coal the mine is

producing that isn't bituminous is lignite. And lignite is an extremely low grade of coal that burns dirty and pumps a lot of carbon dioxide into the atmosphere."

"So without the new antiemission bill passing the operation is in trouble. With it in place, they're dead in the water."

Tracey nodded. "Five years and they're out of business. Unless they come up with another source of coal."

Leona was silent for the better part of a minute. She shuffled a few papers about, reviewing the high points. Her staff straightened their papers and began refiling their reports in briefcases and file folders.

"Each of you has a full copy of the reports you submitted today," she said, and they all nodded. "Thank you for a job well done. Everyone." She looked up from the stack of paper. "There's one more thing. Everyone knows about the CEO of Coal-Balt, Reginald Morgan, disappearing from a cruise ship. As his company is a major client of ours, we've been asked not to talk about it outside the office, but among ourselves we can certainly acknowledge what happened. Mr. Morgan has been a client of DC Trust for almost forty years. He's a well-respected businessman and philanthropist. That his company is experiencing some bumps in the road does nothing to detract from his character."

"I met him numerous times at different functions around the city," Angela Samarach said. "He was a true gentleman."

"Yes, he was," Leona said. "I had the privilege of meeting him once. Both he and his wife, Amelia, were wonderful people." She glanced around the table. "So let's keep any comments about Mr. Morgan, even to friends, to what a warmhearted man he was."

The group split up, Leona heading for her office down the hall, the other four retreating back to the eleventh floor. She stopped in the staff room and grabbed a Diet Coke from the fridge. A noise from behind her caused her to turn. Bill Cawder was entering the room, coffee cup in hand.

"Hey, Bill."

"Leona. How's life on the twelfth floor treating you?"

"Love it," she said, lifting the can. "There's never a shortage of the good stuff."

"I think you're the only one up here who drinks that," he said, then asked, "What was the meeting all about? Saw you and a few others sequestered in the boardroom for a couple of hours."

"Coal-Balt. The results of a feasibility study for their conversion to an income trust."

"How'd it go?" He filled his cup and added a touch of sugar.

"I'd rather not say anything until I submit my report to Anthony Halladay," she said. This was her first assignment as vice president and the last thing she needed was for her findings to hit Halladay's desk before her report.

"Whatever you say," Cawder responded. He stopped for a second, then said, "You junior or senior vice president?"

"Just a run-of-the-mill VP, I think. Why?"

"Well, if you were senior vice president, I'd have to call you sir, or ma'am." He grinned and disappeared into the hallway.

Leona stood in the staff room, with its plush rugs and teak table and chairs, and thought about Cawder's comment. All her life she had pushed her way to the top, trying to be the son her father had always wanted. Why couldn't she be the one looking for help? Just once. Why did she always have to be the strong one? The one with the answers.

For once, she didn't have an answer to the question.

## 21

Derek Swanson watched the ball arc toward the green, then land within twenty feet of the pin. He smiled and gave the rest of his foursome a wave, slipped his seven iron back in the bag and walked toward the eighteenth green. Even with a two putt he was still only six over par. A damn good round for a twelve handicap. The summer grass felt spongy under his feet and he had a renewed confidence ebbing from his pores. His mind wandered from the last hole on the course to the office.

Senator Claire Buxton wasn't going to derail his plans. Her bill would never pass fast enough to kill the conversion and he would start dumping stock in the weeks before it became law. The real obstacle to his forty-or fifty-million-dollar windfall was Reginald Morgan. And the old man was shark food. They had never found his body, probably never would. Amelia was doing all right. She had her family and a hundred million dollars to help her grieve. Not that the money meant anything to her. She and Reggie had been filthy rich for so long she didn't know any other way to live.

Swanson reached the green and waited for the rest of the group to putt out. He had this for a birdie and his best round of the season. There was a slight left to right break and the hole was downhill—not an easy putt. He lined it up from a couple of different angles, then tapped the ball with an even stroke. It appeared to be too far left, then as it slowed the slope took over and the ball broke to the right. A foot from the hole it didn't seem to have enough speed, but the slight downhill angle gave it enough to reach the hole and drop. Swanson pumped the air with his fist, Tiger style. He shook hands with the rest of the foursome and headed for the clubhouse. What a way to spend a Saturday morning. He dropped his clubs off for cleaning, then opened his locker and changed out of his soft spikes and golf pants and shirt. He had finished changing when another man came around the corner and leaned against the lockers. The space around them was deserted, save for the two men.

"What the hell are you doing here?" Swanson asked, his voice low and threatening.

Darvin stared back at him with dark eyes. His light brown hair was slicked back and sprayed and he had a double chin that Swanson had never noticed before.

"Needed to talk with you," he said in a dry voice.

"I have nothing to say to you. Our business is concluded." Swanson snapped his locker shut and spun the combination lock. He hoisted his tote bag and started for the door. The killer fell in behind him.

"You shouldn't treat people so poorly, Derek. Especially when they know stuff that could send you to jail."

Swanson stopped in his tracks and spun about. "You've got nothing on me. There is no paper trail linking me to you, or to Reggie's death. Nothing. Go back to whatever it is you do when you're not killing people and leave me alone."

A smile spread across Darvin's face. His eyes danced with darkness. "Tying you to Reginald Morgan's murder is easy." The smile disappeared and the eyes turned cold. "We need to talk."

"All right," Swanson said. "We can stand out by the driving range."

He pushed through the doors and walked briskly past the putting green to a bank of trees that bordered the practice range. Two men and one woman were hitting balls, but they were a hundred yards or more from the trees. Swanson glanced about to make sure they were alone and hidden from sight by the foliage, then turned to face the killer.

"What do you want?" he asked, his voice terse.

Darvin leaned against a tree and looked about. "This, Derek, this is what I want. The country club, the yachts, the million-dollar summerhouse—the lifestyle of the rich but not necessarily famous."

"You're well paid for what you do. Buy a membership."

Darvin clucked and shook his head. "A half million a year doesn't buy anything anymore. Prices are through the roof. And I have no benefits, no pension plan, no way to build for the future. No, I need something else. Something more profitable. And that's where you come in."

"What the hell are you talking about?"

Darvin's tongue flicked out and licked his lips. "You're got a lucrative deal on the table right now. I know what you're doing with Coal-Balt—the conversion to an income trust. That's why you had me kill Reginald Morgan. He was opposed to the conversion. And that would have cost you a lot of money."

Swanson's face surged with color. "Who the fuck do you think you are? You stay out of my life and away from me. What I do and why I do it are none of your business. Do you understand?"

"No, it's your turn to understand something," Darvin hissed. "I'm part of your life and I'm not going away. When you had me kill Reginald Morgan, you tied the knot. Now you get to live with the Pandora's box you opened."

Neither man spoke for the better part of a minute. Darvin finally continued. "And now I want in. I want a share in whatever you take out of the increase in the stock prices."

Swanson was shaking with rage. He thought of grabbing the smaller man and choking him, killing him on the spot, but his mind cooled as the moments passed. He waited until his breathing returned to normal, until his brain was processing what was happening properly.

"The conversion isn't going to happen," he said.

"Sure it is," Darvin said. "I have sources that say it's a done deal."

"You should get better sources. There's a problem with new legislation that's going to kill it."

"What sort of legislation?"

"A senator out of Utah, Claire Buxton, is submitting a new bill that will require us to completely revamp both the mine and the power plant. The regulatory boards won't approve the conversion with the new legislation in place."

"But it's not in place now. And you've already got regulatory approval."

Swanson was impressed with the accuracy of the man's research, but stayed the course. "Buxton's bill will pass. I hired lobbyists to crater it but they were unsuccessful. The conversion is dead in the water. It's over. Take your hundred thousand dollars and call it a day."

Darvin was thoughtful. "We'll see," he said, then added, "You know what pisses me off, Derek?"

"What's that?" Swanson sighed. He was tired of the conversation and could have cared less.

"That a woman wields such power. How the hell did that happen? There was a time not so long ago when men made the decisions in Washington. Now look at it. Hillary Clinton and her ragtag bag of political bitches. Giving women this kind of control is bad. Very bad."

"We're done here," Swanson said curtly. "I've got other things to do with my day."

Darvin's face darkened again. "You should learn to be nicer, Derek," he said icily. "I don't like being treated like one of your casual employees."

Swanson glared at the man. "That's exactly what you are," he said. "And now, as The Donald would say, you're fired."

Swanson walked back to his car, alternating between seething anger at the man's audacity and being petrified with fear at the thought of being linked to Reginald Morgan's murder. He had little doubt that Darvin could link him to the killing. The hundred thousand dollars was partially traceable to a withdrawal from one of his accounts. The remainder had come from his safe at his house. He hadn't been careful enough. He had never foreseen this happening—that he would be essentially blackmailed by the killer. And of all the people to go up against, a hired hit man was probably the least desirable. Nonetheless, no piece of trash that crawled out from under a rock when summoned was going to dictate terms to him.

Things were moving ahead. Without Darvin. That was the way things were, plain and simple.

Swanson gunned the motor on his Porsche and squealed the tires on the hot asphalt. Asshole, he thought as he raced past the killer on his way to the main gate. But even accelerating out of the parking lot, he still got a quick glimpse of the man's eyes. They were cold—cruel.

Darvin watched the rear end of the Carrera fishtail as it swung out onto the main road. What a fool. If Derek Swanson thought this was the last time they would meet, he was completely out of touch with reality. In fact, they would meet again soon, and often. Darvin knew this because he was already planning it.

He walked back to his car and thumbed the key fob. The lights blinked and he opened the door and slid behind the wheel. Senator Claire Buxton. The bitch. Tabling new legislation that could crater the deal and cost him millions of dollars. Millions of dollars that Derek Swanson would gladly pay to keep a secret if the conversion went through. Couldn't let that happen. He turned over the ignition and followed the tire marks Swanson had left on the asphalt out to the main street. He needed to take care of this wrinkle. And quickly.

Time was of the essence.

# 22

Easy jazz piano played on the stereo and the gentle aroma of vanilla drifted through the town house. Light streamed in from the bay window fronting Caroline Street, and a handful of tropical plants swayed with the breeze from the air conditioner. The living room was an eclectic mix of steel-and-leather furniture and antiques. A couple of brightly colored abstract paintings hung on one wall, a plasma television on the other. Outside, the Saturday morning sun warmed the busy street scene.

Leona sipped her tea and stared at the stack of paper on her coffee table. The reports on Coal-Balt, the evidence supporting her initial intuition that the company was not soluble as an income trust. She buried her hands in her thick ringlets and closed her eyes, letting the soothing piano notes sink into her soul. What to do? The bank had a vested interest in Coal-Balt's financial health, and a fiduciary duty to the shareholders. Their two-hundred-and-eighty-million-dollar debt was secured and was probably safe. The reasons, from the bank's perspective, to give the conversion a thumbs-down, were nominal at best. Over the short term, switching to an income trust was probably a good thing, as the share values would definitely rise. It was the long term she was worried about. And the shareholders. Which was absolutely crazy. There was no upside to her worrying about what happened to some schmuck ma and pa in Iowa, who invested part of their retirement portfolio in Coal-Balt. And she certainly had no allegiance to the giant investment firms that bought up huge chunks of stock. So why the trepidation? Why not just okay it?

She had come so far, from the fat kid in the school cafeteria who ate lunch alone, to the successful woman who fit a size eight. The teacher's pet, with great marks and few friends, none of them the cool kids, and none of them boys, was gone. It hadn't been easy. Nothing in her life had been easy. Watching her parents divorce after forty-one years had torn her apart emotionally. Always feeling that no man would want her. Fighting off what she knew in her heart to be untruths.

Leona opened her eyes and sucked in a deep breath. She had finally made it, had reached a point in her life that, to her, represented success. And now she was poised to throw it all away. Anthony Halladay had made it quite clear that he expected the bank to back Coal-Balt's new business plan. Maybe Halladay's allegiances to the energy company had waned a bit with Reginald Morgan's death. Maybe, but there was no guarantee of that. Going against the CEO's wishes was going to ruffle some feathers. Big feathers. But if she gave the conversion a thumbs-up, all that vanished.

It was almost ten and she got up from the couch and switched off the music. Tyler would be waiting, ready to go over the new menu at the restaurant. They met every Saturday morning when she was in Washington. It was a meeting she looked forward to—Tyler's exuberance about the food he served was refreshing. She rinsed the cold tea from her cup, locked up the town house and backed her Saab 9-3 out of the garage. The restaurant was less than ten minutes in the light traffic and parking was easy. It was five minutes after the hour when she sat down with her chef at one of the tables close to the front window.

"What's wrong?" Tyler leaned back in his chair, coffee in hand.

Leona didn't answer for a second, then said, "That obvious?"

He nodded. "Oh yeah."

"Bit of a problem at the office."

"Want to talk about it? It helps sometimes. Gives perspective to things."

"It's privileged information. I can't discuss it."

Tyler propelled himself forward, his elbows resting on the table. "Give me a hypothetical. Nothing with any substance. No names, no details."

She eyed him for a minute, then said, "Okay, tell me what you would do." She gave him the situation, the premise, then sat back, sipped her diet Coke and waited while he mulled it over. Her chef was an intellectual without a degree. He had a sharp mind that could have breezed through college-or university-level courses if he'd taken that route. He had simply chosen a different path in life. One that he loved—his passion.

"Give it the thumbs-up," Tyler said after a couple of minutes. "But on a condition. The company has to place x amount of dollars from the share price increase in a separate fund to allow for updating the equipment and rebuilding the plant. If the new legislation comes into effect, they go ahead with the work, if not, they continue on like nothing happened. That way the shareholders don't take the full hit. And you get to continue on as Leona Hewitt, vice president."

Leona raised an eyebrow. "Very well done," she said. "Probably not all that easy to implement, but an excellent line of thinking."

"That's because I have no idea what I'm doing," he said. "Outside the forest, so to speak."

"Well, who knows where it's going to go. There's a bit of a wrinkle."

Tyler leaned forward. "A wrinkle. I like wrinkles. What sort?"

She grinned. His enthusiasm was contagious. "Someone died."

He leaned back and ran his hands through his short hair. "Now it would be really interesting if it was that guy who disappeared off the cruise ship. You know, the one that's all over the newspapers these days. Was it murder? An accident? Someone removing the old guy so they can manipulate the company he owned? Coal-burning plant, from what the newspapers reported. Nasty shit, burning coal to produce electricity."

"What made you think that?" The color drained from her face.

"I don't know. It was in the newspapers." Tyler stared at her for a few seconds, then said, "Holy shit. It was him, wasn't it? That was the guy. And the plant you were talking about is the one in the papers."

Slowly, she nodded. "It goes no further than this table."

"Jesus Christ, no. Never." His body twitched about, like a surge of electricity had shot through it. "Damn, this is exciting."

She couldn't help but grin at his excitement. "The police think Reginald Morgan fell overboard. He was elderly and could have misjudged his balance. It would be easy enough to do."

Tyler leaned back and his eyes narrowed. "You really think that?"

She finished her soda. "No."

She glanced at her watch and said, "Let's get the menu sorted out."

"Yeah, let's do that."

An hour later, Leona closed the door of her restaurant behind her and stood facing the street. A wide selection of cars drove past—sedans, sports cars, SUVs. It struck her that each one was a capsule, insulated from the world outside its windows. Unique little environments. She watched an older women driving slowly, enjoying a piece of classical music. Behind her was a group of teenagers, the sound system turned up and the bass thumping. Young families drifted past with small children strapped in car seats, staring out the window at the strange and new sights. Each car its own little world. The people inside with their lives, their loves, their fears. None of them the same.

She walked to her car and slipped behind the wheel. This was her world. The one where the young woman could never do enough to earn her father's approval. The college student who drank red wine because women were expected to drink white. The woman in her early twenties who bungee-jumped off a bridge in New Zealand to prove she wasn't scared of heights. The vice president of a bank who knew only unfulfilled dreams and desires. She felt the leather on the steering wheel, warm and smooth to the touch. Her life was one of great privilege; she knew that. She could easily have been born a black child in one of the small Kenyan villages her foundation was pumping money into. Scraping for the necessities of life. But her course in life had been easier.

So why did she still feel so unaccomplished?

Leona gave her head a shake and turned the key in the ignition. The motor came to life and she shifted into first gear and pulled out into the traffic. Some things in her life were uncertain, but one thing was rock solid. And that was her decision on the Coal-Balt income trust conversion. She'd made up her mind and there was no moving her.

Time would tell whether she'd made the right decision.

## 23

For over a week they told him nothing, gave him no reason for throwing him in a squalid jail cell and locking the door. Meals were sporadic, and when they did arrive they were almost inedible. And Mike Anderson prided himself that he could eat almost anything, including a few of the larger bugs that wandered in under the door. At least when he ate them he knew what he was getting. There were no windows in the tiny cell, and he had lost track of time. It could have just as easily been noon as midnight when the door finally opened and a solitary man, dressed in paramilitary clothes, entered. He stared at Anderson for a full minute, his jet-black skin blending into the darkness, the whites of his eyes floating in the dim light. The man motioned for Anderson to get up and follow him.

There were four other men in the hallway leading from the cell, all armed with automatic weapons. Anderson shuffled behind the first man, his bare feet sloshing in the cold puddles of water on the uneven stone floor. They had taken his shoes and socks before shutting him away from the outside world. The cell was cold and damp and Anderson could feel the first stages of hypothermia setting in. They reached a narrow staircase, well illuminated from above. As they climbed the wooden risers, the sun came into view through a barred window. The warmth felt good and he squinted against the first light over twenty-five watts in a few days.

"Sit there." The man in the uniform pointed to a wooden chair on one side of a table.

A second chair sat on the other side, and both were identical. Anderson was tempted to sit on the other side of the table just to see the response, but didn't. He had no idea what level of trouble he was in and aggravating the police was never a good idea, let alone in Nairobi. He sat and waited. The man who had led him to the room picked up a file from a cabinet on the far side of the room, then sat in the other chair so they were facing each other. The other four armed men filtered to the edges of the room and leaned against walls. A solitary fan moved the stale air about a bit, but did little to cut through the humidity or the heat. Anderson didn't mind the warmth; it felt good.

The guard perused the file for a minute, his eyes narrowing at times, his brow furrowing as he read the contents. "What are you doing in Kenya, Mr. Anderson?" he asked. His voice was soft, but conveyed authority.

"I work for a nonprofit organization." Mike resisted the temptation to tell the man he was an idiot if he didn't know that already. "We raise money in the United States and use it to protect the elephants from poachers in a region near Samburu. The government has approved our work."

"Ah, yes, I see this now. You are doing good work in our country." There was a touch of English accent to the voice.

"We're trying to help."

"Help comes in many forms, Mr. Anderson. When it comes in the form of money, that is good." He paused, but when Anderson didn't respond, he continued. "It's the amount of money, and to whom it's being given, that we have a problem with."

Anderson wondered who the *we* was. From where he was sitting, it could be a handful of thugs who were using their positions inside the police force to extract bribe money, or it could legitimately be the government. He had no definitive proof, but he strongly suspected option A over B.

"The money is spent very carefully," Mike said. "It has to be. We're accountable to our donors in the US."

"I see." The man referred to a different written page inside the file.

"May I ask a question?" Mike asked.

The man's eyes looked up from the page without any other part of him moving. "That depends on the question, Mr. Anderson."

"Why am I in jail? Am I under arrest?"

The officer leaned back in the chair and thoughtfully scratched the day-old growth on his chin. "That's two questions. Which one would you like an answer to?"

"Why am I in jail?"

"You brought a large sum of money into the country a few days ago. And when you left the bank, you took a considerable sum in cash."

They had someone inside the bank. An informant. There was no other way they could know. "Yes. I took two hundred and sixty thousand American dollars with me." There was no sense in lying; the police would know the amounts.

"In Kenya, that is a small fortune." The man cocked his head slightly and smiled. His teeth were shocking white against his black skin. "You're lucky to be alive, Mr. Anderson. Most people with that much money in their pockets wouldn't last long on the streets."

"I have friends in Kenya, sir," Mike said. "Friends who protect me from thieves and murderers."

"Is Nikala Shambu one of those friends?"

Telling a lie now would be the next closest thing to suicide. "Yes."

"And you were visiting him when we arrested you?"

Anderson nodded. "So I *am* under arrest. What is the charge?"

His interviewer laughed, a hearty chortle that echoed about the spartan room. "No charge yet. We are simply holding you until we determine if you have done anything illegal."

"Have you figured that out yet? Whether I've done anything bad?"

Again, the laugh. "Oh, I'm sure you've done many bad things, Mr. Anderson. It's all a matter of perspective."

"Perspective?" Anderson asked, impressed with the man's command of the English language, but totally unimpressed by their judicial system.

"Yes, of course. Perspective. From yours, you are simply paying people to ensure your safety, and that of your villagers and the elephants that live inside the tract of land our government has allowed you to police. From ours, you are giving money to a very dangerous man. A man who may use that money to oppose the authorities."

"That would be bad," Anderson said, nodding. "He told me the money was for a new house he was building."

"You can see the problem with perspective, Mr. Anderson. Everyone has one, but only one counts."

"Yours."

"Yes. Mine. Ours, if you wish." The man stared into the American's eyes. "So that brings us to our problem."

"Which is?"

"What to do with you. If we charge you with assisting antigovernment forces, you will never get out of that cell. Except to face a firing squad."

Anderson swallowed heavily. "I don't think I like that option."

"It doesn't matter what you think, Mr. Anderson." Any civility in his tone was gone. "It matters what I think."

"I understand."

Silence settled over the room for a full two minutes. To Anderson, it felt like a week. A week with his balls in a vise. The room was hot now that his body temperature had returned to normal. He was sweating, and felt the droplets trickling down the sides of his ribcage. He avoided his interrogator's eyes, focusing on a loose floorboard instead.

"There may be a second option."

Mike didn't respond. He couldn't. His mouth was too dry.

"There is still a considerable amount of money in the bank." The man's voice was upbeat again. "And you know what they say. Money talks."

Anderson wet his lips, his tongue felt the size of a football. "It's not my money."

"But you may have some influence over how it is spent. For your good, I hope you have this influence."

Mike weighed his answer carefully. Agreeing would only guarantee his death if he couldn't get his hands on the money. Disagreeing could have disastrous results on the spot.

"The money is controlled by a woman in the United States. I have her confidence. She trusts me. There is a possibility I could have some, *influence*, as you put it. I would have to speak with her directly."

Silence cut through the room like a barracuda in cool water. Finally the man said, "I am not so sure that will work. I'll have to think about it." He looked at the other guards. "Take Mr. Anderson back to his cell."

Anderson stood and bowed his head respectfully toward the other man. He wanted to leap across the table and snap the bastard's neck, but that would only serve to get him killed. No upside to that. At least he had a chance to get himself out of this mess. Probably not a great one, but right now he'd take whatever he could get.

# 24

It was early for the phone to ring. Too early. Nothing good ever came from phone calls in the middle of the night. Leona glanced at the clock beside her bed as she picked up the receiver. Four-eighteen on Sunday morning.

"Hello?" She tried to sound awake, but sleep resonated through her voice.

"Miss Leona." The voice was commingled with heavy static, but recognizable as Kubala Kantu.

"Kubala?"

"Yes, it's me."

"Is everything all right, Kubala?" she asked, waking up quickly now.

"Mr. Mike didn't show up at the village, Miss Leona."

"He's not there? You haven't seen him?"

"No. You said he would be arriving again sometime last week, but no one has seen him."

"Where are you?"

"Nairobi. I drove to the hotel where he usually stays, but he wasn't there."

"Did he check in?"

"Yes. Friday afternoon, nine days ago. But he left the next morning and the desk clerk said he never came back."

Leona rubbed her eyes and thought for a moment. "Have you checked with the police?"

There was a pause. "That might not be a good idea."

"Why?"

"You know my country, Miss Leona. If I speak with the police, they will be interested in why Mr. Mike is in Kenya."

"Yes, of course." She flipped on the light next to the bed and ran her hands through her hair. "Is there any other way of finding out what happened to him? He has two men who drive him around Nairobi. Maybe you could talk to them."

"I know these men. I've met them. Momba and Tuato. I've tried to find them, but have had no luck."

"Is there anyone else?"

"I could talk with the man he delivers the money to, but I don't know who that is."

Leona racked her brain. It was early and her thought processes were barely working. "It was something like Nike. Nike Shamba."

"Nikala Shambu?" Kubala asked.

"Yes, that's it. That's the name." When there was no response, Leona said, "Do you know this man?"

"Yes. He is very bad. Very dangerous. The most violent man in Nairobi."

"Could you ask him about Mike?"

"It would be very dangerous. This man, he is powerful, and ruthless. I have heard many stories of how he kills people who get in his way."

"Don't go near him if you think it will put you in danger," Leona said. "I'll think of some other way. Mike is an American citizen. Maybe the American embassy can find out what happened."

"Maybe, but I doubt it. If no one on the street is talking, there will be no information."

"I'll contact the embassy, Kubala. You do what you can to find him."

"Yes, of course, Miss Leona."

"Be careful."

"This is Nairobi. I am always careful when I'm in the city."

"Call me back in a day or two at the most. Or when you get some information." She thought for a second, then added, "Can you leave me a phone number where I can reach you? In case I find out something through the embassy."

"My friend has a phone. The one I am calling from." He recited the country code, then the number. "Ask for me when you call. If I'm not here, they will get the message that you called to me. I will call you back."

"Good. I'll talk to you soon."

"Yes. Have a nice day."

Leona hung up, Kubala's final words echoing about her head. *Have a nice day*. It was merely a colloquialism, but it stuck with her. How was that possible? Mike Anderson had disappeared, swallowed up by the mass of deceit and corruption that was the Kenyan capitol. She had worried about this happening from the first time Mike left the United States with money destined for Kubala and his village. Was he being held captive? Or dead? There was no way of knowing. Either was possible. Probable, in fact.

Leona slid out of bed, no longer tired. Her mind was alive with possible scenarios, all playing out like movies on the big screen. So vivid, so real, so brutal. The chances of Mike taking a detour before he visited the village and handed over the money were zero. After, maybe. But he didn't care for Kenyan beer, and would have nothing to do with the women because of the high rate of AIDS and HIV. Mike took his job seriously and had always found some way to deliver the money. Something was wrong. But what? Standing in her town house in Washington DC, a world removed from the violence of Nairobi, she had no idea. It was Sunday, but there had to be some way of contacting the American embassy. And with the time difference, now was probably the best time. She had a quick shower and put on a rare pot of coffee, calling the international operator and getting the embassy's number while the dark roast

Colombian blend brewed. She dialed the number and waited.

A voice answered and she said, "My name is Leona Hewitt. I'm calling from Washington, DC. A business associate of mine has gone missing and I need your help."

Kubala replaced the cracked handset in its cradle. Nikala Shambu. He knew Mike Anderson was paying off someone in Nairobi to ensure his safety and keep the conduit for the money open. He suspected it might be Nikala Shambu. He hoped not. The man was a monster. A legend that had evolved from a trail of mutilated bodies, murdered families, and young women violated to the point of suicide. If Shambu had his hooks into the American, he wouldn't be letting go. But it made no sense that Shambu would kidnap or kill the American. Shambu was collecting money on a regular basis from Miss Leona's foundation. He wouldn't kill the messenger of good tidings.

Which meant something else had happened to Mike Anderson. And even if Shambu weren't involved, he would probably know who was. Kubala shuddered. If he wanted to find out, he would have to approach the most feared man in Nairobi. His life would be in the man's hands. If Shambu decided to kill him for poking around, asking questions, he would die. If Shambu's decision was to humor him and tell what he knew, then the chances were good he would live. And find out where Mike Anderson was.

Or his body.

Kubala looked around his friend's tiny house, the paint peeling from the walls and the floor a jumble of old tiles and pieces of wood. Poverty. They all lived with it, every day. Parents worked sixteen-hour days under horrible conditions, and their children still went hungry. Violence was everywhere. Clean water and food difficult to attain.

But Leona Hewitt had taken an interest in the elephants of Kenya, and its people. She sent money and expertise that improved lives. She was making a difference to so many families that would have little, or nothing, without her. And Mike Anderson was the man who brought the money into the country. A dangerous job at any time, yet almost suicidal in Kenya. He risked his life . . . for them.

Kubala's hand was shaking as he realized he had made a decision. A life-or-death decision. He couldn't leave Mike Anderson alone in a time of need. He was going to see Nikala Shambu.

# 25

Sunday morning dawned brilliant blue, not a solitary cloud scarring the sky over Salt Lake City. Claire Buxton woke at six, a half hour before the alarm. She rolled out of bed and tiptoed to the shower, careful not to wake her husband, who usually slept soundly until seven. A quick shower invigorated her and by the time her kids and husband rolled into the kitchen a few minutes after seven-thirty, she had breakfast prepared and on the table.

"Since when does this happen?" Deirdre, her seventeen-year-old daughter, asked. "You never cook in the morning."

"Special day." Claire removed her "Kiss the Cook" apron and draped it over the back of a chair. She sat with her family. "Dad gets to golf and we head out for a day trip to the mountains."

Her son, Abraham, said. "I like going to Logan. It's cool up there. Lots to do."

"For a fourteen-year-old," Deirdre said. "Things change when you get older. Like you get a life."

"You're a witch," Abraham said. "If we lived in Salem, they'd burn you at the stake."

Claire gave her daughter a sideways look. "Don't start anything, honey. It's not often I get to spend time with you two. It would be nice to have a fun day."

Deirdre smiled. "Okay, Mom. Logan's not so bad. The canyon is neat."

"We'll visit it. After lunch."

Eric Buxton finished his breakfast and kissed his wife on the cheek before loading his golf clubs and heading out for an early tee time. Claire and the kids were twenty minutes behind him. They took her van, a Chevy Uplander, and headed north through the city. The prominent spires of the Salt Lake Temple flashed through the thick canopies of leaves, and the State Capitol rested on a hill to the north of the downtown core. The Georgian marble in the Ionic columns glistened in the sunlight. They passed the central part of the city and headed north on Highway 89.

Dry expanses of scrubland greeted them and the temperature rose as the sun heated the arid land and sent undulating heat waves drifting up from the hard-packed sand and dirt. Claire sat alone in the front, the kids watching a Jennifer Lopez movie on the DVD screen in the back. They pulled into Logan, home of Logan State University and a stunning Mormon Tabernacle, slightly before noon. Claire found a parking spot two blocks from the Bluebird Restaurant and they ducked in for lunch.

"Love this place," Deirdre said, standing near the soda fountain. The inside of the Bluebird was a throwback to the fifties and early sixties, with checkered tiles on the floor and vinyl-covered stools lined up along the counter. "Was this really what it was like when you grew up?"

Claire laughed. "Pretty much. Times were simpler. Nobody had much money, we lived in smaller houses and drove old cars, but I think growing up when I did was easier. Not as many diversions or pressures."

"And no video games," Abraham said.

"Not true, we had Atari."

"Pong, or whatever they called it," Abraham said, laughing. "I saw something on TV the other day about that game. It was a paddle you moved up and down and a ball that bounced across the screen. Totally lame."

"Like I said, times have changed."

They ordered and ate lunch, followed by a dessert from the soda fountain, then walked down Main Street for an hour. The bookstore, complete with a musty smell that told of old tomes on the shelves, was a favorite. It was closing in on two o'clock when they returned to the van and traveled northeast from the city, parallel to Logan River and toward the canyon. The slope of the road increased as they climbed into the Wasatch Mountains, the river and canyon to the south side of the winding road. They crested the plateau at Bear Lake Summit and Claire pulled the van over at one of the many roadside stops.

"It's weird breathing up here," Deirdre said as they picked a trail and hiked.

"Air's thinner," Abraham said. "We're almost eight thousand feet above sea level."

"This would be tough enough even if I could breathe normally." Claire picked her way along the narrow trail. Her cell phone rang and she answered it, surprised that there was service in the area.

"Senator Buxton, it's Bradley."

"Things okay in Washington?" she asked. The phone she carried with her was her private line—only her husband and the staff in her DC office had the number.

"Fine. No problems. But I've got something for you. The information you wanted on Reginald Morgan's death."

"Go ahead," she said, breathing deeply. Her lungs never seemed to fill and her body craved more oxygen.

"The Mexican police came aboard *Brilliance of the Seas* when the ship docked. They spent the entire day walking each of the decks, looking for traces of blood. One of their team was a forensic specialist and she gave Morgan's room a thorough search. They came up empty and allowed the ship to sail on schedule. When *Brilliance* arrived in Miami, the FBI boarded and repeated the procedure. Again, nothing."

"So they're looking at the incident as an accident."

"Yes. There's no proof of any sort that would point to foul play. Their stance is that Mr. Morgan slipped and fell overboard. The investigation is closed."

"Interesting," Claire said. "The timing is certainly suspicious."

"There's probably never a time when a rich guy dies that the timing doesn't look that way," Bradley said. "That's the problem with being rich. Everyone trying to kill you for your money."

"And you'd know about that?" Claire asked.

"Not yet. Maybe someday."

"Okay, thanks for looking into that. Anything else on the go while we're talking?"

Bradley took a few more minutes to run over a few things that had come up since Claire had been in her office. He wished her a good day in the mountains and she tucked the phone back in her pocket. She buttoned her coat against the wind, cool even on a beautiful summer day. The kids were a hundred yards ahead of her and she quickened her pace. No sense appearing any more out of shape than she was.

★ ★ ★

Claire Buxton's van was parked halfway along a row of eight spots, facing an outcropping of rock. Five minutes after she and her children left the parking lot, a rental car pulled in next to hers. The driver remained in the car, tinkering with something. After a few minutes he looked around the empty lot, then opened his door and got out. That simple action put him inches from the van's passenger door. He pulled out a thin piece of metal and slipped it between the window and the rubber and pushed down. A few seconds of fishing for the locking mechanism and he pulled sharply upward. The door opened to his touch. He set the tool back in the front seat of his rental and slid into the van, closing the door behind him.

Darvin glanced about, but there was no one in the parking lot and the vehicles were far enough from the road that it was impossible for anyone to have noticed him breaking into the vehicle. He removed a canister with a small metal and rigid plastic mechanism attached to one end from under his windbreaker and leaned across and down so he could see under the driver's seat. The space was cluttered with wires running to the motors that moved the power seat. He tucked the device in among the jumble of wires and activated the receiver on the remote control. A tiny red light glowed.

Darvin straightened up and looked around. Nothing. The parking lot was still deserted. He slipped from the van into the front seat of his rental, then backed up and pulled into a spot at the far end of the lot. He turned off the car and settled in with the latest Dean Koontz paperback. Now it was time to wait. Utah's representative to the Senate would be back soon enough.

## 26

Deirdre could hardly walk when they arrived back at the parking lot. Her open-toe shoes were fine for cruising Main Street, but next to useless for hiking on the uneven mountain paths that rimmed Logan Canyon. She fell into the backseat of the van, unfastened the straps on her shoes and gingerly slid her feet out.

"Oh, my God, that feels good," she said, lying flat and wiggling her toes. "I thought I was going to die."

Claire caught the language but let it pass. "We'll find something to rub on them when we get to Logan. You can survive until then."

"I doubt it," she said.

Abraham jumped in the front seat. "Shotgun."

"Like I care," Deirdre said.

Claire started the van and backed out. The forestry road wasn't busy and she pulled out, heading south toward Salt Lake. Hiking with the kids was fun; they were still young enough to enjoy spending time with their mom, but old enough that she didn't have to worry about them. Memories of her children as toddlers sifted through her mind and a hint of a smile crept across her lips. Kids grew up too quick. One minute they needed their parents, the next they wanted to walk on the other side of the mall. The gap between the two stages was a lot smaller than she could ever have imagined. She glanced in the rearview mirror but Deirdre was lying down. Next to her, Abraham was playing a video game on his Game Boy, his fingers tapping the buttons like he was a concert pianist.

She looked back to the road, a series of twists and switchbacks under the afternoon shadow of Naomi Peak, a ten-thousand-foot wall of rock to the west. The road was a challenge, even on a clear summer day. She'd never traveled it in the winter and had no desire to try. They were only twenty miles out of Logan, then she'd be back on Highway 89. From there it was easy driving back to Salt Lake. Claire relaxed her grip on the wheel slightly. No problem, everything was fine.

Darvin kept Claire Buxton's van within his line of sight for the first three miles, losing it on some of the twisty sections of road. He wasn't worried. Following someone on a highway was easy. Unless they turned off on one of the tiny secondary roads, or into a campground, they weren't going anywhere but straight. Four miles from the parking lot he touched the accelerator and closed the distance between his vehicle and the van.

"Almost there," he said to himself. "What's it like to have a minute left to live? But then, you wouldn't know that, would you, Senator?"

He slipped a remote control from his windbreaker pocket. He entered a four-digit code and waited. The road climbed slightly, then crested and began a long downward slope. His index finger touched one of the buttons, triggering a deadly sequence of events. A tiny receiver under the driver's seat in the van picked up the radio signal, electronically closing a circuit and sending a current from the battery to the solenoid coil. A small electric magnet opened the canister, releasing the pressurized cyanide gas into the passenger compartment of the van.

"Good-bye." He set the remote on the seat behind him.

Claire shook her head, trying to clear the cobwebs. Beside her, Abraham's fingers were slowing down and his head was drooping. Then he stopped altogether. She turned back to the road and swerved sharply to the left. The van's tires caught the edge of the road and gravel spit up, peppering the side of the vehicle. She brought the van back under control, but her reaction times were slow. Too slow. She misjudged the next turn, going over the center line and almost hitting a car coming the other direction. The look on the man's face registered for a brief second, then she forced her attention back to the road.

Another corner. This one coming fast. She steered into it, but her actions were sluggish and the van's passenger tires caught the gravel and slammed into the guardrail. It held, forcing the vehicle back onto the road. Claire's brain finally sent a message to her foot. *Get off the gas. Slow down. Stop. Something's wrong.* Her foot lifted off the gas pedal, and without power driving the van into the turns, it started to skid. The passenger-side rear wheels slid forward until the van was traveling almost sideways down the center of the road. Then the rubber caught on the pavement, sending the van directly into a rock wall on the wrong side of the road. The air bags deployed, but the force of the crash was too great. The impact crushed the front of the van, driving the motor into the passenger compartment and impaling the driver with the steering column. The van bounced off the wall and careened across the road, hitting the guardrail head-on. The posts and metal were designed to keep a car on the road when it sideswiped the rail, not a frontal impact. The van cut through the guardrail and flew off the road into the ravine.

It crashed through the first row of trees, each of the thick trunks taking its toll on the battered piece of metal and plastic. When one of the trees finally stopped the van's forward motion, there was little left of the front section and the entire passenger side was ripped apart. A couple of branches snapped, and there was a grating sound as one of the wheels slowly rolled to a stop. Then a surreal quietness settled over the forest.

Darvin overshot the accident scene by a couple of hundred yards, then ran back to where the van had left the road. His car was far enough down the road that no one would notice the make or the license number. He would be some guy at the scene, nothing more. But now, he had to move quickly. The car Claire Buxton had almost hit had stopped and turned around. He had less than a minute. But that should be enough.

He jumped over the destroyed guardrail and slid down the steep slope, grabbing tree trunks and branches to slow him. The van was almost a hundred feet below the road and hung up on a couple of large spruce trees. As he reached the vehicle, a smile spread across his face. The driver's door was forced open and he could see inside the compartment. It was completely destroyed, Claire Buxton's battered body visible, crushed between the seat and the steering column. Since the door was open, the threat of any cyanide gas lingering in the vehicle was almost nil. He approached the vehicle with caution, then, convinced that the gas had dissipated, slipped his hand under the seat and found the canister. He pulled and it came free. The device he had activated from his rental car was still loosely attached, but the solenoid was missing. It must have fallen off onto the floor. He cursed under his breath, slipped the empty canister into his windbreaker pocket and knelt down to search for the trigger mechanism. It was impossible to see under the seat, it was too tight to the floor. He moved his hand carefully across the carpet, feeling from one side where the seat was bolted in to the other. Nothing. Time was running out. He tried again, quicker and pushing harder with his hand in case the tiny mechanical device had sunk into the carpet pile. He felt a sharp piece of the seat cut him before he could react. He swore under his breath but ignored the pain and kept searching. It took another fifteen seconds to locate the device and he squeezed it between his index finger and his thumb and pulled. Some carpet fibers came out with it and he tucked everything in his pocket and jumped back to his feet. He had the evidence. His finger was bleeding slightly, and he wrapped a tissue around it, dabbed at the blood, then stuffed it in his pocket.

He glanced over at the body in the front seat. It was Buxton's son. He was dead, his head almost severed by an impact with some part of the van or a tree. It angered him that the boy had died. If his mother wasn't such a power-seeking bitch, he would still be alive. Another decent life snuffed out by the walking vagina that had brought him into the world. Like it was their birthright to destroy the lives they had created. He traced his finger across the boy's cheek, his flesh still warm.

"Sometimes they kill us fast. Other times they take a whole lifetime," he whispered to the corpse.

A low groan emanated from the backseat and he peered in. The daughter was still alive. Barely. He would have preferred they all died, but there was nothing he could do now. She must have been lying down on the seat otherwise the roof of the van, which was caved in, would have hit her in the head, probably breaking her neck.

He leaned into the cab slightly, so he was only inches from Claire Buxton's bloodied face. He stood motionless, staring at her. His expression changed, mutating into a cold mask. His eyes went dead, all emotion drained from the pupils, like a flower left without water. His mouth turned down into a sneer, devoid of hate, but also of empathy. Color drained from his face, giving his already white skin a pasty texture. His hand snaked through the air, tracing the outline of her face.

"Dead now, dirty thing," he said, his voice a low whisper. He was careful not to touch her. "So close, but you can't get me. Dead dirty things are helpless."

Above him were voices. The glazed-over look slowly dissipated from his eyes as people coming down the hill toward the crash site. Within a few minutes the scene would be crowded. Do-gooders all over the place. Trying to save the girl. Throwing up at seeing a body impaled by a steering column. Then, once the scene was sufficiently overrun, he would leave. A quick jaunt through the trees, then up the hill to his car. And gone.

"Holy shit," the man said as he reached the vehicle. "Is anyone alive?"

"I think so," Darvin said, not meeting the man's gaze, but keeping his focus inside the van. *If they don't see your eyes, they'll never remember what you look like.* "The girl in the back. I think she might still be breathing."

More people arrived, scrambling down the slope, cell phones pressed to their ears. Emergency crews and police would already be dispatched, but Logan was fifteen miles to the south. At least fifteen minutes from the time the first person called in the accident. And by that time he'd be gone. A ghost in the forest.

# 27

The American embassy in Nairobi was of no assistance. They had no idea who Mike Anderson was, or where he might be. If he was even still in the country. And until someone could produce proof he wasn't shacked up in one of the many brothels in the sprawling city, they weren't prepared to start looking for him. Leona was frustrated, but not surprised. If embassies and law enforcement agencies jumped every time someone went missing for a couple of days, their workloads would double or triple. She had spent most of Sunday on the phone, but with little to show for it. It was after midnight when she fell into bed. Her favorite movie, *Chariots of Fire*, was in the DVD player and she burrowed into her pillow and watched it for the $n^{th}$ time. What fascinated her about the film was all the characters doing the same thing, but for different reasons. Maybe fundraising was the same—so many people looking for money for so many good causes.

When she woke on Monday, the skies had clouded over and a light rain was falling on the nation's capital. Leona drove to work, the wipers beating a steady cadence as they cleared the water from the windshield. She took the stairs to the twelfth floor and was breathing deeply when she finally reached the upper stairwell. It was early, before seven, and the hallway was deserted. Her breathing and pulse returned to normal as she stopped by the staff room and grabbed her morning Diet Coke. Can in hand, she settled into her office with the reports for the Coal-Balt income trust conversion in front of her.

Her decision to approve the trust conversion was a bit of a shock—even to her. The company was going to face problems in the near future, even more so if Senator Claire Buxton's bill passed. But her job was to assess risk and determine whether the bank would find its investment in jeopardy if the conversion were successful. Nothing in the reports indicated that the bank's loan would be compromised. Would she buy shares in the company? Absolutely not. The medium-to long-term prospectus for the company was okay, but not rosy. Short-term gain drove the deal; she knew it. But had the company compromised any regulatory or accounting standards? Not that she could see. And that was the basis of her decision. They had done nothing wrong.

"You're in early."

The voice shocked her and she spilled soda on her desk and one of the printouts. She looked up to the door. The bank's CEO, Anthony Halladay, was leaning on the door jamb. "Are we still on for two this afternoon?" he asked.

"Yes. Two is fine. Sorry, you gave me a bit of a start. I didn't think anyone was in yet."

"Just you and me." He moved into the office, his footsteps inaudible on the thick carpet. "Have you finished the reports on Coal-Balt?"

Leona pointed at the papers on her desk. "Everything is done. Ready for the meeting."

"And . . ."

"Things are fine," she said.

He smiled. "Excellent. That's good news." He turned toward the door. "I'll see you at two."

"Two o'clock."

Halladay vanished into the dimly lit hallway and Leona finished dabbing the errant liquid off the papers. A few needed to be reprinted, but that was easy. She made a note of the page numbers and walked it out to her executive assistant's desk, then retreated to her office. The sun was up and light flooded through the easterly facing window, but the dark wood closed in the space around her. She sucked in a few deep breaths and felt the anxiety decrease. Damn the claustrophobia. She was, and always had been, a tomboy. Tough to the core, her father's son he never had. But she couldn't fight the pure fear she felt when the world closed in on her. Elevators were a nightmare. Even public washroom stalls felt confined. And there was no upside to the phobia. None at all. She glanced at the door as another face appeared. It was Bill Cawder.

"Big day." Steam wafted from the cup he held in his hand.

"How's that?" Leona asked.

"The Coal-Balt report is due. Your first test as VP."

Leona shook her head, her mouth open slightly. "That's amazing. How did you remember that?"

"Like a steel trap." He touched the side of his head. "That, and the fact that my report on Nabisco is due today as well."

"Ahh," she said, nodding. "And how did that go?"

"A no-brainer. Easiest decision I've had to make in six years. Yours?"

"Probably not as easy, but it went well. Anthony Halladay should be pleased."

"Good to hear. He's the one who counts. See you later."

"'Bye."

More staff were arriving and the hallway lights came on. Ruth, her executive assistant, poked her head in the door.

"Did you make any changes to the files you want me to reprint, or are we using the same ones we used to make the original copies?"

"Same files. I spilled pop on them."

"Give me ten minutes."

"No rush, I'm not due in Halladay's office until two."

There were a few small details she needed to take care of on the Coal-Balt file, some e-mails that required a response and a handful of voice mails on her phone. It was approaching noon when she wrapped everything up and cleared her desk. She walked down the hall to the staff room and picked up a copy of the *Washington Post*. She sat down, flipped open the paper and stopped dead. Staring back at her from the front page was Senator Claire Buxton. The caption under the photo explained the article in five words.

*Senator Killed in Car Crash.*

Leona read the copy, quickly at first, then reread it, looking for any hints that Buxton's death might have been something other than an accident. Nothing. The reporter kept to the facts, stating that the weather conditions were optimum, the pavement was dry and there was no fog or low cloud obscuring the road. A driver was quoted as saying that he had passed her going in the opposite direction and she had crossed the center line, almost hitting his vehicle. She crashed a few hundred yards down the road, her van traveling through a guardrail and down a steep embankment. The senator's son died in the crash, but her seventeen-year-old daughter survived, and was in serious condition in the intensive-care ward of Salt Lake Regional Medical Center. The remainder of the article was on Claire Buxton's contributions as a senator and a mother.

What was going on? Reginald Morgan, CEO of Coal-Balt, disappears from a cruise ship sailing through calm waters. Senator Claire Buxton, the author of a new bill that would deeply impact Coal-Balt, is killed while driving in the middle of the afternoon under ideal conditions. And all this just before Coal-Balt was scheduled to convert to an income trust. What were the chances?

Slim, she thought, but possible. She set the paper on her desk and leaned back in her chair. Who stood to benefit from the conversion? The company's common shares would increase dramatically, and that played in Reginald Morgan's favor. It also benefited Derek Swanson, the second-largest private shareholder behind Morgan. But did it benefit him enough for him to murder two people, three if you counted the senator's son? She flipped through the file, looking for the information on Coal-Balt's major shareholders. When she found it, she recalculated the value of Derek Swanson's shares with the projected figures after the conversion. A touch over thirty-five million dollars. Plus bonuses. Corporate executives always tied their stock options and bonuses into the company's performance on the market. And Swanson's bonus would be substantial. Maybe another ten million. That totaled to the mid-forty-million mark and gave Derek Swanson a whole lot of motivation to keep the trust conversion on track.

Leona stood up and walked to the window and stared down at the street. What the hell was she thinking? Murder? A company president killing off people for his own personal financial gain? How totally ridiculous was that? Stupid thinking, that's what it was. Reginald Morgan had fallen over the edge of a cruise ship and Senator Claire Buxton had perished in a traffic accident. It was simple. Don't read any more into it.

But still, her intuition was telling her that something wasn't right.

# 28

The low-pressure front had settled in over the entire eastern seaboard, then pushed inland, and West Virginia was socked in under low cloud cover. Derek Swanson stood at a second-floor window in the front of his house, staring over the small city of Morgantown. How much longer would he have to live here? One year, maybe two. Then he could bow out of his position at Coal-Balt and return to Richmond. That day couldn't come quick enough.

He turned away from the window and slipped on a suit jacket. Morgantown was okay, and he was a big fish in a small pond, but his life was in Richmond. He missed the restaurants, the theater, the culture that a smaller center could never provide. He hadn't dated anyone since he moved to Morgantown, at least not with any degree of regularity, and missed the women. A handful of images flashed through his mind—one stayed.

Jill. Jill Brower. A stunning brunette with a wide smile and a quick sense of humor. The last time he had called she was still single. Maybe when he returned to Richmond . . .

His cell phone vibrated and he checked the number. It was an internal number from DC Trust. He knew exactly who it would be. This was one call he was expecting.

"Hello," he said. "I hope you have good news."

"Yes," the voice said. "She's going to approve the conversion."

"That's what I wanted to hear," Swanson said, allowing himself a smile. "What happens from here?"

"Leona Hewitt submits her report and the bank goes on record as backing the change in accounting practices. You already have regulatory approval from the stock exchange, pending the bank's decision, so it's a done deal. Your legal team will handle things from here."

"Excellent. How long will it take?"

"That's a question for your lawyers. I can only speak for the bank."

"I understand. Thanks for letting me know."

"Not a problem."

Swanson killed the line. Having a contact person on the twelfth floor of the bank was crucial to his success. He relied on the man to feed him inside information and steer decisions his way whenever possible. That connection would come in handy later, when Coal-Balt needed hundreds of millions of dollars to upgrade their facilities. But that would be someone else's problem, not his. He set the alarm and exited his house through the garage, backing the Porsche into the circular drive, then winding out the gears as he steered through the tight turn leading to the street. His cell phone rang again as he pulled out from his private drive. He answered without looking at the number.

"Good morning, Derek."

Swanson tensed. It was Darvin's voice. "What do you want?" His tone was cool, bordering on uncivil.

"Having a good day?"

"Tell me what you want or I'm hanging up."

"You haven't seen the newspapers today, have you?"

"What the hell are you talking about?"

Darvin's voice was aloof, almost condescending. "You really should read the early morning paper, Derek. Especially a man in your position. How can you be a leader if you don't know what's going on in the world?"

"Stop fucking around," Swanson said, his anger rising. "I'm busy. I have to go."

"Read the paper, Derek. You'll be very pleased."

A dial tone followed the final word and Swanson flipped the phone shut. What the hell was the demented fool talking about? What could be in the papers today that would interest him more than any other day? He touched the accelerator slightly and the sports car surged ahead. He'd be at the office soon enough. Then he would find out what Darvin was on about.

Darvin set the phone on his kitchen counter and grinned. What a dumb fuck. Derek Swanson was so screwed . . . and he didn't even know it yet. Soon enough. This time it would be Swanson calling him.

The house was dark, every blind drawn against the sun. A solitary light hung over the tiny island in the kitchen, the light illuminating a stack of dirty dishes and empty pizza boxes piled on the counter and overflowing onto the floor. The stench from the rotting food was overpowering and every breath was an affront to his senses. He left the kitchen and navigated a narrow staircase to the upper floor. The odor dissipated as he reached the second floor and was almost unnoticeable as he opened the door at the end of the hall. The heavy drapes were open a crack, allowing enough sunlight in to showcase a surreal scene.

It was a bedroom, with an armoire and a matching dresser and night table. An old-style alarm clock, with two bells and a ringer, sat on the night table, positioned beside the single bed. The covers were pulled up and the pillow shams smoothed—no wrinkles. A wheelchair sat motionless against the far wall. Darvin walked across the room and threw back the curtains.

"Good morning, Mother," he said.

The sudden influx of light flooded the room and color sprang from the darkness. The comforter was bright pink, the wallpaper a muted rose with lavender flowers. The corpse sitting in the wheelchair remained pale gray.

Darvin strode over to where the emancipated cadaver sat, its elbows resting on the arms of the chair, its bony hands grasping the wooden curls like eagle's talons. The eye sockets were empty holes, and any skin that was left over the skeleton was stretched tight with long vertical creases and cracks. Yellow teeth protruded from the petrified jaw. Jagged bones protruded from the dried skin on both legs, evidence of compound fractures inflicted before death.

His eyes fixated on the broken bones, then he kneeled and ran his finger along their sharp edges. "You're all broken," he hissed. "Broken and withered and weak. Never thought the day would come when you were the one begging for a doctor . . . begging for your life." He stopped touching her and leaned forward, his face only inches from the hollow eyes.

"Weak, Mother. Pathetic and weak." His voice changed,

higher in pitch and demanding. "And your tears. I never knew you could cry. But I gave you something to cry about, didn't I? You felt what it was like to be brutalized. To be humiliated. Poor baby. Poor Mother." He stood up, a malicious leer etched on his face.

"Another dirty thing is dead, Mother. And Darvin never touched it." He pushed on the safety brake and silently wheeled the chair about the room. The corpse's thin hair swayed in the stale air. "Never touch the dirty things. That's what you told me. I listened well. I don't touch them, and I never let the dirty things touch me. Never."

He returned the chair to its original spot, walked over to the window and looked out. The farmhouse was nestled into a large square of hickory and black oak trees, invisible from the secondary highway that ran by a few hundred feet to the north. In the summer, when the foliage on the trees was full, he felt safe from the world. In the winter, when the leaves dropped and the snowy fields were visible from the window, he felt naked. Exposed. He hated the winter.

"The meal I had last night was wonderful." He continued to stare out the window. "Cajun chicken with risotto and asparagus. Very different from when you were doing the cooking. And I didn't clean the kitchen yet. It's quite disgusting. I think you would be very angry with me." He turned from the window and looked into the hollow sockets that at one time had held hateful eyes. "But you don't care, do you? You're dead."

He stared at her for a few minutes, then added, "Thank God for that."

Derek Swanson breezed through the outer office and said the perfunctory good mornings to the admin staff in the bullpen. He walked down the hall and stopped for a moment at his executive assistant's desk.

"Do we have a copy of today's newspaper?" he asked.

"*USA Today* and the *Richmond Times-Dispatch*," she responded, handing him both.

"Thanks."

Swanson headed straight into his office and threw the papers on his desk. He powered up his computer and checked his e-mail. Sixteen new messages had come in over the weekend and he scanned them to see if any were high priority. None were. He sat back in his chair and picked up the *Richmond Times-Dispatch*. The usual drudgery covered the front page—terrorist bombings, murders and high-profile court cases. He flipped through most of the first section, wondering what Darvin had been talking about. He stopped on page twelve, his eyes fixated on one of the articles:

UTAH SENATOR DIES IN CAR CRASH.

Slowly, he allowed his eyes to drop from the headline to the copy. He read it, all the while knowing he was reading a lie. Senator Claire Buxton didn't die accidentally. She had been murdered. He didn't know the details, but he was sure Darvin was responsible. Swanson set the paper on his desk and closed his eyes. He felt sick. The twisted bastard had taken things into his own hands and removed the senator before her bill was introduced to Congress. And now he was tied in with her death. He would never be able to convince anyone that Darvin had acted unilaterally when he killed the politician and her son. The same brush would paint both of them. Tar and feather them, rather.

He stood on shaky legs and walked to the window. Why had he involved Darvin? The man was a complete psychopath. He had seen something in the killer's eyes the first time they had met, when the union rep had to die. Something that had bothered him. A coldness that went beyond any vestige of normalcy. A tiny window into a sick and troubled mind. But he had opened the latch and let the man into his life. Now, with everything at stake, that mistake was coming back at him like a runaway boulder crashing down a hill. And there was little he could do to stop it. What did the twisted bastard want? Money, to be sure. But how much? A specific figure, or a percentage of the net gain in the common shares after the conversion? Either one was too much. He had brought the man in to take care of a single task and had paid him well for it. But what would be the final figure? That was the question. And to that, he had no answer.

# 29

The air was absolutely still, no hint of a breeze. Sweat dripped off Kubala Kantu's forehead onto his cheeks, but he made no move to wipe his brow. He sat quietly, under the intense African sun and the watchful eyes of six heavily armed men. None of them smiled. And every one of them was staring directly at him.

A door opened and a middle-aged man swaggered across the dusty courtyard to where Kubala was perched on a small stool. He carried an automatic rifle and a revolver was stuck in his belt. As he approached, Kubala could see the line of a jagged scar that ran from the man's right eye to his jawline. It had been stitched up, but very poorly. The scars from the suture formed a crisscross pattern over the gash. His eyes were yellow and piercing. He reached Kubala and poked him with the business end of the rifle.

"You can see Mr. Shambu now." He leaned forward, closing the distance between them. His breath reeked of rotting teeth and bad gums. "If you make any sort of movement that I do not like, I will kill you. Understand?"

"Yes, I understand," Kubala said.

"Keep your hands where I can see them. At all times. Do not put your hands in your pockets."

Kubala nodded that he understood. They had already subjected him to a strip search, but there was nothing to be gained by reminding Nikala Shambu's bodyguard that he could not possibly have a weapon. He walked toward the door, then through it and out of the sun into an air-conditioned room. From the outside, the building was simply another shanty on one of Nairobi's many side streets. But inside, it was anything but a dump. The walls were brightly painted and the floor was inlaid tile covered with thick Persian carpets. Heavy leather furniture and modern glass end tables were arranged in two separate groupings. Smoke hung in the air, but through the haze, Kubala could see three men sitting on one of the couches. He approached them and stood a few feet back, unmoving and quiet.

"What do you want?" Nikala Shambu asked, picking his teeth. A half-eaten plate of food sat on the coffee table in front of him. Smoke trailed from a thick cigar he held between his fingers.

"I am Kubala Kantu," he said, his voice even and with cadence. "I work with an American organization called Save Them, keeping elephants safe from poachers in the Samburu district."

"I know who you are," Shambu said. "I asked what you wanted."

Kubala cleared his throat. "A man who works for this organization has disappeared. I was wondering if you might know where he is. His name is Mike Anderson."

Nikala shifted slightly on the couch and picked up a revolver that was sitting next to him. "It bothers me that you would come looking for this man." He caressed the gun, almost a loving touch. He paused, then continued when Kubala didn't respond. "Why do you care about him?"

"He works for Save Them. I also work for this organization. When Mr. Mike didn't show up in Samburu, I phoned the woman in New York who runs the charity. She asked that I speak with you, to see if you had heard anything about what might have happened to him."

"Why would I know anything?" Shambu leaned forward, his eyes dark.

Kubala knew his life was in the man's hands. Any mistake at this point would be fatal. "Mr. Mike told me that he had set up safe passage for the money from the United States. In order to do that, he needed to have the most powerful man in Nairobi working with him. He told me you were that man."

Shambu relaxed into the couch. "You keep a lot of information in that head of yours, Kubala Kantu. Information that could be dangerous to your health."

"I have known of this since you and Mr. Mike first struck your deal. I have never said a word to anyone. There's no reason to start now."

"I see." Shambu reached out and picked up a date from the plate of fruit on the table. "So you want to know what happened to Mike Anderson."

"Yes, sir."

"The police have him. They picked him up after he and I met. That was a little over a week ago."

Kubala looked at the floor, trying to piece together why the police would have taken the American. "I don't understand. Mr. Mike was in Kenya legally. What would the police want with him?"

Shambu smiled. "Come now, it can't be that difficult."

"Money."

"Of course. But what is troubling is how quiet the police are being. I was able to find out where they were keeping him, but that is all I know. Other than they think he is the key to a large amount of money."

"That is impossible. Mr. Mike doesn't control the money. Ms. Leona, the woman in America, set things up so that once the money is in the bank, it can only be released to the local bank in Samburu. And that requires three signatures. It is very difficult to get the money. She did that so no one could steal it."

Shambu nodded. "Mike Anderson told me this some time ago. He said that the only time he could access money was when he first deposited it. After that, he wasn't authorized."

"Yes. Ms. Leona arranged that so he could take money to pay you."

Nikala Shambu chewed on the date and spit out the pit. "It troubles me that you know so much."

Kubala was terrified, but simply shrugged. "As I said, sir, I've known since you first began dealing with Mr. Mike. I've never said a word to anyone."

Shambu pondered that thought, the gun in his hand. Finally, he said, "Mike Anderson is in a basement cell in the old jail on Ngariama Street. Do you know this building?"

"Yes, but it's no longer a police station. Not for many years."

"Not an official one." Shambu waved at the door. "You have the information you came for. Leave. And do not say one word of my involvement, or you and every person you know are dead. Do you understand?"

"Yes. Very clearly. This will not be a problem."

"Good."

Kubala returned to the afternoon heat and walked back to the main road and his Jeep. He slipped in behind the wheel and dug in his pocket for the keys. He was shaking so badly that it took him three tries to insert the key into the ignition. The traffic was thick and he concentrated on driving as best he could. But foremost in his mind was what had just happened. He was now known to Nikala Shambu, and if there were ever any doubt if he had said something Shambu considered confidential, his life was over.

But even more troubling was Mike Anderson's predicament. The Nairobi police had grabbed him and thrown him in jail. But not a regular jail. One that had been decommissioned a long time ago. And that meant the American was being held unofficially. Without charges. And in Nairobi, that was serious. They wanted money—that was the easy part. The not-so-easy part was how to contact these people. How to tell them that Mike Anderson did not have access to the money sent over from the United States. And then, how to get him out of the jail.

First things first. He had to call Leona Hewitt and deliver the news.

# 30

The Salt Lake City police would release no further information than what was in the newspapers. That came as no surprise to Leona—she wasn't family, and her request for additional details on Senator Buxton's crash was a long shot that went nowhere. She thanked the officer, hung up the phone, walked to her window and stared out at the gray sky and the drab buildings across the street from the bank.

What to do?

Her two o'clock meeting with Anthony Halladay was fast approaching, and now she was unsure of herself. Of her decision. She had already indicated to the CEO that there would be no problems. But now, with Claire Buxton's death, she was rethinking things. The phone rang and she turned away from the dreary day and checked her call display. It was Jacquie Cole, her friend who worked in the legal department at the U.S. Department of the Interior.

Leona had placed a call to the lawyer first thing in the morning, asking about the status of Claire Buxton's bill now that the senator was dead.

"Hi, Jacquie," she said. "What have you got for me?"

"Tough to tell right now. But it looks like Buxton's bill will go on a back burner for a while. At least until a new representative to the Senate is elected. The general feeling is that no one wants to push ahead with what is a controversial issue."

"Controversial? How is getting these companies to clean up their acts controversial?"

"The lobbyists are all over this, Leona," Jacquie said. "Jack Dunn is already in front of a camera, expressing deep regrets at losing such a great stateswoman with one breath, and attacking the bill with the next. This initiative was Buxton's and hers alone. She was the driving force behind it. Without her, it could well die on the vine. Everything depends on who replaces her. Will they be an advocate of her stance and the work she's put into this, or will they have their own agenda? No one knows. And it's going to be some time before a new senator moves into her office."

"So it's going to die," Leona said.

"No guarantees, but that would be my best guess right now."

"Okay, thanks."

Leona set the phone back in its cradle and leaned against her desk. What were the chances? First Reginald Morgan disappears, then Claire Buxton dies in a car crash. Both were opponents of the income trust conversion in one form or another. And both dead. Who stood to gain? Derek Swanson was the logical choice. He was the largest shareholder outside Reginald and Amelia Morgan. Amelia probably controlled the shares now that the CEO was dead, but her influence on the company would be far less than her husband's. That left Swanson. Alone in first place.

She glanced down at her desk. Her cell phone was moving across the surface, silently vibrating. She picked it up and looked to see who was calling. Unknown number. She thought for a moment, then answered.

"Miss Leona," a voice said through the static. It was Kubala.

"Hello, Kubala." She sucked in a nervous breath. "Did you find Mike?"

"I know where he is," he answered. "The police have taken him."

Leona stood beside her desk, listening as Kubala detailed his trip to see Nikala Shambu. The prison, closed years ago— the captors, police working outside their official boundaries. None of it good news. Mike Anderson was in serious trouble. She had always suspected this day may arrive, but had chosen to think of it as conjecture more than fact. Now it was fact.

"Is there anything else you can do?" she asked when he finished talking.

"This is very dangerous, Miss Leona. Nikala Shambu is a ruthless man who would think nothing of killing me and my entire family. And the police who are holding Mr. Mike will not be happy if I knock on their door. I don't see how I can be of any help."

"What if you went to the regular police station and filed a report. A missing person's report. Tell them that you expected Mike to show up over a week ago, but you haven't seen him. The report will probably get to the people who are holding him. They may come looking for you."

"And that's a good thing? These men are kidnappers and murderers, Miss Leona."

"They want money, Kubala. You could promise them money if they released Mike."

"Where do I get the money? The cash Mr. Mike brought with him is already in the bank and they're not going to release it without the proper signatures."

"Can we get the right people to sign something that will allow the bank to release the money?"

"That means I have to travel to Samburu, meet with them, have them sign documents, get the money from the local bank and bring it back to Nairobi. This will take two weeks, maybe a month."

"Why so long?" Leona asked, shocked. "You can travel back to Samburu in a day."

"Yes, but getting everyone together takes a few days. And then the bank has to bring in the money."

"The bank doesn't have enough money?"

"No. They keep very little money on deposit. And almost no foreign currency. We are always waiting for the money, even after all the documents are signed."

"I never knew this," Leona said.

"That is one of the reasons Mr. Mike stayed in Kenya after he had deposited the money in Nairobi—to be sure we could access it."

"I see. So what can we do? We have to help him."

"Can you send more money?" Kubala asked.

"No. That doesn't work. The money needs to be brought in by courier. That's why Mike always traveled to Nairobi with negotiable bearer bonds."

"Yes, of course."

"I wonder if sending someone from the American Embassy to speak with the police holding him would be a good idea," Leona said.

"I would think that might get Mr. Mike killed."

"It probably would. The kidnappers would know they'd been uncovered."

Silence filled the line for a few seconds, then Kubala said, "I could try filing the report."

"Only if you think it's safe to do so, Kubala. I do not want you to risk your life. Is that understood?"

"Yes. I'll be careful. If I think it's too dangerous, I won't go to the police station."

"Okay. Can you keep me informed? Let me know what's happening?"

"I'll try, but finding a telephone I can call you on is difficult. Most phones don't allow long-distance calls. Not overseas, anyway."

"You're resourceful. You can do this, Kubala."

"I'll do my best, Miss Leona. I should go now."

"Call me the moment you get news."

"Immediately."

Leona snapped her cell phone closed and dropped into her chair. She stared blankly about her office, her mind a mess of conflicting thoughts. Mike Anderson's life in jeopardy. The possibility that Derek Swanson was murdering people to keep the income trust conversion on track. Crazy times, crazy thoughts. But one was very real. Mike Anderson was in serious trouble. And there was little she could do to help him. Jumping on a plane to Nairobi was foolish. She would be equally ineffective once there, perhaps even more so. At least while she was in the US, she could access money and wire it to an account in a country that wasn't as convoluted and corrupt as Kenya. If Kubala could initiate contact with the kidnappers.

The alarm on her computer beeped. Quarter to two. Fifteen minutes. She closed her eyes and thought about Senator Claire Buxton and Reginald Morgan. Both involved with Coal-Balt. And both dead. There was something else, some other place in the reports that she had seen a notation of a death. Where was it? Who was it? Leona opened her eyes and dug into the pile of reports. It took her five minutes to find it.

Four years ago a business agent with one of the unions had been stirring up a lot of resentment against the company. He had disappeared. But six weeks later he showed up—when the rope someone used to tie his ankles to a heavy weight came loose and his corpse floated to the top of a lake a few miles from the mine site. No one had ever been arrested for the man's murder. Leona fixated on the single paragraph describing the incident. This one was definitely a murder. And right at the time when the union rep was making waves for Coal-Balt. Coincidence again knocking at the door?

She checked her watch, then closed the folder. Time to present her report to Anthony Halladay. She stood on shaky legs and picked up the file from her desk. For a moment, she stood, unmoving, her eyes focused on the thick document. What was happening? The edges of her well-ordered life were fraying—like an ill-kept book. Chaos was creeping into her world. Somehow, this wasn't how she had envisioned success.

# 31

The twelfth-floor boardroom was a testosterone-charged bastion of the good old days in banking when pinstripe suits and cigars were the order of the day. Thick carpets covered the floors and four low-hanging chandelier-style light fixtures were evenly spaced over the mahogany table. The walls were dark walnut from floor to ceiling, with pictures of every man who had served as president of DC Trust. Almost to a person they were white males in their sixties or early seventies. Only one had made the grade while still in his fifties. And he was the son of a previous president. It was a good-old-boys network if there ever was one.

Leona walked in, the file tucked into a leather briefcase, and took a seat two chairs down from Anthony Halladay. Also present were two other vice presidents, James Maher and Robert Grist, and she acknowledged all three men as she pulled out copies of her report and set them on the table. The final version was eighty-one pages, bound with a glossy cover. Once each man had a report, she started her presentation with no preamble.

"This was not an easy process," Leona said as the men flipped through the pages. "Coal-Balt is a major source of carbon dioxide emissions, and their equipment at both the coal-mining facility and the power-generating plant is quickly becoming antiquated. Major work is necessary to bring it back to acceptable standards."

"I understand the work at the plant is ongoing." Anthony Halladay crossed his arms and leaned back in his chair.

"It is, but each renovation is less than twenty percent of the power plant's current value, which allows Coal-Balt to circumnavigate the Environmental Protection Agency's laws. In essence, the work being done is to improve production, not to reduce emissions."

"Is the plant still within acceptable government standards?" Robert Grist asked.

"Yes. But that could change if new legislation is introduced that would close certain loopholes that Coal-Balt currently uses to continue burning coal in an environmentally unfriendly manner."

"Does that legislation exist?" Halladay asked.

"No, not yet. But it appears inevitable. At some point, Coal-Balt is going to be backed into a corner and the cost of the upgrades will be astronomical. Those figures are noted on page eighteen." She waited while the men perused the documents, then continued. "The mining facility is depleting its resources at an alarming rate. The Demonstrated Reserve Base is detailed on page thirty-one, and the projections show that the mine will be completely depleted of usable reserves in five years, give or take six months. And a high percentage of what they are mining is low-grade bituminous coal. It burns dirty and produces a lot of carbon dioxide. That means even bigger problems when the legislation to control fossil-fuel power-plant emissions is introduced."

"Do you have anything good to say?" Halladay shut his report.

"Of course. At present, the company is profitable, has adequate cash reserves and owes no outstanding taxes. The labor situation is currently in hand, although they will be entering negotiations with five unions later this year. This could be a tough time for the company, as the unions want concessions on wages and pensions. Coal-Balt is not in a position to sweeten the pension pot, as the plan is only fifty percent funded at present."

Halladay tapped the report. "What's the bottom line, Leona? Is the bank behind the conversion?"

"My initial thought was to exercise caution and not approve Coal-Balt's application. But then I took time to look at the picture strictly from a risk perceptive. The increase in Coal-Balt's net worth due to the anticipated share price increase substantially diminishes our risk. Strictly from a risk point of view, the bank's position is safe. That led me to approve the conversion," she said.

Halladay's face brightened. "Good news, Leona. And a job very well done."

"On one condition," she continued.

The room was deathly silent. "What would that be?" Halladay's voice was suddenly cool.

"The senator drafting the bill calling for stricter emissions controls died in a car crash on Sunday. Claire Buxton. You may have read about it in the paper this morning. We need to wait for the coroner's report on the accident before giving this the green light."

"Why? What does her death have to do with the issue we have on the table?" Halladay asked.

"Public perception," Leona responded. "We have a fiduciary duty to our shareholders to ensure every company we fund is entirely above reproach."

Halladay leaned forward on his elbows. "Are you suggesting that there was something suspicious about the senator's death?"

"Absolutely not. What concerns me is the public's perception, nothing more. The chances are probably a million to one that Senator Claire Buxton's death was anything but an accident. But what would happen if there were something strange about the crash? The press would be all over it. Especially if they could somehow tie in Reginald Morgan's disappearance from the cruise ship. And the first place they would look is at the companies fighting her new bill. Coal-Balt is front and center. It's due diligence to wait for the results on the accident."

"How long will that take?" Halladay asked.

Leona shrugged. "I don't know. A few days. Not long."

Anthony Halladay stood up and walked to the south-facing bank of windows. Sunlight illuminated his face and reflected off his eyes. He remained motionless for a minute, then turned back to the table. "I don't like the delay, Leona. Coal-Balt has regulatory approval, but that can be rescinded at any point. I think we should move ahead right now."

Leona shook her head. "If a decision has to be made one way or the other today, I can't okay it. There's too much risk for the bank if the police find something unusual in their investigation."

"Are you saying that if you were pressed to give a firm decision today, you would reject the proposal?" Halladay asked.

"That's exactly what I'm saying."

No one spoke for a full minute. Finally, Halladay said, "I could override your report, Leona. Veto any objections you have and use my position as CEO to okay this project."

Leona swallowed. This was a shaky limb on a skinny tree, and Halladay had a saw. But it was exactly where she had foreseen this going and she was ready. "Anthony, you and I both know that vetoing something like this doesn't make the report disappear. It gets filed with the application. And then if something goes wrong, it's not hard to figure out who everybody is going to be looking at for making a poor decision."

Halladay was thoughtful. "You're sure it won't take long for the police to wrap up their investigation?"

"Not positive, but my best guess is about five days."

He nodded, a slight and very slow motion. "Then we wait for the results from the Utah police."

"And if they come up empty, you'll give this a green light?" James Maher said.

"Yes."

"All right," Halladay said. "This is your file, Leona. Your career. I trust your judgment when it comes to protecting the bank." It was all lip service. He didn't sound overly happy.

"Thanks," she said, packing the report back in her briefcase. "If there are no other questions . . ."

There were none. Leona left the room and headed directly back to her office. She closed the door behind her and sat down, her heart beating fast. What had she done? Her decision was to approve the conversion, but once she was in the boardroom, she had waffled. The simple way out was to give Halladay what he so obviously wanted. But she couldn't do it. Reginald Morgan disappearing was strange, weird even. Claire Buxton dying was bizarre. And then the union rep. How often did one hear of bodies floating to the surface of a quiet lake in rural West Virginia? Not often. If there were something dark going on with Coal-Balt, she didn't want her name associated with it. Or the bank's.

Leona ran her hands through her curls and rubbed her temples. She had bought some time, but ultimately she would have to give Anthony Halladay her firm decision. If it mirrored what he wanted, her new job was safe. And her father would be pleased. If not, she could well lose what she had worked so hard to achieve. But what was that? What had she worked so hard for? The job? That was what her father wanted. Maybe she already had what was important to her. Integrity. Honesty to herself and her convictions. A clear conscience.

There was a knock on the door and she called for the person to enter. Bill Cawder stuck his head in and smiled.

"Things went well?"

She shrugged. "Not really. Halladay didn't get what he wanted."

Cawder pushed the door open and stood a couple of feet inside the threshold. "What happened?"

"Bad timing on a couple of things. I had to attach a caveat to the approval. He didn't like that."

"I thought you said it was a go," Cawder said.

"I thought so, but like I said, things happened that changed the outcome."

"That's too bad. Is it fixable?"

"Maybe. Time will tell. Can't really say any more than that."

"Of course."

"At least things went okay for one of us today."

Cawder gave her a slight nod. "This was important for you. I wish it had gone smoother."

"Me, too."

"Got to run. See you Monday."

"Have a good weekend."

Cawder closed the door behind him and quiet settled over the room. Why was her father in that boardroom with her? How the hell did he get in there? Never physically, just in her head. Telling her to okay the deal, keep her job, move ahead, make something of herself. Christ, why didn't he realize the greatest impact she was making in her life was thousands of miles away in the sticky jungles and sweltering savannahs that bordered Samburu? There, she was changing lives, helping feed hungry children and saving a few hundred of the world's most regal mammals from being slaughtered for their tusks. Here, she was just another banker in a city full of lawyers and politicians and bankers. No matter how high she climbed in DC, her greatest achievements would always be on the other side of the world. She closed her eyes as the tears began as she realized that an opportunity to make a difference on this side of the world had been handed to her, and that she had dropped the ball. She should have stopped Derek Swanson in his tracks when she had the chance. Now she had painted herself into a corner and left no way out. If the police investigation turned up nothing suspicious, she had to okay the conversion. And the curtain was drawn back on exactly what it was. A well-orchestrated business maneuver that would make a few people very rich—and eventually wipe out a whole lot more.

She felt sick. Even sicker when she thought that this was the one moment when she would have her father's approval.

## 32

"What do you mean she's reneging?" Swanson asked. His face was crimson and his hand was shaking with rage, threatening to crush the plastic telephone receiver.

"She's not going to approve the conversion. Without her onside, you probably won't get regulatory approval," the voice said.

"Who the hell is this woman?" Swanson yelled. His voice echoed about his house.

"Leona Hewitt. She's no pushover. I warned you she could be trouble."

"We are a couple of days from closing this deal and you tell me some bitch named Leona Hewitt is going to fuck everything up? I don't think so." Swanson stopped yelling for a moment, regained his composure, then said, "She needs to okay this. And quickly."

"I'm doing what I can at the bank," the voice said, "but this is her show. There's nothing you can do right now but wait and hope she comes around."

"Jesus Christ," Swanson said, sinking into an arm chair, his shoulders sagging. "All right. Keep me in the loop."

"Of course."

Derek Swanson let the phone dangle from his hand as he sat in the silence of his living room. After a minute, the cordless phone started beeping. He pushed the end button and let it drop to the floor. Early evening sunlight filtered through the thick trees and shone in the west-facing windows, reflecting off the Swarovski crystal on a sofa table. The cut glass bent the light, fracturing it into a menagerie of color. Everything so ordered, each color separate from the others. No overlapping, no problems with one of the colors trying to overpower the rest. No color sticking their nose in another color's business. Order and harmony, just as his business should be.

Something changed in the room. A shadow that shouldn't be there. He turned and looked behind at the entrance from the dining room. A figure was moving from the other room toward him. He jerked around to face the other man as the light illuminated his facial features.

"What the fuck are you doing in my house?" he said, his voice a blend of fury and loathing.

"Not happy to see me?" Darvin moved forward at a steady pace.

"You arrogant little puke. Get the fuck out of my house right now," Swanson yelled, jumping up off the chair. He started toward the other man, then stopped when he saw the gun.

Ten feet separated the two when Darvin finally stopped and stood in the center of the room. "Who is Leona Hewitt?"

"I want you out of my house. Right now."

Darvin cocked his head slightly. "You don't get it, Derek. You answer to me now. You're my bitch. And if I decide you're a liability rather than an asset, I'll kill you. And if you piss me off any more than I already am, I'll torture your ass before I finally end your pathetic little life." He motioned at the chair with the gun. "Sit down, or I'll shoot you in the balls. I'll castrate you with a bullet, you stupid bastard. Three seconds. Two. One." He stopped counting as Derek Swanson sat in the chair.

"That's better." Darvin slowly looked about the room, taking in the décor. "Nice stuff," he said, touching a vase. "This looks likes something from the Qing dynasty, back when Emperor Kangxi controlled China. This is a museum-quality piece. It must have cost you a few dollars."

Swanson swallowed heavily. "It was expensive."

Darvin grinned, a sadistic curl of the lips. "I should break it. What do you think?" He hoisted the vase in his hand and held it out in front of him. "Won't be worth much if I drop it."

Swanson's throat was dry. "No, it won't."

Darvin glanced at the sofa table and something caught his eye. He set the near-priceless porcelain down and picked up one of the picture frames. Inside was a photo of an elderly man and woman. "Your parents?"

Swanson nodded, glad to have the art back on the table. "Yes, those are my parents."

"Nice-looking couple."

Swanson didn't know what to say. The killer was all over the map, no sense to what he was doing or his questions. "Thanks."

"What did your father do? For a career, I mean. He must have done something to buy you all of this."

"I bought this myself," Swanson snapped, immediately wishing he hadn't used a harsh tone. Darvin's eyes darkened, but he didn't speak. Finally, Swanson said, "Dad was an investment banker. He made a good living. He provided very well for my mother and I."

"Ahh, I see. An investment banker. Big money in that profession. A lot of stress, though. Working on Wall Street and all that."

"I suppose."

Darvin set the photo back on the table and took a couple of steps toward Swanson. "I don't like you, Derek. Never have. You use people. You're a condescending prick. You haven't changed the slightest since I killed that union rep for you. Not one iota. I'm not sure you realize how badly I want to kill you. I don't need much of a reason. But while this gig is still on the go, you're worth more to me alive than dead.

So, for right now . . ." He let the sentence tail off as he sat on the arm of the couch. "Now if seems we have a bitch who is sticking her nose in things that she should leave alone. Who is Leona Hewitt, and why is she fucking everything up?"

Derek Swanson stared into the killer's eyes and for the first time felt total fear. Darvin had always irritated him, maybe even scared him a bit, but this was different. There was no emotion in the killer's gaze—the eyes were dead. "She works for DC Trust. She's the person assigned to our income trust file."

"And she's a problem?"

"I have a source at the bank. They phoned and told me that she's not ready to okay the deal."

"And what does that mean?"

"We could lose regulatory approval and the conversion would die."

"And we would lose all that money from the increase in the share prices."

Swanson caught the use of *we* rather than *you*, but ignored it. "Yes."

"Then Leona Hewitt is a problem. Perhaps she's a problem that should be removed."

"You've killed enough people."

"Apparently not," Darvin said sarcastically. "You keep coming up with new glitches in what appeared to be a very good idea. Glitches that need my attention."

"Killing Leona Hewitt is not going to solve anything."

"Nor is leaving her alive. She's obviously a stumbling block."

"Look, this has gone far enough. I'll give you some money. I want you to go away."

Darvin's eyes flashed with anger. He stood up and walked toward Swanson, chambering a round in the pistol. "I don't want to go away, Derek," he said, drawling out the name.

"I'm having too much fun. The money is almost secondary at this point." He reached the chair. "Almost." He raised the gun so it was pointing at Swanson's head.

"Open your mouth."

Swanson slowly opened his mouth and felt the cold metal against the back of his throat as the killer rammed the gun in and pushed.

"Don't ever defend her again, Derek. She's a useless bitch who is standing between us and a lot of money." He twisted the gun slightly and Swanson grimaced in pain. "You have no idea how badly I want to kill you. I should, simply to show you how easy it would be." His face was only inches from Swanson's, his eyes locked in and feeding on the fear in the other man's eyes. A minute passed with neither man moving an inch. Finally, Darvin said, "But that would really screw things up. End the quest for our fifty million."

He extracted the gun from Swanson's mouth. "Did you catch that? *Our* fifty million?"

Derek Swanson nodded, his throat too dry to speak.

"You have a partner now, Derek. That's how it works. You handle the legal end of things, like the stock exchange and the bank, and I take care of any problems that pop up. Like Leona Hewitt."

Swanson's voice was a mere whisper. "You can't keep killing people associated with this or someone is going to catch on."

"Then what?" Darvin asked, moving back a few feet and sitting on an oversize ottoman. "Who will they come looking for? Not me. You. That's who will be on the front line. You. They'll suspect you of murder. And what can you tell them? That you hired some guy named Darvin to kill a union rep four years ago, then asked him to take care of Reginald Morgan. But you never told him to kill Senator Claire Buxton or Leona Hewitt. Pretty weak, don't you think? And the moment you open your mouth, they've got you for murder. Premeditated murder. And a US senator at that. You'd be lucky to escape with consecutive life sentences. My guess is that they'd put you in the chair and fry you." His eyes reflected light from the living-room window, and for a moment they came alive. "Is that what you want, Derek?"

"No."

"Then stop being such a wet dishrag. Get with the program. We're in this together and we'll reap the profits together. Right?"

"Yes."

"Great. Now what can you tell me about Leona Hewitt?"

"I don't know the woman. I'd never heard her name until she was handed the file."

"That's okay." Darvin rose from the foot stool. "I have my resources. I'll find her easily enough."

He walked to the entrance and slipped the pistol in his waistband. He pulled his shirt down over the handle and said, "You know, you should be careful about that source in the bank. You can get in a lot of trouble these days for insider trading."

He walked through the doorway and left the house.

# 33

A ceiling fan turned slowly, moving little to no air. Flies buzzed about and the strong aroma of freshly brewed coffee clung to the silence that enveloped the room. The officer working the desk occasionally turned a page and the sound carried through the dead air. Someone shuffled their feet on the gritty tile floor and all eyes turned.

Kubala sat on the wooden bench without moving. Two hours and counting. And three of the other six people in the room had arrived before him. How much longer? And when they finally called him in, what would they say? He had already filed the missing person report, so they knew why he was here. But did they care? He doubted it.

A short man in a crisply pressed uniform made his way to the gate that separated the visitors from the working portion of the police station. He glanced at the sheet of paper in his hand.

"Kubala Kantu?"

"Yes," Kubala said, standing. "I am Kubala."

"Come."

He held open the gate and Kubala passed through, catching a quick glimpse of the rest of the people still waiting. The look was the same: *Why are you being called out of order? It's our turn.* No one said a word. He followed the short man down a long hall, past numerous painted wooden doors, all of them shut. They reached the first open door and he pointed into the room. Kubala entered. Inside were two uniformed police officers, standing and talking. Both were armed with pistols. They turned to face him as he entered.

"Sit, please, Mr. Kantu," one of the men said. The short officer closed the door behind Kubala.

"Would you like something to drink?" the other officer asked.

"Water, please." Kubala eased himself into one of the hard-back chairs.

The cop departed through the door Kubala had come in and was back in thirty seconds with an unopened bottle of spring water. He handed it across. The water was cold and the outside of the bottle was sweating.

Both officers sat opposite him at the table and the one who had gone for the water opened a light gray file folder that rested on the scarred wooden surface. He perused the contents for a minute, then closed the file and leaned forward.

"You filed a most interesting missing-person report," he said. His words came out slightly nasal, probably a result of numerous broken noses from years spent in the boxing ring. "Mike Anderson is a friend of yours."

"We work for the same charitable organization."

"Save Them," the officer said, the name fresh in his mind from reading the file. "What is it?"

"We work with the park rangers in Samburu to protect the elephants."

"Worthy cause," the other man said. His voice had an accent. English. "So that is why you are filing the report? Because you know this Mike Anderson from work?"

"Yes. I don't think he knows anyone else in Kenya, so if I wasn't to make the report, I'm not sure who would."

"And he's been missing for eleven days—since July twenty-first?"

"Yes."

"I see." The officer opened the file and flipped through a couple of pages. "What did Mr. Anderson do for the charity?"

"He brought money into Kenya from the United States. US dollars from fundraising events."

The policeman raised an eyebrow. "What do you know about this money?"

"That it was his job to bring it into Africa. I don't know what he did with it once it arrived."

"You never saw the money?" the man asked, surprised.

"The only money I saw was what I received every month for my wages. But I did see the results of what happened when the money made it to Samburu. Part of it was used to expand the protection for the elephants, and the rest was used to improve the villages near the game preserve. We built a hospital and a school with the money."

"Did Mr. Anderson carry cash with him?"

"No. Not that I am aware."

Miss Leona was right, he thought as they grilled him. They wanted the money. In fact, it wouldn't surprise him if the man he was speaking to was the one who had orchestrated the kidnapping. The man who knew exactly where Mike Anderson was being held, and had the power to release him.

"We'll be in touch if we need anything further," the policeman said, rising. "Please leave your contact numbers in Nairobi and Samburu with my associate." The interview had taken over an hour and they had not touched on where Mike Anderson could be or what might have happened to him. Not once.

Kubala rose from his chair as well. "I didn't catch your name, sir," he said to the officer who had asked most of the questions.

"That's because I never told you." The man walked to the door, then stopped and turned. "I'm Inspector Rack-isha." He smiled, the white of his teeth in contrast to his black skin. "Now you know."

Kubala followed the police inspector out of the small room. By the time he reached the hallway, the policeman had disappeared through one of the many doors on either side. Kubala made sure the inspector's aide had his contact information, then left the station and stood on the street corner, feeling the warmth of the sun on his skin. It felt good. He needed to find a phone that could call overseas and inform Leona Hewitt of his meeting with the inspector—a meeting that had convinced him that someone in the police department had Mike Anderson and was holding him in hopes of a large payday. He hurried down the street, unaware of the dark Mercedes with tinted windows passing him in the traffic.

Bawata Rackisha sat in the backseat of the Mercedes and gave Kubala a perfunctory glance as his driver drove past him on the busy street. The man had been honest and to the point. That was good. What was even better was that they now had a conduit to the money. He wanted to check with Anderson and see if Kubala Kantu was as reliable and honest as he appeared.

The American Embassy slid past on the right side of the road. For Mike Anderson it was so close, yet so far away. They passed the National Archives and turned onto Latema Road for six blocks, then onto Ngariama. Both streets were a collection of three- and four-story buildings in varying stages of disrepair. His driver pulled up in front of a disheveled stone building with no number. Rackisha walked slowly across the sidewalk, looking both ways to see if anyone was watching. There were only a handful of people on the street and none looked his way. The less they saw, the healthier for them. The door opened as he reached it. Inside was a serious-looking cop in plainclothes, an Uzi submachine gun slung over his shoulder.

Rackisha made his way to Anderson's cell and the jailer twisted the key in the lock. The door groaned as it swung open. The stench of feces and urine hit the inspector immediately. He almost gagged, but entered the room anyway. Inside it was dark, but he could make out a figure crouched in the corner.

"We may be making progress in getting you out of here," the inspector said.

"Good. The sooner the better. I'm getting tired of eating

bugs." Anderson's voice was still strong. He didn't rise to greet his visitor.

"Do you know a man named Kubala?"

"Yes."

"What is his full name?"

Mike dragged himself up off the cold stone floor and walked stiffly over to Rackisha. "I'm reluctant to say. I don't want to get him in any trouble."

"Loyal to your friends. That's a good trait in a person. But I already know this man's last name and how to contact him. He came into the police station today and filed a missing person report on you. I want to make sure he's legitimate."

Mike pondered the request. There was no upside to refusing to answer, but probably a huge downside. "Kantu. Kubala Kantu. He works for the same charity that I'm with."

Rackisha nodded. "So he said. I think maybe this man can help us. What do you think?"

"I've told you, no one can access the money in the bank. That includes Kubala."

Rackisha's face contorted with anger. "This is getting very frustrating. I'm almost ready to end our arrangement."

Reading what the inspector was saying was simple. Without a reasonable ransom, Mike Anderson was a dead man. Killed and dumped in a shallow grave somewhere outside the city. Not difficult to do. Easy, in fact.

"Maybe there is something Kubala can do for us," Mike said, scratching at a spot on his arm were a mite had burrowed under his skin. "But I need to speak with him."

"Impossible."

Mike shook his head. "Then I can't help you get any money."

Rackisha studied the American. He was in total disarray, filthy with a thick growth of dirty facial hair. Yet his eyes still burned with life. The man's spirit wasn't broken. Not even close.

"What good will it do for you to meet with your friend?"

"There may be a stash of money outside the bank, but I need Kubala to go for it."

"My men and I can retrieve it," Rackisha said.

"No, Kubala is necessary. I need him."

Rackisha hesitated for a moment, then said, "How much money?"

"Seventy-five thousand US dollars."

Again, the hesitation. "You are sure of this?"

"As sure as I can be. I'm in here and the money's out there. If it's where I left it, then it's all yours."

Rackisha edged closer to the American. "Perhaps I should persuade you to tell me where it is."

"Much simpler to have Kubala get it for you," Anderson said, trying to keep the tone in his voice from showing any fear.

"All right, I'll arrange for a meeting. But if you try anything stupid, I'll kill both of you."

Anderson nodded. "Okay, now we're talking. My schedule's pretty open these days. I'm ready anytime you are."

# 34

The request to visit the Washington police station came at ten on Tuesday morning in the form of a plainclothes cop at Leona's office door. She powered down her computer and switched off her light, then joined the young detective by the elevator. They rode down together in silence. In fact, they didn't speak until they were at the precinct and he asked her to follow him. They both entered a well-lit corner office where two men and one woman were sitting and talking in low voices. The room went silent when she entered, then the man behind the desk stood and introduced himself.

"Detective George Harvey." He extended his hand. Harvey was DC Homicide, and had been DC Homicide for twenty-three years. The job had taken two wives, but not his hair. At forty-seven, he still sported thick dark hair that was the envy of the department. Even the young guys in their twenties were envious. His face was taking on some age—character wrinkles he called them, and the creases were getting deeper and more pronounced every year. A goatee, graying slightly, added a few years to his look. "This is Marion Jeffries and Hank Trost. Hank and I are both local; Marion is from Salt Lake City."

"Pleased to meet you." Leona sat in the offered chair after shaking hands.

"I'm sure you're wondering why you are here," Harvey said.

"It crossed my mind. I don't think I have any unpaid parking tickets," she said, then spoke directly to Marion Jeffries. "Salt Lake City. This has to do with Senator Claire Buxton."

"Yes. You called the Salt Lake police and asked some very interesting questions about the Senator's accident. We'd like to know why you did that." Jeffries pushed a few errant strands of short dark hair off her forehead. At five-nine she was tall, and kept her figure slim and her weight down to a respectable one thirty-six. Her eyes were dark brown, to the point where delineating the iris from the pupil was almost impossible. She was forty-two, a mother of three teenage kids, and didn't believe in wasting time.

"I don't remember leaving my name," Leona said coolly.

"We like to know who's calling," Jeffries replied. "For times like this."

"Perhaps you can tell me why you're so interested in me—in why I was asking questions about the accident."

"We'd prefer to hear your side of things first, Ms. Hewitt."

Leona glanced about the room. All three cops were staring at her and she could feel the temperature dropping. No sense antagonizing them. "I'm with a local bank and recently had a file dropped on my desk. It was to okay a change in accounting practice for one of our largest clients. If the deal gets a green light, a handful of people stand to make a lot of money, very quickly. While I was collecting information on the company, one of their senior executives disappeared while on a cruise ship."

"Was that the fellow who fell overboard on *Brilliance of the Seas*?" Jeffries asked.

Leona nodded. "Yes. Reginald Morgan. He was the CEO of Coal-Balt, the company in question. And I had heard from some reliable sources that Mr. Morgan was not in favor of the income trust conversion. That made the timing of his death kind of suspect."

"How does Claire Buxton figure into this?" Jeffries asked.

"She was drafting a new bill that would require coal-burning power plants to clean up their acts. The impact on Coal-Balt, if her bill was passed and became law, would be huge. They would have to upgrade almost all their equipment within a very short period of time. If Senator Buxton's bill passed through the Senate and Congress, Coal-Balt was poised to be in dire straits financially. Whether or not I approved the conversion depended on the status of her bill."

"So, much better for the company if her bill were to never make it to the Senate," Jeffries said quietly.

"Absolutely."

"Who stands to gain most from the conversion?" she asked.

"There are a lot of pension funds and large American corporations, a few multinationals and a handful of individual people."

"Who are the people?"

"Reginald Morgan and Derek Swanson are the two most obvious. CEO and president of the company, respectively. They were the largest private shareholders.

"I don't think we have to worry about Reginald Morgan," George Harvey said. "What about Swanson?"

Leona shrugged. "I don't know the man. Never met him."

"How much money does he stand to make if you okay the deal?" Harvey asked.

"I'm not sure, but my best guess would be around forty million dollars. Could be more, but I doubt it would be any less."

Hank Trost let out a low whistle. "That goes to motive."

"Certainly does," Marion Jeffries said. She directed her question to Leona. "So that's why you called Salt Lake asking about Senator Buxton's accident?"

Leona nodded. "It was too coincidental. Nine days separating the deaths of two people, both connected to Coal-Balt."

Marion Jeffries tapped her pen against one of her knuckles. "Your insight has been invaluable. I'm sure we wouldn't have picked up the connection. It was too remote."

"The only reason I noticed it was because they were both on my radar screen right at that moment. Dumb luck is all." She asked the Salt Lake detective, "Did you find something suspicious in your investigation?"

"I'm not at liberty to say, Ms. Hewitt. It's an ongoing investigation and we can't disclose our findings."

"I understand."

"Can I ask you a question concerning the bank?"

"That depends on the question," Leona said. "We have confidentiality agreements with our clients."

"Of course," Jeffries agreed. "Did you approve the conversion?"

Leona pondered her answer for a few seconds. Perhaps quid pro quo could come into play. "That's a difficult question to answer, Detective. Actually, the answer depends on your answer to my previous question."

"Really."

"Yes. I tied my decision to the results of your investigation."

"So if we found clues that could point to some sort of tampering, then you wouldn't approve the deal. Something like that?"

"Something like that."

"Well, we'll be releasing our results in about a week, maybe two. We need time to work with what we found."

"Interesting," Leona said. Jeffries's choice of words was purposeful and very clear.

"One thing," the Salt Lake detective said. "You should be careful for the next little while."

"Why is that?"

"Every person who has appeared to be a threat to Coal-Balt is dead. If you nix the deal, you immediately fall into that category."

The color washed from Leona's face. "I never thought of that."

"It might be nothing," Jeffries said, "but I'd be careful just the same."

George Harvey cut in. "If you need anything, if you see anyone or anything suspicious, Ms. Hewitt, let us know." He handed her his business card.

"Sure, I'll do that."

The interview lasted another twenty minutes, and when Leona finally left the corner office, she was in shock. Marion Jeffries had done everything but tell her outright that Senator Claire Buxton had been murdered. The Salt Lake City police had found something that led them in that direction. Jeffries had used that exact word: *found*. She was giving what she could without breaching the confidentiality aspect of the investigation. Reginald Morgan on the cruise ship. Claire Buxton while driving her car. Both murdered.

Was she next?

# 35

The meeting was set for Wednesday at one in the afternoon in a coffee shop on Biashara Street, three blocks from the center of the City Market. Kubala was to come alone and unarmed. Mike Anderson would be waiting.

Kubala sat on a bench overlooking St. Paul's Chapel and Central Park, and checked his watch. Fifteen minutes until the meeting. He was nervous. Scared, actually. The Nairobi police were not people you wanted to spend time with. They were corrupt, dangerous, and since they *were* the law, they operated with impunity. Almost everyone in Nairobi had a story about the police. None of them were pleasant. Kubala stood and stretched, then headed away from the riverbank and into the congested and violent streets. A group of thugs taunted him as he passed, but he refused to make eye contact and they left him alone. Committing suicide in the Kenyan capital would be so easy—just insult a gang member by staring at him.

He turned the last corner and walked halfway down Biashara Street to where a Mercedes sat outside the small café. Two men in street clothes lounged against the car, but Kubala instantly sensed they were police. The condescending look in their eyes and their stiff body language simply confirmed it. He avoided making prolonged eye contact with them and pulled open the battered door to the café.

Inside it was dark and smelled of grease and smoke. There were six tables, but only one was occupied. Mike Anderson and Bawata Rackisha were seated on the wobbly wooden chairs. Both had water bottles in front of them. Anderson was freshly shaven and looked clean and alert. His eyes were energized pools of brown and Kubala knew the reason. His American friend was experiencing freedom for the first time in almost two weeks. Kubala knew the feeling from personal experience. A very bad personal experience with the Kenyan army.

"Thank you for coming, Mr. Kantu," Inspector Rackisha said as Kubala approached the table.

"Not a problem, Inspector." He focused on Mike Anderson. "It's good to see you again, my friend."

"And you, Kubala," Anderson replied.

Kubala sat and a moment later a man appeared from the kitchen area with a fresh bottle of water. He set it in front of the newcomer and disappeared into the back room. Kubala unscrewed the top and took a short drink, glancing about the café as he set the bottle back on the table. There were three other men inside the room, standing back in the shadows, almost hidden from view. It was hard to discern their facial features, but not difficult to see the bulges in their suit jackets under their left arms.

"Could I have a minute with Kubala in private?" Anderson asked.

The inspector shrugged his shoulders. "That's fine. Keep in mind what we discussed."

"Of course."

"You look well treated," Kubala said when Rackisha was out of earshot.

"Looks can be deceiving. I have been treated very poorly. I need to get out of the cell where they're holding me, and I may be down to my last few days to do so. The window of time where I am useful to them is shrinking very quickly."

"What do you need me to do?" Kubala asked, leaning closer.

"They want money. But the funds I've already deposited are untouchable. It would take too long and involve too many people in order to access the money."

"What can we do?"

"I have an idea."

"What is it?"

"When I first arrived in Nairobi, I kept two hundred and sixty thousand dollars in cash. I gave one hundred and eighty of that to Nikala Shambu. That leaves eighty thousand dollars."

"Where is it?" Kubala asked.

Mike Anderson stared into Kubala's eyes. "This could get very dangerous."

Kubala smiled. "This is already very dangerous. There is no guarantee they will let either one of us live."

"Then why are you here?"

"You need help. Without it, you will not survive. I am your knight in white armor."

"Shining armor, Kubala. Knight in shining armor. And yes, you are, my friend."

"I thought it was white."

"Your horse is white. White horse, shining armor."

"Yes, that's it. Very good. You know this saying very well."

"English as a first language has its benefits." Anderson glanced over at the police inspector, then continued. "The money is tucked up under the driver's seat of Tuato's car. It's the one he and Momba always use to drive me around

Nairobi. Once you find the car, the easiest way to get at the money is from the backseat."

"Where does Tuato live?"

"Kariokor, on the north side of the river. On Jairo Owino Street."

"I know this place. Should I bring the money to the inspector when I have recovered it?"

"No. Absolutely not. Once you give him the money, there's no upside to him letting me go. When you have the money, you come back and talk with the inspector. Tell him you'll give him twenty thousand up front and fifty-five once I'm free and at the airport with a ticket in my hand, or inside the American Embassy. Either one is fine."

"You said eighty thousand. That's only seventy-five."

"Five for you. Something for you to live on while hiding out. You'll need to stay out of sight for a few months until things calm down. These guys will eventually forget about you."

"Thank you," Kubala said. "Do you need me to buy your plane ticket?"

Anderson shook his head. "No. Just get me out of here with my passport. I have an account at First Kenyan Bank with a couple of thousand dollars in it in case something like this happened."

"All right. I'll try."

"I need you to do this, Kubala. There is no one else."

"There is Tuato and Momba."

"I trust Tuato to keep me safe while I'm paying him, Kubala. But I don't trust him to make a good decision if he finds out about the money. Eighty thousand dollars is a lot of money. I think he would keep it and let me rot in jail. He can't know what you're doing. The same thing with Momba."

"Yes, I agree." Kubala took a long drink of water, his eyes

focused on Anderson's. "But you trust me with eighty thousand dollars."

"Completely. There is no doubt in my mind that if it's possible, you'll get me out of here."

"Your trust is a great compliment, Mr. Mike. I'll do my best."

"I know, my friend."

Kubala stood up. Inspector Rackisha returned to the table. "Do you have everything worked out?" he asked.

Anderson nodded. "You will have your money soon."

Rackisha grinned, but more warmth would emanate from an open fridge door than from his smile. "That's good news. For everyone."

Kubala left the café immediately. There was nothing else to say. He retraced his steps to the park, then cut back through a series of alleyways and narrow warrens, watching for any sign he was being followed. Nothing. When he was sure he was in the clear, he returned to his Land Rover. It was an older model, covered in mud, with a smashed front bumper and many dents, and fit nicely into Nairobi's traffic. He knew the area of town where Tuato lived and steered toward the neighborhood. It was a rough part of town, as were most, and surviving long enough to find the car and grab the money was going to be a challenge.

He had one stop to make: to call Leona Hewitt and tell her what was happening, that he had met with Mike Anderson and that he was alive. Not all that well, but alive. And that they had a plan to free him that didn't require trying to pry money back out of the Kenyan bank.

He allowed himself the hint of a smile. Mike Anderson trusted him with eighty thousand dollars. What made him happy, proud even, was that he had earned that trust. It was an incredible feeling to know that Mike Anderson, a man he liked and respected, had placed his life in his hands. That trust was not misplaced. He would do everything possible to save Mike Anderson, just as Mike and Leona Hewitt had done everything they could to save the elephants and villagers in Samburu.

What worried Kubala was the question of whether his best would be good enough.

# 36

The doorbell rang at 9:18 on Wednesday morning. Derek Swanson was expecting his landscaper and didn't bother checking to see who had rung the bell before answering the door. He got quite a shock.

On his doorstep were two people; a man and a woman. They didn't have to show any credentials for Swanson to realize he was looking at two cops. As it was, they both had their creds out and flashed them in his direction. The man spoke first.

"Derek Swanson?" he asked.

"Yes."

"I'm Detective George Harvey, Washington DC Police. This is Marion Jeffries. We'd like to ask you a couple of questions. Do you have a few minutes?"

Swanson looked at the outstretched badge. "Washington. You're a ways from home."

"Can we come in?"

"A few minutes, but that's it," he said, glancing at Jeffries's badge and motioning for them to enter. "I have a meeting at ten."

"That should work fine," Harvey said, walking through the foyer into the great room. "Nice place."

"Thank you." Swanson pointed to the couches. "Would you like to sit?"

The two cops sat on a couch and Swanson settled into

one of the wingback chairs. There was a brief silence while George Harvey slipped his notebook from his pocket and silently perused one of the pages.

"You are the president of Coal-Balt, is that correct?"

"Yes."

"What exactly does your company do, Mr. Swanson?"

"We mine coal seams here in West Virginia and ship the coal to our power plant where it's burned to produce electricity. Then we sell that electricity to various companies that distribute it to business and residential customers."

"And Reginald Morgan was the Chief Executive Officer of Coal-Balt."

"Yes. He was the CEO."

"I would imagine you knew Mr. Morgan quite well."

"We interacted almost daily for a number of years. We discussed issues relevant to running the company. I saw him at the office mostly, but we attended functions together as well. Golf tournaments, fundraising dinners, that sort of thing."

"It must have been quite a shock when he disappeared from the cruise ship."

"Yes. It was unbelievable. It still is."

"Have you assumed his duties at the office?"

"Our job descriptions always overlapped, so it was only natural for me to take on the additional workload."

"Was Mr. Morgan well liked?"

"I'm not sure I understand the question," Swanson said, scratching his chin.

"Do you know anyone who would want Mr. Morgan dead?"

Swanson cracked a small smile and slowly shook his head. "Well, there's no misunderstanding that question." He shifted slightly in the chair. "Reggie was a fine man. He spent a lot of his life, and his money, giving back to the community. He was philanthropic on many levels. He was honest in his business life and believed a good deal was one where both parties felt they had been treated fairly. When you uphold those sort of principles in your business and family life, you don't make people mad. So, to answer your question, no, I didn't know anyone who would want him dead." Swanson looked back and forth between the two cops. "I thought Reggie's death was an accident."

"Yes, that's the official result of the investigation by both the Mexican police and the FBI," said Marion Jeffries, speaking for the first time.

"You don't believe it?" Swanson asked her.

"It seems strange that a man, an elderly man at that, would fall over a railing on a perfectly calm evening. He was hardly at the age where foolish drunken acts result in accidents like this one."

"No, hardly. I can't see Reggie climbing on the railing."

"So it makes you wonder." Jeffries pursed her lips, then said, "I understand Coal-Balt was in the midst of a financial restructuring."

"Not really a restructuring," Swanson answered. "We were converting to an income trust."

"Were you and Mr. Morgan on the same page about this business move?"

Swanson rubbed his chin thoughtfully. "We had different opinions on some of the details, but ultimately we both wanted the same thing."

"And that was . . ."

"A financially solid company. By converting to an income trust we would substantially raise the value of our common shares, and that would inflate the company's book value."

"I'm just a dumb cop when it comes to that sort of stuff," Harvey said. "What does that mean?"

"The higher your common shares are pegged on the stock exchange, the more financial clout the company has. It would allow us to pay out our investors and have additional money left over to upgrade our facilities, strengthen our pension plan, and possibly even expand."

"That's pretty simple," Harvey said.

"It's not rocket science."

"And this conversion—it's finished? In the bag, so to speak?" Marion Jeffries said.

He shook his head. "Not yet. But it should be in about a week or so."

"What effect will that have on you personally?" Jeffries asked.

"My net worth would increase due to the rise in the share values."

"Considerably?"

"Considerably."

"What could derail it?"

"You mean keep the conversion from happening?" he asked, and she nodded. "Lack of regulatory approval from the stock exchange, but that's already done. That's the big one. There's a handful of smaller things that might have an effect, but nothing that could unilaterally kill the proposal."

"Things like proposed legislation requiring coal-burning power plants to upgrade their equipment?"

Swanson's eyes narrowed slightly. "Yes, that could have an effect. It wouldn't be enough to cause the deal to falter or fail."

A brief silence settled on the room, and Swanson used his right forefinger to pull back his shirtsleeve and look at his watch.

"I'm out of time," he announced, rising from the chair.

"Thank you for inviting us in," George Harvey said.

They walked to the door and left with a simple good-bye.

Neither party told the other to have a nice day. Derek Swanson closed the door and stood in the foyer, unmoving. What had just happened was not good. Not good at all. The woman, Marion Jeffries, was from Utah. The printing on her badge was small, but readable. Salt Lake City. Homicide.

He cursed Darvin under his breath. The stupid little bastard had blown this thing wide open. There was no reason for him to kill Claire Buxton. But he had. And now they had to deal with the repercussions. Including police from Washington DC and Utah showing up at his door. He was halfway to the garage when another thought hit him. There was no reason for a police detective from DC to be at his door. New York, because of the tie in to the stock exchange. Florida, as that was where the cruise ship docked. West Virginia, for obvious reasons. But Washington DC? The only tie that Coal-Balt had to the nation's capitol was the bank. DC Trust.

Leona Hewitt.

His legs almost gave out on him as the full impact hit him. The only possible way those two cops arrived together on his doorstep was if Leona Hewitt had pieced this together and called them. She was the common link. And Darvin, that demented little prick, was going after her. If he managed to find her and kill her, the police would be back. And they would have a warrant.

Swanson reached the great room and picked up the cordless telephone. Then he slowly set it down. What if they were monitoring his phone line? The same thing with his cell and his office number. He'd have to call Darvin from a pay phone. And then, he'd better be damn sure no one was watching him. He ran his hands through his hair. They were shaking almost uncontrollably.

His life was unraveling. And quickly.

## 37

Leona Hewitt was predictable. And predictability made his job easy.

He had been watching her for four days and her routine was the same. Leave for the office a few minutes after six-thirty, work until five, then head for her restaurant. Some days she was in and out, others she closed the place. That was the only inconsistency. It didn't matter. He already had three different ways of killing her.

Darvin sipped coffee and watched her interact with the staff at her restaurant. She was the owner, he had established that easily enough, and visited often to help out wherever she could. The chef was in complete charge of the kitchen, and she had little input there. The front end of the restaurant was more her domain. She worked alongside the serving staff when it was busy, and spent time sitting at one of the tables near the back working on paperwork after the dinner rush.

She was interesting, for a woman. Not a thin beanpole like all those skinny fashion queens, and not fat, just sturdy. He liked that. And she had a nice smile. Lots of teeth—some of them a bit crooked—not the product of orthodontics. There was life in her eyes and her hair bounced about when she moved.

It was too bad she had to die.

He finished his coffee and set two twenties on the edge of the table to catch the server's attention. The woman was busy and the money sat for a couple of minutes. Leona noticed the cash and started toward his table. He felt a slight adrenaline rush as she walked over to him. The Christian coming to the lion.

"I'll get you some change," she said, smiling.

"No, that's fine. The young lady who served me was great. She can keep the change."

Again, the smile. "It's a generous tip. That's kind of you."

Darvin returned the smile. Kind wasn't a word he heard all that often. "Nice place."

"Thanks. It keeps me busy."

"You own it?"

"Yeah, and work full-time. I must be nuts."

"You work full-time at both jobs?" Darvin acted surprised. Keep her talking, she'll give her schedule.

"No, I'm only here off and on. The staff run the place."

"You're lucky to have good staff."

"Very. I don't do much in the kitchen, which is too bad because that's why I opened the place to start with. I like to cook."

"Not me," Darvin said. "I don't mind paying for a good meal." Then he added, "Do you help with the menu? It's quite eclectic. And different, especially the sauces."

"That's my chef's doing. He's brilliant in the kitchen. I come in every Saturday morning and we go over the menu for the week, but other than that, it's all him."

He had what he needed. Time to leave. "Well, thanks for the meal. It was very good."

"You're welcome," she said. One more smile and she was gone.

Darvin took his time leaving, visiting the men's room, then walking slowly through the restaurant to the front door. By the time he reached the sidewalk, he knew exactly how he was going to kill Leona Hewitt. Some things were not all that difficult. This was one of them.

His rental car was parked a block down on M Street. His phone rang as he approached the parking spot. The caller ID registered as *unknown*, but he decided to take the call anyway. Derek Swanson's voice came across the line.

"Why are you calling?" Darvin asked him, his voice cool, detached.

"The police were at my house yesterday. They were asking a lot of questions."

"That's what they do, Derek. They get paid to ask questions."

"One was from Washington, the other worked Homicide in Salt Lake City. A little too much for coincidence, don't you think?"

Darvin leaned against the car. This was fun, listening to the fear in the man's voice. "Was that a question? Am I supposed to answer it?"

"They're on to us."

"Us? They're on to you, Derek. They have no idea who I am. In fact, *you* have no idea who I am. You have one phone number that will never lead to the real me, you don't know my last name, and you're probably not even sure if Darvin is my real first name. So how is this supposed to worry me?"

"This wouldn't be happening if you hadn't killed Claire Buxton and her son. That was stupid."

"This wouldn't be happening if you hadn't asked me to kill Reginald Morgan. You started this. Now you're getting scared because things aren't going all that well."

"Scared? I'm pissed off. I'm fucking furious is what I am," Swanson yelled into the phone. "This whole thing is over. It's finished. Pull your goddamn claws back in and go crawl under a rock."

"That was a mistake," Darvin said. "You just fucked up, Derek. Real bad."

He hung up and turned the phone off. A smile crept across his face as he envisioned Derek Swanson hitting redial. The man was a mess, fear oozing out every pore of his body. His pampered lifestyle was hanging by a very thin thread. If he thought things were bad now, wait until Leona

Hewitt died. The shit was going to hit the fan and when it did, most of it would be heading in Derek Swanson's direction. The money was history, he had already accepted that. Once the banker was dead, the conversion to an income trust would come to an abrupt stop. Now it was partially for fun. Swanson had insulted him, ridiculed him, lied to him and tried to cut him out of the deal. Payback was due.

No one had ever crossed him and walked away without paying some sort of price. Ever. And that was one thing that wasn't going to change. He was going to take everything that Derek Swanson valued away from him. His position in society, his money, his freedom. Perhaps even his life. Derek Swanson deserved it more than he knew. But he'd find out soon enough.

# 38

For two days Kubala had watched the house. A handful of people had come and gone, but Tuato was not one of them. And the car that held Mike Anderson's ticket to freedom was nowhere to be seen. The midday heat was stifling, dangerous even. He had spent a considerable amount of his meager supply of money on bottled water. Dehydration was a very real threat when you spent the day in an enclosed space superheated by the African sun. He took a long draught on his final bottle of water and set it on the seat beside him. This wasn't working. He needed to do something else. Waiting for Tuato to come to him was not the answer.

As far as he knew, there was one person at home, a young woman in her midtwenties. He had identified three other people as regulars—one woman and two men. None of them over thirty. And no children. The three who were gone were always well dressed, left early and returned at dusk in the same car. The regular hours and choice of clothing suggested they all had some sort of office job, perhaps in the business district. It was Friday afternoon. If they worked Monday to Friday, they would be off on the weekend, which meant all four would be at home. If he were going to approach the house, now was the time, when the woman was alone. One person would give up information easier than four.

He slipped out of the Land Rover and walked the half block to the house and knocked on the door. The paint was fresh and the adobe façade was in good repair, making it one of the best cared for houses on the run-down street. It took a full minute before the woman answered. She stared out through a crack between the door and the jamb. Her eyes were filled with mistrust and anxiety.

"What do you want?" she asked. There was fear in her voice.

"I am looking for Tuato," Kubala said in a soft voice. "I work with Mike Anderson, the American he drives for, and I have a paycheck to deliver. Will he be home soon?"

The woman hesitated before answering. "He doesn't live here. He moved."

"Oh," Kubala said, a tinge of concern creeping into his facial features.

"I can take the check and give it to him," she said.

Kubala smiled. "Yes, in most cases that would be fine. But not with this one. Mr. Mike has asked me to deliver this personally to Tuato, along with a message."

"What message?" She opened the door a few more inches.

"One for Tuato. It is of a personal nature."

"Let me see the check," she said.

"The check is in the car," he answered. "Where it's safe."

"Who are you?" she asked suspiciously.

"Kubala." He licked his lips, dry in the intense heat. "I'm due to return to Samburu tomorrow. I want to give Tuato his money before I leave. Otherwise he will have to wait until I come back to Nairobi."

"You are the man who comes in from Samburu? The one who works with the elephants."

He nodded. "I am."

She gave the matter serious thought, then said, "Yes, I suppose it's okay. He lives on Weruga Lane."

"Ah, yes. Near the railway station."

She nodded. "Number eighty-two."

"Thank you." He smiled and dipped his head slightly.

Kubala returned to the Land Rover and turned over the ignition. He needed to get moving quickly, as time was now a factor. The woman at the house would tell the others who lived with her of his visit and someone would travel to the nearest telephone to call Tuato. If Tuato had a phone. And even if he did, there was no guarantee they would be able to reach him. Phone service in Nairobi was not the best when one was trying to reach the slummier areas. The phones in the upscale villas and five-star hotels worked fine. Still, Kubala figured he had one, maybe two days to find the car and get the money. When he didn't show with the check, Tuato would be on edge, watching. Then getting to the car would be more difficult.

He had only met Tuato and Momba once, and briefly at that. Usually Mike Anderson had cut the two men loose by the time it was his turn to transport the American to the game preserve. Anderson always spent a couple of days in Nairobi, between depositing the money in the bank and heading out to Samburu, sampling the various brands of liquor. The lack of personal connection between him and Tuato was probably a good thing. Kubala didn't want to come face-to-face with Tuato again, as it would entail making up some sort of story about why he was there. Telling the man there was eighty thousand American dollars under the driver's seat of his car was not an option.

Traffic was normal, which meant insane by almost all other standards. No one obeyed the laws and traffic lights were more of a suggestion than an actual authority. A battered Renault scraped the side of the Land Rover as the driver tried to fit through a narrow gap, but Kubala waved the man on. He wanted to get where he was going and nothing would be done about the scratch anyway. The police were too busy drinking strong coffee, or kidnapping people, to care. He stayed off the ring road and stuck to the secondary streets, crossing under Haile Selassie Avenue and entering the down-trodden subdivision of Muthurwa. The buildings were three-story tenements, decaying with age like a rotting carcass in the heat. The stench of garbage and sewage was strong.

Kubala turned off Railway Avenue onto Weruga Lane and cruised slowly down the street, watching the building numbers and scanning the parked cars for Tuato's ride. He passed number eighty-two, another dilapidated hellhole filled with desperate families and street-level thugs looking for an easy way out of their poverty. It was nothing new. He'd seen the same scene every day of his life. There was a parking spot near the end of the block and he pulled in. He switched off the ignition and stepped out onto the pavement. A pack of dogs cruised past, showing some teeth, tails down. Like the punks on the street, Kubala thought. Tough kids, scared to death of the life they were living.

He walked the street, another black man in a black nation on a continent of unfulfilled dreams. He drew no attention, no second looks as he sat on a door stoop across from Tuato's apartment. The man would return home at some point. And then the challenge of getting at the money would present itself. Nothing easy. Like Africa itself.

## 39

"Has he made any outgoing phone calls?" George Harvey asked the technician working the electronic surveillance on Derek Swanson's house and office.

"A few from the office, none from home. I'll print you a list."

Harvey waited a minute, then took the paper from the tech. "Thanks," he said, heading back to his corner office where Marion Jeffries waited. By the time he arrived, the detective knew they had drawn blanks on their surveillance.

"Anything?" the Salt Lake City homicide detective asked.

He shook his head. "Swanson made no calls from home, and very few from his office phone. Fewer still from his cell phone. Almost like he was trying to stay off the line."

"Think he suspects we're watching?"

Harvey shrugged. "Who knows. The guy isn't dumb. He's probably being careful."

"Think he's involved?" she asked.

"Oh, yeah," Harvey said. "I think he's in this up to his asshole. He didn't kill them, but his fingerprints are all over the murders. What about you? What do you think?"

"He's the motivation behind it. Has a trigger man of some sort."

"Think he'll go after Leona Hewitt?" Harvey asked.

Jeffries shook her head. "No. He knows we're watching him. She's safe."

"I agree." He consulted his notes, a compilation of what his department, working with Jeffries, had accumulated since Leona Hewitt had visited them four days ago. He recounted what they had to date. "Reginald Morgan disappears off *Brilliance of the Seas*. That means premeditation.

Swanson had someone on the ship. We've pulled the passenger manifest, concentrating on late bookings. Swanson's person will be one of the last to secure a cabin, and that narrows our search to a reasonable number. Somewhere around two hundred people."

"That's workable," Jeffries said.

"Swanson knows that Morgan isn't coming back, and that allows him to push ahead with the trust conversion without internal opposition. Then he runs into another problem. His lobbyist, Jack Dunn, is unable to convince enough of the decision makers to reject Senator Claire Buxton's bill. It looks inevitable that it'll pass. And that means Buxton has to go. Another call to his hatchet man."

"Or woman," Jeffries said. "You know us women these days. Nothing we can't do."

Harvey gave her a sour look, the kind only a man twice divorced can master. He rubbed his hand across his goatee. "That gives us some approximate dates for outgoing calls from Swanson's phones."

"You've pulled his phone logs?"

"Yesterday. I've got two people working them. He made a lot of calls, local and long distance, over the past few weeks. It's going to take some time. This is a slow one."

"Well, maybe we've got one clue from the crash in Salt Lake."

"What?" Harvey asked.

"Our forensics found a bit of blood in the wreckage that doesn't belong. Under the driver's seat. The impact of the crash impaled Buxton on the steering column and she bled out directly below onto the floor mat. From the positioning of her body, there was no way it got there as a result of the accident. We checked it out. It's not Claire Buxton's or either of her kids'. We asked her husband for a sample, just in case, but it's not his."

"Under the seat? That's weird."

"Very. Makes you wonder how the hell that happens. Someone reaching for something and cuts himself?"

"Could be the killer," Harvey said.

"Could be," she agreed.

"The report said traces of hydrogen cyanide were found on the carpet. Once we found that we ran a tox screen on the bodies. Cyanide bonds to an enzyme called cytochrome, and once that happens, oxygen transfer is inhibited at the cellular level. We found traces of cyanide in Buxton and her son. There's little doubt that the crash was a result of her reaction to the cyanide."

"Dizziness, loss of consciousness."

"Exactly. So the question that has to be asked is how does the van cabin fill with cyanide, yet leave no clue as to how it got there? No canister. No crushed glass from a vial. Nothing. Perhaps he grabbed the evidence."

Marion Jeffries nodded. "That's a legit line of thought. If the blood is legit and not one of the kid's friends or something like that, then our best guess is that whoever planted the gas was the first to arrive at the crash site."

"Anyone see this person?" Harvey asked, leaning forward.

"The first man on the scene who came forward as a witness remembers another guy being there, but has no recollection of what he looks like. White and male, that's it. But that doesn't necessarily mean he's our killer."

"Guy is first on the scene, then doesn't hang around to make a witness statement. Makes you wonder." He closed the file on his desk. "When are you heading back to Utah?"

"I fly out tomorrow morning."

"When is your office going to release the results of Senator Buxton's autopsy?"

"A few more days at least. We don't want to stir the pot until we've exhausted every lead, like what we've got here in

Washington. Once we're sure there's no upside to keeping her cause of death under wraps, we'll hold a press conference."

"That's going to make the headlines," Harvey said.

"Precisely why we don't want to let it go public too quick. Everyone and their dog will have a smoking gun. High-profile cases always bring out the nutcases. What would be really nice is if the Derek Swanson angle worked and we nailed him and the person who planted the gas in the van. Then when we make the announcement, we've already got someone in custody."

Harvey nodded emphatically. "We've got something to work with on this end. If there's a trail, we'll find it. And once we do, I'll be on the phone. First thing."

Jeffries smiled. "Thanks."

"Not a problem. I think we all want to get this guy."

"The killer or Swanson?"

"Both," he said.

# 40

Leona sat at the bar, sipping a glass of red wine. Tyler poked his head out of the kitchen to see if she was still there, then stripped off his apron, poured himself a draught beer and came out to sit with her. It was after one and the last patrons had left the restaurant an hour earlier.

"Quite the night." Leona set down her pen and closed the cash-out book. She pushed it and the function sheets for the weekend to the side.

"Fridays always are." Tyler downed half the beer in one long draw. "Man, we got slammed about nine o'clock. I think the whole place ordered entrées in less than half an hour. Boozy was crashing on the grill. Janet came over from the salad line to help or he would have gone down."

"You'd never have known it from out here," she said. "Everyone left happy. Lots of compliments on the food tonight, especially the tuna feature."

"We sold out by ten on that one," Tyler said, grinning. "Thirty-six specials. At thirty-eight dollars. Told you tuna was the flavor of the week."

"You know what they want." She gave him a pat on his arm. "We make a good team. You think so?"

"Damn right," he said with a lilt to his voice.

Leona reached for her wine, but her finger touched the stem and the glass wobbled, then crashed on the bar before she could grab it. It smashed, and shards of glass mixed with the spilled wine. Tyler leapt up and ran to the kitchen for a cloth.

"Damn it." Leona picked the largest pieces of broken glass out of the wine as it slowly spread across the shiny wood. Tyler returned with a cloth and paper towels and they wiped up the spill. He wrapped the broken glass and paper towels in the cloth, disappeared through the kitchen doors and returned a minute later with a fresh glass of wine. He set it on the bar.

"No spilling this time," he said.

"Promise—and thank you." Leona took a drink and glanced at her watch. "Can you come in half an hour early tomorrow? There's something I want to run past you."

"Sure. Not tonight?"

"Nah, you enjoy a few beers and go home and get a solid night's sleep. I'll see you at ten-thirty."

"Sure."

"Make sure the rest of the kitchen staff get in on that beer," she said. "Keep track so I can subtract it from the day's sales."

"Thanks. Could be a few pints. I think the guys are pretty thirsty."

"Thirty-six specials at thirty-eight dollars each. Plus another two hundred entrées and wine and drinks. I think I can afford to get my kitchen staff drunk."

"Well, in that case . . ."

"Good night." She placed the almost-full wineglass on the table. She couldn't help laughing at the fox-with-the-key-to-the-chicken-coop look on his face.

Outside it was muggy but still warm. The low-pressure weather front had dissipated, gone wherever they go, and normal temperatures were back. She walked the half block to where her car was parked in its underground stall. The parking structure was quiet, only a few cars left at the late hour. She hit the open button on the key fob and the parking lights blinked once. A movement to her right caught her eye and she turned quickly. Nothing. She stood a few feet from her car, concentrating on the line of concrete pillars fifty feet away. There was no sound, no motion to indicate anyone was hiding. She kept her eyes riveted on the area as she slowly edged toward her vehicle. When her hand touched the side of her car she looked down and grabbed the door handle and pulled. She swung through the open door, closed it and locked it, sliding the key in the ignition and turning. The motor caught and she shifted the car into gear. She glanced in her rearview mirror before backing up and screamed.

The man standing beside her car jumped back, startled at her yell. On his shirt was the insignia of the building above the parking lot. Clipped to his front pocket was an identity card with his photo.

Leona touched the button and the window silently slid out of sight. "I'm sorry," she said. "You scared me."

He gave her a half smile. "You scared me when you yelled. Is everything okay?"

"Yes. I thought I saw something moving behind those pillars." She motioned to the long line of concrete posts.

"I was a bit nervous and all of a sudden you were right beside my car."

"Sorry about that. I didn't mean to scare you." He looked over to where Leona had indicated. "I'll check it out. I'm doing my nightly rounds."

"Sure."

She rolled up her window and pulled out of the garage onto the deserted street. What was wrong with her? Spooked by her overactive imagination. Reginald Morgan's disappearance and the death of the Senator from Utah may or may not be tied together. The police weren't sure. They suspected, but had nothing more than that. Suspicions. She had to pull it together.

Her cell phone rang, startling her again. She pulled it from her hip holder with shaking hands and flipped it open. The incoming call was a mass of static, but through the wall of white noise was Kubala's voice.

"I can hardly hear you." She cranked on the wheel and pulled over to the side of the road. The static diminished a touch and she could make out his words with little difficulty.

"I have found Tuato's car," he said excitedly.

"What took you so long?" Leona asked, her tone inquisitive, not accusatory. "It's Friday night. You called me two days ago."

"He moved, Ms. Leona. I had to find his new house."

"And you did?"

"Yes. This afternoon. It's in a rough part of town. Very dangerous. I watched his house for a few hours until he arrived, about five hours ago. But getting to the car will not be easy. Tuato parks it behind his apartment building right by his window."

"If it's too dangerous don't try. I'll fly over tomorrow with the money."

"No, Ms. Leona. It's worse for you to come here, to Nairobi, with a large amount of money. It is very likely you would be killed. Do not try that, I beg of you. Let me see if the money is still under the seat."

He was right. There was no upside to running directly into the fire. Her life would be in jeopardy the moment the plane's wheels touched the runway.

"All right. But be careful, Kubala."

"Yes, of course."

"When will you try?"

"Maybe tonight, but it's almost dawn here. Probably to-morrow night. I would have tried earlier, but there were homeless people sleeping a few feet away. Maybe they won't be there tomorrow."

"Call me. I want to know what's happening."

"I'll call. Tomorrow." The international line went dead.

Leona closed her phone and pulled away from the curb. She needed to get home and pour herself a glass of wine. One that she could drink without having to drive after-ward. She was a banker, in Washington DC. How could so many things be happening all at once? Mike Anderson kid-napped by the police and in danger of being killed. Kubala skulking around a Nairobi slum waiting for an opportunity to grab eighty thousand dollars from a car. Eighty thousand dollars in Nairobi. Eighty dollars was enough to earn a knife in the ribs. Eighty thousand was beyond belief. Kubala was in great danger since he had signed on with the foundation. Someone killing everyone who opposed the Coal-Balt deal. Now, her own safety threatened.

She felt the car closing in on her, the panic building. There was no stopping it. She slammed on the brakes and skidded to a halt in the curb lane, opening the door and jumping out, almost into the path of an oncoming SUV. The headlights were right in her face, coming fast. The driver swerved sharply and laid on the horn, missing her by inches. Leona slammed the car door and ran to the sidewalk, grabbing a streetlight for support. She was sweating and her hands shook uncontrollably. For five minutes she stood immobile, breathing the night air, relaxing. She concentrated on soft music and friendly memories. Anything to drive away the massive surge of anxiety that accompanied her claustrophobia. Finally, when the shaking had stopped, she walked slowly back to her car and eased into the seat. The panic attack was over, the car no longer felt constricting. She took more time than necessary to start the car, fasten her seat belt, and adjust the mirrors. She shoulder checked and merged back into the threadbare traffic.

That glass of wine was looking better all the time.

# 41

"Fucker," Darvin whispered under his breath.

He watched the security man check the other side of the parking structure. The beam from the flashlight poked behind the concrete pillars and cast long shadows across the smooth cement floor. After a couple of minutes the light abruptly disappeared. A second later Darvin heard the click of a fire door closing. The man was gone.

Leona Hewitt had dodged a bullet. Literally. His first choice had been to take her out in the parking garage and make it look like a carjacking. Easy enough to do. A bullet in the head, tire marks next to the body, and no car. But that opportunity had vanished the moment the security guard had walked onto the scene. He slid out from behind one of the posts and walked to the stairwell, taking a moment to hook the wire back into the surveillance camera he had previously disabled. He headed back to street level.

He was breathing a bit deeper after climbing the three flights of stairs. The door to M Street opened next to an alley and he ducked into the darkness and made his way toward the restaurant. Always good to have options. And while his second choice on how to kill Leona Hewitt was his favorite, it was also the riskiest. He reached the back side of Gin House and stopped, backing into a small alcove. The door from the rear of the restaurant to the alley was open, and two men in cook's uniforms were sitting on the stoop smoking cigarettes and drinking beer. He recognized one of the men as Leona's head chef, his blond-red hair and facial features highlighted by the glow from his cigarette. Their voices drifted across the lane, empty but for garbage bins and a few broken bottles. He settled in to wait.

It took forty minutes for the kitchen staff to finish their beer and lock up. Once he was sure the restaurant was deserted, he crossed the alley and jumped up on the metal Dumpster. A plastic conduit pipe ran up the side of the building, tight to the brick exterior. He slipped a penknife from his pocket and levered open one of the joints, exposing the thin wires inside. They were the main telephone feed to the building. Holding a small flashlight in his teeth, he selected the correct wire and snipped it. Then he slid the cover back in place, hopped off the garbage bin and slipped back into the shadows. Darvin had noticed the alarm the one time he had visited the restaurant, and from the control pad he suspected it was an older model without a radio frequency backup. The system was tied into the telephone lines and without the backup to alert the alarm response company or the police, simply cutting the phone line disabled it, giving him full access to the restaurant. He'd know soon enough whether he had guessed correctly. Fifteen minutes passed and there was no sign of the police. He slid out of the shadows and walked across the garbage-strewn alley to the door.

It was closing in on two o'clock when Darvin slipped a thin strip of tensile steel into the deadbolt lock and felt for the tumblers. After about thirty seconds the lock clicked open and he pulled on the door. It swung outward, revealing a small storage area. Immediately inside, on the right side of the doorjamb, was an alarm pad. It was armed, but not beeping. Cutting the telephone line had definitely disabled it.

The interior of the restaurant was almost entirely dark, lit by a solitary twenty-five-watt emergency light in the main eating area, and a few shards of ambient light filtering in from the front street. Darvin moved with caution through the smattering of tables and chairs and pushed open the door to the kitchen. It creaked with the slowness of the motion, the sound drifting through the silent space like a single note on a piano. Inside the kitchen was another emergency light, which lit the twenty-by-forty-foot room enough for Darvin to see what he was doing.

He concentrated on the ceiling, which was about sixteen feet above the tile floor. Numerous unlit lights hung down a few feet from the roof on thin wires, positioned to illuminate the work area for the kitchen staff. One of the lights was directly over the prep area, which had a metal hood that extended above the counter. He flipped a couple of light switches until he found the one that controlled that particular light, then turned it off and jumped up on the chopping board. He climbed onto the hood, stepping cautiously on the frame. It held his weight without buckling and raised him to a level where he could reach up and touch the light. He unscrewed the bulb and held it in his left hand while he withdrew a syringe from his right coat pocket. He pulled the plastic sheath off the needle with his teeth, then placed the tip against the metal base of the bulb and pushed. The sharp point pierced the thin metal and he continued to push until the tip of the needle was visible inside the glass. Then he thumbed the plunger and squirted the accelerant into the bulb. When the syringe was empty he withdrew the needle and rubbed the tiny hole with his index finger to seal it. He replaced the bulb and carefully stepped down off the hood onto the chopping block, and hopped down to the floor.

Darvin unscrewed the switch cover and detached one of the wires connected to the circuit that controlled the tampered bulb. He bent it so there was a downward pressure on the wire, then slipped a tiny plastic device between the loose wire and the one still attached to the switch. Remove the device, which he could do by remote control, and the wire would move down and complete the circuit. The bulb would light, and that's all it would take to trigger the explosion. He replaced the switch plate and glanced over at the cooking area.

The stove-oven combination was against the far wall and he knelt in front of it. It was a commercial-grade, 30,000 BTU natural-gas Garland stove and griddle. He extinguished all the pilot lights on the stove and oven, then located the incoming gas line and carefully sliced through it with a razor blade. The odor of natural gas drifted into the still air. The low-pressure line would continue to leak the deadly gas for the next few hours, filling the entire room. All the variables were now in place to create a blast that would obliterate the entire restaurant. Natural-gas explosions or fires were rare, but they did happen. Especially in commercial kitchens, where there was so much activity and open flames on the stove top and in the oven. And when they happened, they were usually so violent that they completely destroyed trace evidence. The chances of the fire department discovering the tiny cut in the gas line were minimal to nonexistent.

He walked across the kitchen to the swinging doors that

led to the eating area of the restaurant. He removed a roll of cellophane tape from his pocket and carefully sealed the narrow gaps between the two doors, and then between the doors and the floor and the frame. The heat from the blast would melt the tape, leaving virtually no residue. The odor of gas would stay inside the kitchen until someone pushed open the doors in the morning and broke the seal. When they did . . . he would be ready. Close by, with the remote control in his hand.

Darvin exited through the back door, locked it behind him, then jumped up on the garbage container and reattached the telephone wires. He pulled the plastic cover over the joint in the conduit and rubbed a bit of grease from the Dumpster hinges on the split in the plastic. Even from two feet away, it was impossible to tell that the conduit had been tampered with. He climbed down from the garbage bin and took one last look at the backside of the restaurant. Every detail of his plan played through his mind, and once he was sure everything was in place, he turned away and didn't bother looking back.

The night was quiet, the city asleep. He walked back to his rental car and drove to his hotel. The night desk clerk glanced up as he entered, and other than a forced smile, showed little interest in his arrival. He took the elevator to the fourth floor, undressed and slipped under the covers. He needed some rest. Tomorrow morning was fast approaching and he knew from talking with her that Leona Hewitt would be at the restaurant in the morning, going over the menu with her chef. He closed his eyes, a smile on his face.

It would be the last thing she ever did.

## 42

The sound came to him like snippets of a dream, fading in and fading out, never quite real. It had a certain cadence, a rhythm of slow African drumbeats. Like the ones that floated around the campfire when he visited Kubala's tribe in Samburu. He blinked and saw nothing but blackness. The sound continued, creeping through the murky darkness with a regular beat.

Footsteps.

Mike Anderson wiped a dirty hand across his face and licked his cracked lips. Someone was coming. He had seen no one for many days. Three, if he had counted the number of meals correctly. Three days with just a plate coming in under the door. Three more horrible days of cold and dank, no sun, no communication. He was beginning to lose hope. He suspected that Kubala had not been able to secure the money, that time was running out.

A key slid in the lock and there was a scraping sound. The door swung in and a light cut through the dark. It was like looking directly into the sun and he shielded his eyes. A voice resonated off the slick stone walls. A voice he knew. Bawata Rackisha, Inspector Rackisha.

"You're not looking very well, Mr. Anderson." Rackisha's voice was soft, almost like a lullaby. "You need to shave again."

"There's a certain lack of facilities," he answered. His own voice sounded strange. It was the first time he had heard it in days.

"I had a phone call from your friend today," the inspector continued.

"And . . ."

"He's doing well. He called to tell us he had found the money. Now he needs to wait until it's dark to get it."

"That *is* good news," Anderson said. His throat hurt, every word excruciatingly painful.

"I'm thinking that this little venture is coming to a close. One way or the other."

Anderson fully understood what he meant. "Kubala will get the money. This will end well." He could see the man's features now, reflected in the yellow glow from the small electric torch. His eyes had lost their whiteness—they appeared jaundiced, sick almost. "Kubala has never failed me."

"There's always a first time. We have to be ready for that possibility."

"What are you saying, Inspector? That you're going to kill me? That's not difficult to figure out."

Rackisha leaned over, his face close to Anderson's. "How can I let you go? You know who I am."

"And dead men don't talk."

Rackisha didn't move for a few seconds, then leaned back slightly. "That is correct. Not a word."

Anderson leaned toward the Kenyan policeman. "Why would I tell anyone? What would that accomplish? Once I'm out of here, I'm at the airport and back to the United States. Nobody in the US could give a shit what happened here. No one. Not one fucking person. Even if I did tell someone, they would just blow it off. Like it never happened. So, to me, it never happened."

"Kubala still has to find the money."

Anderson nodded. He could feel his will, his strength, returning. "He'll find it. And you'll get it."

Rackisha straightened. "Well, we will see. He told me he is going to try and get it tonight. If he does, I'll have to decide what to do."

"You will not get that money if you kill me," Anderson

said. He surprised himself with the determination in his voice.

"Is that a threat?"

"It's the truth."

"You're very brave, for being in such a place. A place that you may never leave."

"I've been through a marriage and a divorce. I can take this."

Rackisha's hand snaked out and the barrel of his gun caught Anderson on the side of the head. It made a dull thud, so soft it was almost inaudible. The impact threw Anderson sideways too quickly for him to react and he smashed the other side of his face on the floor. He lay on the cold stone, unmoving.

"Do not mock me, Mr. Anderson. Or I will kill you right here, right now."

"My apologies," Anderson said softly. One of his teeth was embedded in his cheek but he did nothing to dislodge it.

"Pray your friend can get the money."

Rackisha left the room and the darkness returned. It was getting harder with every day. His mind was coming apart, sane thinking beginning to elude him. Visions appeared when he closed his eyes. Strange moving pictures of wildebeests being brought down by lions. Of deranged and angry chimpanzees in trees, throwing fruit at him. Somewhere in the madness was reason, maybe a moment from his life that some clinical psychologist could decipher. Or maybe he was going crazy.

His wife floated across the room, her eyes inviting, her mouth soft. God, he loved her. Even with the hell she put him through, he couldn't shake the feelings. It was in his nature, something he couldn't kick. Like an addiction. Her image slowly dissipated and Leona's face found its way through the fog. She was smiling and her eyes were windows to a soft soul. She was so kind, so giving. The foundation was proof of that. It gave so much to the villagers who lived around Samburu, yet she asked for nothing in return.

Save Them was dead. He knew it, and by now, Leona knew it. Rackisha would never let the flow of money arrive in Nairobi without him getting his share of the pie. And there could be no justifying any additional payments to warlords, gangsters or corrupt police. Nonprofit foundations had expenses, but there was a limit. He felt like he'd let her down. That he'd gotten complacent in a very dangerous country.

And now he faced the consequences. Alone, in a tiny, wet cell, held by a rogue cop and an inch from death. Everything, whether he lived or died, now rested with Kubala.

# 43

Leona rolled over and buried her head in the pillow. The last thing she felt like doing was dragging herself out of bed, getting dressed and heading for the restaurant to work on the menu with Tyler. Friday night had taken its toll. She had arrived home at one-thirty, still shaking from the close call with the SUV and worried about Kubala and Mike Anderson. Even with two glasses of wine, sleep hadn't come until after four. She lifted her head slightly and focused on the alarm clock. Nine-thirty. Time to get up.

She switched on the coffee machine and showered while the coffee was brewing, towel drying her hair into a maze of ringlets. The aroma from the coffee was inviting, but it tasted bitter. She gulped back a cup, the caffeine clearing her head, then backed her Saab from the garage and drove through the quiet Saturday-morning streets to Georgetown. She parked underground and walked the short distance, arriving at twenty minutes after ten. Tyler was sitting at one of the tables in the center of the restaurant, drinking coffee and reading the *Washington Post*.

"You're here early," she said, rubbing the top of his head as she walked by him, heading for the bar to grab a Diet Coke.

"Trying to wake up." He lifted the coffee cup an inch or two.

"Is it working?"

"No."

She poured the soda into a glass and added a slice of lime. When she returned to the table, she couldn't help but laugh at the dozy look on Tyler's face. "Not a morning person, are you?"

"Hardly. Hate the fucking things." He took a sip of coffee. "Look who's talking."

"I live for the day when I can sleep in," she said. "Nothing to force me out of a nice warm bed."

"You're a vice president with a bank," Tyler said. "That's not an overly rough life."

"It's not everything it's cracked up to be." She ran her fingers through her hair and shook her head, the ringlets all falling into some sort of disjointed order. "I wanted to talk with you about something."

"What's that?" He cupped his coffee in his hands.

"Things have been going very well here. I couldn't be happier with how we're doing financially, but even more importantly, we're serving some of the best food in Washington and the word is spreading. We're building a clientele that will keep coming back. I think we're here to stay."

"That's good."

"Very good. And most of the success is because of your work in the kitchen."

"Not just me." Tyler held up an index finger. "The whole team."

"You manage the kitchen. When I say you, I mean

everything that happens behind those doors." She paused for a second, then said, "I want to bring you on as a partner, Tyler."

He didn't move or speak as he let the words sink in. Finally, he swallowed and said, "How would that work?"

"Simple. We draw up some papers that give you thirty percent of the restaurant for a very reasonable price. Then, because you own a percentage, you're eligible for the profits on that thirty percent. But rather than taking cash, you put it back into the mix to cover the cost of the initial purchase."

He let it sink in for a few seconds, then said, "So I pay no money up front, and nothing comes off my paychecks. I pay back the money for the percentage I now own from the profits off that percentage. Is that it?"

"That's it. There's a few other details, but that sums it up."

He didn't speak for a minute. When he did his voice was muted. "You're giving me thirty percent of the restaurant"

She wanted to object, to tell him he'd earned it. That the success they were experiencing would never have happened without him. She didn't bother—just nodded.

"Holy shit," Tyler said. "Man, this meeting was worth coming in early."

"Then it's a deal?"

He stuck out his hand. "Absolutely."

She smiled and shook his hand. "You deserve this."

"Thanks."

Both their heads turned as the front door opened and two young men walked in. Tyler glanced at his watch. "Boozy, Eric, fifteen minutes early. I'm impressed."

"I need coffee," Eric said, heading straight for the half-full pot of medium roast. Boozy nodded good morning and pushed open the doors to the kitchen. The unmistakable odor of natural gas filled the room seconds after the door swung inward.

"Gas," Eric yelled, and started into the kitchen.

"No." Leona was out of her chair and racing toward the kitchen immediately. "Get out," she yelled. "Eric, Boozy, get out of here." She spun to face Tyler, who was directly behind her. "Where is the gas line?"

"It comes in on the upper level. There's a shutoff up on the roof."

"Upstairs?" Leona asked. "Are you sure?"

"Yes. They had to run the line from next door and the city wouldn't approve it at ground level. Remember?"

"Yes. Yes. I do. I remember the hassle." She started through the door into the kitchen. "Eric, Boozy, move it. Out the front door." She continued into the kitchen area, Tyler immediately behind her.

"Don't turn on any lights," Tyler yelled as they ran into the stairwell that led to the roof. "The spark could cause the gas to blow."

Darvin watched from the driver's seat of the rental, parked across the street. He could clearly see Leona Hewitt seated at a table, talking with one of her employees. They were both intent on the conversation, neither looking around nor distracted. That was good. Focus on one thing that was happening, miss all the others. Like the incredibly high concentration of gas building in the kitchen. Two men reached the front door of the restaurant and entered. Kitchen staff, in early to prep for the day. It was showtime. His finger tightened on the remote control as one of the men pushed open the kitchen door. As he entered, Darvin's finger rested on the button.

The tape he had placed on the kitchen doors must have been completely airtight, because the second the door cracked open, everyone reacted. He could see the panic in the room. They could smell the gas. The man who had pushed open the door started into the kitchen, then stopped and backed off. Leona and the man she was talking with jumped from their seats and ran into the kitchen. The two kitchen staff moved hesitantly for the front door. They kept looking back and Darvin knew exactly what they were thinking. *There must be something we can do to help.* He smiled and started the car.

"She's a dirty one, Mother" he said, wiping at the saliva dripping down on his chin. "And now she's gone. One less who can hurt Darvin."

He pulled out onto the street and when he was a hundred feet down the street he pushed the button. The front of the restaurant was gone in a matter of two seconds. The blast surge pushed out from the kitchen and obliterated the dining area, the hostess station and the bank of windows fronting onto M Street. Glass and wood showered the passing cars and the fireball that blew out from the building ignited two vehicles parked directly out front. Seconds later the gas tank in one of the cars ignited and it exploded, sending a second wave of glass and metal flying across the road. A delivery van swerved to avoid the blast and hit a parked car, sending it up on two wheels and careening into the storefront opposite the restaurant. It smashed through the window and came to rest on its side inside the store. The force of the explosion triggered car alarms and in scant seconds the street was transformed into a battle zone.

Darvin watched the carnage in his rearview mirror, then accelerated and turned the corner. He drove at the posted speed limit into the city center, melding with the other Saturday morning traffic. He hummed a favorite tune, "Fields of Gold," until he reached a quiet area where he could pull off the road and park tight against a leafy hedge. He backed up so there were only a couple of feet between the rear bumper and the hedge and hit the button to open the trunk.

He slipped out, ducked in behind the car and quickly un-screwed the license plate, replacing it with the one that was registered to the car. He wiped any fingerprints off the stolen one and dropped it in a trash bin next to the hedge, taking the time to cover it with garbage. He reentered the Washington traffic and drove toward the car rental return.

"Another dirty one is dead, Mother," he said, spittle form-ing at the sides of his mouth. "Dirty ones should all die. That's what they should do. Just die." His eyes grew cold, his mouth turned down and when he spoke again there was venom in his voice.

"You should have died much before you did. I should have killed you before you murdered my father. I should have picked up the shovel and done it. Whacked you with it. But I didn't know . . . I didn't think you'd actually kill him."

He drove with the traffic, another driver alone in his car, lips moving, singing with the music or talking on a cell phone.

# 44

The moment before the blast, everything in the restaurant was normal, save for the smell of natural gas. The second Darvin pushed the button, everything changed.

The trigger mechanism inside the light switch housing was simple. A tiny servo rotated the nonconductive material a fraction of an inch and the exposed wire slipped down and touched the one still connected to the post. The fila-ment in the light above the prep station glowed, igniting the accelerant Darvin had injected into the bulb. The glass shat-tered and thin tongues of flames shot into the air. The high concentration of natural gas exploded, sending a shock wave equal to a tsunami through the kitchen. It blew the room apart, the fireball completely enveloping the entire kitchen in less than a second. The blast flattened the wall that separated the kitchen from the dining room and the front windows shattered into thousands of deadly glass shards, spraying across the street a split second before a wall of fire erupted from the mouth of the restaurant.

Leona and Tyler were halfway up the back stairwell, the one the staff used to run food and drinks from the main floor to the upper tables, when the gas ignited. The wall between the kitchen and the stairwell was part of the original structure of the building and solidly constructed of cinder blocks, mortar and rebar. It bowed under the pressure, but somehow held, keeping the fatal wall of fire and death inches away. Both Tyler and Leona were thrown sideways into the opposite wall and Leona slipped and fell backward down the stairs, landing on top of her chef. He grabbed the railing with his right hand and wrapped his left arm around her torso, pulling her into him, keeping her from tumbling down the steep stairs. A few seconds later the heat and noise dissipated and the sound of car alarms took over. Thick smoke clogged the stairwell and Tyler pulled Leona up.

"Let's go. To the roof. We need to get out of the smoke."

"What happened?" she asked, dazed.

"Gas explosion." He wrenched on her arm. "C'mon. Hurry, let's go. We've got to get out of here."

Within seconds the smoke was too thick to see through. Tyler felt his way up the stairs, Leona behind him. His lungs were bursting from a lack of oxygen, his senses dull. His feet were heavy on the concrete, like it was sticky, and moving upward was more difficult with every riser. He felt Leona going limp behind him and he doubled his efforts. His fingers grabbed the railing like talons, snaking about the wood that was their lifeline. Lose it and they would lose this battle.

Leona was starting to panic, her claustrophobia kicking in as the smoke engulfed them. But she was unable to act on the overwhelming fear, to lash out and try to break free. Her body wasn't responding. The horror of being trapped alive in the smoke-filled space was only in her mind. Her systems were starting to shut down—her breathing, her mind going blank. She couldn't fight it. She was finished.

Tyler pulled her up the last few stairs, her head and body scraping on the rough cement. Finally, his hand hit something solid ahead of them. The door to the roof. He pushed on the handle and it swung open. Tyler dragged Leona semiconscious through the door at the top of the stairs into the fresh air. Black smoke poured out of the stairwell. Tyler pulled her to safety and checked that she was conscious.

"I've got to check on Boozy and Eric," Tyler said, once he was sure she was coherent and breathing. "You okay by yourself for a minute?" She managed a small nod and he ran to the north end of the building and jumped onto the fire escape. A second later he was gone.

Leona could barely breathe, even in the fresh air, and she realized they had both come within seconds of succumbing to the smoke in the enclosed stairwell. She couldn't stop coughing and her eyes burned when she tried to open them. She lay on the ground, thoughts flooding through the confusion of sounds and smells.

What had just happened?

Her restaurant was destroyed. Tyler was okay, but what about the rest of her kitchen staff? Were they dead? How could they have survived the explosion that almost crushed Tyler and her in the stairwell. If that wall hadn't held . . .

Two, maybe three minutes passed and the sirens pierced the morning air, growing louder by the second. Here, she thought. They're coming here. How strange. Sirens had never come to her before, always somewhere else. There was a scraping sound on the far side of the roof and she opened her eyes as Tyler appeared at the top of the fire escape. He jogged over to where she was struggling to sit up. His eyes were red and teary. She knew immediately that it wasn't solely from the smoke or the fire.

"Let's get you down to street level. There's some fire in the restaurant. Not much. I think the explosion sucked most of the air out and the fire never really caught."

"What about Boozy and Eric?" she asked.

He shook his head, then pulled her upright and hoisted most of her weight onto his shoulders and off her feet. When they reached the fire escape, she steadied herself against the edge of the building, her strength and balance returning. Tyler went first on the stairs, below her, in case she slipped. She followed, hand over hand, feeling each rung with her feet, careful not to fall. The last of the fire trucks, police and EMS were pulling up as they touched the ground. Hoses snaked from the trucks, barricades were quickly erected at each end of the street, and medical crews attended to the wounded. An EMS woman checked Leona, then went on to other, more seriously injured people. A uniformed policeman took their names and when he learned they were both in the restaurant when the explosion occurred, asked them to wait across the street. Tyler sat beside Leona on the curb and they watched the hub of activity in the burnt-out shell that twenty minutes ago had been one of Washington's most popular restaurants.

"There's no way they survived," Tyler said quietly. Tears pooled, then drifted down his face, smearing the soot and dirt. "Boozy was twenty-three, for Christ's sake. Best guy I ever knew. And Eric had a wife and a kid—little girl about two years old."

Leona fought back the tears. She'd seen Eric's girl a few

times, when his wife dropped in on him while he was working. Now the child would grow up without a father. Amid the chaos on the street, she envisioned how different her life would have been if her father had not been around. No one driving her to succeed. No one to tell her that her best wasn't good enough. No one pushing her to her limits.

Was it that bad? Would she really have wanted a life without her father's influence? His relentless rejection of everything she accomplished in life was simply his way of saying he loved her. That he knew what she was capable of, and that she should go for it. No halfway measures. Commit to what she was doing or go home. He had given her a strength of character that none of life's lessons had come close to matching. His love, his caring, although bordering on fanatical, was real. It was tangible. Something that Eric's little girl would never have.

Leona buried her face in her hands and cried. The explosion, the two young men dying in such a horrific manner, a little girl growing up without her father—it was too much. She felt Tyler's arm around her shoulder and leaned against him. They sat motionless on the curb as a tide of activity whirled about them. A new vehicle caught her attention as the police pulled back the roadblocks and let it proceed onto the street. It was a cube van with CRIME SCENE INVESTIGATION in block letters on the side. Two men exited the truck after it was parked. They stood on the sidewalk, talking to the police, who occasionally pointed at the burnt-out building.

CSI was here to determine the cause of the explosion. That was easy to figure. But it raised a very good question. What *had* caused the blast? Buildings didn't just explode every day. It was the exception, not the norm. And the timing. The smell of gas, then she and Tyler leaving the main dining area and running through the kitchen to the back staircase. Five seconds earlier and they would have been in the kitchen, not the stairwell. They would have joined Boozy and Eric in body bags.

Scant seconds. The difference between life and death.

What were the chances? What were the odds, that four days after she sat in a police precinct talking to detectives from DC and Utah about two suspicious deaths, her restaurant would be obliterated by a fireball? Very slim. Next to nonexistent, in fact.

The pieces were falling into place. Reginald Morgan opposed the conversion to an income trust and disappeared from a cruise ship. Senator Claire Buxton drafted a proposed bill that would require Coal-Balt to substantially upgrade their facilities, thus placing the conversion on shaky ground. And Claire Buxton died in a suspicious car crash. Now her, the banker with ties to the coal and utility company, decides that the trust conversion is shaky, and refuses to give the okay until Buxton's death is determined accidental. And her restaurant blows up.

This was no coincidence. Someone had tried to kill her. The more she thought about it, the surer she was. Derek Swanson was trying to remove her from the equation. And he had almost succeeded.

Would he try again?

She was shaking, her already frayed nerves pushed too far. What could she do? The police probably couldn't protect her. The only person she knew who was capable of that was in Kenya. And Mike Anderson was in enough trouble himself. If she were right, and Swanson or someone in his hire was trying to kill her, there would be no help there.

She was alone. Alone, and facing a killer.

## 45

Night drifted over the Kenyan capital, danger growing as the light of day diminished. Darkness drew the thieves and muggers out from their shanties, like venom sucked from a festering snakebite. Streets that were marginally safe under the harsh sun were transformed into nests of vile shadows. Gangs of young men, unemployed, broke and angry, wandered the narrow roads and alleyways looking for marks. The air was thick with the pungent smells of cooked meat and sewage. Nighttime Nairobi—dark and dangerous.

Kubala waited until six hours after sunset before driving to Tuato's apartment. He parked the Land Rover a few blocks south on the main road and walked the rest of the way. His dark-colored clothes were ragged and dirty, his curly hair unkempt. He shuffled slowly along the cracked sidewalk, dragging one leg slightly with each step. To everyone he passed, he was a homeless cripple. A man of no consequence, and no money. They left him alone.

He limped past the front of Tuato's building at two in the morning. Lights burned in a solitary window on the second floor. The remainder of the building was dark. But darkness was no guarantee the people inside were sleeping. It was hot and air-conditioning was a luxury this part of Nairobi did not have. Sleep was difficult and electricity was expensive. Many times people sat in their apartments with the lights off, watching, listening. Taking anything for granted—that because the lights were off the inhabitants were sleeping— was folly. Fatal even.

A full block to the north was an access to the alley and Kubala turned in. Total blackness enveloped him. He shuffled ahead, the stench of rotting garbage harsh on his nostrils.

A sound to his left startled him and he glanced over. Outlined in a tiny swatch of pale moonlight were a boy and a girl, neither more than fifteen, having sex. The boy turned and glared, his body still moving. Kubala looked away and hastened his pace. He reached the corner and headed back south toward where Tuato parked the car.

Every sense, every nerve went into overdrive as he approached the small alcove off the alley. He shortened his steps and passed the opening at a crawl. The car was there, pulled tight against the building. He stopped a few feet farther along and pressed his back to the rough cement wall. He was sweating and his shirt stuck to his skin. His hands were trembling, his heart racing, the blood pumping through his body like surges of water from a well. After five minutes he walked back the other way. Nothing happened. No movement, no opening and closing of doors or windows. Nothing to indicate Tuato was still awake. Kubala moved into the alcove and sat against the wall, barely visible in the darkness. He remained motionless for half an hour, searching the black windows for movement. If anyone were watching from above, they would have come down by now to find out what he was doing. He took a few deep breaths. It was time.

He figured the time to be almost three in the morning. Other than a few mangy dogs and two homeless people passing by in the alley, there was no activity. Sounds filtered through the thick night air; babies crying, men yelling at women, men yelling at other men, empty liquor bottles smashing on the cement. But no gunshots. It was a quiet night.

Kubala shifted onto his belly and crawled to the car. He tried the driver's side front door handle. It was locked. Then the back. Also locked. He dragged himself around the car to the passenger's side. It was close to the building. Too close to open the door and slide in. He tried the rear door handle and it opened to his touch. He pulled it out until the metal touched the stone wall, then slid his hand in and felt for the window crank. He rolled the window down an inch at a time, turning the handle slowly to keep it from squeaking. Beads of sweat formed on his forehead and dripped down his face. He ignored the distraction, and when the window was fully down he hoisted himself up and squeezed between the car and the wall. It was too tight. He didn't have enough room to arch his body and slide in through the window. Kubala stood motionless, jammed between the car and the building, thinking. Maybe if he tried coming in from the roof.

He slid out of the narrow gap and climbed on the trunk of the car, staying on the rear quarter panel where the metal was rounded and wouldn't buckle under his weight. If it did cave in, and the dent popped back out after he removed his weight, there would be a noise. And in the quiet of the night, any sound would be amplified. He bellied his way onto the roof of the car, trying to keep his weight evenly distributed and not create a dent. Then he spun ninety degrees so he was perpendicular to the side of the car, grabbed the top of the window housing and jackknifed his body through the opening. He went in headfirst with no hands to break his momentum, landing on his back in the rear seat. His spine hit something hard and there was a sharp crack. He swore under his breath and pulled his feet in through the window. Underneath him was a thin walking stick that had snapped under his body weight. He rolled off the seat onto the floor and lay facedown without moving.

Seconds later a door opened and there was the sound of footsteps crunching on gravel. Then silence. Kubala stayed facedown on the floor of the car, barely breathing. Seconds ticked by with no sound. Above him someone pulled on the door handle. Once, then twice. The locking mechanism held and the handle clicked but didn't open. Kubala, on his belly, had no idea if the person trying the door was now staring in the window. Or if his dark clothes and black skin would keep him invisible in the darkness. Again, the seconds moved by, inexorably slow, time frozen. Then the back door to the building opened and a voice cut through the silence.

"What's up, man?"

"Nothin', maybe. Don't know. Thought I heard something."

More footsteps on the gravel. "You see anything?"

"Nah, nothin'."

"Smoke?"

"Sure."

The acrid smell of cigarette smoke trickled into the car, catching in Kubala's nose and throat. The men continued talking, and Kubala was sure that one of the voices was Tuato. He had no idea who the other man was, nor did he care. He just wanted them to leave, to return to the house. The interior of the car was stifling hot and breathing was becoming more difficult with each minute. He let his mind drift, back to Samburu where his wife and young son were waiting for him. Where the vast Maasai Mara met the forests and the sky was clear of the choking smoke that hung over Nairobi. Where fifteen-year-old boys and girls spent their leisure time playing soccer on dusty fields, not having sex in dirty back alleys. He made himself a promise, that if he got out of this alive, he would stay out of Nairobi, away from the madness that was consuming the city.

The voices continued, Tuato talking about some woman he had met at a club the week before, the other man laughing at the story of drink and uninhibited sex. It was forty minutes from the time Tuato had walked through the door before both men returned to the house. Kubala waited another fifteen minutes, his head up off the floor so he could breathe, then slid his hand under the front seat. The under-side was a jagged metal frame covered with cloth, and Kubala was careful not to cut himself on any of the sharp edges. The gap between the floor and the bottom of the seat was too narrow to give him any line of sight, and he felt blindly for a slice or tear in the cloth. He found one and slid his hand in, holding his breath.

The money was still in place, tucked up in the springs that gave the seat support. He fished it out, one bundle at a time until he was sure he had all of it. The enclosed space where he lay was too dark to count the money, and he double-checked the hiding spot, then tucked the cash inside his shirt and carefully unlocked the door. He pulled slowly on the handle, holding the armrest to keep the door tight to the car. When he had the handle all the way down, he re-leased pressure on the armrest and the door silently swung open. He slipped from the car onto the gravel, pushed the door closed, but not shut, and crept quietly across the small courtyard to the alley. His feet made a slight crunching sound, but he was treading lightly and it was barely loud enough for him to hear. He turned the corner into the alley and started walking.

He had the money, but getting Mike Anderson to safety was not going to be easy.

# 46

The street was cordoned off for seven hours while a police forensic unit worked the scene in and around the restaurant. There was little left of the main floor, and the kitchen was completely destroyed. Two charred bodies were found in the rubble, so badly burned that DNA identification was necessary. No one doubted that they were the remains of

Boozy and Eric, and the corpses were sent to the morgue for autopsy and identification. It was six-thirty Saturday evening before the street was cleared of debris and opened to pedestrian traffic. The yellow tape remained in place and no vehicles were allowed.

Leona spent part of her day at the hospital for a perfunctory checkup and the remainder at home, nursing a few bruises, sore lungs and a feeling of incredible vulnerability. Her worry was equally divided between her own safety and what was happening in Nairobi. There had been no news from Kubala and that was not good. There wasn't a fifteen-minute stretch went by without Mike Anderson's situation running helter-skelter through her mind. She knew the city and how dangerous it was on the surface. She could only guess at what kind of hellhole he was in.

It was eight in the evening before George Harvey was finished at the scene and the morgue and back in his office. Leona and Tyler met with him and Hank Trost in Harvey's office at the main police precinct at twenty minutes after the hour. The mood was somber, and they spent the first half hour going back over what happened prior to the explosion, and immediately afterward in the stairwell. Trost made notes as they talked.

"What caused the explosion?" Leona asked after Harvey had wrapped up their eyewitness statements.

The DC cop shook his head. "The gas line to the stove severed, gas escaped and ignited. That part is pretty simple. The tough part is trying to determine why the line failed. The explosion damaged it to the extent where we can't tell. The CSI techs removed whatever shreds of evidence they could find and are working on it in the lab, but so far they have no proof that the line was tampered with prior to the blast."

Tyler looked puzzled. "Why would it be?"

"Checking things like that is a routine part of the investigation," Harvey said to the cook. Then he added, "Tyler, I'd like to have a few words with Ms. Hewitt. In private, if you don't mind." The tone of his voice indicated that he didn't care whether Tyler minded or not.

"Sure," he said, rising.

Leona let her gaze run across the pictures on the wall behind George Harvey's desk. People pictures, every one of them. Mostly of cops, in uniform, posing for the camera. Smiling, no guns in sight—none of the dirty and dangerous side of being on the force. She focused on one of the photos. A young George Harvey was standing beside an older man, whose facial features were similar to Harvey's now. His father.

When the door closed, Leona said, "Your dad must be proud of you."

Harvey saw where she was looking, took a quick glance at the picture and nodded. "Yeah, he's retired now. But I think he's pleased I went into law enforcement. Justified what he'd done with his life."

"What do you mean?"

"Being a cop is a lot of things—dangerous, unrewarding, disturbing. You get to see the negative side of society on a daily basis. It wears on you. I think my dad wondered why he did it—why he devoted his life to it. When I joined the force it somehow made him feel that the time he spent as a cop was worthwhile." He shrugged. "That's what I think, but I'm no psychologist, just a cop."

Leona nodded, thoughtful. "Interesting concept." There were a few seconds of silence, then she looked away from the picture and back to him. "You think the timing of the explosion is suspect." It was a statement, not a question.

He didn't respond with a yes or no, but his eyes told the story. "You and Tyler were sitting at a table in the restaurant talking and drinking coffee, but neither of you smelled gas before the man who was killed in the blast opened the door to the kitchen? Is that correct?"

"Yes."

"Are the doors airtight?"

Leona shook her head. "I doubt it. They open and close hundreds of times every day. If they were that tight, they wouldn't swing shut easily."

"That was our line of reasoning as well. That and the fact that this happened at the precise moment you and Tyler headed into the kitchen. The odds of you not noticing a heavy concentration of leaking gas and the timing of the explosion are next to impossible. I think you're lucky to be alive. And with what's going on at the bank, it certainly makes one wonder. But so far we don't have any definitive proof that the explosion was rigged."

He paused for a minute to flip through a file on his desk, then continued, "There are two details about Claire Buxton's death that point toward foul play. Even in this room, off the record, I'm still not going to say that we're convinced she was murdered. But what I will tell you is that I'm heading back down to West Virginia to collect a DNA sample from Derek Swanson."

"You have blood spatters at the crash scene that don't belong to the victims," Leona said after a five-second gap. "You think Swanson was there."

"Can't confirm that. But I will say that we're going to be looking at where Mr. Swanson was at the time the senator was killed in the crash."

Leona nodded. She didn't speak for a minute, then said, "This may sound crass, but I'd like to ask you a question about the insurance on my restaurant."

"I don't know much about that," Harvey said. He turned to Hank Trost. "How about you?"

Trost shrugged. "Not really. What's the question?"

"Will it affect my coverage if they find out someone blew up the restaurant in an attempt to kill me?"

Trost looked at Harvey. "Good question. I'm not sure."

"Very good question. I think you're probably best to offer them the least you can until you know for sure. I mean, *we* don't know. Nobody knows right now. Until we do, it's an accident."

"Thanks. I was thinking about asking for an officer to watch my house, but that's probably not a good idea. If the insurance people found out, they might disallow the claim. If it's not covered, I'm ruined. I don't have a million or million-five to fix up the place."

"Best if you don't make a formal request for protection, then," Harvey said. "I don't think we could justify it at this point anyway."

"Okay."

George Harvey stood up. Hank Trost and Leona followed suit. "Be careful. Watch everything that's going on around you. And if you feel threatened, call immediately." He handed her his card.

Leona left the precinct and turned her phone on as she walked back to her car. It showed five missed calls, each caller unknown. Someone was trying to contact her. She found out less than five minutes later when the phone rang. It was Kubala.

"What's going on? Have you been trying to call?" she asked the moment she recognized his voice.

"Yes, but you weren't answering. I have the money," he said excitedly. "I'm on my way to meet with the men who are holding Mr. Mike. I wanted you to know."

"Kubala, be careful," she said. It was a trite thing to say, but conveyed her feelings, her anxiety.

"Yes, of course. I think they will let him go. Mr. Mike thought of a good way to give them the money."

"How?"

"I will give them twenty thousand dollars now, and the remainder when Mr. Mike is on an airplane or in the American Embassy."

"Excellent idea." She reached her car and leaned on the passenger-side door. "When do you think Mike will be out of Kenya?"

"I would have to guess."

"That's fine."

"Twenty-four hours, maybe forty-eight at the most."

"Oh, Kubala, that's good news. Keep me posted on how things are going."

She snapped the phone shut when the dial tone kicked in and sucked in a couple of deep breaths. Mike might get out alive. She had consciously kept herself from dwelling on his predicament for a very good reason. Until this phone call had come through, she didn't think he would live. She knew Kenya, knew the corruption and violence. She knew the value of life, and that value was very low. Her world and Kubala's were so different. Vastly different.

Yet someone was trying to narrow that gap. Whatever value society placed on her life, there was one person who thought it was considerably less. Nothing, in fact. They had tried to kill her. Of that she was certain. To Derek Swanson, or his flunky, she was expendable. A thing that was in their way. Something to be removed, like a burr from inside a sock. And in trying to kill her, they had taken a young girl's father. A woman's husband. A family's son. She tried to disassociate herself from blame, but it wouldn't happen. Boozy and Eric had died in the explosion because of her. If she had okayed the conversion without any conditions, they would be alive. Two men dead, a direct result of her decision not to give Derek Swanson what he wanted. She shook her head in disbelief as she fished the car keys from her purse and thumbed the fob. The car lights blinked and she reached for the door handle.

She stopped, frozen.

Something was wrong. Very wrong. No one knew what her decision was except the men in the boardroom. And Bill Cawder. Swanson had an inside man. She closed her eyes and pictured him, standing inside her door at the office, smiling. What had he said to her? *I thought you said it was a go.* She had answered that it wasn't; then he had asked if it was fixable. Christ, why hadn't she seen what was happening right then? The questions. And the results of those questions. Derek Swanson had been fed information that ended up with two more people being killed during an attempt on her life.

She opened her phone and thumbed through it until she found a number. Then she dialed it and waited. Anthony Halladay answered.

"It's Leona Hewitt," she said.

"Yes, Leona. What can I do for you?"

"I need to see you. Immediately."

# 47

Sunday morning at the open market on Mfangano Street was a busy time—a sampling of every region of Kenya thrown into a finite number of city blocks. Maasai villagers, in from the great plains of the Maasai Mara, sat elbow to elbow with locals from the city, displaying their wares on rickety tables. Small children ran through the throngs of shoppers packed into the narrow streets. Pickpockets worked the crowd, searching out targets by instinct more than sight. No one with any common sense dressed well or wore jewelry in the tight confines of the marketplace. A menagerie of odors drifted in the stale morning air; sweet cabbage, pungent spices. It was business as normal for Nairobi's working class.

Two men pushed through the crowd, the thieves and beggars melting into the crowd as they approached. Police. Even without their uniforms, the men were like red flags to the unsavory. Something about the swagger in their step, the ruthlessness and arrogance in their eyes, told of power. Something bordering on evil.

Bawata Rackisha and his flunky slowed as they neared a booth selling cabbages, rice and potatoes. Sitting next to the vendor was Kubala Kantu. Rackisha's aide stopped fifteen feet from the booth and stood with his back to a wall, his hand perched near his unseen handgun. Rackisha waved off the owner of the stall and waited until he was behind the ripped curtain that gave the man and his family a modicum of privacy. When the vendor was out of sight, the police inspector leaned over the baskets of food.

"I don't like meeting here," he hissed. His face was twisted with anger. "And I don't like being told what to do."

Kubala's bowels were ready to let loose, but he maintained an easy posture and kept his voice level. "This is a safe place."

"For whom?" the inspector asked. His eyes were glittering with contempt.

"For everyone, of course." Kubala adjusted his stance and continued, "I have twenty thousand American dollars with me. I will release the other fifty-five when Mr. Anderson is on a plane out of Kenya."

Rackisha ground his teeth and leaned closer to the Maasai. "I could grab you right now and take you somewhere very private and convince you to tell me," he whispered. "Don't play games with me, Kubala Kantu, or I will kill you in a very ugly and very painful way."

Kubala wanted to run from the booth. Run and never

look back. He simply shrugged. "No offense, Inspector, but I have taken certain precautions to protect myself. I do not know where the remainder of the money is hidden."

"How is that possible?"

"I have a friend who hid the money. Then he left Nairobi. He has a cell phone with him and is waiting for my call. I have his phone number, a password, and a certain time when I must call him. If I am incorrect with any of these three things, he will not release the location of the money."

"I could easily torture you and get the information."

"You do not have enough time. I have to make the call soon," Kubala said. He picked up a cabbage and pulled off an overripe leaf. It calmed him to have something in his hands. "The moment Mr. Anderson is on a plane, I will phone this man."

"That may be impossible. There may not be a flight."

Kubala reached inside his shirt pocket and slipped out a solitary piece of paper. He handed it to Rackisha. "This is a printout of all the flights departing Nairobi Airport today. Six of them are international. Any one of the six is fine. I highlighted them for you."

Rackisha glanced at the page, then back to Kubala. "You have twenty thousand on you right now?"

"Yes."

"And fifty-five thousand later."

"That is correct. Seventy-five thousand US dollars."

"That doesn't seem like very much," Rackisha complained. "I think the American is worth far more than that."

"The only way to get more money is to contact his government."

A woman stopped at the booth to sample the produce, but one look from the inspector and she left. Rackisha rubbed his hand across the stubble on his chin. "I am not happy about this." When Kubala didn't respond, he said,

"All right. Twenty thousand dollars now, fifty-five at the airport."

"That is fine."

"Where is the twenty thousand?"

"You are leaning on it. The money is under the cabbages."

Rackisha rolled away a few of the vegetables and extracted a brown paper bag. He glanced inside, then folded the top flap back over. He held up the paper with the plane schedules on it and scanned the highlighted entries. Two morning flights, four later in the day. He needed time to get Anderson cleaned up—it would have to be a night flight. "Nine-fourteen to Paris," he said, dropping the paper on the ground. "I'll have the American at the airport. You make the call."

Kubala nodded. "This is not a problem."

Rackisha's voice was filled with contempt. "It will be a very big problem if you don't have the money." He turned and walked back through the crowd. In seconds he and his associate were gone, swallowed by the sheer number of people.

Kubala didn't move. He was too scared to try his legs. Everything he had told the police inspector was a load of bullshit. There was no other person to call. The bulk of the money was ten feet from him, stashed in a bin full of white maize meal called *ugali*. He had come within one command from Rackisha from being tortured to death. Only the worthless cop's greed had kept Kubala alive. He knew that. He also knew that Rackisha was not to be trusted until his American friend was safely on the plane. And then, with the money in hand, Rackisha would be at his most dangerous. The path to freeing Mike Anderson was still a hazy one, with much treachery and deceit. Timing was going to be the key to whether Mike Anderson and he lived or died. And that timing had to be perfect.

Kubala finally stood, tentatively at first, testing his strength in increments before putting his full weight on his legs. He was shaking so badly he almost fell. Many difficult situations had arisen over the years, but nothing like this. He scanned the crowd to see if Rackisha had someone watching, then scooped the money from under the *ugali* and tucked it back inside his loose-fitting shirt. He paid the owner of the stall twenty American dollars and left, walking in the opposite direction from Rackisha. A chance meeting at this point would be a death sentence.

He had important things to do, and little time. And two lives depended on how well he took care of the details.

# 48

Leona pulled her Saab off Foxhall Street in the upscale DC subdivision of Wesley Heights and into the secluded driveway. She punched the button under the security camera. Nothing happened for ten seconds, then the wrought-iron gate clicked and drew back on its track. She drove into the private estate, along the winding road bordered on both sides by ash and walnut. The foliage ended abruptly, revealing a Civil War–era stone house set on a slight knoll. It was large, but not massive, and the expansive grounds made it look smaller than it was. The road ended in a circular driveway, and she stopped in front of the heavy oak door.

Anthony Halladay appeared in the doorway. He was dressed in khaki shorts, a golf shirt and an impatient expression. "I have a nine thirty-one tee time. I'd like to make it."

"This is important, Anthony." Leona climbed out of the car and glanced at her watch. Three minutes to eight. The morning air was still, the mercury rising as the sun warmed the parklike surroundings.

"Come in." He motioned for her to follow him into the house.

The interior of DC Trust's Chief Executive Officer's house was exactly what she expected. Dark wood covered the walls and heavy draperies hung over small windows. Leona felt a touch of panic, the house drawing in around her, sucking the air out of her lungs, suffocating her. She followed Halladay into the great room in the rear of the house. It was much lighter, with a bank of windows that overlooked a small ravine filled with indigenous trees and shrubs. The claustrophobia diminished and her breathing returned to normal. She sat in a chair Halladay pointed to and waited until he had taken a seat opposite her.

"What's on your mind?" he asked.

"The Coal-Balt file."

"You have a definitive answer?"

"I do. But I wanted to speak to you about something else. Something I think you're going to find rather disturbing."

"What is it?"

"I think one of our staff is feeding Derek Swanson information."

"Who?"

"Bill Cawder. He showed up in my office a few minutes after our meeting to discuss my report. He wanted to know how things went—whether we approved the conversion."

"And that was the information he passed along to Swanson?"

"Yes. Swanson knew about my decision not to approve the conversion before he should have. And I think he acted on that knowledge."

Halladay cocked his head slightly and said, "That's a serious allegation, Leona."

"I know."

"What sort of action did he take?"

"He tried to kill me."

Halladay's eyes flickered, then narrowed. "What did you say?"

"Derek Swanson, or someone in his hire, tried to kill me. They blew up my restaurant." She glanced over at the *Washington Post*, sitting unopened on the coffee table. "I take it you haven't read the newspaper yet. It's all over the front page."

"I don't bother reading it on Sunday. There's no worthwhile business section," he said, standing and walking over to the table. He picked up the paper and flipped open the first section, scanning the headlines, then reading the first few lines of copy. "This is your restaurant?"

"Was. There's not much left."

"And you think Derek Swanson was behind this?" He returned to his seat, the paper still in his hand.

"I do. And I think he was involved in the deaths of Reginald Morgan and Senator Claire Buxton as well."

"Jesus, Leona, this is serious."

"You have no idea. Two of my employees are dead. One of them had a wife and small child."

"Why would Swanson do something like this?"

Leona stared at him, like he had asked a stupid question. Which he had. "Money, Anthony. A lot of money. Fifty million dollars. He wanted the trust conversion to go through, and when it looked like there may be some stumbling blocks, he removed them. He killed people for financial gain."

"Have you been to the police?"

She nodded. "Yes. They think he's involved."

Halladay stood up and walked across to the windows, the light playing off his features. Worry showed in his eyes and the downturn on his lips. "This is not good news. If this is true, we have to break the connection between him and the bank. And quickly. He could drag our name into the press."

"Probably too late to sidestep that one," Leona said. "Someone, somewhere, is going to put this together. Or the police are going to get enough evidence to charge him. Then it'll really hit the fan."

Halladay stared out over the tranquil forest behind his house. The sky was unmarred by clouds and only a hint of breeze tugged at the leaves on the trees. Leona waited, watching the man, measuring his reaction to the inevitable scandal that was about to rock the bank. His shoulders were rounded, his head down. The pose of a man who knew of difficult times to come.

"Thank you for coming today." He turned from the window.

Leona stood. "I thought you should know."

"Yes, of course. I take it I have your final decision on the income trust conversion."

"That we won't touch the deal with a very long pole," she said, stating the obvious. "Our shareholders would lynch us if we got behind Swanson with what we know."

"I'll see you out."

Halladay shook her hand at the front door. She pulled away from the house, checking the rearview as she rounded the circular driveway and started into the thick grove of trees that shielded the house from the road. The banker was still framed in the doorway. She couldn't tell the expression on his face or where he was looking. But one thing she could pretty well guarantee was that he wouldn't be golfing anytime soon.

The gentle hum of the car's tires on the pavement diminished, then faded to nothing. Halladay watched the Saab disappear into the trees, and a silence descended on his house.

He stood unmoving for the better part of five minutes, leaning against the doorjamb, staring at the empty road. He retreated into the house, closing the front door behind him. The foyer was bathed in darkness, and for the first time it bothered him that his house was so dimly lit. He walked down the hall into his master bedroom and opened the wall safe hidden behind the plasma television. Inside, tucked away among his valuables, was a cellular phone. One registered to a shell corporation and impossible to trace back to him. He powered it on and dialed a number. Another cell phone—a private one that only he had the number to.

"Hello, Anthony."

"Derek."

"Why are you calling?" Swanson asked, concern creeping into his voice.

"Have you read the paper today?"

"Yes. Why?"

"Nothing in the West Virginia newspapers about an explosion in Washington?"

"No. What are you talking about?"

"Did you tell anyone about Leona Hewitt's decision not to okay the conversion?"

There was a pregnant moment of silence, then Swanson said, "Someone found out. I didn't tell him."

"Is it the man I think it is?"

"Yes."

"Well, it looks like he took things into his own hands," the banker said. "He blew up Leona's restaurant. He missed her, but killed two other people."

"Oh, Jesus."

Neither man spoke for a minute, then Swanson said, "How much does she know?"

"She thinks someone else at the bank is the conduit to you. But it's not us you have to worry about, it's the police.

They're putting all this together. You should never have touched the senator."

"That wasn't my idea," Swanson said angrily. "The son of a bitch acted on his own."

"What about Leona?"

"I didn't even know about the restaurant. I never asked him to take care of her."

"Well, he tried. And he missed. Now we've got a problem. A really big problem."

"I'll phone him. Try to rein him in."

"Do more than try, Derek."

Halladay hung up and turned the phone off. He slid it back in the wall safe, closed the door and spun the dial. The plasma television was on a pivoting arm and he pushed it back tight to the wall, hiding the safe. He took a few steps to the bed and flopped down on his back, staring at the ceiling. Derek Swanson had made a grave error. Bringing in the assassin was a bad idea from minute one. Killing Reginald Morgan was stupid, probably unnecessary, but killing a senator was nothing short of psychotic behavior. Out of more than three hundred million people, only one hundred were senators representing their state. Who in their right mind would think they could kill a US senator and not be hunted down and thrown in jail? It was lunacy.

And now, through no doing of his own, he was caught in the web of violence Derek Swanson's killer had woven. Guilty by association. The truth would come out. He knew it. Their long-term association. The forged financial records in the bank's files to ensure Coal-Balt always had ample operating capital. The cell phones they used to call each other would be uncovered. The times of the calls, perhaps the contents. One thing was certain. His life as he knew it was over. Everything he had worked for. Gone.

He shut his eyes and a wave of blackness closed over him.

## 49

"What the hell do you think you're doing?"

A slow smile crept over Darvin's face. His eyes glittered with a strange mixture of contempt and satisfaction. He gripped the phone lightly, in contrast to the stranglehold he had on the other man. "Just taking care of business, Derek. It's what I do."

"Stop it. Stop killing people."

"No."

"What? What did you say to me?"

"I said no, you moron. I'll stop killing people when I want to. And there is absolutely nothing you can do about it."

"I'm not involved in this. I have no part in what you're doing."

"Of course you do. The District Attorney could care less if you ordered me to kill Claire Buxton and Leona Hewitt. The fact that you paid me to kill Reginald Morgan is enough to put you in prison for life. Or the chair. What is West Virginia's stance on the death penalty?"

"You're psychotic."

"No, Derek, I'm not. I know exactly what I'm doing. You haven't figured it out yet."

"The money from the conversion is gone. You've completely fucked it up. There's no way you're going to get a cent out of this."

"I know that."

"You are fucking mental." Swanson was yelling now, his emotions totally out of control. "The police were here this morning. DC homicide police. They had a warrant for a DNA sample. What the hell is that all about?"

"No idea," Darvin said. He leaned back in the armchair

and sucked in a long, mellow breath. "Perhaps they suspect you of something. That's usually why they take DNA swabs."

"You killed two innocent people when you blew up that restaurant. One of them had a young child, for Christ's sake."

"Shit happens."

"You're insane and you're incompetent. You missed the banker. She's alive."

"Yes, I know. I read about that." There was a pause as he walked over to the window and stared out at the tranquil Virginia countryside, then he added, "She won't be around much longer, Derek."

"Leave her alone," Swanson screamed into the phone. "No more murders. You understand. No more bodies."

"I told you before, Derek, don't defend her. Leona Hewitt is a dead woman. She will not see the end of this week."

Swanson's voice came down twenty decibels and his tone shifted to threatening. "You listen to me. You are not going to kill any more people. I'll go to the police, tell them you're blackmailing me. They'll hunt you down before you can do any more harm."

"A threat. My, I'm scared. But should I be?" Darvin said sarcastically. "You don't know my real name or where I live. You know nothing about me, except what I look like. And do you really know that, Derek? Maybe I wore a disguise. Christ, you really are a rube. How did you ever achieve such wealth and power? Certainly not through any of your own initiative."

"I'm phoning Leona Hewitt and warning her."

"Go ahead. It won't matter. She's already scared and try-ing to hide. I'll find her. I have my ways. You phone her and all you do is give away your involvement in all this."

"I'll get you, you motherfucker."

Darvin leaned forward in the chair, a cruel, remorseless

stare washing over his eyes. "No, Derek, you won't. And that's the beauty of this. I'm going to get you."

Darvin pushed the off button with his finger and set the phone on the end table. He stared at the hunk of plastic, marveling at how much damage he could do with such a simple instrument. Derek Swanson was terrified. His life was coming apart at the seams, like it should have years ago when the union rep floated to the top of the lake. If the police who were assigned to figure out who had killed him weren't so incompetent, none of this would have happened. Derek would have been in jail years ago. Where he belonged.

But the cops had messed everything up. No different from when his mother had caved in his father's skull. She had done it right in front of him. Even with a witness, the police working the file couldn't put it together that his father hadn't fallen getting out of the bathtub. That the woman was a murderer. He tried to tell them, but they never listened. Finally, the police told his mother that her son was having delusions, saying crazy things. He stopped trying after that and let them think that his father had died accidentally. All the while plotting how to kill the queen bitch.

He rose from the chair and slowly climbed the stairs to the second floor. The door at the end of the hall was closed. No light escaped from the thin crack between the door and the floor. It was time to open the drapes. She liked the light. Liked to be pushed around the room in her wheelchair. She was so demanding. He touched the handle and turned.

"Good morning, Mother," he said as he entered.

# 50

Heat waves rose off the runway, distorting the sleek lines of the Air France jet as it taxied to the terminal. Kubala stood at the windows, watching the plane attach to the jetway. A couple of minutes later a steady stream of passengers made their way through the bridge into the terminal. On the ground and under the harsh glare of the night lights, baggage attendants unloaded the plane and a fuel truck parked next to the fuselage on the far side. Two other wide-body jets flanked the Air France 767, and inside the terminal all three gates were crowded with people waiting to board their flights. Despite the late hour, the building was oppressively hot, the air-conditioning units ineffective in such a large space.

Mike Anderson entered the terminal from the street. Bawata Rackisha and his sidekick were tight to either side of him. They stopped at the security checkpoint and Rackisha produced identification that allowed them to proceed without walking through the lone metal detector at the main entrance. There was no doubt in Kubala's mind that both men were armed. He checked his watch as they approached. Ten minutes after eight. Not much time. He raised his hand and Rackisha caught the motion, angling toward where he stood.

"Hello, Kubala," Mike said when they were standing a few feet apart. He was clean shaven and well dressed, in new blue jeans and a patterned shirt. Another foreigner heading home after a safari. His eyes told a different story. They showed pain and distrust, perhaps even a hint of fear. Something Kubala had never seen in the man's eyes before. "Thanks for coming."

"Of course, Mr. Mike."

"Did you make the phone call?" Rackisha asked impatiently.

Kubala shook his head. "Not yet." He reached inside his shirt and pulled out an airline folder. He handed it across to Mike, but Rackisha intercepted it and yanked it out of Kubala's hand.

He flipped it open and scanned the boarding pass, focusing on the flight and time. "Make the call," he said.

"I require Mr. Anderson to at least be through the final security checkpoint and boarding his plane. Then I will make the call."

Rackisha looked like he was going to erupt. After a full minute he finally calmed down enough to hand the folder across to the American. "The sooner you get moving, the sooner your friend can make the call."

"No problem," Anderson said. He grasped Kubala's hand and squeezed. "Thank you so much, my friend."

"It's okay." He held Anderson's hand for a second longer than necessary. "I tried to get you a window seat, but was unable. I had to settle on the airline's second choice. I think you'll be pleased with it."

Anderson nodded. "I'm sure you've done well, Kubala. I'll be fine."

They released hands and Anderson queued up for one of the two metal detectors that delineated the main section of the airport from the gate area, where only ticketed passengers were allowed. He went through without incident and kept moving, disappearing into the throng of people waiting at the gates.

"Make the call," Rackisha said, turning to Kubala.

Kubala pivoted slightly so the men couldn't see the number he was dialing. He hit the send button, waited a few seconds, then said, "Everything is fine. Where is the money?"

He nodded a few times, then said, "Thanks." He clicked the phone shut. As it closed, it slipped out of his hand. He tried to grab it but missed, and it hit the worn tile floor, shattering on impact. "Shit, my phone."

"Never mind your phone," Rackisha growled. "Where is the money?"

"Close," Kubala said. "In Nairobi."

"Where in Nairobi?" the inspector said, growing impatient very quickly. "It's a large city."

"In the arboretum. There is a garden shed on the north side of the road, one hundred yards in from Arboretum Road. Not Drive—Road. My friend was very specific about that. You must come in from the south entrance or finding the shed will be very difficult. Especially at night."

Rackisha looked to his flunky. "Did you understand the directions?"

"Yes." The man turned to leave. "I'll call you when I have the money."

Rackisha watched him leave, then pointed to a couple of empty seats. "Please get comfortable. You're not going anywhere until I have the money."

"I understand." Kubala sat on what looked to be the most comfortable chair.

They waited, watching the people enter and leave the airport. Two of the three flights called for boarding, one of them Anderson's flight to Paris. When the two planes had loaded, and the people in the departure area had thinned out, Kubala scanned the crowd for his friend. There were few white people in the crowd and no Mike Anderson. He had already boarded his flight. Things were looking good. The plane next to the Air France wide-body pushed back, then taxied to the runway. Kubala watched as the bridge pulled back from the French plane. Almost there.

Rackisha's phone rang and he answered it. He nodded

twice, then hung up. "Your friend did well. The money was where he said it should be."

"Good," Kubala said, breathing easier.

"But I have a little something to take care of," Rackisha said. He leapt from his seat and ran to the security checkpoint, police identification in his hand. "Stop that plane," he yelled at the guard.

"Which one?"

"The one to Paris. Gate two."

An airline rep intervened. "The bridge is already pulled back. The plane is ready to leave."

Rackisha shook his head. "It will leave when I say. Attach the bridge."

The employee returned to her podium and spoke into the telephone. A minute passed, then the arm slowly returned to its position against the side of the plane. Rackisha pushed past the gate attendant and disappeared into the walkway.

Kubala grabbed the opportunity and left the terminal, slipping into the backseat of a cab and waving at the driver to get moving. He glanced over his shoulder as he spouted out the address where he had left the Land Rover, half expecting to see one of Rackisha's men coming after him. Nothing. He had escaped. And once he reached the vehicle he was out of Nairobi and back to his village. His wife and child would be waiting. And they would leave for a few months, until Rackisha forgot about him.

There was nothing he could do now to help Mike Anderson. What he could do, he had. The American was on his own. Breaking the telephone by dropping it on the floor was necessary to keep Rackisha from taking it and hitting redial, looking for the last number dialed. There had been no outgoing call. No one on the other end. Just him. And if Rackisha had discovered the ruse, there would have been no stopping his murderous rage. Kubala closed his eyes and tried to force the image of the corrupt and violent inspector heading onto the plane from his mind. It didn't work. Rackisha was on the plane, looking to pull the American off. Looking to take him back to whatever hellhole they had imprisoned him in for over two weeks. To do as he wished with his prisoner now that he had the money.

Would Mike Anderson live or die? The next few minutes would tell how that story ended.

# 51

Someone was trying to kill her.

The realization sunk in slowly, like an iceberg melting as it drifted south. Nothing about it seemed real. How could it be? She was an average person, living a normal life in Washington DC. People like her didn't make it into a killer's Rolodex. They went about their business and 99.99 percent of the world ignored them. Now the question was, what to do? Go home? What if he, or she, was waiting for her? What if her car ignition had been tampered with? What if there was a bomb wired to the starter?

Leona fingered her car keys with one hand and ran the other through her hair. She had been away from her car for an hour, having a bite of lunch with a friend. That would be plenty of time for someone to tamper with her vehicle. Her heart was beating fast, adrenaline surging through her body. All in anticipation of starting her car. Something she had done tens of thousands of times in the past without a second thought. Now everything had changed. Danger, death, could be a fraction of an inch away.

Where was Mike Anderson? She needed him right now more than ever in her life. He was tough and resourceful. Fearless even. Mike would know what to do. But Kubala hadn't called since last night. Eighteen hours. A lot could happen in eighteen hours. Or nothing. She had no idea whether Mike was still alive or if he had been murdered and thrown in a shallow grave somewhere outside Nairobi. Leona leaned against the car and choked back the tears. She couldn't remember the last time she had cried. She tried, more to take her mind off things than anything else, and it finally came to her. Years ago, at her cousin's funeral. She had died of brain cancer at twenty-seven. What a waste. Leona remembered sitting next to her father in the funeral service, looking over at him and seeing the wetness in his eyes. He had cried that day, too. It had never registered with her before, but now she could envision him sitting on the hard wooden pew, struggling to hold back the tears. It was a side of her father she had seen, but had never recognized.

Her phone rang and she snapped back to the present. She checked the caller ID. It was George Harvey of the DC police. "Detective Harvey," she said. "Calling to check up on me?"

"Actually, yes. Everything okay?"

"So far. But I'm a little spooked. I've been envisioning a bomb planted under my car, and that it's going to explode when I turn the ignition key."

"That's probably a little extreme," the DC Homicide cop said.

"Someone blew up my restaurant."

"Point noted."

"What should I be watching for?"

"People who are watching you. The same face in the background more than once. It's not that difficult to pick someone out if you stay alert."

"Do you have anything new? Any sort of lead or clue as to who's doing this? When I was in your office on Friday you were checking the passenger manifest from the cruise ship. Anything come from that?"

"No. If Swanson's person did buy a ticket close to the sailing date, he did it without leaving a trail. But we did get a sample of Derek Swanson's DNA today. It's at the lab now."

"And if you get a match to the blood at the crash scene?"

"Ms. Hewitt, I never said there was blood at the scene other than the victim's. You assumed that."

"Yes, I did. But I think it's a pretty good assumption." She paused. "Will you tell me if it matches?"

Harvey didn't answer for a few seconds, then he said, "I'll give you every bit of information I can without jeopardizing the integrity of the investigation."

"Thank you."

"You have my card. Call me if you need anything."

"I will."

Leona killed the call and slipped the cell phone back in her pocket. She thumbed her key fob and clicked the button to open the doors. There was a thunking sound as the locking mechanisms released. She swung open the driver's door and dropped into the seat, then inserted the key into the ignition and turned. No hesitation. *God hates a coward.* The engine caught and settled into a low idle. Before she could shift into gear, her phone rang. The screen read *private caller.* She took the call.

"Leona." It was her father.

"Hi, Dad." Her hand gripped the stick shift a little tighter.

"I thought I'd call and see how things were going at the bank. With the new vice president."

"May not be doing that much longer," she said, not willing to play games. Her father suffering with the truth would be easier than her forcing a lie.

"Something wrong?" he asked.

"Things went badly with the first file I was handed. I'm not sure the position will be mine much longer."

"Isn't there some way to fix it?" he asked, concern creeping into his voice.

"This one is out of my hands, Dad," she said. "There's nothing I can do but wait and see how things play out."

"Maybe if you talk to the CEO."

Leona didn't respond right away. When she did it was off topic. "Dad, do you remember cousin Sheri? She died of cancer about four years ago."

"Yes, of course I remember her. Why?"

"Did you know her well?"

"Not all that well. She was your mother's sister's daughter. You probably saw her as often as I did."

"I only saw her about twice a year. Christmas and the yearly family barbeque."

"Yes. What's this all about?"

"Nothing. Listen, Dad, I've got to run. I'll tell you about what's happening at the office when I have a few more minutes."

"You're sure everything's okay?"

"Everything's fine. Talk to you soon."

"Okay."

Leona let the phone fall on her lap. She stared out the window at the Sunday DC traffic, but it wasn't registering. Who was this man that was supposed to be her father? Her dad was a man's man—one who would never look for the easy way, and would certainly never offer it. His demands were great, as were his expectations. Perhaps that's what had driven her to overachieve. In fact, she was sure it had. But the other side, the man who cried at funerals, not because he knew the person intimately, but because he perceived an injustice in life. This man she didn't understand. Had he always been there? Had she missed it? Had she lived her life in an emotional bubble because that was where she had put herself? Too many questions, no answers.

She slipped the car into gear and pulled out from the curb, pushing the thoughts from her mind. Right now she had one, and only one, thing to worry about. Staying alive.

# 52

Bawata Rackisha moved down the aisle slowly, enjoying the fearful glances from the passengers. None of them wanted to be the one picked. None of them wanted to be the one to accompany the police from the plane to a small room with no windows or cameras. Sometimes the ones who disappeared never came back. Rackisha looked into every pair of eyes, sensing the fear like a predator stalking trapped prey. He felt powerful, invigorated, aroused even, by the control.

Most of the passengers were African, with varying shades of black skin. Picking out Mike Anderson would be easy. The lone white guy. Rackisha was about halfway down the aisle and he glanced ahead. Many black faces stared back at him, lowering their gaze when their eyes met. He caught a glimpse of white skin near the back of the plane. *You can hide, but you can't escape.* He touched his shirt lightly, the feel of his gun under the cotton reassuring. Not long now. He increased his pace slightly, anxious to have the American back in his grasp.

Would Anderson try anything—to run, to push past him and bolt from the plane? Or would he go quietly? Rackisha didn't know the answer but suspected there may be trouble. Certainly Anderson would understand that this was it. That there was no way he could ever be released. That he would die in a most horrific way under the harshest of conditions. Mike Anderson could never possibly foresee the torture that lay ahead, but if he suspected he was going to die, he may try for the gun. Desperation breeds panic.

The inspector was almost to the rear of the plane. He slipped his hand under his shirt and wrapped his hand around the pistol grip. Two more rows. He could see the brown hair and snippets of white skin. He felt an incredible surge of power as he drew abreast the seat. The executioner had arrived. He steeled himself for a reaction and peered into the row. A white man between two Africans. The man turned and looked upward.

It was not Mike Anderson.

Rackisha stared for two or three seconds, then jerked his eyes back to the last three rows of the plane. He could see every person and not one of them was white. There was no chance he had missed him. Anderson was not on the plane. Rackisha turned and strode up the aisle, moving quickly and with purpose. He cornered the purser in front of the door to the cockpit and stood within a foot of her.

"Michael Anderson. He was supposed to be on this flight. Where is he?"

She opened the passenger manifest with shaking hands, running her finger down the list of names. She stopped, then said, "He was in row nine, seat C, but I can tell you for sure that he's not on the plane."

"How can you do that?" Rackisha asked rudely.

"Our headcount was one short, and we noticed it was him. We called back to the personnel at the gate and they told us he had informed them he wouldn't be taking the flight."

"Where is he?" Rackisha's face was inches from the woman's.

"I have no idea, sir," she said. "He's not our responsibility if he's not on the airplane."

Rackisha considered grabbing her and dragging her down to police headquarters, but came back to his senses. The chief of police and his lieutenants had no idea what he had done, and it was best kept that way. If he were to show up at the precinct with the flight attendant, there would be questions. Tough questions to answer. There was no upside to taking her off the plane.

"Thank you," he said through gritted teeth.

Rackisha returned to the terminal and walked about, searching the crowds for the American. The only group of whites was a safari tour preparing to leave the country on another outbound flight. The inspector looked at all of them closely. Anderson was definitely not among them. He posted a guard on the front doors and searched the bathrooms. Nothing. Anderson had escaped. He walked out into the late afternoon sun and stared at the chaos. Anderson was gone. Somehow, the American had managed to elude him.

Rackisha allowed himself a small smile. Who cared? He had the money. Killing Anderson would have been a bonus. An unnecessary bit of fun. He slid into the backseat of his car and shook his head. Son of a bitch. Tricky little bastard, Michael Anderson.

Mike Anderson accepted a rum and Coke from the flight attendant and downed it in two gulps. God, that felt good. He asked her politely for another one. A wave of exhilaration and relief swept over him as he looked out the window at the scattering of clouds and the vast African tract thirty thousand feet below. He had escaped, only with Kubala's help and ingenuity.

*I tried to get you a window seat, but was unable. I had to settle on the airline's second choice. I think you'll be pleased with it.*

For a few minutes he hadn't understood the message. Then, as he leaned against the wall, waiting to board the Air

France flight to Paris, he realized what Kubala was saying. He hated window seats, much preferred the aisle, and Kubala knew that. That was to get his attention. Then the mention of a *second choice*. Why those words? He opened the folder from the airline and pulled out the boarding pass. Underneath, folded in half and almost invisible, was a second boarding pass, this one on the Lufthansa flight departing for Frankfurt at eight forty-nine.

*Do not be on the flight to Paris.*

The message was very clear. He checked with the Air France airline personnel at the gate and told them he would not be flying due to a problem in Nairobi. Because they knew he would be a no-show, they scratched his name off the passenger manifest and didn't announce his name over the intercom. The boarding area was extremely crowded and it was easy to slip onto the other plane, which left twenty minutes before the Paris flight. Kubala's resourcefulness had probably saved his life.

The flight attendant brought his drink and he thanked her by name. Nancy. It was nice to be back with people whose names he could pronounce. No more Bawata Rackisha. No more sadistic police officers with the power and resources to torture and kill innocent people. No more Africa.

The thought of not returning brought on a dichotomy of emotions. He loved Kubala and his family and the village, but hated the corruption and violence that plagued almost every level of life on the continent. Save Them had worked miracles, but its time was done. Leona had saved some of Africa's wildlife from the poachers, but her real gift had been the difference she had made in so many lives. Schools, churches and hospitals now stood where before had been scrubland and dusty plains. Water flowed from deep wells and crops and livestock were well watered and nourished. He had been a part of it, and there was a pride associated with that.

Anderson finished the drink and closed his eyes. The softness of the seat and the steady drone of the plane's engines were sedatives, and he felt himself drifting off. The last thought he had before his world settled into black was that he would call Leona from Frankfurt. Give her the good news. Soon he would be back in the United States and it would be life as normal. That thought felt good.

# 53

Mike Anderson found an open pay phone and closed the glass door, cutting off some of the noise echoing through the Frankfort airport. It was busy, considering it was the middle of the night. Numerous incoming flights were on the arrival board, most originating at a reasonable hour in different time zones on the other side of the Atlantic. It was nine o'clock in DC and Leona would still be up. Anderson entered his calling card and password from memory, then dialed her number and waited.

"Hello?" It was Leona's voice, but she sounded unsure.

"Leona, it's Mike."

"Mike, are you all right? Where are you?"

"I'm fine. I'm in the Frankfurt airport."

"I almost didn't pick up. The caller ID shows some weird area code."

"Pay phone."

"Kubala never called. I didn't know what was happening. I was worried sick about you."

"Yeah, it was a little tense there for a while. Kubala probably didn't call because he was trying to get out of Nairobi before the asshole who kidnapped me got his hands on him."

"Is Kubala okay?"

"I don't know," Anderson said, watching a stream of people walk by on their way to the baggage carousel. "He's pretty resourceful. I imagine he's fine. He'll probably call you when he gets back to Samburu and has his family with him."

"What happened?" she asked.

"Later, Leona. When I'm back in the States. It's a long and ugly story."

"Okay. When are you flying in?"

"No idea. I just got here. I have no money, no credit card, no clothes . . ."

"Naked in the airport. That's interesting."

He chuckled—the first time in weeks. "Funny girl. I need you to wire some money so I can buy a ticket."

"I have a better idea. Go to the airline and book the flight, then call me and I'll put it on my credit card."

"Yeah, that might work," Anderson said, his head swiveling as an attractive woman walked past the booth.

"It has to work, Mike," Leona said. "I need you back in DC. Fast."

He stiffened at the words and her tone. "What's wrong?"

There was a pause, then, "Someone's trying to kill me."

"What the hell? You're kidding, right?"

"No, I'm not."

"Leona, what's going on?" His grip tightened on the handset and he turned away from the concourse and stared at the phone, concentrating on every word.

"It's all tied in to the Coal-Balt income trust conversion. It looks like the president of the company is killing anyone who stands in his way. The company's CEO and he weren't seeing eye to eye on the conversion. He's dead. Then a senator in Utah tabled an antipollution bill that could have cratered the deal. She's dead. Yesterday my restaurant exploded, killing two of my staff, missing Tyler and me by inches. Things are not good over here right now."

"What about the police? Are they protecting you?"

"From whom? We have no idea who's doing this. We suspect that Coal-Balt's president, Derek Swanson, has hired someone, but there's no proof. The forensics crew is still piecing together what caused the explosion at the restaurant. Could have been an accident."

"Are they saying that?"

"No. They're pretty sure it was intentional."

"What are you doing to protect yourself?"

"Nothing, really. I'm not sure what to do. The police call every now and then. They told me to watch for suspicious people. Try to notice faces, and if I see the same one more than once to call them."

"I want you to get out of your house. Right now."

"Where do I go?" she asked, panic rising.

"My place. There's a key under the flowerpot on the stoop."

"That's original."

He ignored the attempt at humor. "Wait until we get this plane ticket sorted out, then leave. Use the time to pack."

"How long will it be before you call back?"

"It's three A.M. over here. It may take me a few minutes to find an airline rep. There should be someone here who can sell me a ticket. I'd guess in a half hour, maybe less."

"Okay, I'll get ready to leave."

"Good. I'll be as quick as I can."

"Thanks."

"You stay safe."

Leona set the phone back in its cradle and stood motionless in the middle of her living room. Darkness was settling in, the streetlights throwing a deepening yellow hue over the trees and cars parked along the curb. Branches swayed slightly in the evening breeze and shadows danced about on her front window. Silence crawled into every corner of the town house, air entering and escaping her lungs as she slowly breathed in and out, the only sound in the rapidly darkening room. A couple walked by on the opposite side of the road, their dog pulling at its leash. A solitary car drove past, then nothing. Just the shadows.

Leona moved to the stairs, her bare feet soundless on the hardwood. She set one foot on the bottom riser, feeling the carpet on her toes. Every sense was heightened, every nerve on edge. She left the light off, not wanting to illuminate herself in case someone was watching. Step after step, she walked up toward her bedroom. She reached the top of the stairs and contemplated turning on the hallway light. This portion of the house wasn't visible from the street. Her hand went to the light switch, then stopped. There was some sort of security with being in a dark space that she knew well. She had walked every inch of her town house a thousand times with the lights off, getting water, using the bathroom, heading downstairs to the kitchen on winter mornings. If anyone else were in the house, they would be at a disadvantage.

She left the lights off and moved ahead, closer to her bedroom door. She glanced in the second and third bedrooms as she passed. They appeared empty, but there were many places to hide if someone were already here, waiting. Leona reached the door to her bedroom and stopped, listening. There was a light scraping sound, but she recognized it as a branch on the tree that brushed against the garden doors leading to the small second-floor balcony off her bedroom. How many times had she lain in bed listening to that sound, vowing to take the pruning shears to it the next morning? She always got busy and forgot about it. She slowly tilted her head, keeping her body behind the wall. The room came into view.

Her bed was made, the duvet smooth, the pillows puffed up and carefully arranged against the wrought-iron headboard.

A half-full glass of water sat next to her alarm clock. The clock's red numbers were now very visible in the almost total darkness. Pale moonlight backlit the tree tucked against the rear of her town house, casting shadows into the room, much like the scene in her living room. She let out a slow and deliberate breath, then relaxed and moved into the room.

She froze.

The outline of a hand, then an arm, followed by the shape of a man's body, materialized outside the garden doors leading to the balcony. The hand reached for the handle and twisted. The door was locked. The intruder slid effortlessly into a position directly centered on the doors and crouched in front of the handle, working on the lock.

Leona backed into the hallway, her breath coming in short gasps. If she had turned on the light, he would have known she was there, would have stayed out of sight. Her eyes would have adjusted to the brightness, allowing him to stay invisible in the low light. She hugged the wall, her mind spinning with a tangle of disjointed thoughts. Did he know she was in the house? Was it the same person who destroyed her restaurant? What to do? She had to escape. Time was of the essence. She had to react, and quickly, before he gained access to her house. She had seconds, not minutes.

She turned and raced down the stairs, her bare feet soundless on the carpet. Once on the hardwood she slowed and ran on the balls of her feet, not wanting to send vibrations through the house. Her car was in the garage, but she bypassed the keys, hanging on a hook on the wall. Opening the garage door was a giveaway to her location, something she was not going to do. She was thinking clearer now, focusing on one thing. Survival. Don't give the intruder anything to work with. No clues to where she was. She reached the front door and silently turned the deadbolt. She felt a presence behind her, then a noise. A loose floorboard. She grabbed the door handle and twisted as she turned to look. He was at the end of the hall, coming toward her fast. Running. Close, very close. She pulled on the door and scrambled onto her stoop, then down the stairs to the street. Her heart was pounding as she frantically looked up and down the road. A car turned on from Fifteenth Street and she jumped into the headlights, waving her arms and screaming. The driver slammed on his brakes and the taillights flashed as he thrust the transmission into park. He opened the door and stepped halfway from his vehicle.

"Are you all right?" he asked. He appeared to be around thirty and solidly built.

"Someone's in my house. A robber. He tried to grab me." She ran to where he stood, fear in her eyes.

The man made a snap decision. "Get in." He motioned to the passenger's door.

Leona slipped into the car and looked back at her condo. The front door clicked shut as she watched. A moment later a shadowy figure appeared in the front window, staring out onto the street. She could see his outline, but no features. Then he was gone. Hardly any motion, a flicker, then nothing.

"Damn." The driver had his cell phone to his ear. "I'm on nine-one-one hold."

"Here." Leona dug in her pocket and retrieved George Harvey's card. "Dial the cell number. He's a cop."

The man took the card and flipped on the overhead light. He dialed and when it rang, handed the phone to Leona. A couple of rings and Harvey answered.

"Detective Harvey, it's Leona Hewitt." She sucked in a deep breath as she motioned for the driver to pull up the street, away from her condo. "He just tried to kill me again."

# 54

Darvin watched the taillights on the car until it turned the corner and disappeared. His mouth was twisted into a sneer and his eyes glowed with anger.

"Dirty, dirty, dirty," he said through clenched teeth. "Goddamn dirty bitch keeps getting away."

He turned back to the room. There was much to do and little time. He picked up the phone and hit redial, then jotted down the number that appeared on the display. The phone had an up-down button and he pushed it, recording every number Leona had called until it reached the bottom of the list. Twenty numbers. He tucked the paper in his pocket and went in search of her mail. He found a stack of unopened envelopes on the narrow table in the hallway and stuffed them in his waistband. Her office was on the main floor, and he tried the computer. The monitor glowed when he touched the mouse. A quick click on Microsoft Outlook and her e-mail program opened. He went to contacts and hit print, rummaging through her drawers while the printer warmed up. Two minutes later he closed the back door behind him and blended into the blackness of Leona's backyard.

His car was a block over on Hampshire, facing toward Dupont Circle. He merged in with the traffic, muttering curses under his breath. Two steps closer and he could have slammed the door and snapped her neck. A couple of seconds had saved her. *Not for long*, he thought. *People are entirely predictable*. Leona Hewitt wouldn't disappoint him. Somewhere in the list of names he had taken off her phone and computer was the person she would turn to for help. He'd know it when he saw it. That was one of his gifts.

Not one that would ever win him a philanthropic award, but a gift nevertheless.

It was getting late and he opted to pull into a small road-side motel and register for the night. No sense driving and getting pulled over, his license scanned into the police computers. The less you gave the cops to work with, the less likely they were to catch you. It was so simple. He checked in, paid cash for the room and spread the printouts from the woman's computer on the bed. The answer was there. He just needed to find it.

Mike Anderson replaced the handset and pushed open the door to the phone booth. The concourse was quiet; most of the people from the arriving flight had already collected their luggage and headed for customs. He walked quickly past the baggage carousels, cleared German customs and immigration, and went in search of a ticket agent. The American airlines were all closed, but Lufthansa was open. The women spoke fluent English and found a flight leaving Frankfort for Washington, DC, at 11:16—a little over eight hours. It was the best he could do.

"I need to call my friend in Washington and have her put the charge through on her credit card. I was robbed yesterday. I lost everything but my passport."

"I'm not sure we can make the long-distance call," the woman said.

"I know my calling-card number. I can bill it to my account."

She thought for a moment, then nodded. "Yes, that's fine." She handed over the phone and Mike dialed Leona's number, then input his calling card number and password when prompted. The phone rang six times, then went to voice mail. He tried again with the same result. Nothing changed on the third attempt. He stood at the counter, the phone in his hand, wondering where she was. Another customer approached the counter and he handed the woman the phone and stepped off to the side.

No more than twenty minutes had passed since they had spoken. She told him she would wait for his call, yet she was gone. Gone or dead. He felt helpless, useless. Trapped on the other side of the world from a friend who needed him. The ticket agent finished with her customer and he stepped back up to the counter.

"Do you have an Internet connection?" he asked. "I can book the ticket through the site I use back in the US. They have my credit card number on file."

"Not here. Our ticketing system is tied into our mainframe computers. But there is an Internet café in the airport. One level up. Use the first set of escalators and turn right."

"Thanks," Mike said. He headed for the café at a brisk pace. Even if he could get a flight, the best he could hope for was to arrive in Washington in twelve to fourteen hours. That would be about midmorning in DC. Monday morning. People heading back to work after the weekend. A normal day for most. Except Leona Hewitt.


George Harvey thanked the motorist for assisting Leona and staying with her until he arrived. They exchanged cards; the man gave Leona a grim smile and wished her well, then drove off. Leona joined the DC detective in his car as a light rain began to fall.

"Nice fellow," Harvey said, twisting about in the seat and leaning his left elbow on the steering wheel. "You're lucky he was driving by."

She nodded, watching the tiny drops of rain splatter against the windshield. "I'm not sure lucky is a good adjective to describe me right now."

"Did you get a look at the guy? Any sort of description?"

She shook her head. "All I saw was an outline. He was on the second-floor balcony and the only light was from the moon, which was directly behind him."

"Nothing that stands out?"

She watched the rain. Random little concentric circles against the glass. A bit like life—countless tiny happenings, all linked together to form one giant patchwork quilt. The ultimate menagerie. "His hair," she said, her voice surprising even herself.

"What about his hair?" the detective asked.

She closed her eyes and tried to piece it together. Why had she said that? What was it about his hair? There was something, but what? The moonlight, reflecting off his shape, his head. It was light, blond almost, and perfect. That was it. Not a strand out of place. Too perfect.

"I've seen his hair somewhere before," she said, turning slowly to face Harvey. "I can't remember where, but I know I've seen him. In fact, I think I've been face-to-face with him."

Harvey was silent for a while, letting her work with the thoughts spinning about her head. When she didn't continue, he said, "Sometimes if you forget about it for a while it comes back to you."

She nodded. "Maybe."

"Have you got somewhere to stay? Some place you know is safe?"

"Yes. I can go to a friend's house. He's in Europe tonight, heading home tomorrow. Ex-cop, in fact."

"DC?" Harvey asked, thinking they may have crossed paths.

"New York."

"You sure you'll be okay at his place tonight?"

"I'll be fine."

A cruiser pulled up beside the unmarked car and two

uniforms exited. Immediately behind them was another un-marked car. Two plainclothes cops walked over to George Harvey's vehicle. Harvey opened his door and turned back to Leona before he got out to meet them.

"I'm going to give these guys the key to your place." He held up the key she had given him a few minutes earlier. "They'll open it up and check things out, then wait while the CSI guys look for fingerprints on the balcony doors. I'll give you a lift to your friend's place, then meet them back at your town house and call you. Let you know what we found."

"Thanks," she said.

"Not a problem." He slid out of the car and the five men stood in a circle, talking and nodding. He handed the key across to one of the detectives and then brushed the rain off his coat and got back in the car. "Where to?"

"Brookland area. On Sargent Road. I think it's a little northeast of Brookland actually. Michigan Park maybe."

"Good part of town. Have a couple of buddies who live in Brookland. Lots of history."

She smiled. He was talkative, trying to take her mind off what had happened. "I think Mike said his house was built in the late thirties."

"Sounds about right." Harvey launched into a tirade about building standards and how tough it was to get a new home built without wanting to kill the builder by the end of the process.

They talked as he drove and by the time they arrived her nerves were settled a bit and she'd stopped shaking. Harvey had her wait in the car while he retrieved the key from un-der the flowerpot and made a thorough search of the house. For a few minutes, she was alone with her thoughts. What had just happened was still like a bad dream. She had been stalked in her own house, inches from the outstretched fingers of a killer. It was absolute insanity. But not everything on her landscape was bleak. At least the Washington police were aware of what was going on and were there for her. Mike Anderson was free and would find his way back to the US. He was resourceful and she wasn't too worried about not being in the house for his call from the airport. He'd find another way to get a ticket home. She had a safe place to stay, and Detective Harvey had been watchful on the drive over that no one was following them. The killer had no link to Mike Anderson's house. She was okay for a few days.

But what about after that? What about her job? She couldn't go in to work. That was the one place where she would be highly visible. There was absolutely no doubt the killer knew where she worked. Hell, every problem—every danger—she faced now, was as a direct result of her job. The damn income trust conversion. She loathed the day Anthony Halladay had walked into her office with the promise of a vice presidency. At that time she hadn't recognized what accepting that file would mean to her. Looking back now, the writing had been in a large, easy-to-read font.

She remembered the moments leading up to her presentation in Halladay's office, to a word that had flashed through her mind: chaos. Her life had every appearance of coming apart at the seams, but in retrospect, that had been mild. Everything had spiraled out of control almost from that time on. It was as if someone were trying to douse the fire with gasoline. Everything but an outright admission by the Salt Lake police that Senator Claire Buxton had been murdered to keep the income trust conversion on track. Her narrow escape from death in the stairwell. Two of her staff killed in the explosion.

And her restaurant? What was going to happen there? She should be contacting her insurance company, meeting them at the site, going over damage estimates and figuring out what her policy would cover. She couldn't do it. There was too great a danger that the killer would be watching. She had to stay away from anything predictable right now. No routine that he could figure out and be waiting.

George Harvey appeared on the porch, closed the front door and made his way back to the car. "All clear inside the house."

"Thanks for coming out tonight," she said. "I don't know what I would have done."

"You're okay, that's what counts. I'm going back to your place to see if the guys found anything. I'll call you on your cell phone."

She nodded and gave him a quick hug. The action surprised him, but as they broke apart he smiled. She walked up the concrete steps to the older brick town house and let herself in the front door, locking it behind her.

Safe, for now.

# 55

The phone rang at eleven-thirty. It was an older model with no call display, and Leona considered not answering it. But who would be calling a half hour before midnight? Mike Anderson was the only person she could think of. She answered, relieved to hear his voice on the other end of the line.

"What happened?" he asked. "Why did you leave your place?"

"Someone was in the house. I barely got out. Detective Harvey, he's the homicide cop I met when I went to the police about Reginald Morgan and Senator Buxton dying, picked me up and drove me to your place."

"Christ, this guy was in your house? Who is this asshole?" He sounded furious.

"I don't know, Mike," she said with a sigh. "The police think he's Derek Swanson's paid killer. Swanson insists he's innocent, says he doesn't know anything, but the cops are trying to find out who the killer is and tie him back to Swanson."

"Why doesn't he stop? He must know the cops are on to him."

"That's what George Harvey is wondering. It doesn't make any sense. The income trust conversion is dead in the water. There's no upside to these guys killing anyone else."

"Something about all this is wrong," Mike said. Years of experience with the police department had taught him that people didn't commit crimes without a motive.

"You still in Frankfurt?"

"Yeah. I managed to get a ticket on Lufthansa. Bastards only had executive class left. You wouldn't believe what the ticket cost me."

"I'll reimburse you," she said.

"It doesn't matter who pays for it. It's robbery."

"When are you back in Washington?"

"Ten-sixteen tomorrow morning. I'll call you when I arrive."

"I'll be here."

"You okay in the house?"

"Sure. This is fine. Thanks for the offer."

"It's okay. The sheets in the guest room are clean."

"Which one is it?"

"Top of the stairs, turn right, first door on the left. The place is hardly the Taj Mahal. It won't take you long to find it." There was a moment of silence, then he said, "There's a gun under the seat cushion on the couch in the living room. It's loaded. Snap off the safety and you're ready to go."

"I don't like guns," she said. "Dad used to encourage me to shoot gophers, but I always missed on purpose."

"If this asshole comes anywhere near you, just point and pull the trigger. Don't miss."

"Guns scare me."

"Guns scare me, too. That doesn't matter. Take it upstairs with you. Tuck it under your pillow."

"You're lucky your cleaning lady never shot herself when she was vacuuming the seat cushions."

"She did. I had to get another one. Turned out to be very bad. The new gal won't touch the windows."

His humor hit the mark and she smiled. "See you about noon tomorrow."

"Yup."

Leona walked slowly through the living room to the kitchen. Mike Anderson's house was early-bachelor, with no sense of décor. The walls were pale green and the carpets teal. Wood paneling covered one wall, and his commendations from the time he spent on the force hung randomly against the dark wood. The kitchen was worse, with flowered wallpaper and patterned linoleum that clashed with the harvest gold appliances. She grimaced as she opened the fridge, expecting mold monsters. It was empty except for a six-pack of beer and a tub of margarine. She closed the door and sat at the kitchen table, staring at the opposite wall. A solitary picture hung in the space. It looked small, silly almost. Leona focused on the people. Mike and his ex-wife, both smiling. Better times. They were holding hands and there was a sparkle in his eyes. How could he forgive her—still love her like he did? She cheated on him, slept with another man. Yet he'd take her back in a minute.

Her father's face drifted through her subconscious. Why couldn't she just accept the man as he was? What stopped her from opening her heart? He was a good man, hardworking and intelligent. Funny sometimes. Not often—mostly he was businesslike and gruff. Maybe that was the key. They were different from the most basic chromosomes outward. She was creative, giving, and acted on what her heart told her was right. He was money and material things. Accepting the fundamental differences between them was the key. Could she do it? She had no idea.

Leona walked into the living room and stared at the couch. Aside from being butt ugly, it looked normal enough. She tentatively lifted the middle cushion. A section of the material was cut away and a thin wooden box jammed between the metal coils. She pulled it out and opened it, revealing a revolver. She touched it. The metal was cold. She wrapped her hand around the handle and lifted. It was heavier than she expected. The bullets were visible, each sitting in its chamber like little torpedoes loaded in their tubes and ready to fire. She placed her thumb on the hammer and cocked the gun. It made a clicking sound, a low noise in the quiet room that didn't carry very far. She carefully released the hammer and let it settle back in its housing. The gun hung from her hand, pointing at the floor.

Is this what her life had come to? Standing in a strange house, holding a gun. Waiting for a hired killer to track her down and murder her. Even as a dream, this would be a good one. Too bad it was real.

# 56

Darvin hated the room. It reeked of hotel sex.

Not present-time sex, but of the hundreds of times men and women had sweated and cum all over each other on the bed. He could smell it, like a festering sore on rotting flesh. Six hours in the room and he was long past the point of thinking clearly. He closed his eyes and saw women bent over the bed, men behind them, hammering their weapons

into hot, willing pussies. He forced his eyes open, hating
every graphic image.

At six o'clock, Darvin got up and showered. His penis
hung like a limp rag and he tried to make it hard by thinking of the one time he'd put it in a woman. Nothing. He
finished washing and turned off the water. As he rubbed the
towel over his skin he remembered slicing her neck open
and watching her gasp for air. Her arms flailing about as she
died, and her body going slack as he ejaculated inside her.
He glanced down. His manhood was fully erect.

"Mother wouldn't have liked her," he said as he jerked off.
"She was so dirty." He moaned as he climaxed, then pulled
on his underwear and walked back into the bedroom. The
smells were still overpowering and he felt nauseous.

It took him less than five minutes to pack and leave the
room. The sun was up and burning off the morning haze.
He drove to the outskirts of the city before stopping at a
roadside diner for breakfast. He spread the papers from
Leona Hewitt's town house on the table as he picked at his
bacon and eggs. The last incoming call was from a European
number. The country code indicated the call had originated
in Germany, and less than twenty minutes before he pulled it
off her phone. He scanned down the other nineteen numbers on the list. Seven were the same, and he checked the
phone book for the number to her restaurant. It matched.
He scratched them off the list. Two other entries were the
same and he recognized the number—the main line to the
Washington Police Department. The calls that had tied
Derek Swanson to the murders of Reginald Morgan and
Senator Claire Buxton. Smart girl, this Leona Hewitt.

He drew a line through another five numbers, all from
her office at DC Trust. Her support staff calling her to
check on things. One was from a 1–866 number—probably

some telemarketing firm. That left four numbers, all different. She didn't use her home phone all that often, and the oldest recorded number went back a full month to July 6. Darvin circled the four remaining numbers and dialed out on his cell phone. A man's voice answered.

"Greg, it's Darvin."

"Oh, you," the voice went up an octave. "Where have you been? You disappeared. Gone in the morning. I was devastated."

"Get over it," Darvin said icily. "Listen, I need a favor."

"If I didn't know better, I'd think you were using me." There was a teasing tone to the voice.

Darvin ignored the flirting. "Can you run four numbers through your system and get me names and addresses?"

"When I get to the office. I'm at home right now."

"Sometime today would be good."

"Just because I work for the phone company doesn't mean I have nothing to do."

"How long will it take you to pull four numbers off your computer?" Darvin wanted to leap through the phone line and strangle the talker.

"I can do it today. I was just teasing. Why are you so abrupt? It doesn't suit you."

"Sorry. I'm busy. I don't mean to be rude."

"That's okay. What are the numbers?"

Darvin recited the phone numbers and hung up. He had other things to do today. Important things. It was time to close a chapter of his life. One that should have been closed years ago. He paid the waitress and left her a decent tip for keeping his coffee topped up. A gas station was attached to one side of the diner and he pulled up to the pump and filled the car. He had a three-hour drive ahead of him. The road was familiar and the weather was nice. Perfect day for an outing.

In fact, it was a perfect day to take care of something that had been burning inside him for over thirty years.

Leona woke and looked about the room, wondering where she was. It took a few seconds, then she remembered. Mike Anderson's guest room. She glanced at the alarm clock on the night table. Seven-twenty. She rolled out of bed and headed for the bathroom.

The shower invigorated her and twenty minutes later she was wide-awake. At eight she called the office and asked for Anthony Halladay. The receptionist rerouted the call to his private line.

"Leona," Halladay said. "What can I do for you?"

"I won't be in today," she said. "Something's come up. I need to take a few days off."

"What's wrong? Is this to do with Derek Swanson—with what you told me yesterday?" the CEO asked.

"Yes. It's related. I'd rather not say any more. I need some time off. You can mark it down as holidays."

"Usually we get some advance notice."

"Sorry, not this time."

"When will you be back?"

"Next week." It was lip service. She had no idea when it would be safe for her to return.

"Is there anything I can do?"

"No, I don't think so. I've got to go. I'll see you next Monday."

"Okay." He sounded hesitant, confused.

She set the phone back in its cradle and stiffened. There was a noise from the front of the house. Boards squeaking under weight. Someone was on the porch. She peeked around the door frame between the kitchen and the living room. The door handle was turning and she could see a shape outlined through the window in the upper half of the door. The gun—it was upstairs in the bedroom and impossible to retrieve in time. She raced across the kitchen to the butcher's block on the counter and pulled out the largest knife. The blade was ten inches and the edge looked clean and recently sharpened. She moved back toward the door as the sound of footsteps echoed through the living room. The knife was at chest level, horizontal, ready to slash across the chest area. Even if he could get his hands up, she'd cut his arms, try to disarm him if he had a weapon.

Leona reached the doorway as the man entered. The knife flashed forward, then she pulled back. It sliced harmlessly through the air. He yelled and took a sluggish step back, banging into the far side of the doorjamb and tumbling to the floor. He lay there, staring wide-eyed at her.

"Sorry," she said, letting the knife fall to her side.

"Who are you?" He was at least sixty-five, with thinning gray hair and dressed in light green work pants and a plaid shirt. He looked terrified.

"Who am I? Who are you?" Leona asked.

"John Fisher. Mike's neighbor. I come in to check the place every day."

"Leona. I'm Mike's boss. Sort of."

"Oh, the elephant charity lady." He leaned on one hand and pushed up onto his knees, then stood up. "What's with the knife?"

"I didn't expect anyone. You scared me."

"Ditto," he said. Fisher looked around and shrugged. "Everything looks okay."

She nodded. "It's fine. Thanks for checking in."

"Sure. When will Mike be back home?"

"A couple of hours."

"Oh, he's back today."

"Yes. I'm killing a bit of time, waiting for him."

"Okay." Fisher walked to the front door. He gave her a final smile and left, closing the door behind him.

Quiet settled in again. Leona shuffled to the couch and dropped onto the cushion. She looked down at the knife, dangling from her hand. Upstairs, under the pillow she'd slept on, was a loaded gun. It was Monday morning and she had called in because a killer might be watching her office. Not exactly a normal start to a workweek.

Anthony Halladay sat at his desk, staring out the window at the surrounding buildings. Sun glinted off the reflective glass across the street. How many times had he looked at those windows, thinking of the mundane lives of the office drones who worked there? Now, that anonymity looked pretty good. He was at the top, poised to crash. There would be no stopping it now. If Leona Hewitt was too scared to show up for work, Swanson's man was still after her. Derek hadn't been able to reel him in.

Leona Hewitt was not going to survive.

When she died, the DC homicide police would be all over the case. His connection back to Derek Swanson would eventually be uncovered. He was ruined. Financially, he would survive, but socially, he would be a pariah. Shunned, the one left standing when the music stopped.

He thought of the gun in his home safe. The easy way out. Maybe, but not yet. He'd wait until Leona was dead and the police were at the door.

## 57

"Anything happen last night?" George Harvey asked.

The detective, a junior in the department, shook his head. "All quiet. Lights went out about midnight and there was no activity. The next-door neighbor went in through the front door about ten minutes after eight this morning. He had a key. Came out five minutes later."

"Checking on the place?"

"I'd say."

"Thanks for staking it out overnight," Harvey said. "Submit the overtime hours. I'll make sure it gets through."

"Sure. I'm going home to sleep for a couple of hours. I'll be back in after lunch."

"See you then."

Harvey leaned back in his chair, his hands cupped around the crown of his head, fingers interlocked. He hadn't told Leona Hewitt a man was watching Mike Anderson's house for good reason. He wanted her alert, not dropping her guard because she felt protected. It was impossible for one man to watch the front and rear of the house, but getting one of his detectives on short notice for an unauthorized surveillance had been tough. Two would have been impossible.

Leona's friend, the ex–New York cop, was due home today. That took some of the pressure off his department. If he were in town and close to her, the killer would have to deal with him. It was almost like having one of his men shadowing her, but without the cost.

He tipped forward, unclasped his hands and dialed the number Leona had given him. She answered on the second ring, her voice uncertain.

"It's George Harvey," he said. "I wanted to follow up on what we found at your house last night."

"Anything to identify him?" she asked.

"No. No fingerprints on the upper balcony doors and no fingerprints on your telephone. Including yours. It was wiped clean. You don't have a habit of wiping off your telephone after you use it, do you?"

"No."

"I didn't think so."

"What does that mean? That he wiped off my telephone?"

"Your phone holds the last twenty incoming numbers. I suspect he touched the buttons necessary to pull those numbers off your phone, then wiped it off to erase his prints."

"Why would he do that?"

"Anyone who called you, aside from telemarketers, know you. If he could trace their numbers, he may get your location. Has your friend where you're staying called you recently?"

"Not in the last month. He's been in Africa since the second week in July." She was about to tell him that her home phone wasn't a busy line as most of her calls came to her cell phone, but he was already talking.

"That's good. We're probably okay then." He paused for a moment, then asked, "When is your friend arriving?"

"He should be here by noon."

"Call me when he gets there. I'll feel better knowing he's with you."

"Sure. Thanks, Detective Harvey. I appreciate your concern."

"You're welcome."

A CSI tech entered the room as he replaced the phone. The midthirties woman was carrying a thin folder and wearing a puzzled expression. Her name was Arlene, and she worked a lot of the homicide cases. Harvey liked and re-spected her.

"What's that?" he asked.

"Results of the two DNA samples." She flipped open the file. "Derek Swanson's and the blood traces in the van that Claire Buxton was driving." She handed him two sheets of paper. "Take a look at this."

He took the papers and scanned the contents. After twenty seconds, he looked up at her. "Are you sure this is right?"

She nodded. "When we saw the results, we ran the entire analysis again. There is no error."

"This is incredible."

She nodded again. "Very."

Mike Anderson cleared customs and headed for the closest phone. He dialed his home number and waited. When Leona picked up, he breathed a quick sigh of relief.

"You made it through the night okay?"

"I did. A little glitch in the morning when John showed up. I almost ran him through with one of your knives."

"Oh, shit, I forgot about him. He okay?"

"Yeah. What about me? I could have been killed."

"You could have . . ." Silence, then, "Funny. Glad you've still got your sense of humor."

"You at the airport?"

"Yup. I'm going to grab a cab. I'll be at the house in about an hour."

"See you then. Make sure you knock. I have a knife in one hand and a loaded gun in the other."

"My kind of gal."

"You wish." She set the phone down and collapsed back into the armchair. Her gaze was angled up, toward the ceil-ing and she focused on the light fixture in the foyer. It was a chandelier-style piece with little dangly crystal balls that refracted the light and threw faded spectrums across the upper walls. Hideous was a mild word for it.

"If I get out of this alive," Leona muttered under her breath to no one. "I'm going to redecorate this place."

# 58

Darvin pulled up in front of Derek Swanson's house midafternoon. Traffic was moving well and he had made good time on the 165-mile trek from Washington to Morgantown. Swanson's Porsche sat in the driveway. That was good, although he would have waited for the man to return home from work if necessary. He pulled up beside the car and walked to the front door. A quick touch on the doorbell set the chimes in motion. He could hear them through the thick, wood door. After about thirty seconds there was a noise from inside the house, then the door swung open. Derek Swanson stood in the doorway, his cell phone attached to his ear. Shock registered on his face, then anger.

"I've got to go," he said into the phone. He snapped it shut and slipped it in his pocket. "What the hell are you doing here?"

"Killing you," Darvin said, shoving Swanson back into the house. A gun appeared in his hand, and he flipped the safety off and pushed the end of the barrel against Swanson's head. "But not quite yet."

They were inches apart and Darvin could smell the fear. He loved the odor—thrived on it. He had yet to kill a person up close who didn't reek of fear just before they died.

"Move." He pushed the gun against Swanson's head so hard it left a red circle when the other man broke away and walked backward into the house. Darvin spun Swanson around and lowered the gun to his back. "The kitchen."

They walked through the formal dining room to the kitchen; an open expanse with a central island and walls of cabinetry. Stainless-steel appliances were tucked into the maple cabinets and the granite countertops reflected the mid-day sun pouring in the windows.

"I'm thirsty," Darvin said, leaning against the island. "Get me something to drink." He waited a second, then added, "Please."

Derek Swanson's hands were shaking as he opened the fridge and took out a pitcher of lemonade. He set it on the counter, removed a glass from one of the upper cabinets and poured. He held it out but Darvin shook his head.

"Set it on the counter and back off. And get another glass down while you're there. I don't like to drink alone."

"It's lemonade, not alcohol."

"I don't care. Pour a glass for yourself."

Swanson complied, then backed off a few feet. Darvin kept the gun leveled and pointing at the other man as he walked over to the counter. He stared down at the two glasses of lemonade for a few seconds, then opened the cabinet and took out another glass. He set it on the counter and pushed. It slid along the smooth surface to Swanson.

"Put some ice in the glass and slide it back," Darvin said.

Swanson turned and filled the glass from the ice dispenser on the front of the fridge, then pushed it along the counter to the killer. Darvin tipped the glass and added ice to both glasses. He took a sip from his and backed off to the island, glass in one hand, gun in the other.

"Drink your lemonade," he said.

"What do you want with me?" Swanson took a couple of steps and picked up the glass. "Why don't you go away?"

"What do I want with you?" Darvin repeated. "That's a good question. I don't think I'm quite ready to answer it yet. But I can tell you why I won't go away." He sipped the lemonade and puckered his lips. "Not enough sugar, Derek."

"You don't have to drink it." Swanson downed a third of his glass in one draught. His throat was suddenly dry.

"You irritate me. That's part of the reason why I'm not leaving. You think that because you have money, you can do whatever the hell you want. *Things aren't going well with the trust conversion—I think I'll have someone murdered.* That kind of thinking pisses people off. Maybe not everyone, but it pisses me off, and right now, that's what counts."

"I never asked you to kill Senator Buxton or Leona Hewitt. You undertook that all on your own."

"Are you saying that independent thinking is bad? You were poised to make a quick fifty million dollars. I saw an opportunity to help make that happen and I went for it. In your business they call that entrepreneurship. People are rewarded for that sort of thinking."

"I produce electricity. You murder people. There's a difference." Swanson took another drink, then said, "Stop killing people. There's nothing to gain from it."

Darvin wagged the gun at Swanson. "Why don't you stop thinking like an executive? Not everything is based on the bottom line. Money isn't always the motivator."

"Why else would you kill someone, Darvin?" Swanson asked. "Rage, jealousy, hate might work, but Leona Hewitt is none of those to you. There's no upside financially and there is no other reason to want her dead. Leave her alone."

Darvin shook his head. "Pride. You forgot pride."

"What's pride got to do with this?" He finished the lemonade and set the empty glass on the counter.

"I have never taken on an assignment and not completed it."

Swanson's mouth dropped open. "What? You're going to kill an innocent person to keep your record of consecutive kills intact? Are you insane?"

Darvin's eyes clouded over and his voice changed pitch—deeper, and the words were clipped, his mouth contorting into a sneer as he spoke. "You can't save it. No one can save it."

Swanson instinctively backed away from his unwelcome visitor. "*It?* You called her *it*. What the fuck is that all about? Serial killers talk like that." Swanson grabbed the counter and ran his free hand across his forehead. "Holy shit, what's going on?" His knees buckled and he fell to the floor. He tried to get his hand out in time to protect his face. He failed and smashed headfirst onto the tiles.

Darvin hooked his foot under Swanson's chest and rolled him over on his back. "Gamma-Hydroxybutyric acid. GHB as it's often called," he said. "Date-rape drug. Totally incapacitates you by depressing your cerebral metabolism. Wondering how I did it? When you got the ice. Only took a second to drop it in your drink. Shaking the ice into your lemonade helped mix it. Christ, you really are dumb. Dumb and helpless." His voice had returned to normal, but his eyes burned with madness.

Darvin pulled a pair of handcuffs from his pocket, gathered Swanson's arms behind his back and snapped the cuffs over the prone man's wrists. Then he hoisted the dead weight over his shoulder in a fireman's carry and trudged out to his car. He dumped Swanson in the front seat and stretched the seat belt across his chest and snapped the buckle shut. The last thing he needed was an overzealous state trooper stopping him because his passenger didn't have his seat belt on. He returned to the house, spent five minutes wiping down any surfaces he had touched, then locked the front door and slid behind the wheel.

"Anyone need to use the facilities before we leave?" he asked, looking over at Swanson. He laughed at the blank expression. "No? Okay, but it's a long drive and I'm not stopping."

He started the car and pulled out of Swanson's private drive, humming an Eagles tune.

# 59

There was a soft knock on the door, then the sound of a key in the lock. A moment later Mike Anderson appeared in the open doorway. He closed the door behind him and grinned at the sight of Leona Hewitt sitting on the couch with a gun in her lap.

"Nice touch," he said, nodding toward the gun.

"My newest best friend," she said, rising and walking over to meet him. She wrapped her arms around her friend and they hugged. When they finally broke apart, she said, "What happened to your face?"

"A guy named Bawata Rackisha happened to me." He took ten minutes to recount the story of kidnap and neglect in the dank cell, sparing her a lot of the more horrific details.

"You ate bugs?" Leona asked.

He laughed. "Lots. They're tasty. Kind of crunchy, too. Filled with protein."

"That's awful."

His face turned serious. "It kept me alive, Leona."

She nodded. "You're probably going to want some sort of a bonus for this. Danger pay."

The light returned to his eyes and he smiled. "Whatever you're offering, I'm taking." He leaned back on the couch. "What about you? Give me the whole story."

Leona continued the story from the last time they had spoken face-to-face, in Kinkeads, in mid-July. She wrapped it up with the attempt on her life the previous evening.

"The police think this guy is tied in with Derek Swanson, the president of the company that was doing this conversion thing?"

"Yes."

"But you've already given your boss the thumbs-down. It's a done deal. There's no way this thing is moving ahead."

"No, it's over."

"This makes no sense at all." He shook his head.

The phone rang and Mike walked over and picked up. He said hello, listened for a minute, then held the phone out. "It's for you. George Harvey."

"Is that your friend?" Harvey asked when she answered.

"Yes, he's back from Africa."

"Good. Listen, I need to speak with you. Are you going to be there for a while?"

"I'm not going anywhere. Are you coming over now?"

"Soon. I have one other thing to take care of on another case. Give me about forty minutes plus the drive. Less than an hour and a half."

"What's this about?" she asked.

"I'll tell you when I see you."

"Okay." She hung up and turned to Mike. "This keeps getting weirder. The detective handling the case is coming over."

"Did he tell you why?"

"No."

"Hmm, that's not good."

"Why not?"

"We cops are a secretive breed. Mundane things, we use the telephone. The zingers get a house call."

"What now?" Leona asked. "What the hell else could go wrong?"

"Don't tempt the fates," Mike said seriously. "You're still alive. Worst-case scenario is that changes."

# 60

Darvin stayed on the main highway from Morgantown to Hancock, a small border town sandwiched between Pennsylvania, Maryland and West Virginia. Then he turned south on a secondary road that sliced through the heavily wooded foothills encircling the northern fringe of the Appalachian Mountains. He was close to the boundary of Shenandoah National Park when his cell phone rang. It was Greg Stiles, his connection at the phone company.

"I have names and addresses for the numbers you gave me," he said.

"Well done. What are they?"

Greg repeated the four numbers, then a name and address for each one. Darvin scratched the information down on a piece of paper while he drove. He thanked his friend, promised to call soon and killed the connection. He glanced at the passenger's seat where Derek Swanson was sitting, watching him.

"You seem more coherent now, awake almost. But you don't have any control over your muscles, do you? Neat drug. One of my favorites." He looked back to the road. "We're almost there. Forty-five minutes, an hour tops."

Darvin alternated his attention between the road and the list of names. One of them, Mike Anderson, rang a bell, but he couldn't remember why. He had an entire file on Leona Hewitt at his house. Maybe when he got home something would click. It usually did. Patience and organization were two important keys to doing well in the assassination business. He respected both, and gave them due diligence. As a result, not much got by him. If he was having a feeling about Mike Anderson, it was for a good reason. He needed to pull the information in his file and look for the connection. It was there. He knew it.

Traffic was light and he made good time on the secondary roads through Fauquier and Culpepper Counties. At Jeffersonton he cut south for eight miles, then turned east onto Oak Shade Road. The fourth drive on the south side of the road was mostly obscured by thick hickory and black oak, and he slowed and turned in.

"Almost home," he said as the car bounced up the gravel access road. The house came into view, a white clapboard structure with dark shutters. The grounds were landscaped, but poorly kept, with weeds growing in the flower beds and patches of brown on the grassy areas. Paint was peeling and the edges of the shingles were beginning to curl. A porch ran across the entire front of the house, a handful of the railing slats cracked or broken. Darvin pulled up and stopped a few feet from the wooden stairs leading to the main entrance. He turned off the ignition and an instant silence settled over the scene.

"Let's get you comfy, shall we?" He walked around to the passenger's door and dragged Swanson out by his shirt. Swanson cleared the seat and crashed to the ground on his back. Darvin let him hit the gravel hard. "Whoops," he said, smiling.

"You fucking psychopath." Swanson labored with every syllable.

"Ahh, you're waking up," Darvin said. "That could be dangerous." He picked up a rock the size of his fist and smashed it into the side of Swanson's head. Swanson's body went limp.

Darvin dragged him up the stairs, across the porch and

over the threshold. He closed the door, shrouding the foyer in darkness despite the clear skies and sun almost directly overhead. A trickle of blood ran from a cut on Swanson's head and pooled on the hardwood as Darvin rummaged about in the kitchen for something to drink. He returned to the foyer and hoisted the inert body up the staircase and down the hall to one of the bedrooms. Inside, he dumped Swanson into a solid wood chair that was bolted to the floor and lashed him securely to the seat and arms. Then he sat in a recliner facing the unconscious man and waited.

When Swanson first woke he was groggy and rocked his head back and forth, obviously in agony from the pain shooting through his brain. Darvin watched him, a wry smile on his face. After ten minutes of watching Swanson drift in and out of consciousness, Darvin took a plastic bottle of water and shot a spray directly in the man's face. He sputtered and gasped a few times, his eyes wide open and filled with loathing.

"Where am I?" he asked, his voice like acid.

"Always the CEO," Darvin said, leaning back in the recliner and dropping the empty water bottle to the floor. "Always the one in charge."

"You have no idea how far over the line you are," Swanson said. "You can't kidnap people and get away with it."

"Oh, this is much worse than kidnapping. I think you know that," Darvin said. He leaned close to Swanson and whispered, "It would be murder if I were to kill you."

Swanson shook his head, water flying from his hair. His voice was still strong but his eyes had lost their defiance. "If you want money, I'll get it for you."

Darvin smiled. "I don't need money. It's the one thing I have plenty of. What I need is a little respect."

Swanson stared at him for a few seconds, speechless, then looked away. The room was large for a bedroom, twenty feet square. The floors were hardwood and the walls covered with embossed wallpaper. Aside from the perfunctory bed, night table and armoire, one other piece of furniture, oddly shaped and covered with a white drop cloth, sat about six feet from his chair. There was a closet set into one wall and a window seat in the gable that protruded into the roofline. The blinds were drawn and the view was of green fields, treetops and a gravel road bordered by a line of trees. They were in a farmhouse, and the scenery reminded him of North Virginia.

"All right. Respect. Let's work on that."

Darvin shook his head. "You can't just work on it, Derek. It's something you have or you don't. Like class. Some people have class. They may not have a lot of money, but they have class. It's in the way they move—how they walk and their body language. Others have a real problem with it. They may have money, but they don't have class. Never will. You know the old adage—you can take the girl out of the trailer, but you can't take the trailer out of the girl. It's so true."

"What's your point?" Swanson asked.

"Do you think class is hereditary?" Darvin asked.

"I really wouldn't know."

"See, you think you have class. I don't. You also have arrogance and a host of other rotten traits, but that's a whole different program on Dr. Phil. We need to stay focused."

"I'm flattered," Swanson said facetiously. "But I still don't see what this has to do with anything."

Darvin's eyes flashed with anger. "It has everything to do with why I kill people. With why I have no friends. With why I'm borderline psychotic."

"At least you can admit you have mental problems."

"Influenced entirely by environment," Darvin said, regaining his composure.

"Not genetics," Swanson said.

"No."

"You sound very sure of yourself."

"I am. You see," he leaned close to his captive, only a couple of inches separating their faces, "you're my brother."

Absolute silence descended on the room. Neither man moved nor spoke. Tiny specks of dust floated between them, highlighted by the sun pouring in through the window. Darvin slowly pulled away, his eyes still locked on Swanson's.

"Bullshit," Swanson finally said. "Absolute bullshit. I don't have a brother."

"Yes, you do. A younger brother. Ever notice how similar our names are? Derek—Darvin. Mom and Dad having a little fun." Darvin pulled a rickety wood chair close to Swanson and sat so they were facing each other. "Would you like to know the story?"

"Sure, why not."

"Your mother and father were human garbage. Mom was the most dominant bitch with a vagina on the planet. Dad was a feeble excuse for a man. He couldn't stand up to her. She beat him with yardsticks, electrical appliance cords, even a sock filled with three or four baseballs. I remember once he tried to tell her no, and she beat him so bad they had to hospitalize him for almost two weeks. She finally killed him. Hit him too hard."

"She murdered him?"

Darvin nodded. "While I watched. Whacked him with a bowling pin. Then she dumped his body in the bathtub and told the police he fell. They believed her. The dumb bastards actually believed her. They're useless. The police are completely useless."

Swanson couldn't help smiling. "A bowling pin. This just keeps getting better."

Darvin's face turned dark. "Don't mock me, Derek. Or I'll kill you before you hear the whole story."

Swanson shook his head vigorously. "But you never found

*me*. I found *you* when I went looking for someone to kill the union rep."

Darvin smiled. "That's exactly what I wanted you to think. I'll get to that in a minute. Anyway, our parents had a kid—you—and they decided they were too young and too fucked-up to raise you properly. So they gave you up for adoption. They knew who adopted you and watched as you grew up. Then, when they were able to properly raise a child, they had me. But there was a slight problem."

"What was that?"

"They were still completely fucked-up. Dad worked at the bowling alley, repairing the machines and pins. Mom was a waitress in a crappy little diner on the highway a block from the shit hole I grew up in. Both were alcoholic, Mom was violent, Dad was a sissy, and they both gambled. Growing up in that house was a nightmare that you can't even begin to imagine. I'm not especially fond of women, courtesy of the queen bitch. And I hate weak men. I don't like overly strong men, either. In fact, there are very few people I actually like. But while I was being subjected to a hideously cruel childhood, you were having a great life. A membership to the country club and money to burn. Nothing but the finest college for your sorry ass. Polo. You played polo for Christ's sake. What the hell is polo? Riding around on a horse hitting a ball. How fucking inane is that? Your family was loving and wealthy, ready to hand you whatever you needed to succeed in life. Everything was given to you. Everything. Me, I got nothing."

"Explains the bitterness," Derek said, wondering where the man professing to be his brother was going with this.

"So I decided to destroy you. Slowly and methodically. To pull you apart like a bug—a wing here, a leg there. The first thing I needed to do was to get in your life. It was so easy. Remember the redhead at the bar in Clarksburg? I paid her to sleep with you. She was a dirty little whore, Derek. And you screwed her. How many times? How many times, Derek?"

Swanson shook his head. "I don't know. It was a long time ago."

"Sixty-seven. Sixty-seven times, you fucker. At five hundred dollars a shot, that was over thirty thousand dollars. But it was money well spent. She connected me to you. And I needed to be there for you when you wanted someone roughed up. But you went even further than I thought you would. You hired me to kill the union guy. Never thought you had it in you."

"You sick bastard. You paid her?"

Darvin laughed, a strange chortle that echoed about the room. "You should have been in jail years ago, you prick. I dumped the body, then waited a few days, suited up in some scuba gear and untied the rope that attached the guy's body to the concrete I used to weigh him down. Man, he was gross. Underwater for a couple of weeks really does a number on a body."

"You unfastened the rope so he'd float to the surface? So the police could tie the murder back to me?"

"Yup. But they messed up the investigation so bad they never managed to connect it back to you. Dumb asses. I gave them everything they needed to convict you, but they were too stupid."

Swanson swallowed hard. He said, "I have to go to the bathroom."

"So go."

"Untie me."

"Fuck you. Go in your pants."

Swanson was trembling with fear. "Darvin, I'm your brother. The only family you have left. If I'd known, I would have come for you. Saved you. I didn't know. How could I?"

"You would have saved me," Darvin sneered. "You would have left your life of privilege to help a worthless speck of trailer trash. I don't think so."

Swanson took a couple of deep breaths. "You've had it tough. I can fix that. Whatever you want, just ask and I'll make it happen."

Darvin crossed his right leg over his left and leaned back in the wobbly chair. "All right. I want my childhood back. I want a normal life growing up. I want what you had."

Sweat beaded on the CEO's forehead. "You know I can't give you that," he said, his voice a whisper.

"Then I guess you can't make it happen." Darvin rose and walked to an antique dresser pushed up against an interior wall. He opened a drawer and withdrew a black satchel, then set it on top of the piece of worn furniture and opened the lid. He lifted two knives and held them up, one in each hand, the sun reflecting off the steel. He walked back toward Swanson. "So now we do it my way."

The odor of urine filled the room.

"I've wanted to watch you suffer for so long. I couldn't wait any longer. I couldn't wait for the police to arrest you for Morgan or Buxton's murder. So here we are. You and I, bro."

"Darvin, don't do this."

"Oh, I almost forgot." Darvin set the knives down on his chair and walked the short distance to where the drop sheet covered the piece of furniture. "Before we begin, I'd like you to meet someone."

He pulled back the sheet. A dried corpse sat in the wheelchair, bony elbows resting on the arms. The empty sockets were staring directly at Derek Swanson, the mouth twisted in a grotesque scream. Lifeless lips were pulled back and yellow teeth hung from the jawbone.

"Say hello to your mother," Darvin said.

# 61

"He didn't say what he wants?" Mike asked, as the doorbell sounded.

Leona shook her head. "Not a word. Just that he wanted to meet."

Mike answered the door and introduced himself to the man on the stoop. They returned to the front room and George Harvey sat on the couch next to Leona.

"We've had a bit of a break on Claire Buxton's case," he said.

"I thought Claire Buxton died in Utah," Mike interjected. "Strange you should be working the case."

Harvey nodded, then spoke directly to Mike Anderson, bringing him up to speed on the file. "The Salt Lake CSI team found some blood in the van that didn't belong to the senator or her children. On a long shot, we got court approval for a sample of Derek Swanson's DNA. We never expected them to match."

"Was it his DNA in Buxton's van?" Leona asked.

Harvey shook his head. "No, but the two samples were very similar. Far too close to be random." He asked Leona, "Do you know anything about DNA testing?"

"Not really. What I've seen on television."

"Each of our cells contains a complete strand of our DNA, with the exception of platelets and red blood cells. But blood can still be used as a DNA fingerprint by typing the white blood cells. The Utah police used those cells and came up with a set of thirteen regions, or markers as we call them. We did the same with Derek Swanson's DNA sample. Then we compared the two."

"And . . ." Leona said, leaning forward.

"Think of the thirteen markers as lottery balls. To match one out of thirteen is reasonable. Two is still within reason. Three is starting to push the limits of probability. Four and above is beyond random chance. We had a match on nine of thirteen."

"Nine?" Leona said. "But if it were the same person, wouldn't all thirteen match?"

Harvey nodded. "Allowing for some contamination in the testing, the match would be very close to thirteen. Nine is low for an exact match, but too high to be random."

"Whoever was at the van was related to Derek Swanson," Mike Anderson said. "Father, brother, sister—someone from the same gene pool."

"That's what we think," the DC detective said.

"Any idea who this person is?"

"We're checking into it. Swanson has no brothers or sisters. At least that's what we initially thought. Then we found something interesting." He paused for a moment. "Derek Swanson is adopted. His parents couldn't have children."

"Have you found his biological parents?" Mike asked.

Harvey shook his head. "Not yet, but I have a team working on it. I suspect we'll know sometime today who they are."

"So if Derek Swanson has a brother or sister, they could be the killer," Leona said.

"That's what we're thinking."

"So why would this person, this sibling, still want to kill Leona?" Mike asked. "Taking her out of the picture isn't going to resurrect the income trust conversion."

"Maybe they still think the deal is on," Harvey said without conviction.

Leona shook her head. "No way. Swanson has an inside man at the bank. He knows the deal is dead."

"Then there has to be some sort of motivation. Or he would stop."

"Maybe he's crazy," Leona said. "Nothing would surprise me now."

"Whoever is killing these people is far from crazy," Harvey said. "Disturbed, sick, demented, without empathy, dangerous—but not crazy. Nutcases don't plan and implement murders with this degree of precision."

"Why would he want Leona dead?" Mike asked, thinking out loud. "Money is out. Revenge perhaps?"

"Revenge?"

"He thinks you've wronged him—or Swanson."

They talked in circles for the better part of an hour, no further ahead when they finally wrapped up. Mike and Leona stood on the front stoop with the detective and shook hands.

"You won't let her out of your sight until we get this guy?" Harvey said.

"Only if she needs to use the ladies' room," Mike said.

"Good. I'll keep you in the loop."

Mike and Leona returned to the house and he put on some coffee. They sat at the kitchen table talking, mostly about Africa. Save Them had been such a bright light in a country that needed illumination. Now it was gone, courtesy of one man's greed. But that was Africa, where the ones at the top of the food chain ruined lives on the lower rungs. So many innocent and decent people victimized by so few.

"What will you do about the restaurant?" Mike asked, returning the conversation to more local geography.

She shrugged. "I have to talk with the insurance adjusters. If they hedge on paying out I'm finished. I need the money to rebuild."

"Why wouldn't they pay?"

"Someone was trying to kill me when they blew up the place. Not exactly the kind of thing that's covered under clause five, subparagraph nine."

"I suppose not."

Leona shook her head. Tyler was so happy when she offered him part of the business. He was young and eager, and she knew the relationship would pay off. Now it was all in jeopardy of disappearing. She closed her eyes and envisioned the dining room before the explosion. Everything in its place—knives and forks carefully positioned by the plates. Water and wineglasses. Crisp, white tablecloths and soft music playing on the sound system.

She sucked in a breath and her eyes flew open.

"I know who it is," she said. "I remember where I saw him."

"Who?"

"The person trying to kill me. I'd seen him somewhere before. I recognized his hair. It was so perfect, every individual strand in its place."

"Where did you see him?" Mike asked.

"At the restaurant. He was in for dinner about a week ago." She wracked her brain, trying to remember. "Thursday night. I spoke with him." She went pale. "Oh, God."

"What?" Anderson asked.

She slumped down in her chair. "I told him everything he needed to know to kill me. We were talking about the restaurant and he asked about the menu. I said that my cook designed it, but I went over it with him every Saturday morning."

"Saturday morning," Anderson said quietly. "He used that to time the explosion."

"Oh, God." She fought back the tears. "I gave him what he needed to kill my kitchen staff."

Anderson's facial features hardened. "You didn't do this, Leona. He did. He set the explosion and pushed the button. He killed those men, not you."

"Mike, that poor woman. Her husband dead. Her child's father."

Mike Anderson slipped his arms around her and pulled her close. She burrowed her face into his chest and felt her body jerking as she sobbed. She was a dear friend, and it hurt so much to see her in such pain. Leona was a strong woman, but he knew better than most that everyone had their breaking points. As he held her close, he prayed that she hadn't reached hers.

# 62

Mike Anderson.

Darvin smiled and pushed the paper aside, then took a drink from the glass of wine. Drops of blood ran down his arm onto the table. One of the droplets merged with another on the smooth wood surface. He would have to clean the red splotches with disinfectant. The kitchen table was no place for blood, even if it was his brother's. He stared at his hands, covered with spatters and streaks of dried and fresh blood. His session with Derek Swanson had taken almost three hours. That seemed long, even for him. He wondered how long it had seemed to the grotesquely disfigured man in the chair. Probably like a year.

Good. He deserved it.

Darvin looked at the paper and read the name again. Mike Anderson. Yes, it was the one. He was sure of it. When his contact at the phone company had called with the four names, he thought Anderson's sounded familiar. Now he knew why. When he had researched Leona Hewitt, the one aspect of her life that was in the public domain was her charity. Save Them was a nonprofit organization with ties to Kenya. And Mike Anderson was an employee of that charity. The liaison to Kenya. Which would explain the call on her phone that had originated in Germany. Anderson was on his way home.

*Stay in Africa*, Darvin thought. *It's much safer.*

The blood was beginning to crust over and having it on his skin was no longer a nice feeling. He set the empty wineglass on the table and headed for the shower. Half an hour later he walked out the front door of his house with Mike Anderson's address in his pocket, courtesy of Leona's Microsoft Outlook contact list. It was six-thirty. An hour into Washington, then time to find Mike Anderson's house. Lots of time for dinner. He settled into the driver's seat, then turned to look at the house. A simple-looking farmhouse from the exterior. Yet inside was part of a man, hovering close to death. Darvin hoped he wouldn't die before he took care of business in the city and returned. Round two would be fun.

He drove with the car on cruise, five miles an hour over the speed limit. Cops got suspicious when you drove exactly the posted speed, and they pulled you over if you exceeded it by more than ten or fifteen. Five was perfect. Don't weave and keep to five over—they'll never stop you. He glanced at the gun and knife sitting on the passenger's seat. This was not one car they wanted to stop anyway. Go have a donut and a coffee, finish your shift and head home to see your wife. There was a good chance none of that would happen if they stopped him.

He skirted Alexandria on the 495, then cut north on the 295 into the city, paralleling the Anacostia River. At the end of the park he backtracked slightly on the 50, then turned onto Dakota Avenue. He stopped at the Franciscan Monastery to check where he had to turn. It was dusk and the street signs were difficult to read. He passed Sargent Road on purpose, but missed the turn at Twelfth Street. He continued on another block and turned right on Eleventh, then doubled back two blocks to Sargent. He squinted until he saw a couple of house numbers in the low light. From that he figured out which way to turn, then scanned the street intently both ways before pulling out. He cruised at the speed limit past Mike Anderson's house. The living-room light was on and the shades were pulled tight. He drove two blocks farther, turned around and checked it out one more time. If the lights were on, the chances were that Mike Anderson was home. And Leona Hewitt was most likely with him.

Darvin accelerated slightly after he passed the house. This would be so easy. But first he needed to eat. Never kill on an empty stomach. It was a rule. His rule. There didn't have to be a reason for it to be a rule. It just was. He smiled. What a great business. No boss. No set hours. The only real downside was no benefits. And twenty-five to life if he ever got caught.

Leona watched Mike check his gun. It fit perfectly in his hand, just the right size so it didn't look too large or too small. The wood grip molded to his hand, the smooth curves fitting every crease in his time-worn palm. An untouched glass of whiskey sat on the table next to him. When he was finished oiling the weapon and checking the action, he set it on the table and picked up the glass. He took a small sip, then set it down.

"Nerves," he said to Leona. "Helps calm them."

"You? I'm surprised. Ex-cop and all. I thought this would be old hat to you."

He managed a slight smile. "Never gets to that point. If it does, you get hurt or killed. Every cop will tell you that complacency is dangerous."

"So we sit here and wait?" she asked.

"We could check into a hotel if you want."

"Is that necessary?"

Anderson shrugged. "I don't know. Now that they know the guy trying to kill you is Derek Swanson's relative, George Harvey and his guys should be able to track him down in a reasonable length of time. Probably quicker than he can find us."

"You think so?" She sounded worried.

"I hope so. No guarantees." He held up the gun. "That's what this is for."

"They're horrible things," Leona said. "Guns."

"Depends entirely upon which end is pointing at you."

George Harvey gripped the phone like a vise, listening to the woman's voice, and despising everything about it.

"I can't release the information without checking with my superior, Detective." There was a slight drawl in the singsong chatter. "And there's no way that will happen until tomorrow morning at the earliest. Even then, you may need a court order."

"Please have your boss call me the moment she gets in," he said civilly. "A woman's life is at stake."

"I'll pass the information along. Whether she calls or not is up to her, Detective."

"That's not good enough. What's her direct line?"

"You'll have to go through the switchboard. We don't give out direct lines."

"What time do you open in the morning?"

"Eight o'clock."

"Please put a note on her desk that I'll be calling at one minute after eight. I need a name and an address, and I need it quickly." Harvey's face was red and his teeth clenched. He was struggling now to keep his cool.

"Her office is locked. I'll put the note in her mail slot."

"Listen to me." His voice finally cracked and took on a menacing tone. "People are going to die if we don't get this guy. And if you read in the newspaper that two or more people were brutally murdered because we couldn't get the necessary information from the clerk who controlled the adoption records, you'll know that person is you."

"Well, I don't see what else I can do."

"Tape the damn message on your boss's door. Stand in the foyer when she arrives and tell her she has to get me that name by eight-fifteen. Don't leave her side until she does it. That's a good start."

"I'll do what I can."

George Harvey slammed the phone back into its cradle. "Bitch," he screamed at the phone, his emotions exploding. "You stupid, fucking, pencil-pushing, bureaucratic bitch."

Leona Hewitt and Mike Anderson were in danger. Of that, he was sure. He felt it, like cops always feel bad things that are about to happen. The sixth sense they covet some days and hate on others. Whether their lives were in jeopardy tonight was debatable. He didn't know how quickly the killer would track Leona, but he suspected it would be fast. He briefly considered pulling one of his men off a sanctioned stakeout, but nixed that thought. The man was needed where he was, and Leona was with Mike Anderson, a resourceful ex-cop.

They should be okay for one night. He kept telling himself that, but it wasn't working.

# 63

Darvin parked six houses down from Anderson's, on the opposite side of the road. He checked his watch. Eleven-fifteen. Dinner had taken a long time, but he was partially responsible, having sipped his solitary glass of wine before ordering a steak and finishing with dessert. His hunger was sated, his predatory urges stimulated. A perfect combination.

He exited the car without locking it. The keys were next to the console, out of sight but easily retrieved if a quick getaway were required. He'd learned years ago not to take keys or change into a quiet environment—for obvious reasons. The sidewalk was deserted and he walked to the street corner at a leisurely pace, counting the number of houses. Ten. Mike Anderson's was the tenth from the corner. He crossed the street and walked to the alleyway that bordered the rear of the subject property. With a quick glance in both directions, he entered the lane and blended in with the darkness.

Gravel crunched softly under his feet as he hugged the fence line. A tabby cat hissed at him, then leapt onto the fence and disappeared into an adjacent yard. Darvin counted the houses carefully. Mistakes at this point were very ugly—either for him or whoever was in the house. It was best if he found Leona Hewitt with a minimum of hassle. In—kill—out. Everything was so simple.

He reached the back of Anderson's house and crouched by the fence. There was little sound, mostly traffic noise from the nearby roads. A small child's cries carried through an open window in one of the town house–style homes and the odor of fresh-cut grass floated on the night breeze. There was a small knothole in one of the boards and he peeked through. The yard was narrow, but long. A solitary tree was tucked in the corner of the lot, useless as concealment. Once he opened the gate, he would be completely visible to anyone watching from the rear of the house. He retreated to the fence bordering the house next door, found a small crack in the boards, and peered in. The windows were dark and kid's toys were visible in the faint moonlight. He tried the handle on the gate. It opened to the touch and he slipped inside the yard, sidestepping the tricycle and sandbox. He flattened himself against the side of the house and waited, listening. The bricks felt rough on his skin.

Ambient background noise drifted into the yard and he took a couple of cleansing breaths. It would happen soon. The adrenaline surged and his heart raced. His gun was tucked into a shoulder holster and he quickly checked the clip, then snapped it back in place. His hand touched the cold metal of his knife, hidden in a sheath against the small of his back. The time was now. He grabbed the fence boards and jackknifed his body onto the upper horizontal board. A quick roll and he was over the top and sliding down the opposite side. He landed silently on the grass and tucked himself up to the house. There was no reaction from the house—no exterior light coming on, no footsteps on the rear porch.

He waited thirty seconds, his pulse even. It was quiet, very quiet, and he screwed the silencer onto the gun barrel. Silencers were heavy, and when attached, shooting accuracy was severely diminished, but he was going to be in close quarters and the sound of a gunshot would carry through the neighborhood. The benefits of using the silencer far outweighed leaving it in his pocket. Six short steps and he was at the stairs to the back door. He counted seven risers as he started up. His eyes remained focused on the door and the handle, not the stairs. When he had counted seven he didn't need to look down. The porch was wood and his steps were light. If a board creaked now, the sound would transmit into the house. He reached the door and tried the handle. It was locked. No surprise there, and inside five seconds his lock-picking tool was in his hand, working the tumblers. A low click resonated across the porch. He slipped the thin metal back into his pocket and twisted the handle. It turned and he pushed the door inward.

The aroma of coffee was faint in the air as a crack appeared between the door and the jamb. That meant they would be awake, caffeinated and on edge. Not good news. The view through the crack was of a small, unlit mudroom. He worked the door open a few more inches, the gun firmly gripped in his left hand. He knelt on the porch and slid his left hand through the opening, feeling for anything that Mike Anderson may have set against the door to warn him if it opened. His fingers touched something smooth and he wrapped his hand around it and pulled it back so the door could open without tipping it over. He could see it was a glass vase with a handful of marbles—just enough to cover the bottom. A well-planned warning device, but rendered useless by his skills. He pushed open the door and entered the house.

The mudroom was tiny, only six feet square, with hooks on the walls for coats and a shelf for boots. Darvin stood in the muted light, every sense on high alert. A low sound drifted to him—voices. Hushed tones, probably a normal conversation in a room near the front of the house. He quietly closed the door and moved into the kitchen. The lights above the counters and over the eating area were off, but illumination filtered through a doorway about halfway along the far wall and threw enough light for him to see. He moved toward the door leading to the front of the house, the voices becoming clearer. He reached the entrance to the living room and paused.

The time had come, as it always did.

Mike Anderson felt the presence before he saw the movement. He scrambled for his gun, on the arm of the chair. That simple motion saved his life. A slug tore into the couch where his torso had been a split second earlier, ricocheting off the metal springs and blowing stuffing out the front and back of the couch. Mike's hand hit the gun and it skittered off the arm onto the floor. He rolled onto the floor and grabbed Leona's arm, yanking her out of her chair and sending her sliding across the floor and into the stairwell leading to the basement. She bounced off the first couple of stairs and came to a stop in a heap on the landing. A second later, Mike flew through the doorway and landed half on top of her, half on the landing.

"Down," he yelled. "Get downstairs."

She tumbled off the landing, caught the handrail and managed to take a few steps before missing one in the dark and crashing headfirst into the concrete wall at the bottom of the stairs. The impact knocked her sideways and she fell to the floor, somehow managing to get her hands out to break the fall. She crawled blindly across the floor, like a crab searching for a hiding spot on the beach. Behind her, she heard Mike coming down the stairs. She turned, just in time to see a second figure appear on the stairs. A muzzle flash lit the room for a split second and Mike's head snapped back from the impact, his body careening sideways into the wall. He slid to the floor and lay unmoving in the darkness.

The figure on the stairs continued down to the basement floor. She could see his features, barely lit in the soft glow of light from the upper floor. The hair, the face—it was the man from the restaurant. The whites of his eyes reflected the shards of light in the darkened room, and they looked to be on fire. He walked to where she lay and looked down at her.

"Mother warned me about girls like you," he said. His voice was a low hiss.

Leona skittered backward until she hit the wall. He came toward her, a shadow with the outline of a gun in his right hand. He stopped a couple of feet from her and squatted down. Despite the darkness, she could see the face clearly, the evil in the eyes. She pushed back but there was nowhere to go. Her hands ran across the rough concrete, searching for anything to use as a weapon.

"Dirty thing." He raised the gun. The words sounded detached from reality, like he was functioning more by instinct than reason.

Leona scrambled to one side and her hand touched something lying on the floor. It had a handle and four long tines. A handheld tool for tilling the garden. She grabbed the handle and swung it at his arm. The tines hit him in the fleshy part below the elbow, puncturing the skin and slicing into the muscle. He screamed in pain, a wolf's howl that resonated through the dank cellar. She released the tool and it hung from his arm, the tines embedded deep in the muscle. She tried to get up, but he kicked her in the rib cage, a roundabout boot that cracked a couple of ribs and sent an excruciating wave of pain up her side and into her brain. She fell back to the cold cement, writhing in agony. A second later his face was inches from hers.

"You bitch. You dirty, fucking bitch. Now you don't die so easy. Now you're going to suffer. I'll make you wish you were dead, you whore."

She saw the gun butt coming at her head, then nothing.

The room was spinning, wild and out of control.

Mike Anderson fought to bring his equilibrium back in check. What had happened? The scene replayed in his mind—the figure on the stairs, the gunshot, then waking up. He had been shot. How bad? He had no idea. He struggled to his feet, his head pounding at the exertion. He glanced about, taking in the surroundings.

Leona.

Where was she? He used the wall as a support and flicked on the light. There was no body on the floor. A fresh blood trail snaked across the cement to the stairs. Drag marks accompanied it. Leona or the killer, one of the two was injured. And she must be unconscious. He had dragged her to the stairs then carried her up to the main floor.

Anderson started up the stairs and fell backward. He grabbed at the railing but missed and landed in a heap at the foot of the stairwell. Standing up was impossible—he had no sense of balance. He crawled up the stairs on his hands and knees and followed the blood droplets through the kitchen and across the front room. They led to the main door. The window was closer and Mike pulled himself up on the jamb and stared out into the street.

Across Sargent Road and down a few cars was the killer, loading Leona into a car against the far curb. The thought of going after them ran through his head but he immediately discarded it. He was barely hanging on to consciousness and they were already at the car. He must have been out for a couple of minutes, no more, or Leona would be long gone. There was one chance. The license plate. He steadied himself on the window ledge and concentrated on the vehicle as it pulled out. For a split second the plate was visible. He recognized the insignia immediately as West Virginia. The series of letters and numbers registered in his brain, then the car was gone.

Anderson let himself sink to the floor and pulled a coin from his pocket. He used the metal edge to score the drywall under the window, scratching the plate number into the wall. He looked at what he had written, the room getting dimmer and dimmer. He fought the impending unconsciousness, but it was no use. Slowly, his brain shut down and a quiet darkness settled over his still form.

## 64

The first rays of the new day woke him.

Mike Anderson shook his head to clear the cobwebs and almost screamed at the pain. This was like no other headache he had ever suffered from. Even the slightest movement was excruciating. He used the arm of the couch to drag himself onto his feet, then staggered across the wood floor to the bathroom. Visions of the previous night flooded back. The shadowy figure. He and Leona crashing down the stairs. A gunshot. Then the car pulling out from the curb, with Leona, unconscious in the front seat.

He reached the bathroom and stared at his reflection in the mirror. If he had wondered why he had a headache, he now knew the reason. His head was a mess of scrapes and blood. But the places where his face had slid on the concrete were not the worst. It was the bullet wound. The flash of light from the top of the stairs was a gunshot, and the bullet had hit him in the head. A groove at least a quarter of an inch deep and four inches long ran down the left side of his scalp. That impact had jerked his head and sent him crashing into the wall or the floor. It had knocked him out and saved his life. The killer would have seen the impact and in the poor light had assumed it was a killing shot. Mike had been lucky. Very lucky.

Mike carefully washed the wound and applied some antibiotic cream. Then he popped three extra-strength Advil and sat down by the phone. He dialed a number from memory and waited. A deep voice answered.

"Billy, it's Mike Anderson."

"Holy shit, Mike, what's up? I haven't heard from you in over a year."

"I need some help, Billy. I need you to run a plate for me."

"Where are you, Mike?" the voice asked.

"Washington. But I don't know anyone on the force here. Can you access West Virginia plates from your New York precinct?"

The response was guarded. "Yes, but I need an authorization. I can't run a plate for no reason."

"Billy, this is me. When I tell you I need this guy's address, I mean now. Not three minutes from now. You do this or a woman is going to die."

"Jesus, Mike. I don't see you for a year, then you call out of nowhere. Ask me for something sketchy."

"I can't take the time to explain, Billy, but she's going to die."

"Christ, Mike . . ."

Silence hung on the line.

"What's the plate number?"

Anderson repeated the letters and numbers and waited while the homicide detective pulled the information from the government computers. The minutes dragged, then the voice came back on the line.

"Got him."

"Go ahead." Mike held the pen in his hand, poised over a sheet of paper.

"His name's Darvin. I'm going to spell the last name—it's unpronounceable." He recited the letters over the phone and Mike repeated them. "That's right. His address is Forty-five Oak Shade Road in Culpepper County, West Virginia. I've got the GPS directions to the house. You ready?"

"Yeah."

"Take sixty-six west and cut off on fifteen/twenty-nine at Gainesville. Stay on it to Opal, then head west five miles. Turn south on the first secondary highway, then take a right about half a mile down the road. That's Oak Shade Road. His house is a few hundred yards down on the left."

"Got it. Thanks."

"What are friends for?"

"You got that straight, Billy."

Mike hung up and headed for the door. The Advil was starting to kick in and the pain was diminishing by the minute. He checked his watch. Eight-fourteen. He pulled the door closed behind him and walked unsteadily to his car. He had an hour of driving to regain his senses. And he was going to need every one of them. His mind wandered to Leona as he turned the key in the ignition. Whether she was alive, or already dead.

He didn't want to know the answer to that question. Not yet.

# 65

"The room's a bit messy. I didn't have time to clean up. But I don't think it cares."

Leona slowly opened her eyes, the light from the window like tiny daggers pushing into her brain. She focused on the man in front of her. It was the same person who had visited the restaurant. The man with the perfect hair. She glanced down at his arm. It was bandaged where she had impaled him and fresh blood soaked through, staining the white gauze a deep red. Her head rolled on her neck and the rest of the room appeared, like the horizon from the deck of a steeply pitching ship. She sucked in her breath and tried to hold back the bile. It didn't work and she vomited on the floor beside the chair to which she was tightly lashed.

"Christ. As if I didn't have enough to clean. Now look at

what it's done." Darvin's voice was unemotional, almost clinical.

Next to her, still lashed to a chair, was Derek Swanson's body. His skin was sliced off in strips and the white of bone showed through the mess of severed tendons and muscles. Both eyes were cut from the sockets and dangling by the optic nerve. Beyond the horror that had been a living person was a wheelchair occupied by an emaciated corpse, its mouth locked in a primal scream.

"They were bad," he said as she looked at him with fearful eyes.

"You're one sick bastard." Her lips and throat were almost too dry to speak.

His hand shot out and punched her in the face. Blood spurted from her nose. "That's not polite. Not nice at all."

Leona spit out the blood that trickled into her mouth. "Why? Why did you kill these people? Why did you kill my staff?" She stared him straight in the eyes. "One of my cooks had a baby. Now that kid doesn't have a father."

The coldness melted from his eyes and fury took over. His jaw clenched and his hands balled into fists. "Don't talk to me about not having a father. The man who said he was my dad was spineless. Useless. Pig shit."

"Everyone has good in them," Leona said. "Your father included."

"You know nothing about him." His voice rose in pitch and volume.

"Nobody's parents are perfect."

"Perfect." Spittle flew from his lips. "I never wanted perfect. Anything but what I had."

"My father was too busy for me. I grew up alone. No friends. No parents. No brothers or sisters."

"Brothers," Darvin shook his head in disgust. "This is what I got for a brother." He waved his hand at the bloody corpse a few feet from her. "What a piece of shit he turned out to be."

"At least you had a brother. I had no one."

Darvin lowered his face to her level. He was merely inches from her. "I don't care about your family. I don't give two shits about you. Other than to kill you."

"Why? What does it matter if you kill me?" She was shaking with anger. "I did nothing to you. Nothing. Yet you went out of your way to find me. To take me. What's with that?"

"You're a mouthy bitch." The coldness returned to his eyes. "It wants to die."

Leona's breath quickened. She could see the shift in him—from angry to psychopathic. A veil that dropped down over his eyes, his face, his entire body. Everything in the man changed. The tenseness in his muscles disappeared, replaced by a slack body language that scared her far more than his anger. It was as if every shred of empathy had dissolved into the primordial mix. Anger she could work with, could talk to, try to reason with. But the cold, detached part of him was impossible. *It.* She shuddered at the word. The moment he slipped back into the detached persona, he called her *it.* No empathy. No chance for her to negotiate. She had to get him angry, keep him angry. He might beat her, but he wouldn't kill her. The psychopath took care of that.

"Why did you kill your brother?"

Darvin circled her, a predator sizing up its prey. When he came back into view, he was holding a long, curved blade. "He was never much of a brother."

"Maybe you never gave him a chance." Leona kept her eyes from focusing on the knife.

"I watched him. I saw his life. His parents cared for him."

Leona cocked her head slightly. "You and your brother never met? He didn't know you?"

Darvin smiled, a crooked grin that resonated evil. "We met. He didn't know who I was."

"So you watched him, cherished his life, and never let him know you existed. Then you complain because he wasn't a great brother to you. How could he be? He didn't know you were related."

Darvin's mouth curled into a sneer. "Funny you should say that—it's exactly what Derek said. *If I'd known, I'd have saved you.* What a crock of shit that is." He tapped the knife against his palm and it sliced into the skin. Blood pooled in the creases but he was totally oblivious. "You think you're smart. That you can twist things around and make me feel responsible for this."

"You *are* responsible," Leona said loudly. "You killed him. You probably killed whoever that is in the other chair. And you killed a whole bunch of other people. Don't try to pass the blame on this. People have bad childhoods. They don't all become murderers."

He leapt across the floor and grabbed her by the throat, the knife an inch from her eye. "I'm going to carve you into little pieces. Slowly, so you feel every bit of pain."

"You don't scare me."

"I should."

"You revolt me. There's nothing you can do to me that will change that. Nothing."

He lowered the blade slightly and drew it across her neck. It cut through the skin but not deep enough to slice the trachea. "It wants to die. But not yet. It has to suffer first."

Leona felt the blade cutting into her skin. The cold, detached look flooded back into his eyes. The anger was gone. She was powerless against this part of his personality. Tied to a chair, with a madman slicing her into strips, she knew she'd lost the battle. She closed her eyes and refused to scream.

## 66

Eight-thirty and no response at Mike Anderson's house. George Harvey hung up and dialed the number again. It rang and eventually went to the answering machine. Something was wrong. He swore under his breath. He should have pulled the man off the other stakeout. He knew it, felt it, and didn't do it. Now Mike Anderson and Leona Hewitt were either dead or missing. That's what his gut told him, and this time he was listening.

"Marnie," he yelled across the squad room. "Take Ed with you and get to Sargent Road." He recited the house number, then added, "Mike Anderson is the owner's name. He's an ex-cop. New York. Leona should be with him. If they're still in the house and okay, they'll answer the door. Be careful going in if there's no answer."

"Okay. She scribbled down the address and grabbed her keys. She and the other detective disappeared through the door into the hall.

The fax beeped and a solitary sheet glided through the printer. Harvey waited until it was all the way out, then yanked it out and scanned the contents. It was from the woman at the adoption department. His conversation with her a half hour earlier must have hit a chord. She'd moved fast to get him the information he needed.

"These are Swanson's birth parents." Harvey slammed the sheet of paper down on the desk. "I need everything you can get on them, and I need it now."

One of his detectives grabbed the paper, ran it through the copy machine and handed the pages to the other detectives. They scattered to their computers and started working the names. It took less than three minutes to get a hit.

"Parents lived on a farm in West Virginia before they passed on. Address is on Oak Shade Road. Number forty-five."

"Run the land title," Harvey said. "See if the son still owns it."

Again, the response time on the computer was almost immediate. "It's in his name," the man running the request said.

"Tony, you and Alan come with me. Alicia, you stay and watch the phones. I want to know what Marnie and Ed found at Mike Anderson's house the moment they call in."

"You got it."

"Let's go."

Harvey ran from the squad room. He was too late. There was nothing telling him why, but he knew it. Knew that he had failed Leona Hewitt. The question now was whether she would die because of his miscalculation. He should have shifted the man to watch Anderson's house. Then a second thought hit him. If he had, there was a good chance one of his detectives would have been on a slab this morning. There was little consolation with the revelation.

Mike saw the house on his left, a white clapboard two-story with dark shutters framing the windows. Trees surrounded the house and the graveled area between the main residence and two oversize sheds that probably functioned as workshops. Parked on the gravel, near the entrance to the house, was the car that had pulled away from his place the night before. A decrepit barn, the roof in disrepair, sat a hundred yards from the house and sheds. He drove past the entrance to the farm, to a spot where there were enough trees between him and the house to block anyone from seeing him pull over. He switched off the ignition and slid out of the vehicle, every sense on high alert. Between the intermittent chirping of unseen birds, it was deathly quiet.

His wife's face flashed through his mind. She was smiling, a warm glow in her eyes. And then, in a single millisecond, it hit him. He still loved her, couldn't shake the connection to a woman who was no longer in his life, but that was okay. He didn't love her as a husband loves a wife, but as a friend who cares for someone so deeply it hurts. The same kind of love he felt for Leona. He closed his eyes for a few seconds and her image dissipated into the blackness. He felt the closure and knew that her memory would stay with him forever, but he would never feel the pain of separation again. He opened his eyes, pushed off from his car and started walking back toward the house on the edge of the asphalt.

His balance was better and the pain from the bullet that had scorched the side of his head was gone, courtesy of the Advil. He angled off the road into the woods and headed toward the house. Where would he keep her? The barn was in such poor condition that he doubted the killer would choose that building. Not when he had three others to pick from. That left the house, or possibly one of the workshops. The woods were thick, which slowed him but gave good cover in case the son of a bitch was watching.

Mike reached the tree line and stopped. Ahead of him were the three buildings, and from his angle he could see the front entrances to all three. Luck more than planning. He squinted at the oversize sheds. One of them had a padlock on the front door. Unless there was a back entrance, there was no way anyone could go inside and lock the door behind them. He looked hard at the second shed, but the distance was too far and he couldn't tell if it was locked.

What were his options? Running across the open area was dangerous. Staying in the trees and skirting the house was his best option, but it would take time and at some point he'd still be racing across open ground to the house. He estimated the distance from the trees to the front porch to be ninety, maybe a hundred feet. Four to five seconds in the open, then his body would be hidden from view by hugging the house. He slipped his gun from its holster and checked the chambers. Loaded and ready. He flipped off the safety and took a deep breath.

Mike pushed out of the undergrowth and ran across the gravel, his feet making light crunching sounds. He reached the house in less than five seconds and flattened himself against the siding. The boards were warm from the sun and he could feel the heat through his shirt. Ten feet to his right and elevated about five feet from ground level was the end of the front porch. He watched for a face to poke around the corner. His gun was aimed at the point where someone of normal height would appear. Nothing. Not a sound. He inched forward to the edge of the deck and peered around the corner. The porch was empty. He glanced across the graveled area to the second shed. He was close enough now to see the front latch. It was also secured with a padlock. The killer was in the house. He knew it—he felt it.

And he felt Leona. She was here. Alive or dead, he didn't know.

Mike slipped his revolver into his waistband, grabbed the porch spindles and pulled himself up high enough to hook his foot on the wood deck. He scurried over the railing and crouched, the gun back in his hand. He duck-waddled the length of the deck and set his hand on the front door handle. He slowly twisted and it turned. The door pushed in a fraction of an inch. He sucked in a deep breath to calm his nerves. It was time.

## 67

The darkness was as terrifying to Leona as the knife.

Her captor had untied her from the chair and dragged her down the center stairwell, past the main floor to the basement. She wanted to scream, to beg him to take her back up to that horrible room, filled with death. Anywhere but in the black confines of the basement. She did nothing. Just sat on the chair that he had lashed her to and stared at him in the dim glow from the single twenty-five watt bulb swinging from the ceiling on the other side of the room. The shadows moved back and forth as the bulb moved—inanimate monsters as sure to get her as the one with the knife.

"You don't like it down here, do you?" Darvin said. "You're shaking now. You liked it more in the room with Derek and Mom." He walked across the room to a table and rummaged through a few rusted garden tools. "You didn't think I was going to kill you up there, did you? That room is reserved for family. Dirty things like you get the basement."

"I am not a thing," Leona said, struggling to find the air to form the words. "I am a person."

"You're nothing," Darvin said cheerfully. "A corpse that still talks. It won't be alive long now."

"Fuck, you're totally insane." Anything to get the anger back. The anger may slow the inevitable.

"You have a dirty mouth," he said disgustedly. "Girls aren't supposed to say fuck."

"Now I'm a girl. Thanks for that."

He moved close to her and leaned over, his breath in her face. It smelled of rancid meat. "I'm going to carve you into a lot of small pieces. You're going to beg me to kill you."

"Never," she said, her words braver than her thoughts. "You'll never get that satisfaction."

"We'll see. Let's get started." He ran his index finger along the side of the blade.

The smell of death hit Mike Anderson the moment he pushed the door open. He involuntarily gagged, then swallowed back the bile. Death was no stranger, and he moved into the house, ready for the worst.

The main floor was divided into numerous rooms with a central staircase leading to the upper floor. He bypassed the living room and headed to the rear of the house, walking on tiptoes and feeling every footstep with the ball of his foot before applying weight. A squeaky floorboard could spell disaster. The kitchen was clean and empty. Beyond it was a mudroom and laundry. He retraced his steps to the foyer and started up the stairs, the revolver gripped tightly in his hand. At the top of the stairs, a hallway stretched in both directions, giving access to the bedrooms and bath. All the doors were open but one. Anderson stood still, listening for an indication someone was in one of the rooms. Nothing. He crept down the hall, away from the closed door, and checked the other rooms. Each was empty. He reached the final door and gripped the handle with his left hand, the gun leveled at chest height. He twisted the handle, then pushed hard.

The door swung open, revealing the entire room. He stared, his chest heaving as his lungs labored to feed oxygen to his tense body. Before him was a slaughter. The remains of a human being were tied to a chair, stripped of skin. He could tell from the size of the form that it had been a man. Blood was spattered and streaked around the chair, the outline of footprints dried onto the hardwood. A few feet from the rotting flesh was another body, a mummified woman

frozen in a moment of agony. An empty chair sat a few feet
to one side. Fresh drops of blood stained the floorboards
close to the chair legs.

Mike wrestled his eyes from the scene, his stomach still
churning. Leona had been here, recently by the look of the
blood, but the killer had taken her. Where? The car was still
parked out front and both the sheds appeared to be locked.
That left the barn or the basement. His money was on the
basement. He retraced his steps to the main floor and
walked on his toes to the kitchen, to where there was a door
directly under the central staircase. Access to the basement.
He sucked in a couple of deep breaths and slowly pulled it
open.

"It doesn't bleed much," Darvin said, a touch of drool on
his lips.

Leona's head swayed from side to side as he rocked it
back and forth, surveying the cuts he had made to her neck.
Her eyes were almost closed, slits in a bloodied face. She
stared beyond him, at the far wall where an open door led
back to the staircase. To freedom. To the warmth of the sun
and the gentle caress of soft winds. Simple things she would
never feel again. Something in the room behind the door
changed for a second. A dim shaft of light, a movement,
then the light was gone. What was that? Concentrate. What
could have caused that? She forced her brain to move beyond the pain and piece together what had just happened.
Light, shadow, then darkness. The stairwell he had dragged
her down was out that door. And the kitchen was filled with
sunshine.

Someone had come through the door to the basement,
then shut it behind them.

She felt a surge of adrenaline as what she had seen hit her.
Someone was here. Someone who didn't want Darvin to

know they had arrived. But subtly, and alone. That eliminated the police. They would never send in one man against an armed psychopath. The only other person who could possibly know she was here was Mike Anderson. She had seen him shot at his house, go down hard against the wall, but nothing else made sense. It had to be. Mike Anderson was here and coming for her.

"It's waking up," Darvin said as he felt the difference in her body.

"I'm not going to die," she said softly. *Talk to him, mask any noise Mike may make coming in.* "I'm going to live through this."

"I don't think so," he hissed, working the knife.

She could hardly feel the cuts anymore and had no idea how badly injured she was. He had sliced her throat once upstairs, and was toying with her in the basement. She felt the cold steel against her skin, but had no idea if it was cutting, or if it was, how deeply. He was in tight to her and she was able to work the ropes that bound her hands without him noticing. His knots weren't as tight as in the chair upstairs and there was some movement.

"Your mother was an ugly bitch," she said.

His head snapped back, and even in the almost nonexistent light she could see the loathing in his eyes. "What did you say?"

"I said, your mother was ugly. Small chin, wide face. You can tell what dead people looked like from their bone structure. I saw it on Discovery Channel."

"You fucking whore," he roared. "You think you have the right to tell me anything about my mother?"

"Simply stating a fact," she said, locking eyes with him. *Keep him focused. Make noise. Give the rescuer a chance.*

His hand snaked out toward her face and she ducked. The fist hit nothing but air and he stumbled to the side. At exactly that moment a figure appeared in the doorway, less than fifteen feet away. Leona could see the man's features. It was Mike Anderson. Darvin saw him at the same time. He spun sideways and dived behind her chair. Anderson's gun was leveled, his finger on the trigger, but she was between him and the killer. Instinct took over and without thinking, she tipped the chair on its side, crashing onto the cement and exposing the hidden man.

Two flashes lit up the room for a fraction of a second, then the surreal darkness settled in. The roar of both guns going off simultaneously was deafening, but the sounds of the slugs tearing into flesh was still discernable. Anderson's gun flew out of his hand and he dropped to the floor, his hands clutching at his side. Darvin struggled to stand, a rapidly expanding red splotch on his left shoulder. He walked unsteadily toward Mike Anderson.

"What the fuck are you doing here?" he yelled. He reached Anderson and stared down at him. "In fact, what are you doing alive?"

"You missed last time," he said through clenched teeth.

"I won't this time." Darvin raised the gun.

Leona yanked her hand free from the ropes and staggered to her feet. Darvin's head twisted, looking her way. She had one option. Only one. She dived at the lightbulb and hit it with her outstretched fingers. The room was immediately plunged into total darkness. Panic gripped her, tearing at her core, constricting her lungs, cutting off her air supply. She forced air down her throat, gulping it like a thirsty person drinks water. She rolled on her side until she hit the wall. A gunshot crashed through the room, a split second of light blasting out of the pistol barrel. The scene registered in her memory in that collection of milliseconds.

"Bitch," Darvin screamed. His face was a mask of unadulterated rage and hate. "Where the fuck are you?"

Leona lay against the wall, replaying the scene in her mind. Darvin, standing with the gun at forty-five degrees, aiming at where he thought she should be. Mike Anderson, severely injured and struggling to get up. Tools, benches, boxes piled against the far wall—and a gun. She saw it clearly. It was on the floor about ten feet to her right. Mike's gun, laying where it had come to rest after skittering across the floor. She needed to get her hands on the gun.

A second later, there was the dull thud of something hard hitting flesh. Darvin's voice cut through the darkness. He was yelling at Mike Anderson as he pistol-whipped him. Mike was too badly injured. This was up to her now. She felt the panic subside as she focused on the image of the gun. All she saw was the weapon on the cement. Nothing else mattered. Her claustrophobia was in her mind, nothing more. The darkness was her ally—it shielded her from him.

She crawled toward the gun, hearing the horrible sounds of Darvin beating Mike to death. Her hands patted the ground, searching for the weapon. Her hands touched something and she wrapped her hands about the gun's wood handle. She curled her finger around the trigger and pointed it toward the thuds. Then she closed her eyes, degrading every sense in her body except her hearing.

"Shithead." Her voice was level and calculated.

The sounds stopped. Total silence settled on the room. Leona kept her breathing even and low, no sound for him to zero in on. He would eventually say something. She knew it. And when he did, she was ready.

"You're going to die in this room," he said, his voice a whisper.

She adjusted her aim a bit to the left and angled the gun up ever so slightly. "I don't think so," she said, opening her eyes and pulling the trigger.

The muzzle flash was intense. What she saw in that speck

of time was terrifying. He was moving toward her, covered with blood, the gun stretched out in front of him. The frame of light only gave her that one moment, no more. She heard the bullet's impact and knew from the elevation of the gun that she had hit him in the thigh. A guttural scream shot through the blackness and she heard him hit the ground. Leona adjusted the gun to the sound of the thud and pulled the trigger again. Then again. The gun kicked back and the acrid odor of gunpowder filled her nostrils. She stopped firing and listened. A wheezing sound penetrated the dark, like air escaping from a punctured air mattress. She had hit him in the chest and collapsed his lung. She sat motionless, listening to the primal sounds of a dying animal.

Leona had no idea how long it took before the labored breathing stopped. He was dead. The monster was tamed the only way it could be. She stood on shaky legs and felt her way along the wall to where Mike Anderson lay. When she reached him, she knelt and felt his chest. His heart was beating. She moved her hands up toward his face.

"That hurts," he said quietly.

"You're alive."

"Alive, but very sore."

"I heard him hitting you with the gun. I thought he'd caved in your skull."

"I got my arms up over my head. He never got a good shot at my noggin. But both my arms are broken, Leona. I'm a mess."

She felt the tears in her eyes, and knew they were falling freely even though she couldn't see them. "He's dead."

"I heard. Thought it was best to stay quiet, though. Just in case."

"You saved my life, Mike," she said.

"And you saved mine. Looks like we're even."

"Sure. Even is good."

"Didn't know you could fire a gun that well."

"I'm more than just a pretty face," she said, then added, "Don't go anywhere. I'm going to call for help."

"I'll hang out down here with the dead guy."

"You do that."

Leona worked her way through the basement until she could see the tiny sliver of light under the kitchen door at the top of the stairs. She gripped the handrail and pulled herself up step by step. She was weak from blood loss and coming down off the adrenaline rush. She had next to nothing left. Sunlight flooded over her as she opened the door, but it felt no different. The darkness no longer had a grip over her. A fear she had lived with her entire life was now in the past. She walked across the kitchen to the telephone and dialed George Harvey's cell phone number. He answered almost immediately.

"It's Leona," she said.

"Where are you?" Panic commingled with relief in his voice.

She looked out the kitchen window, across the gravel to the old decrepit barn. "I don't know. A farm of some sort."

"Okay, I know where you are. We're almost there. Five minutes. Are you okay?"

"I think we're going to need an ambulance for Mike Anderson."

"Are his injuries life threatening?" Harvey asked.

"He's still talking, but he's really beat up. And shot. He might be in worse condition than he thinks. An ambulance is probably a good idea."

"What about Darvin?"

"Dead," she said without emotion. There was no victory in having killed him.

"Okay, Leona, we're turning onto Oak Shade Road right now. I'm going to hang up and call for an ambulance."

"Sure."

She set the phone back in its cradle and returned to the basement. She sat in the darkness, cradling Mike's head in her lap and talking softly to him. He was conscious, but barely. Shards of light flashed about as the police made their way down the staircase with their flashlights. She found the bright beams intrusive. This was her moment with a man who had always been there for her. In Africa or here in America, she had absolute trust in him. That felt good. But there was one more man who had always been there as well. She had never seen it before. It was time to right that.

One of the flashlights illuminated Darvin's corpse, but she refused to look. Her life was not about misery and suffering and negative thoughts or images. It was about the positive things that surrounded her. It was about goodness and caring. It was about living.

# 68

Leona closed the door behind her and looked up and down the hospital hallway. The hour was late and a solitary nurse, making her rounds, was the only person in sight. She walked to the elevator, clutching the novel she'd just finished reading. Music drifted down the hall, barely audible, but she recognized the tune. U2, Bono and the boys—"I Still Haven't Found What I'm Looking For." She felt a warm glow creep through her bones. Her theme song for so many years. Now it was just great music.

Mike Anderson was finally ready to be released from the hospital. Twenty days since George Harvey and his men had carried him from the house and the paramedics had rushed him to the nearest emergency room. The doctor on call had told them another fifteen minutes, half an hour tops, and

Mike would not have made it. The bullet had carved a path of destruction through his lower intestine, but it was massive blood loss that almost killed him. He was on the mend, and that was what counted. She'd known he was going to make it the moment he started objecting to her ripping the wood paneling out of his house. He'd finally given in when she described his décor as early-rumpus-room.

She took the elevator to the main floor and stood outside the main doors, a warm August breeze on her face. Her hand held the business section of the daily newspaper and she glanced at the headlines. Anthony Halladay had been charged with insider trading. The Securities and Exchange Commission had determined he was the conduit to Derek Swanson. Leona shook her head at the irony. She had gone to his house, to warn him of the leak. Not the smartest decision she'd ever made.

Leona slipped her free hand in her purse and touched the cell phone. It was time to make the call. She dialed the number and leaned against one of the concrete planters as it rang. A man's voice answered.

"Hi, Dad," she said.

"Leona. How are you? I haven't talked to you for a while."

"I'm fine. Couldn't be better actually."

"That's great to hear. How are things at the bank?"

"Better than you could imagine." Great because she had quit. She'd deliver that news later, face-to-face.

"What ever happened with the insurance on the restaurant?" he asked.

"They agreed to pay. Tyler and I are working with a guy who has some new ideas on redesigning the interior." With the bank out of her life, she was totally focused on building the restaurant into a very successful venture.

"Good news."

"I have something on my mind. Something I want to tell you."

"What's that."

"I love you, Dad."

There was a no hesitation. "I love you too, sweetie. Nice to hear you say it."

"Feels good to say it." She tilted her head back and stared at the stars. "I don't think we say how we feel often enough."

"No kidding."

"Listen, Dad, I was thinking . . ."

"Yes?"

"Would you like to go fishing sometime?"

There was a definite pause. "You want to go fishing?"

"I do. But only with you."

"Sure, that would be fun. When?"

"Give me a couple of weeks. I need a bit of time to myself right now."

"I know a lodge in Northern Ontario, and September is the time to go. The walleye and pike will be big and hungry."

"I'm in. Remember, give me at least two weeks."

"Okay, honey."

"I do love you, Dad."

"Love you, too."

She hung up, a hint of a smile on her lips. It had always been there, she had just never seen it. Her father loved her unconditionally. It was her perspective that had clouded the emotions he kept locked in his heart. She had tried to fit her father's affection inside the box that defined *her* emotions, but that wasn't how it worked. If she wanted to see the forest, she had to get out of the trees. Pretty simple, really.

She loved her dad and he loved her. Mike Anderson was going to live, all appendages intact. Everything as it should be. Her well-ordered life had teetered on the brink of chaos, then pulled back from the chasm. But while she was on the edge, she had looked down and seen inside her own heart, her soul. Life was for the living and she was back. With a vengeance. Maybe that's what it took—a little chaos to realize what was really important in her world. Like the moment when she had knocked over the glass of wine in the restaurant. Broken glass—spilled wine. A small disaster, easily cleaned up. Not a lot of chaos. Just a little.

A delicate chaos, of sorts.

# GREGG LOOMIS

### The newest secret is about to be uncovered....

A scientist in Amsterdam—murdered. Another scientist in Atlanta—murdered, and his journal stolen. Lang Reilly worked with them both. And when someone took a shot at Lang, it only made him more determined to find the truth. Lang's search will lead him along a twisted trail to Brussels, Cairo, Vienna, Tel Aviv...and deep into the secrets of the past. What's the connection between the murdered scientists and an ancient parchment, recently unearthed? What revelations does it contain, and what powerful group is willing to kill to make sure its secrets remain hidden? With the balance of power in the Middle East at risk, Lang has to stay alive long enough to find the answer to a mystery that has puzzled historians for centuries.

# THE SINAI SECRET

**Available March 2008 wherever books are sold.**

ISBN 13: 978-0-8439-6042-6

# THE JULIAN SECRET

## GREGG LOOMIS

Don Huff was Lang Reilly's friend, and now he's been brutally murdered. Could someone be willing to commit murder to pre-vent the book he was writing from ever seeing the light of day? What secrets are worth killing for? Lang is determined to find the truth, but the organization that killed his friend is just as eager to kill him if he gets too close.

The trail of secrets leads Lang on a deadly chase across Europe, deeper and deeper into a mystery that has been concealed since the days of the founding of the Catholic Church. Danger follows Lang with every startling revelation. But at the end of the hunt lies a final secret that will shock even Lang—if he survives long enough to find it!

ISBN 13: 978-0-8439-5691-7

# TRIPLE IDENTITY

## HAGGAI CARMON

Dan Gordon used to work for Mossad, the Israeli intelligence agency. Now he works for the U. S. Department of Justice. All of his intelligence training is coming in very handy in his current mission—tracking a mysterious Romanian who might have fled the U. S. with ninety million dollars stolen from a failed California bank.

Just as he thinks he's getting close, Gordon discovers this is no ordinary mission, and the Romanian is no ordinary money launderer. He'll need all of his training, contacts, resources and cleverness to unravel a Byzantine plot that will lead him across Europe and into the Middle East in a frantic race to stop a rogue nation…before its operatives can stop him.

ISBN 13: 978-0-8439-6040-2

# THOM AUGUST

Twenty years ago, the Boss of the Chicago Mob thought Franco was having an affair with his wife. He couldn't prove anything, but the Boss still told the pianist to get out of town and never come back. As a reminder, he cut off Franco's little finger....

Vinnie Amatucci is a part-time Chicago cabbie and part-time jazz musician. Things have never been easy for his band, but lately they've been downright deadly. A professional killer known as the Cleaner has been hired to hit first one musician...then another. As members of the band get whacked one by one, a disgraced homicide cop may be their only hope. Will he stop the Cleaner before the whole band is wiped out? And is there any connection between the killings and the new guy sitting in with the band, the one with only...

# NINE FINGERS

ISBN 13: 978-0-8439-6025-9

---

# SIMON WOOD

## PAYING THE PIPER

He was known as the Piper—a coldhearted kidnapper who terrified the city. Crime reporter Scott Fleetwood built his career on the Piper. The kidnapper even taunted the FBI through Scott's column. But Scott had been duped. The person he'd been speaking to wasn't really the Piper. By the time the FBI exposed the hoaxer, time ran out…and the real Piper killed the child. Then he vanished. But now he's back, with very specific targets in mind—Scott's children.

ISBN 10: 0-8439-5980-0
ISBN 13: 978-0-8439-5980-2

To order a book or to request a catalog call:
**1-800-481-9191**
This book is also available at your local bookstore, or you can check out our Web site **www.dorchesterpub.com** where you can look up your favorite authors, read excerpts, or glance at our discussion forum to see what people have to say about your favorite books.

# STEVEN TORRES

The big party in the town square should have been one of the happiest moments of Luis Gonzalo's life, celebrating his twenty-five years as sheriff. But in the middle of the ceremony a blaze is spotted on a nearby hill. The Ortiz home is on fire. Inside is what's left of the Ortiz family—bound and shot. This isn't just a murder...it's a message. But who's it for? As the violence continues and Gonzalo digs deeper and deeper, he starts to worry that his twenty-fifth year of service might be his last.

# MESSAGE IN THE FLAMES

ISBN 13: 978-0-8439-5998-7

# THE
# WATER
# CLOCK

# JIM KELLY

A mutilated body found frozen in a block of ice. A second body perched high in a cathedral, riding a gargoyle—hidden for more than thirty years. When forensic evidence links both victims to one crime, reporter Philip Dryden knows he's on to a terrific story. What he doesn't know is that his search for the truth will involve a mystery from his own past. As his investigation gets increasingly urgent, he will come face-to-face with his deepest fears...and a cold-blooded killer.

ISBN 13: 978-0-8439-6000-6